Pr

"*Voyage of the Mourning D*... characters and an intriguing mystery. I can't wait to see where Rich Wulf takes his story in *Flight of the Dying Sun*."

—Don Bassingthwaite
Author of *The Killing Song*

Eberron's fragile peace hangs in the balance.

The only hope to prevent war from igniting the Five Nations is a harried band of adventurers. Their quest: To track down the last creation of Ashrem d'Cannith, a man whom some named the greatest mind of his age and others called a madman.

"I have no sons. My only legacy is a prophecy that should never have been revealed. My heirs believe I have forsaken them. I have no legacy. Only ash."

THE HEIRS OF ASH
BY RICH WULF

Voyage of the Mourning Dawn

Flight of the Dying Sun

Rise of the Seventh Moon
(2007)

HEIRS OF ASH · BOOK 2

FLIGHT OF THE DYING SUN

RICH WULF

FLIGHT OF THE DYING SUN
The Heirs of Ash

©2007 Wizards of the Coast, Inc.

All characters in this book are fictitious. Any resemblance to actual persons, living or dead, is purely coincidental.

This book is protected under the copyright laws of the United States of America. Any reproduction or unauthorized use of the material or artwork contained herein is prohibited without the express written permission of Wizards of the Coast, Inc.

Published by Wizards of the Coast, Inc. EBERRON, WIZARDS OF THE COAST, and their respective logos are trademarks of Wizards of the Coast, Inc., in the U.S.A. and other countries.

Printed in the U.S.A.

The sale of this book without its cover has not been authorized by the publisher. If you purchased this book without a cover, you should be aware that neither the author nor the publisher has received payment for this "stripped book."

Cover art by Philip Straub
First Printing: February 2007

9 8 7 6 5 4 3 2 1

ISBN: 978-0-7869-4316-6
620-95974740-001-EN

U.S., CANADA,	EUROPEAN HEADQUARTERS
ASIA, PACIFIC, & LATIN AMERICA	Hasbro UK Ltd
Wizards of the Coast, Inc.	Caswell Way
P.O. Box 707	Newport, Gwent NP9 0YH
Renton, WA 98057-0707	GREAT BRITAIN
+1-800-324-6496	Save this address for your records.

Visit our web site at www.wizards.com

For Kat
I owe her a story.

PROLOGUE

War had returned to Cyre.

She had only just begun to recover from the last series of battles, and the Karrnathi invasion had devastated the proud nation once more. Homes and villages lay in ruins. What had once been green fields were now rendered desolate. It was as if all the color in the land had been drained. Even the afternoon sky was polluted with greasy smoke. The sun was little more than a slightly brighter smear in a field of gray. Across the tortured earth, a line of dimly shining yellow stones marked the path of a lightning rail. A cloud of shimmering sparks erupted from the line as a coach sped on its way west, towing a line of cars on a path out of Cyre.

The scattered citizens and wounded soldiers glanced enviously as the coach sped on its way to a better place, then continued to trudge across the land. Suddenly a dash of unaccustomed color turned their gaze heavenward. A splash of flame pierced the gray, burning brightly and moving swiftly through the pallid sky. At first it seemed as if the sun had returned, but the fire glowed green in a solid ring. It was the elemental flame that marked the passage of an airship.

The dead eyes of the refugees watched the ship soar past. Some watched with faint hope, wondering if a new ally had arrived. Others, more pessimistic, worried that this might only be the herald of some new enemy. Most watched only for a moment then returned to their hopeless march, too beaten down by tragedy to care one way or another. After all that had been lost, what did one more airship matter? Soon enough it would be gone, like everything else.

Aboard the vessel, Captain Orren Thardis paid no mind to those below. His hands gripped the ship's helm, knuckles white. His eyes were fixed upon the churning sky as the ship soared onward. His brow furrowed at the rattling hum that grew deep within the ship's hull, but he paid no other mind. The sparse crew exchanged worried looks, yet only one dared speak up.

"We need to slow down, Captain," snapped a sharp voice. The first mate stamped across the deck to Orren's side, glaring up at him in irritation.

Orren's eyes narrowed as he glared down at the gnome, but his expression quickly faded into a pained frown. "We can't, Haimel," he said. "Too much is at stake."

The young gnome folded his arms across his chest and sighed back at Orren. "You don't have to tell me," he said, "but it'll do us no good to tear the ring off its struts before we even catch sight of Metrol. We'll do no one any good if we crash."

"I fear we won't do any good in any case," Orren replied, though his voice was softer now. His grip loosened a bit on the ship's controls. *Dying Sun* slowed her mad pace, and the rattling warning lessened.

Haimel smiled weakly. "We'll catch him, Captain," he said. "The ship was built for speed."

Orren nodded, though it was clear he did not believe his friend's comforting words. His gaze was fixed on the course again, searching for the distant city's skyline. The gnome paced the deck, mumbling orders to the crew or pausing to study the ravaged lands below.

"Haimel," the captain said, his voice low, "there is something you should see."

FLIGHT OF THE DYING SUN

The gnome peered back with a quizzical look. His eyes widened as Orren changed. His skin became a dull gray, his face smooth and nearly featureless. Blonde hair and green eyes both faded to ghostly white. Thin lips quirked in an ironic grin. The crew muttered among themselves and stopped their work to stare at the captain.

"Back to work, you lot," Haimel barked at them sharply. "We're to be in Metrol within the hour!"

Some of them cast a final, uneasy looks at their inhuman captain, but none of them argued with the first mate. The gnome glared at them pointedly till every one of them had returned to his duties.

"You aren't surprised, Haimel," Orren said calmly. "So you knew I was a changeling?"

"I suspected," Haimel said. "I've known a few of your kind. You showed all the signs."

"Signs?" Orren asked. "What signs?"

Haimel shrugged. "Little things," he said. "Sometimes you take on odd gestures and mannerisms, then never use them again. It's like little bits of lives you've led before were peeking through. Your face is always clean shaven, even if by all rights you've had no time to wash up in days. Mostly, though, it's your past."

"I never talk about my past," Orren said.

"That's what I mean."

"Is that really so unusual?" Orren replied. "We're all old soldiers here. I think a lot of us have done things we don't want to dwell upon."

"That's true," Haimel said, "but you never let anything slip. Nothing. Ever. Changelings are better than most at burying things they don't want to think about."

"I only hide things you would not wish to hear," Orren said bitterly. "I must confess I am surprised. I thought I was rather good at hiding what I am."

"Like I said, I only suspected," Haimel said.

"You never said anything," Orren said. "Did you not fear I was a spy, or worse?"

"Well, I always figured Ashrem must have known," Haimel said. "You can't fool Ash. It just isn't possible. And if it was all right with him for you to pretend to be someone else, there must be a good reason for it. After everything we've done in the name of peace, letting a changeling hide behind another man's face really wasn't such a big deal."

"I see," Marth said. "Well, the illusion is done. I am tired of lying to friends."

"Me, too," the gnome said. His brow furrowed as he followed the captain's gaze to the horizon. "What do you think the old man is up to out there?"

"Trying to save the world," Orren said softly.

Haimel looked at him curiously. "You said he was in danger."

Orren did not answer at first. He finally cleared his throat loudly and called out to the crew. They gathered quickly, watching their captain with obvious unease.

"No more lies," Orren said. "It is time we all knew our purpose here. What do you know about the Draconic Prophecy, Haimel?"

"Not much," the gnome admitted. "I know Ash puts a lot of stock in it, but then magic makes a man adopt a lot of odd habits. Ash says the Draconic Prophecy is never wrong, but then again it's very old and very long, isn't it? Babble long enough and you're bound to be right sooner or later, and the Prophecy has been babbling for a long, long time."

Orren chuckled. "That is true of most prophets and prophecies," Orren answered. "The Draconic Prophecy is different. It is a living thing, a thing woven through the fabric of this world, but that exists outside of the constraints of what we recognize as reality. The Prophecy can be misunderstood or misinterpreted, but it cannot be wrong."

"And what does it say is going to happen to Ashrem d'Cannith in Metrol?" Haimel asked.

FLIGHT OF THE DYING SUN

"The Prophecy says that Cyre is going to die today," Orren said.

Startled gasps and frightened mumbling rumbled through the crew. Sailors, even air sailors, were superstitious by nature. Prophecy was not a laughing matter.

"So Ash is flying to the capital to stop the Prophecy from being fulfilled?" Haimel asked.

"I am uncertain what he intends to do," Orren said, "but it will end badly if we are not quick."

The crew was silent for several long moments.

Haimel looked at Orren soberly. "If the Prophecy is never wrong," he finally said, "then there's nothing we can do to save Cyre."

Orren nodded. "Ashrem knows this as well. That is why he told no one why he was leaving."

"So what are we doing here?"

Orren did not answer at first. Finally, a wry grin spread across his pale features and he looked down at his old friend. "Haimel, for years we've been trying to stop the Last War," he said. "We've always known that there was nothing we could do. In the end we're just men, and the world won't change no matter what we do. But have we ever let that stop us?"

Haimel laughed nervously. "No, Captain," he said. "No, I guess we haven't."

"This is no different," he said. "We must save Ashrem, even if he cannot be saved. We must stop the Prophecy from being fulfilled, even if it cannot be stopped. I'm sorry I didn't tell you this before, but I needed you. The *Dying Sun* can fly with a single pilot, but not at the speeds required to reach Metrol in time. Maybe we can't stop destiny, but we don't have to stand aside and accept it, either. We might still reach Metrol before Cyre's doom is revealed. Or, if you want, we can turn back now and flee beyond the borders of Zil'argo. I will not ask any of you to throw your lives away for nothing. If a single soul here is unwilling to risk his life to save

Ashrem d'Cannith and perhaps all of Cyre, say so now and I will turn the ship around."

The crew looked back evenly. Their fear and unease were replaced with grim resolve. Not a single man or woman looked away.

"We are with you, Captain," Haimel said.

Orren nodded. "Then return to your stations," he said. "There is little time."

The crew scattered. Orren urged the *Dying Sun* to greater speed, though not to the same unsafe excess as before. Haimel marched toward the bow, but stopped to look back at his captain a final time.

"Was there ever really a man called Orren Thardis?" he asked.

"No," the captain answered with a chuckle. "Ashrem helped me invent the name and supplied the documents to make him real. Orren is merely a mask"

"What is your name?" Haimel asked.

"The few who ever truly knew me, called me Marth," the captain answered.

"It's been an honor to serve with you, Captain Marth," Haimel said, saluting sharply.

The captain looked at his old friend in surprise. He returned the salute.

And the *Dying Sun* continued on her fateful course.

CHAPTER ONE

Four years later

True storms were rare over the Talenta Plains, but when they came they were swift and savage. Tonight's display was certainly no exception, spurred on as it was by a dryad's righteous anger. Aeven had issued a call to the elements, and they had answered with fury. Wind and lightning gouged the sky. Thunder cracked, the echo returning again and again over the vast plain. Twin rings of fire stood out against the storm as two airships spun in a deadly aerial dance. The larger turned wildly, seeking to bring her weapons to bear against the smaller ship, but the more maneuverable pursuer remained above and behind her larger sister. The leathery flap of wings resounded against the storm as a flock of glidewings spilled from the smaller ship's deck, attacking the larger vessel.

"For the honor of the Ghost Talon!" came a wild cry from the beasts' halfling riders as they dove toward the *Seventh Moon*. The crazed riders lobbed barbed javelins and vials of flaming oil at the airship, bringing screams from the startled crew. Some riders leapt off their mounts onto the *Moon's* deck, drawing swords and flinging themselves into combat against the crew. Jagged lightning erupted from the larger ship's prow, striking two riders who foolishly ventured too far ahead. The furious storm carried their ashes away.

Lightning flashed again, illuminating the night, outlining the unlikely sight of five figures leaping across the void between the two ships. Zed Arthen landed with a grunt, still cursing at the bitter taste Tristam's potion had left in his mouth. Fire shot through the old inquisitive's left thigh. The paladin's magic had healed his earlier wound, but even magic couldn't persuade pain to leave the body. Only time could cure such things. Zed ignored the weakness and drew his broadsword, scanning the rear deck for enemies.

The massive warforged, Omax, landed beside Zed with a crunch of splintered timber. Eraina, the paladin, landed to Zed's right side. She stumbled, unaccustomed to the magic that had carried them here. Zed gripped her arm to steady her. She pulled away with an annoyed sneer, drawing her half-spear and shortsword.

Tristam Xain had been the first one to land. Zed had never really imagined the boy as much of a leader, but then in his experience the best leaders didn't generally reveal their worth until you leaned on them. One day they were in the background, saying nothing. The next, a crisis would hit and everyone was suddenly listening to what they had to say. The boy would do fine, as long as his confidence held out. The best way to ensure he kept it together would be not to give him too much time to think about the impossible situation they were in.

"You ready to do this, Xain?" Zed asked brusquely, forcing Tristam's attention.

Tristam looked past Zed. His worry was replaced with a confident grin when Seren Morisse landed safely behind them. Zed chuckled. As long as Seren was here, Tristam would be too busy trying to impress her to worry for himself.

They'd be fine.

The artificer glanced up at *Karia Naille*, now hovering far above them. "Don't worry, we don't have to jump that," he said. "Pherris will move closer when he sees our signal."

"Unless we die," Zed said, hefting his sword with both hands. He wondered what the boy would say in reply.

"Yeah," Tristam said. "Don't die!"

FLIGHT OF THE DYING SUN

Zed cackled. Yes, Tristam would be fine.

"Good luck, Xain," he said.

"Good luck, all of you," Tristam answered, splitting off with Seren to attend to their share of this mission.

A Cyran soldier stepped around the corner and opened his mouth in alarm, but fell silent as a backhand slap from Omax sent him crashing limp into the wall. Zed allowed himself a little smile. It was good to be fighting beside people he didn't have to worry about, and both Omax and Eraina could take care of themselves. Zed charged past the warforged, surveying the path ahead. Chaos had utterly consumed the *Moon's* deck. Cyran mercenaries and halfling warriors grappled in combat as the storm rains scoured the deck. The Cyrans rallied one another, shouting the name of their lost homeland. The halflings screamed in frenzied rage, slashing and clawing at the men who had murdered their tribe. Zed watched as a Ghost Talon berserker tackled a Cyran warrior, dragging them both over the rail to plummet into the void. There was truly no enemy more fearsome than those with nothing left to lose—and both the Cyrans and the halflings fell into that category.

The time for watching was done. There was no more hesitation. Instinct fired Zed's movements. He charged into the battle, thick blade hewing down a Cyran mercenary. The warforged fought beside him, moving with surprising grace for a creature sculpted of dense metal and enchanted wood. He heard Eraina's smooth voice rising in prayer to her goddess. A wave of dizziness washed through Zed's mind, followed by a surge of renewed strength as the Hearthmother's divine magic flowed into him.

"I don't need Boldrei's help, Eraina," Zed snapped.

"But she needs ours," the paladin answered. "Accept her blessings with grace, and we will triumph."

"If your goddess wants a champion, I'm hardly the best choice," he said, parrying another mercenary's sword and kicking the man away across the slippery deck.

"How can such a brave man have so little faith?" Eraina said.

"Ask Boldrei," Zed said with a scowl. "Which way do we go, Omax?"

Omax pointed at the hatch at the far side of the deck. A half dozen Cyrans stood in a tight group in front of it, watching the fight but not moving from their post.

"Dalan will most likely be held there," the warforged said.

An annoyed sneer creased Zed's weathered features. He had hoped the confusion would leave Dalan's cabin lightly guarded, but at least some of Marth's soldiers were not fools. The Ghost Talons wouldn't be much help. Zed couldn't speak their language and they might not even listen if he could. The halflings didn't care about Dalan d'Cannith. They just wanted to hurt Marth's soldiers as much as possible.

"We need a distraction," Zed said in a low voice. "Wait here out of sight. They probably won't all chase me, but you should be able to handle whatever's left. Don't wait for me. Just grab Dalan and run."

"You will not survive," Omax said.

"Probably not," Zed said, hefting his sword and preparing to charge. "I'll think of something."

Eraina opened her mouth to argue, but no words came. Omax turned and seized one of the huge crates lashed to the deck, lifted it with the sound of snapping ropes, and hurled it past Zed into the group of guards.

"They are distracted now," the warforged said.

Omax released a savage metal roar and ran headlong into the scattering mercenaries. Two had already collapsed from the warforged's improvised missile. A third fell when Omax's heavy fists clapped together over his helmet. Sparks erupted as the others slashed at the warforged with their swords. Omax staggered beneath their attacks but did not fall. Zed rushed in beside him, cutting down one of the remaining soldiers and parrying an attack from another. Eraina was there as well, burying her spear in another soldier.

FLIGHT OF THE DYING SUN

The last man glared at them, eyes narrowed in hate. "You d'Cannith pawns," he said, sneering as he gripped his sword in both hands. "All we want to do is save our homeland. What do you fight for? Gold?"

"No," Zed said, batting the man's weapon away and clubbing him heavily across the face with the pommel of his sword. The soldier stumbled drunkenly. "Right now I'm just fighting to get you out of my way, but I like to keep things simple." Zed punched the dazed soldier in the throat and pushed him aside.

"Dalan?" Omax called out, shoving through the dead and unconscious enemies into the room beyond. The warforged's shimmering eyes illuminated the dark room with pale blue light. Dalan d'Cannith sat cross-legged on the floor. The fat guild master's fine robes were now torn and stained with blood and soot. His face was bruised. His eyes were rimmed with exhaustion. He looked up at them with exaggerated calm, as if unaware of his own pathetic state.

"A rescue?" he asked in a bored voice. "What were you thinking, Arthen? Whose ludicrous idea was this? Xain?"

"It has all the earmarks, doesn't it?" Zed replied. "Now get up. We're getting out of here."

"You should have left me," Dalan said, trembling as Omax pulled him to his feet.

"I agree," Zed said. "You're not worth it. But Tristam really wants to talk to you, and I kind of want to see how that turns out."

"Do you need healing?" Eraina asked, extending a hand toward Dalan's bruised face.

"Nothing urgent," Dalan said, brushing her hand away. "Save your goddess's favor. We may still need miracles."

A hideous roar erupted from somewhere deep within the *Moon*. Sparks of red flame shone between the floorboards, and the entire vessel shuddered.

"Such as that, whatever that new catastrophe was," Dalan said bleakly. "Xain is sabotaging the ship, isn't he?"

"Maybe," Zed said with a nervous cough.

Omax cocked his head. "The ship's elemental has been freed from its bindings," he whispered. "The *Moon* will not survive long."

"Tristam was supposed to banish it back to its own world, not release it into ours," Eraina said.

"Typical," Dalan said with a sigh.

"They get angry when they break loose," Zed said. "We'd better get out of here before that thing kills us all."

"I am too weak to run," Dalan said. "Leave me."

Zed nodded at Omax.

The warforged reached out without another word, grabbing Dalan by the collar and tucking him limply under one arm. Zed ran back out onto the deck, searching the sky for the familiar green flaming ring. He saw her now, the *Karia Naille,* below and to the left of the *Moon,* flying as close as she dared.

"Go now!" Zed shouted.

Zed, Omax, and Eraina ran across the deck, ignoring the chaos. Cyran soldiers scrambled to save their ship. Halfling warriors rushed back to their glidewings, fleeing the doomed vessel. Neither enemy nor ally spared any moment of concern for them as Zed leapt over the rail. The magic of Tristam's potion still lingered, carrying him upward, crossing the impossible distance between the two ships. He landed with a crash. Though nets had been stretched across the deck to catch them, his landing was not gentle. His sword tumbled from his hand and stars swam in his vision. Eraina landed just as he rose, crashing into him. Omax arrived more gracefully, not even needing the nets as he landed nimbly on his feet. The deck buckled under his arrival. The warforged dropped Dalan d'Cannith stiffly on the deck. The guild master's eyes were wide as he stared back at the burning hulk from which they had escaped. *Seventh Moon* plummeted from the sky, her great size making her descent appear agonizingly slow. The

FLIGHT OF THE DYING SUN

Karia Naille dove, struggling to stay beneath the flaming hulk as she dropped.

"Welcome back, Master d'Cannith," Pherris Gerriman said. Though his voice was casual, the gnome captain's hands were tight on the ship's controls. Sweat beaded on his temples. "I see that the rest of you have chosen, as usual, to spontaneously complicate my evening. I thought Tristam intended merely to cripple their ship, not destroy her."

Fire burst from patches within the *Moon's* hull. The elemental ring that surrounded her was now broken in three places and blazed with purple lightning.

Zed shrugged as he retrieved his sword, shoving it back into its scabbard. "I dunno. That looks crippled to me."

"Damn you, Xain!" Dalan shouted, glaring around him as he searched for the artificer. "How dare you take such foolish risks! You could have killed us all. You could have destroyed everything!"

"Tristam isn't here," Eraina said.

"Where is he?" Dalan demanded.

Omax pointed at the burning *Moon*.

"We can't wait for him much longer," Pherris said, eyeing the burning ship above them with a nervous frown. "I will *not* leave him behind, but that ship is going down fast."

"Fly, Pherris," said a soft voice from the ship's bow. Aeven, the dryad, perched beside the figurehead that mirrored her delicate features. Though the rain slicked her golden hair and olive skin, she looked at the crew with a serene smile. "The wind tells me that Tristam Xain and Seren Morisse are safe."

Pherris nodded rapidly. "Aye, Aeven."

"*Mourning Dawn* rejoices," she added, "for Tristam has released her sister from the *Dying Sun*." She turned her face back into the storm.

A triumphant growl surged through the *Karia Naille*'s elemental ring, and for an instant it blazed pure white. The ship gained altitude, banking heavily to port and pulling away from the *Dying Sun*. The brilliant lightning and roaring thunder were answered with the violent explosive cries of the *Moon's* runaway elemental. The triumphant cheers of the Ghost Talon riders filled the night as Marth's flagship plummeted.

A small blue glidewing landed nimbly on the *Karia Naille's* deck, his jeering caw making Zed jump back with a curse. Gerith Snowshale rolled off the creature's back, his eyes wide as he watched the plummeting *Moon*.

"Marth's ship hasn't broken up yet," he reported. "That damned thing was built to last. Are we going to follow and finish them off?"

Pherris looked back at the halfling with a frown. "How uncharacteristically bloodthirsty, Master Snowshale."

"You think so?" Gerith said darkly. "I saw what Marth and his men did to the Ghost Talons. If those had been my sisters and my brothers, I know what I would do."

"Then we are fortunate that the Ghost Talons are not our tribe," Pherris said, "for not only are we now a crew of but seven, but our own vessel is barely airborne. Have you forgotten the damage we sustained the last time we encountered the Cyrans? We fly, quite literally, on a wing and a prayer, Master Snowshale."

"Aye, Captain," Gerith acknowledged, though his eyes still watched the descending warship with silent rage.

"What about Koranth and the halflings?" Eraina asked. "Are we going to rendezvous with them?"

"No need," Zed said. "We don't have any more business with them. I think it'd probably be better for all parties concerned if we just made all possible speed to a town before our ship falls apart."

"Indeed," Dalan said. "Our alliance is tenuous at best. Consider that our previous meeting with their chief ended with an attempt to betray our progress to Baron Zorlan d'Cannith, an attempt that failed only when that mad changeling murdered most of their tribe. I think the Ghost Talons would be quite content to never see us again, and I echo that sentiment. Pherris, plot a course for Vulyar and make all speed that our fragile condition will allow. I can arrange for our necessary repairs there."

Pherris nodded. "Aye."

"Gerith, why don't you get back on your glidewing and go find Seren and Tristam?" Dalan added. "Vulyar doesn't have the facilities to repair the *Mourning Dawn* properly. We shall need Xain's help to arrange what we can. I would not trust any other artificer."

"Aye," Gerith said. He whistled and Blizzard took to the air, flying over the side of the ship. The halfling moved to the railing, preparing to jump overboard.

"Master Snowshale," Pherris said, a warning tone in his voice. "I recommend you restrain your heroic urges and avoid any survivors of the *Seventh Moon*. If the Ghost Talons still thirst for revenge, they shall find it without your aid. Your duty is to return Tristam and Seren to us. You shall have ample time for a pointless and heroic death on your own time."

Gerith sighed, nodded, and hopped over the rail. Blizzard soared up an instant later, his tiny master riding upon his back.

"The rest of you return to your duties," Dalan said. "Get these nets off my deck. It looks like a fishmonger's hut."

"Back to giving orders so quickly, Dalan?" Zed asked, raising an eyebrow.

"She's still my ship," Dalan said with a chuckle. "Next time you plot to save my life, consider the consequences."

"Noted," Zed said. "When you have a moment, I need to talk to you."

Dalan's smile faded, and he looked at Zed soberly. "Captain, please do not disturb me unless you require my dragonmark for emergency repairs," he said.

"Aye," Pherris replied.

Dalan limped back toward his cabin. Zed wondered how badly d'Cannith was truly injured. The guild master could be a proud man and certainly was not one to beg for aid. That he was showing pain at all suggested his time aboard the *Moon* had not been pleasant. Zed closed the hatch behind them. He was surprised to see Dalan kneeling on the floor, a sudden grin spread across his bruised features. Dalan's shaggy dog huddled happily against his master, tail thumping the floor as he licked the fat man's face.

"D'Cannith?" Zed asked, stunned. He had never seen Dalan smile before, save when profit was at hand.

Dalan looked up with amazement. "I . . . I don't understand," he said, his voice thick. "It's just that . . . after the crash, Gunther was so badly hurt. He's a very old dog, I never thought . . . I just expected he would be gone when I returned."

"Eraina healed him," Zed said.

"The paladin," Dalan said, astonished. "I didn't even ask her. I didn't wish to presume. She . . . dislikes me."

"You should have more faith in people, Dalan," Zed said.

Dalan laughed, scratching the dog's ears a final time before rising and composing himself. "Odd advice, coming from you, Arthen," he said. "I shall most definitely thank the Marshal later, and issue a most generous donation to the Hearthmother's temple in Karrnath. In the meantime, I apologize for allowing you to see me in such a state."

"Whatever, Dalan," Zed said. "I'm glad your dog is well, but it's not what I'm here to talk about."

"You wish to report what Tristam learned from Kiris Overwood?" he asked.

"Not really," he said. "I'll let Tristam share that with you himself, if he chooses to."

"If he chooses to?" Dalan asked. "What do you mean? Tristam works for me."

"Tristam knows about Marth," Zed said.

"Tristam knows what about Marth?" Dalan asked pointedly. He settled heavily into the overstuffed chair behind his desk, dipping a silken handkerchief into a small wash basin and patting some of the blood and grime from his face.

"Don't pretend we're both stupid," Zed said. "He knows why I quit working for you the last time. He knows that you were helping Marth decipher Ashrem d'Cannith's work, and that when you found out Marth was a killer, you tried to distance yourself."

Dalan shrugged. "Why should I care?" he asked. "Tristam is a clever boy. He was bound to learn the truth eventually. If anything, learning that he was my second choice will only intensify his burning need to prove himself as my uncle's superior heir. My presence here is ample proof of that. Would Xain have risked all of your lives to rescue me if he no longer trusted me?"

"Don't let your arrogance blind you, Dalan," Zed said. "Tristam didn't rescue you so that you could keep him under your thumb. He rescued you so that Marth wouldn't interrogate you and find out what we've learned."

"Interrogate me?" Dalan said, laughing bitterly as he lit the small lamp beside his desk. "What could Marth possibly learn from me? We know almost nothing." He chewed his thumb thoughtfully for several seconds. "But perhaps that is what Tristam feared. A man moves slowly if he believes an enemy lies in wait, and so it is with Marth. If Marth knew how far behind him we truly are, he would assemble the Legacy with greater haste. He would know we cannot stop him, and would no longer waste time delaying our own quest."

"That sounds more like the way you think than the way Tristam thinks," Zed said. "Maybe the boy just thinks you haven't told us everything yet, and he wasn't ready to let you die until he found out for sure."

Dalan gave a wicked grin. "You're so paranoid, Arthen."

"Am I?"

"Do not take it as an insult," Dalan said. "I approve. Your paranoia serves you well. Each soul builds defenses against hardship. For you, it is your willingness to expect the worst in everyone about you, and you are never disappointed. For me, is the willingness to turn the weaknesses of others to my advantage—for such opportunity is always there. For Tristam, his work is his defense. He is a craftsman. Invention lifts his soul above earthly worries. So long as I can aid him in his work, he will always need me."

"You haven't changed, d'Cannith."

"Oh, but I have," Dalan said. "You may see me as manipulative and arrogant, but these qualities have served me well. Thus I see no reason to discard them. You may not like me, Arthen, but we are allies—and I do sincerely wish to atone for my mistakes."

"Then stop making them," Zed said. He stooped to scratch the dog behind the ears, then left the cabin. Arthen closed the hatch quietly, leaving the guild master to his solitude.

CHAPTER TWO

The sun shone brilliant gold over the plains, as if proud that it had finally melted last night's clouds away. The new light was greeted by the jubilant songs of wild birds and the bass cry of a grazing threehorn herd. It was a beautiful sight, or would have been, if Seren hadn't had such a terrible headache. She squinted, not wanting to wake up, huddling tightly into her blankets and hugging her pillow against her chest. It was only after a moment's consideration that she realized she had not been carrying any blankets or pillows.

Her eyes opened instantly. She released Tristam and rolled away across the grass, blushing furiously. The artificer sat up and straightened his baggy coat with a lopsided grin, his dark brown eyes meeting hers, then quickly darting away.

"Guess it was cold last night," he said. "People in their sleep will naturally move toward one another for warmth."

"Is that what you call that?" she asked with a small smile.

Tristam blushed and shrugged uncomfortably. "It won't happen again," he said.

"Too bad," she answered, rising and stretching with languid care as she studied the surrounding plains. "So we're headed to Karrnath?"

"What?" Tristam blinked, realizing he'd been staring at her. "Oh. Karrnath." He coughed and stood, stumbling as he patted the dust from his coat. "Yeah, we need to head north and a little west. Fort Bones or Vulyar are probably our best bets. If we're lucky we'll meet a halfling caravan along the way and trade for some ponies or something. I don't have a lot of money, but I could probably trade a few potions to pay them."

"Xain, you're an idiot. Do you need her to make it any more obvious?" whispered a mocking voice from the high grass.

Tristam whirled about, wand and sword appearing in either hand. He lowered the weapons almost instantly and laughed.

"Did someone say something?" Seren asked.

"Only an annoying halfling," Tristam said, laughing.

Gerith Snowshale stepped out of the grass and offered them an elegant bow.

"Gerith!" Seren cried happily. She ran over to the little scout, dropping to her knees and grabbing him in a hug. "Are you all right? Is everyone else all right?"

"They're all fine," Gerith said. "I'm doing great." The halfling winked at Tristam over her shoulder. Tristam sighed.

"Where is the *Karia Naille*?" Seren asked.

"En route to Karrnath," Gerith said. "Dalan sent me to find you two."

"Dalan's alive?" Tristam said. His voice was neutral.

"Aye," Gerith said, "and as bossy as ever. Tristam, you need to get back to the ship so he has someone else to yell at besides me."

"I have a lot to talk to him about," Tristam said.

"Then it's settled," Gerith said happily. "I'll fly Blizzard back and let them know I found you. We should be back soon!"

"Be safe, Gerith," Seren said.

"You too, Seren," Gerith said. "Take care of my winsome damsel, Tristam. My story will be terrible without its heroine. I'll just let you two get back to what you were doing."

Tristam made an irritated shooing motion with his sword. Gerith snickered and disappeared into grass again. Blizzard exploded from the plain seconds later, carrying his master aloft with a proud cry.

"You know I was thinking," Seren said. "That ring you used to save us—didn't you tell me that Orren Thardis made it for you?"

Tristam looked at the golden ring on his finger. "Yeah," he said, frowning. "I'm trying not to think about it."

"Is it possible that Marth could be using that ring to track us?" she asked. "The way you used your enchantments to track me?"

"It's possible," Tristam said. "Just unlikely. He made the ring years ago, when we were still friends and he had no reason to spy on me."

"You didn't want to spy on me," Seren said. "You wanted to keep me safe. Would Marth have done the same thing?"

Tristam frowned. "He would," he said. "But those sorts of enchantments only work over short range. Marth wouldn't be able to use it to follow us from Black Pit to Talenta."

"But he would know if you were nearby," she said. "Like he did last night, when you were on his ship."

Tristam nodded gravely. "I should probably get rid of it," he said, clenching his fist around the ring. He looked up at Seren, noticing she was staring at him with faint amusement. "What are you looking at?" he asked.

She nodded at his sword. "You know if you actually knew how to use that thing you might have done a little better against Marth," she said. "He was prepared for your magic, but wasn't ready for steel."

"What do you mean?" he asked, hurt. He stuffed the ring in his coat pocket. "I'm a good swordsman. I once ranked among the most skilled duelists in the Lhazaar Principalities."

Seren gave him a bored look.

He sheathed the sword sheepishly. "Very well, that's a lie," he said. "I've never had any training. Is it that obvious?"

She grinned and kept walking. "Only when you start fighting," she said. "You have the opening stances down pretty well, but once a fight starts you just flail around or fall back on using your wand."

Tristam flipped the ivory wand in his hand and nodded. "I never really had time to learn to fight," he said. "I never thought it was necessary. I'd rather just intimidate the other guy into backing down, or throw out a handful of sleeping powder or a lightning bolt to get it over with." He tucked the wand back into his belt and rubbed the back of his neck with one hand. "I guess I'm just not much of a warrior."

"Not wanting to fight isn't a weakness, Tristam," Seren said, stepping closer to him, "but you may want to learn."

"I don't think I could ask Zed or Eraina," he said, "and Omax doesn't really use weapons."

"Then ask me," she said.

"You know how to use a sword?" he asked, looking at her with surprise.

Seren nodded and grinned. "My dad was a soldier," she said. "He showed me a few things in case I ever needed to protect myself. It wasn't anything much, just enough to get by. I practiced on my own, sparring with the local boys. I think I was hoping to impress Dad when he came back home." She trailed off, biting her lip as she stared into the distance again.

Tristam watched her quietly for a long time. She turned away, wiping something from her cheek.

"My parents served on a merchant vessel," Tristam said, standing next to her and staring in the distance at whatever she was pretending to look at. "Of course, for a Lhazaarite, the term 'merchant vessel' is used pretty loosely. That applies especially if you're on board the ship we've been hired to make an unscheduled trade with."

"Your parents were pirates?" she asked, looking at him with an interested grin.

"Pirate is such an ugly word," Tristam said, though he beamed

FLIGHT OF THE DYING SUN

to see her smile. "Ten years ago, my father's ship was hired to do some scouting for the Aundairian Royal Navy. She sank in a coastal skirmish with the Valenar, in a battle so minor nobody even cared enough to name it. I left home as soon as I was old enough, hoping I might find that mom and dad had survived and were out there waiting for me." He shrugged into his coat.

"Did you ever find anything?" she asked.

"Unfortunately," he said. "I found the gallows where the elves hanged them. If Ashrem hadn't found me soon after, I really don't know what I would have done. I was alone with no way back home. I was lucky to survive as long as I did."

"That's terrible," Seren said softly.

"It doesn't bother me anymore," he said with a sad smile. "I accepted their deaths a long time ago. It hurts to be alone, Seren, but it doesn't have to be that way. I know you lost your father, Seren, so I just wanted to tell you that . . . so that you'd know that *you* aren't alone." He ran one hand through his unkempt brown hair. "That all sounded good in my head, but it's kind of stupid now that I say it out loud."

"Yeah," she said. "It really was."

Tristam blinked.

Seren laughed. "I'm teasing you," she said. "If you think you're still alone, you're blind, Tristam. Now give it to me."

"Excuse me?" Tristam asked.

She sighed. "Your sword," she pointed at the blade sheathed at his hip. "I'll show you a few things."

"Oh," he said, embarrassed. He drew the weapon and flipped it elegantly in one hand, laying it across his arm with the hilt pointed toward Seren.

"So debonair," she said with a giggle. She took the weapon and stepped away, sweeping it in a fluid arc to one side. Tristam sat down, leaning back on his palms as he watched her.

"Your problem is you're too uptight. You need to hold the sword a little more gently, so you can maintain flexibility." Seren glided through several mock swings, parrying and thrusting against an invisible foe.

"Don't I already do that?" Tristam asked. "I thought I was pretty relaxed."

Seren laughed. "No, not really," she said, and she lifted the sword in a one handed stance, holding it at an angle above her head. "You fight like a lumberjack, hewing wildly. That's fine if you're fighting a tree, but if your focus is too narrow, you won't be free to adapt to an opponent's movements."

"Lumberjack?" Tristam asked, hurt.

Seren sighed, lowering the blade. "Don't pout, Tristam," she said with a laugh. "I'm trying to help you. If you take criticisms personally, you aren't going to learn anything."

"Well then maybe you should stop making fun of me," he replied with a crooked smile. He lurched to his feet and moved close to her.

Seren looked into his eyes with a challenging grin, but it vanished as her gaze moved past him, fixing on something far away. Tristam looked at her in concern, then followed her eyes. A plume of column smoke rose in the distance, scarring the flawless sapphire sky. They exchanged worried glances.

"*Seventh Moon*," he said. "That must be where she crashed."

"Do you think anyone survived?" she asked.

"Probably," he said. "Soarwood is naturally quite buoyant in the air. With a decent pilot, an airship can float to a crash, the same way ours did."

"But what about the rogue elemental?" she asked. "Wouldn't it want to destroy the ship?"

"At first," Tristam said, "but it would ultimately want to return home to its own world. Even if it remained, elementals aren't invincible. The *Moon's* crew would eventually defeat it."

"So there are likely survivors," she said.

"Definitely," Tristam answered, still studying the smoke.

"So we should avoid the wreck," Seren said.

"We should," he said, but his eyes still stared at the distant plume.

"But you don't want to," Seren said.

"I know it's dangerous," Tristam said, "but I want to know how Orren Thardis survived the Day of Mourning and became the monster that he is. I want to know who those soldiers are that work for him. I want to know how he brought back Ashrem's flagship. I want to know how much he knows about the Legacy. We still really don't know anything, Seren."

"We might not learn anything," she said.

"But if we don't investigate, we'll never know." He was quiet for a long time. "At the very least, I have to see how many of those soldiers survived. I didn't want to blow the *Moon's* containment and release that elemental. I . . . I probably killed a lot of people. Whoever those men are, whatever brought them under Marth's command . . . they didn't deserve to die, Seren. I have to know what I've done."

"You feel sorry for Marth's soldiers?" Seren asked. "Those are the same men who murdered Jamus, Kiris, and the Ghost Talons. They tried to kill us, too."

Tristam nodded. "And if things had turned out differently, I might have been one of them," he said.

Seren's smiled sadly. She clearly didn't agree, but she understood. "Very well, then," she said, handing him back his sword. "We'll check it out, but you'll follow me, got it? You aren't very sneaky."

"Lumberjack, I know," he said, nodding, sliding the blade into its scabbard with a crack. "I'll do what you say, Seren."

"And promise me that if you see Marth you won't do anything stupid," she said, "until you're powerful enough to face him. His magic is still much stronger than yours."

Tristam looked crestfallen but mumbled his agreement.

She nodded pertly and set off toward the distant plume, gesturing for him to follow. They stepped over a small rise and saw the wreckage of *Seventh Moon* sprawled in a shallow valley before them. A long gouge split the earth, carved by the ship's violent landing. The airship looked to be in relatively good condition considering the chaos she had endured. Two of the four struts that once held her elemental ring in place were now shattered. One lay in two pieces in the gouged earth. The other was nowhere to be seen. The ship lay half buried in the ground, her hull covered with ragged burns. A few dozen soldiers in Cyran armor patrolled the valley, sorting debris or laying bodies on a burning pyre. Seren kneeled in the grass and Tristam nearly collapsed beside her, staring at the pyre.

"Don't blame yourself," Seren said.

"Then who should I blame?" he said bitterly.

"Marth," she said. "He started this."

"Did he?" Tristam asked. "Do we really know that?"

Seren shrugged. "Let's go see what we can find out," she said, crawling away through the tall grass.

Tristam looked around awkwardly and followed, moving with less grace than she. Seren looked over her shoulder with an irritated frown.

"You're jingling," she whispered. "Stop it."

"Jingling?" he asked, confused. "What do you mean?"

"What in Khyber do you have in your pockets?" she said.

"Some flasks, mostly potions, and a few focusing crystals," he said, looking away sheepishly.

"How many?" she asked.

"Um . . . a few dozen?" he said. "I guess I never noticed how much noise they make. I've grown accustomed to it."

"Take off your coat and leave it here," she said.

Tristam stared at her, aghast. "What if I can't find it again? Some of the things I'm carrying are irreplaceable."

"Then leave yourself here," she said with a sigh. "I'll sneak ahead by myself."

Seren started off again. Tristam watched her in silence for

several seconds. With a pained expression, he shrugged out of his long coat, folded it in a tight bundle, and hid it among the grass before following. He crawled after her for several minutes, stopping to crouch next to her in the shadows beside a large boulder at the outskirts of a small camp. He winced at the pain in his knees. He wasn't used to crawling around like this. Seren looked back at him curiously, and he offered what he hoped was not an obviously pained smile. She rolled her eyes and turned her attention to the camp. Three soldiers sat in a semi-circle against the boulder, staring into the pathetic little blaze. Two of them nursed small cups. The third occupied himself by continuously scratching at or adjusting a bandage on his right leg.

"I feel a little foolish," Tristam whispered to Seren.

She looked at him curiously.

"They aren't even talking," he said. "We aren't learning anything. Did we really expect them to be discussing Marth's master plan or something?"

Seren shrugged. "Sometimes you can learn more from what people don't say," she said. She looked at them again.

Tristam studied the soldiers as well. They seemed bored, unconcerned. Many, in the manner of career soldiers, were seizing the opportunity to catch up on sleep. Despite their flagship crashing deep in unfriendly territory, none of them seemed particularly worried. The truth sank in. He backed away from the camp slowly, gesturing for Seren to follow so that he could share his conclusions.

"They're expecting a rescue," Tristam whispered as she joined him. "And if Marth can rescue them here, then the *Moon* is only the beginning of his resources."

"Who are they?" Seren asked.

"Cyran soldiers," he said.

"I know they're Cyrans," she said, "but Cyre is dead. Where do they come from? How did they organize? How do you just build and equip an army without anybody noticing?"

"I don't think it would be so difficult," Tristam said. "Most people don't even want to think about the war or about Cyre in particular. Didn't Dalan say most of them used to be in a Cyran legion stationed in Karrnath at the end of the war? If someone like Marth wants to take in a bunch of Cyran refugees, no one will miss them. If he wants to buy up surplus military gear to outfit them, most merchants would be glad for the business. People are happier pretending that the Last War never happened and that Cyre never existed. It would be very easy."

Seren's eyes widened and she flattened herself in the grass. Tristam tried to follow suit, not even knowing what she had seen. He was too slow. A Cyran soldier who had wandered from the camp now looked nervously toward them, noticing something amiss. Seren's dagger appeared in her hand.

"Stop him before he calls for help," she whispered.

Tristam reached for the pouch of sleeping powder in his pocket, and cursed as he realized his coat was still hidden in the grass behind them. He drew his wand, but hesitated.

"Someone is here!" the guard cried. "Come help!"

Tristam stood up instantly, firing a bolt of searing blue lightning from his wand. It was not intended to kill, but burned the air closely enough that the Cyran leapt for cover. Tristam pulled Seren to her feet and ran back toward the place where he had hidden his coat. Two more Cyran soldiers came from that direction, weapons in hand. Tristam drew his sword and charged.

The first soldier parried Tristam's sword so hard that it flew spinning out of his hands, disappearing in the grass. The Cyran lifted his sword for a killing blow, then keeled over with an anguished shriek as Seren cut his knee from behind. She gave Tristam a disappointed look.

"You said to hold the sword gently!" he said.

"Not that gently," she said, darting aside as the other guard swung at her.

Tristam ran past the man and snatched up his coat, dusting it

FLIGHT OF THE DYING SUN

off with one hand as he shrugged into it. The Cyran soldier turned to follow, but stopped short as Tristam threw a handful of purple dust in his face. The soldier fell to one knee, then toppled on his side, snoring peacefully.

"I don't even see where my sword went," Tristam said, looking around forlornly.

"Forget about it," Seren said, kicking the other wounded soldier in the side as he struggled to rise.

"I've had that sword for years," he said. "I can't just abandon..."

Tristam fell short when he saw the dozen Cyran soldiers now running from the valley in their direction.

"Sentimental value can be overrated," he said, taking one of the soldiers' swords and sliding it into his scabbard.

The two ran desperately across the plains. Behind them, the Cyran soldiers continued their pursuit. Out here on the plains, there was little they could do to lose their pursuers. All they could do was hope that they could run longer. Tristam cursed himself. His foolish curiosity may well have killed them both.

"I hope you have an invisibility potion in one of those pockets," Seren said.

"I left them on the *Karia Naille*," Tristam said, a little embarrassed.

"Dozens of bottles and you didn't bring invisibility potions?" she asked.

"They're usually not as useful as you'd think!" he retorted.

Seren narrowed her eyes at him and kept running.

"Cease your flight and drop your weapons!" one of the soldiers shouted. "In the name of Cyre, surrender!"

Tristam glanced over his shoulder but kept running. His mind raced through the many potions and concoctions he carried with him. Most of them were fairly useless in this situation. There was, however, one possibility. He reached into one pocket and drew out a small bottle, shaking it in one hand. A thin plume of green smoke rose from the bottle's cork.

"Stop!" he shouted, his voice booming as he turned to face the soldiers. "Don't make me shed more Cyran blood today. No doubt your master has shown you what a weapon like this can do!"

The dozen Cyran soldiers stopped dead. Most stared in quiet terror terror. A few spared Tristam bitter, angry glances.

"Retreat!" the leader said. As a unit, they turned and ran back the way they had come.

"I was bluffing." Tristam chuckled, bouncing the bottle in one hand. His chest swelled with pride. "It's just ink. It smokes when mixed, so I guess it looks more impressive than it is."

"I'm sure they were impressed," Seren said with a wry smile. She nodded past him.

Tristam followed her nod. His pride deflated slightly, but he was hardly disappointed. The shimmering green ring of the *Karia Naille* now hovered high above them. The airship, not the harmless bottle, had given the soldiers pause. Tristam eagerly caught the rope ladder as it spilled to hang beside them, offering Seren a hand as they climbed up. A thick, three-fingered hand was extended toward them from the bay doors. Omax quickly pulled Seren and Tristam into the cargo bay, then began hauling up the ladder.

"All hands aboard, Captain!" Gerith cried in a shrill voice.

The ship banked heavily. The whine of the elemental ring intensified as the *Karia Naille* gained altitude. The wind rushed through the bay doors, which Omax slammed once the ladder was stowed.

"Good timing, Gerith," Tristam said with a relieved sigh.

"Good to have you both home," the halfling said, flashing a broad smile before hurrying off to his duties.

"Dalan wishes to speak with you," Omax said. The warforged's hollow voice was grave.

"I imagine he does," Tristam said. His eyes fixed on the deep gouges that crossed the warforged's chest. "Omax, you've been hurt."

Omax glanced down, one hand touching the damage gingerly.

"I was serving as a distraction," he said.

"I'm sure you were," Tristam said, narrowing his eyes as he studied the wounds. "Don't worry, I'll fix it."

Omax inclined his head in silent thanks.

Tristam made his way above deck, Seren following. Pherris was in his customary place at the ship's helm, lost in thought as he guided the *Karia Naille* on her course. Zed and Eraina stood at the port rail, looking over the side. Blizzard was crouched on his perch in the bow of the ship, preening himself fastidiously. Aeven was nowhere to be seen.

"Were those the Cyran soldiers?" Zed said.

"A lot of them survived the crash," Tristam said.

"Marth?" Zed asked.

"I didn't see him," Tristam said, "but he'll have to return to repair the *Moon*."

"Repair?" Eraina asked. "You blew up her elemental core and crashed her into the plains. The ship is dead."

Pherris chuckled. "Don't underestimate Zil'argo craftsmanship," he said. "Remember that you're standing in a ship that survived a similar catastrophe only a few days ago. The *Moon* will fly again."

"But not soon," Tristam said. "The damage was extensive, and binding a new elemental will take time. We've crippled Marth's mobility for the time being."

"If Marth is as powerful as he's shown himself to be, does he really need an airship to follow us?" Zed asked.

Tristam said nothing. Zed's words only reflected his unspoken thoughts.

"Those men were not Cyran soldiers." Dalan spoke from deep within his cabin. "Do not call them that. They wear the Cyran crest. They shout Cyran battle cries. They may have been born in Cyre, but they are no countrymen of mine."

Dalan stepped out of his cabin, his scowl deepening as he squinted at the morning sunlight. He held a thick ledger tucked under one arm. "Cyre was a proud nation, with a tradition of honor and courage. Marth and the murderers who serve him should not cheapen Cyre's memory by calling themselves her sons."

"Dalan," Tristam said, looking at the guild master coldly.

"Xain," Dalan replied, gesturing curtly at the artificer. "Step into my cabin. I wish to speak." Dalan disappeared into his chambers.

"Not in there, Dalan," Tristam said. "Out here, where everyone can hear."

Dalan stepped back out, scowling at Tristam in irritation. "Tristam, this isn't the time to be rebellious."

"No more secrets, Dalan," Tristam said, his voice heated. "Either you talk to me here and now, or I leave the ship."

The galley hatch creaked open and Gerith peered out curiously. Omax climbed up from below deck, watching with interest as well. Eraina folded her arms and leaned against the rail.

"Me, too," Seren said.

Dalan looked from Seren to Tristam, his scowl deepening. Zed laughed softly, drawing a withering glare from d'Cannith. Dalan's shoulders slumped, and he gave a deep sigh as he sat upon a small crate.

"I owe you my life for rescuing me from the *Moon*," Dalan said in a quiet voice. "I can at least offer you my candor."

"Tell me what you know about Marth," Tristam said.

Dalan looked at Tristam blankly.

"Pherris, take the ship down," Tristam said. "I am disembarking."

"Belay that order, Captain," Dalan said. "If Master Xain chooses to leave us, I insist on depositing him in a civilized land. No offense, Snowshale. I am sure the plains are lovely for halflings."

"Civilization is a crutch," the halfling said.

"I'm not bluffing, Dalan," Tristam said. "I'm done with your lies."

"I believe you," Dalan said in a tired voice, "but why do you insist on me telling you something you already know? Does it please you to hear me recite my mistakes and failures? Obviously Zed has already told you most of it and you have surmised the rest."

"I want you to tell everyone," Tristam said. "Tell them about Marth."

"Very well," Dalan said. "After my uncle disappeared, I determined to seek out his lost research. At the time, admittedly, my ends were no nobler than my own promotion within House Cannith. After a brief search, I came into contact with a skilled artificer who also possessed the cunning, discretion, and manpower to help me acquire the information I sought."

"Marth?" Eraina asked, a dangerous edge to her voice.

"How was I to know the sort of man he was?" Dalan asked. "Over the years, as I surmised the true purpose of Ashrem's Legacy, I began to suspect Marth's motives were not as base and simple as my own greed. He is afflicted with a peculiar mix of patriotism and madness. That is when I sought your aid, Tristam. Like Marth, you possessed knowledge of artifice that I did not. When Llaine Grove died, I severed my association with the changeling. There was no doubt in my mind that he was responsible for the bishop's murder."

"You aided a killer, then simply stepped away when your status as his accomplice became uncomfortable?" Eraina asked.

"I did nothing to assist him in Grove's murder," Dalan said. "I had no idea what he planned. My contact with Marth was more limited than you believe. We merely met from time to time so that we could exchange information. Why do you think I have been so careful to keep Tristam close under my observation? I did not wish to repeat the same mistakes. I did not pursue Marth because I could not. However, I did not intend to aid him any further. Quite the opposite. I made it my primary objective to interfere with his quest as much as possible."

"I don't understand," Seren said. "When I stole your fake

journal, you said that you left it as a trap, to lure out whoever else was searching for the Legacy. But you already knew who was searching for it—Marth was."

"An uncomfortable detail that was irrelevant at the time of our first meeting," Dalan said.

"Why would you try to draw him out when you already knew who he was?" Zed asked.

Dalan sighed. "I will be blunt."

"This is a first," Zed murmured.

Dalan ignored him. "I am a man of position and power," he said. "I cannot simply step forward and tell the world, 'I was assisting a murderer, but now I am sorry,' especially when the man in question is as elusive as Marth. He would have fled and my numerous enemies would have exploited my admission of weakness to destroy me. Any aid I could have offered in Marth's capture would thus have been wasted, and my life would be consumed by petty political battles. Honesty, in this case, would have accomplished nothing."

"And this is blunt?" Zed asked.

"I am coming to a point, Arthen," Dalan snapped. "While a straightforward admission of guilt might be outside my scope, there are other alternatives. Such as producing a false manuscript, one that I know Marth would be too tempted not to investigate, and ensuring that knowledge of that manuscript's existence fell into the hands of certain authorities who would find the information useful."

Dalan looked meaningfully at Eraina.

"Such as the Deneith Sentinel Marshals," he said. "Bishop Llaine Grove was, after all, under their protection. They would have a vested interest in pursuing his killer."

"Ridiculous," she snapped. "My father, not you, told me about that book, and only after Marth hired him to help steal it."

"You don't find it terribly convenient, Eraina?" Dalan asked. "Your prodigal father, who had not contacted you in years,

FLIGHT OF THE DYING SUN

spontaneously visits you with a clue to the same murder you were already investigating? Did it not seem strange that Marth, who has proven himself to be cautious and secretive in his dealings, would seek out an unknown like Jamus Roland for help with a petty theft? Come now, Eraina, you're a better investigator than that."

Eraina said nothing.

"I knew your father since the Last War," Dalan continued. "We were information brokers. Seren, did Jamus ever mention Fiona Keenig to you?"

"She was one of King Boranel's spies," Seren said. "Jamus worked for her for decades."

"And I was one of the lovely Miss Keenig's most highly paid informants," Dalan said proudly. "Cyre and Breland had many mutual enemies. I was pleased to aid her when I was able. Jamus and I were thus well acquainted. When Fiona disappeared, Jamus was shattered. The man fell into a sad state. He became a common street thief. I knew he had a daughter in House Deneith but was too proud to contact her. I was all too eager to give him a reason to better himself and serve the cause of peace again."

"So you blackmailed him into being your pawn," Eraina said coldly.

"Blackmail? I offered him a chance at a new life," Dalan corrected. "I always contacted Marth through intermediaries. My association with Jamus had always been secret. It was simple enough to have Jamus present my false information to Marth's agents as well as to you, Eraina, in hopes that the Sentinel Marshals would interfere. If you could not stop Marth, you would at least interfere with his progress."

"The truth would have been so much simpler," Eraina said.

"Perhaps," Dalan said. "My only true mistake was underestimating the amount of aid House Deneith would provide. If they had sent more than one Marshal to investigate, perhaps Marth would not have escaped Wroat."

"I cannot dispute that," Eraina said, not meeting Dalan's eyes. "I warned my superiors that greater vigilance would be required. I tried, but we failed. I think they were embarrassed by my failure to protect Grove and have been unmotivated to pursue the case."

"Eraina," Dalan said. "You pride yourself on your ability to detect falsehood. It is a talent that causes me no end of discomfort. Listen to me now."

The paladin looked up again, meeting Dalan d'Cannith's gaze.

"Jamus Roland was my comrade," Dalan said. "The two of us survived a great deal together. The adventures the *Karia Naille*'s crew share would have been a footnote among our exploits during the Last War. I never intended for your father to die." He smirked, though there was a hint of sadness in the expression. "I . . . never expected the old fool to steal the book from me himself. If I knew that was his plan, I would have simply *given* it to him. I'm still . . ." He coughed, clearing his voice. "I'm still amazed I did not recognize him when he visited me the night he died, but then he was a master of his trade." Dalan offered a weak smile. "Believe me when I say that the only life I was intended to risk against Marth was my own."

"And mine," Tristam said. "You sent Omax and me to look for that damned book, knowing full well what Marth was capable of."

"Only after I recognized all the earmarks of Jamus's work," Dalan said. "Seren used all of Roland's techniques to break into my office. When I realized that Jamus's life was at risk—that was when I sent you to investigate."

"Without having any idea what we were walking into," Tristam said.

"Omax is a warrior, even if you are not," Dalan said. "He is always prepared."

"True," the warforged said.

Tristam glanced from Omax to Dalan angrily. "But you chose

FLIGHT OF THE DYING SUN

not to tell us any of this until now?" he asked, flustered.

Zed laughed. "Not trying to make excuses," he said, "but does any of this really surprise you, coming from Dalan? I'd wager there's a great deal more that he doesn't think is worth mentioning."

The crew was silent for a long time. Tristam glared at d'Cannith in tense silence. Dalan looked back impassively. Eraina folded her arms across her chest and stared at the deck.

"I don't know what to think of all of this," Tristam finally said, an edge of anger in his voice. "Did you know that Marth was Orren Thardis all along?"

Dalan blinked. "No," he said, shaking his head slowly. "I never knew that at all." A wicked smile twisted his jowls. "A very interesting revelation, Tristam. That certainly explains a great deal."

"Who in Khyber is Orren Thardis?" Zed asked. "Why is that name familiar?"

"He was the captain of my uncle's third vessel," Dalan said. "The *Dying Sun*. He followed Ashrem into Cyre on the Day of Mourning. I had assumed he was dead."

"Like you assumed Kiris Overwood was dead," Zed said.

"Hardly a coincidence," Eraina said. "He must have rescued her from the Mournland. That would explain why she was willing to die for him."

"If Thardis is Marth, his obsession with my uncle's work becomes a great deal clearer," Dalan said. "I knew Thardis hid his talents as an artificer, but I never knew he was a changeling."

"What we never knew grows every day," Gerith said.

Omax nodded vigorously.

"Seren salvaged a few of Kiris's journals," Tristam said. "They aren't written in the same impossible code as Ashrem's, so we may be able to learn something from them."

"Excellent," Dalan said. "We will have several days of idle time during our repairs and travel to Korth. To gain ground would be a welcome change."

"I hope so," Tristam said.

"Any more questions?" Dalan asked. "If you wish for truth, ask for it all. I don't like these uncomfortable suspicions."

"Only one," Tristam said, looking at Dalan evenly. "Zed told me you recruited me to replace Marth. Did you really pick me because you thought I was an easily manipulated fool?"

"Those weren't my exact words," Zed interrupted.

"Yes," Dalan said curtly, returning Tristam's gaze. "When you served my uncle you were headstrong, impetuous, and eager to please. The slightest criticism crushed you, while the smallest compliment could buy your loyalty for weeks. I believed you would be the perfect pawn, talented but malleable."

Tristam's face darkened.

"Stay your temper, Tristam," Dalan said. "You've proven me quite wrong, and I am glad for that. Your ability to think for yourself has saved us all, time and again."

Tristam's eyes widened, surprised by Dalan's use of his first name.

"Marshal, am I lying?" Dalan asked.

"No," the paladin replied.

"There you have it," Dalan said. "Now if you will pardon me, I am not a young man, and I am still exhausted from my kidnapping and torture. If there is anything further, I shall be in my cabin." Dalan stood and made to return to his chambers.

"I don't think I trust you anymore, Dalan," Tristam said to the guild master's back.

"Good," Dalan replied. "You've finally caught up with the rest of the world. Thank you again for saving my life." He closed the door behind him.

"Infuriating man," Eraina said, returning to the bow of the ship.

Zed chuckled and strolled off to help Omax with the ship's maintenance. Gerith disappeared into the galley. Tristam stared at the hatch of Dalan's cabin for nearly a minute, then headed below deck, mumbling something about Kiris's journals. Seren started to follow him, but stopped. She moved to Dalan's cabin, knocking quietly on the hatch.

"Enter," said Dalan's voice.

She slid the hatch open a crack and slipped inside. Dalan sat on his cot, a book open in his lap. Gunther lay at the foot of the bed, nose nestled between his shaggy paws. His tail thumped the cot in recognition.

"Seren," Dalan said, looking up over his reading glasses. "What can I do for you?"

"Was Jamus Roland really your friend?" she asked softly.

"A complex question," Dalan said. "As I have told you before, the term 'friend' is not one that I value. It is bandied about too easily. A man who calls himself a friend might draw his sword against you if it serves his purposes tomorrow, particularly during the Last War. We were spies, Seren. Such men do not give or accept trust easily. Yet I trusted Jamus Roland. I fought beside him, and we saved one another's lives on a few occasions." Dalan laughed. "What's more, I even *liked* him. I can count the people I have ever truly liked on less than one hand. So if that is what you call a friend, then yes, he was my friend."

Seren hugged her arms against her chest, chewing over a thought for several moments before speaking. "Is that why you really kept me here, then?" she asked. "Because I knew Jamus and you felt sorry for me?"

"Haha, no," Dalan said. "That would have been my motivation when I quietly arranged for you to be transported home to Ringbriar with a small sum of money, as I initially planned. I was a great deal more pleased when you proved to be indispensable. I find it comforting to have Jamus' apprentice with us. It is as if he is here, in a way, though you smell a great deal nicer than he did."

Seren laughed. "So you fought beside Jamus?" she asked.

"A few times, yes," Dalan said. "I was never much of a warrior, but that man was deadly with a dagger."

Seren nodded. "So you've seen him fight."

"What are you getting at, Seren?" he asked warily.

"The other thing I wanted to talk to you about," she said. "Jamus taught me to fight. I'm not the sort to brag, but he always said I was a talented student—as good as he was in his time."

"How nice for you," Dalan said, looking slightly confused. "What does this have to do with anything?"

"Nothing, I just wanted you to know," she said.

"Why?" he asked, sensing more.

Seren shrugged. "Because I know Eraina's ability to detect lies isn't infallible, and that if anyone is adept at dancing around the truth, it's you. I just hope you're telling Tristam everything. For your sake." Seren looked at him coldly. "If you hurt Tristam, you won't see me coming."

"I'll keep that in mind," Dalan said, his voice breaking a little.

"Enjoy your book." Seren said. She smiled brightly and left the cabin.

Dalan stared at the hatch for a good, long time.

Chapter Three

"Karrnath is your homeland, isn't it, Eraina?" Zed asked as she joined him at the rail.

The paladin nodded, looking down at the approaching town of Vulyar with a solemn expression.

"What can you tell me about this town?" he asked.

"There's very little to tell," she said. "Just another town. Peaceful. Never saw a lot of battle. Invaders usually stop at Fort Bones to the southwest, so Vulyar escaped the Last War virtually unscathed. It is a boring place, unless you're a merchant, but sometimes 'boring' can be a godsend."

"Fort Bones?" Pherris asked, looking at her curiously. "What a dreadful name. Why would someone give that sort of name to a place?"

"It's something of a legend of the Last War," she said. "The fort was razed after a surprise attack, but the Karrns rallied and won the day. They had to rebuild, and quickly. So they used the bones of their enemies to fortify the walls."

Pherris gave her an incredulous look. "Bone hardly seems the hardiest of building materials," he said.

"The Karrnathi military relies heavily on necromancy," Eraina said grimly. "I can't say that I approve, but death magic has quite efficiently protected our people for generations. The fortifications worked surprisingly well, and the improvised defenses held off all attacks until reinforcements arrived and the enemy departed, seeking easier pickings. Since then, it has become tradition. Any time the fort is attacked, the bones of any slain enemies are added to its defenses."

"A grim sort of folktale," Pherris said.

"It's no folktale," Eraina said. "It is a true story. The Karrn are a fierce, stubborn, and unforgiving people. We are prone to making dramatic examples of our enemies, so that others will be loath to challenge us. I find it barbaric, but it is our way."

"What you call barbaric I find admirable," Dalan said as he emerged from his cabin. His face was still faintly bruised, but he wore a freshly pressed black suit and appeared entirely refreshed from his ordeal. "Dramatic examples defeat future enemies before a battle even begins. It is an extraordinarily humane way to conduct a nation's defense. Those bones, after all, weren't being put to any other use."

Eraina looked at Dalan and sighed.

"Pherris," Dalan continued, ignoring the paladin, "please pull in as close as you can to the village. The lightning rail station may have a proper sky tower of some sort. Eraina, if you would be so kind, I request your presence. The locals will react suspiciously to an unexpected foreign airship docking in their town. The presence of a countryman, especially one who bears the mark of the Hearthmother, may ease my attempts at diplomacy."

"Of course," she said, eyeing Dalan with her usual caution.

"And Tristam?" Dalan peered about, seeing no sign of the artificer. He sighed. "If anyone sees Master Xain, tell him to perform only the minimum labor necessary so that we might travel on to Korth safely. I can arrange the rest of the repairs there for lesser expense. The merchants of Vulyar are accustomed to charging inflated prices to their curious halfling visitors, and I would prefer to avoid their greed. In the meantime, I have business in Korth that can be attended while the ship is repaired there."

"Eager to check in with Baron Zorlan?" Zed said.

FLIGHT OF THE DYING SUN

Dalan nodded gravely.

"You plan to face the master of your own House, Dalan?" Eraina asked.

Dalan snorted.

"Zorlan is not the master of House Cannith," Dalan said. "The Cannith patriarch died on the Day of Mourning. Since then, the leadership of my House has been split by petty political squabbles. I respect all of the so-called lords of my House but acknowledge none of them."

"Petty politics, in your family?" Zed asked dryly.

"Surprising, I know," Dalan said. "Zorlan is one of the leading contenders for leadership, but he holds no authority over me. If I were to acknowledge any Cannith as the new patriarch, it would be Baron Merrix."

"Assuming you didn't just make a bid for control yourself," Zed said.

Dalan laughed lightly. "Politics can be unpredictable," he said. "But my own ambitions are not our concern. If what the Ghost Talons told us is true, Zorlan d'Cannith—or, more likely, someone claiming his authority—knows a great deal more about Marth's activities than he ever divulged. Our own progress, such as it is, is also likely known to them. I despise being kept in the dark. I intend to discover if I have been manipulated by my superiors." He sneered at Zed. "You may now make some biting comment regarding the irony of this moment. I am waiting."

Zed only smiled. "I wasn't going to say anything," he said. "I'm just wondering how you're going to handle the baron. He's not a kind man, if rumor serves."

"I shall handle him as I handle all my affairs," Dalan said. "Cautiously and indirectly."

"Riders incoming," Pherris said, pointing at the city gates. The *Karia Naille* slowed to a smooth hover above the Vulyar lightning rail station. A squad of mounted horsemen in grim black armor were already galloping toward the sky tower.

"Why is it every time we go somewhere new, we're always met by armed guards?" Dalan mused.

"Unmarked airships do not inspire trust," Eraina said. "Why do you fly your ship with no marks of nation or house, d'Cannith? You must admit it looks terribly suspicious."

"Because of the weight such colors carry," he said, stepping to the edge of the deck as Omax secured the ship to the tower. "All nations have enemies, as do all Houses. Even worse, they all have allies—allies who may presume that I have come to aid them, or who would seek to ingratiate themselves to us. I haven't the time for such nonsense."

"You would prefer to appear suspicious to everyone you meet?"

"Quite so," Dalan said. "I can deal with suspicion. It can almost invariably be allayed via diplomacy or bribery. At the very least I always know where I stand."

Dalan stepped onto the tower bridge and climbed down the stairs. Eraina followed. Dalan smoothed one hand over the breast of his suit as he stepped out onto the street. The riders surrounded them. They held crossbows at the ready, half of them keeping a wary eye on the hovering airship.

"Speak your name and business," the captain demanded.

"We are here on an official investigation on behalf of the Sentinel Marshals," Eraina said, emerging beside Dalan. She snapped open a metal case, displaying her official seal. "We wish to purchase supplies so that we can repair our vessel and continue on to Korth."

The captain stared at the seal for nearly a minute, with the air of a man who isn't quite sure if he's looking at an official document, and doesn't know if it's worth making a fuss about. "Marshal Eraina Deneith, eh?"

"My commanding officer is Marshal Kirin Galas, currently stationed in Korth," she said. "You may contact him for verification."

"I don't think that will be necessary," the captain said with a

FLIGHT OF THE DYING SUN

bored sigh. He peered up at the airship again, studying the vehicle cautiously. "As long as you move on quickly."

"Expediency is our primary goal, I assure you of that, Captain," Dalan said smoothly. "Now, if I might trouble you, could you please point me in the direction of a local carpenter or lumber mill? I wish to make a few substantial purchases." He dug into his jacket pocket. "If it helps, I have a precisely detailed list . . ."

Dalan strode away with the captain in tow, grinning broadly as he discussed business. Eraina remained behind, noting that two of the Karrnathi soldiers remained behind at a respectful distance, watching the ship.

"That was unexpected," said a gruff voice. "I didn't think you had it in you, Eraina."

Eraina glanced back as Zed Arthen stepped out of the tower beside her. He was wearing his long, shabby coat but had left his sword behind. He clenched a thin pipe between his teeth, drifting a plume of smoke over one shoulder.

"What are you talking about, Arthen?" she asked stiffly.

"Your vow of honesty," he said, keeping his voice soft enough that the remaining soldiers would not hear. He nodded at them amiably.

Eraina glared at him coldly.

"Oh you didn't lie, sure," he said, "but you didn't tell them the whole truth, either. I thought your vows were a little less flexible than that."

"I told them precisely what they needed to know, and no more," she said. "Do not question my dedication to my goddess."

"A hair is a fine thing to split," Zed said, "but it gets easier with practice. Be careful, Eraina."

"Or what?" she said with a bitter laugh. "Am I to endure lessons in maintaining my vows from a knight who could not uphold his own?"

"Why not?" he asked, spitting a puff of smoke at her. "Nobody knows the way down better than me." He straightened his heavy coat over his shoulders and headed off into the city.

Eraina glared after him for a long time, then started down the road leading out of the rail station. She kept her distance behind him, looking pointedly away when he glanced back. Zed stopped and looked back, waiting for her. She moved toward the far side of the road and kept walking.

"I going into town on purely personal business, Arthen," she said. "I do not require your company."

"We're both going into town, Eraina," Zed said, limping quickly after her. "We may as well walk together."

"Go with one of the others," Eraina said. "I have no desire for your company."

"Nobody else is going but you and me," he said. "Pherris is too tired. Gerith is still depressed about the Ghost Talon massacre. Tristam is studying Kiris's journals, so that means Seren isn't wandering too far away either. Omax knows better."

"Knows better?" she asked archly.

"Your people treat his like slaves," Zed said. "Omax could pretend that he belongs to Tristam, but he'd still get treated like a mindless machine here. Karrnath isn't a place where a free warforged feels welcome."

Eraina grimaced uncomfortably. "The law stands for a reason," she said. "Not all warforged are as kind and contemplative as Omax. Karrnath endured many injuries at the hands of warforged soldiers. Many believe that they are better off kept in check."

"Do you believe that?" he asked.

"No," she said. "I believe they would not have been given life without purpose, and to ignore such a miracle is to squander that purpose. The gods smile upon the warforged, even if they did not create them. Yet I serve the law."

Zed chuckled. "You do a good job of juggling all of that ridiculous dogma and still coming out of it a decent person, but I don't envy you one bit, Marshal."

"The others remained behind," she said, changing the subject.

FLIGHT OF THE DYING SUN

"But you did not. What business do you have here?"

"Nothing in particular. I couldn't stand it in that ship any longer." Zed looked up at Vulyar's rough walls, removing the pipe from his mouth for a moment. "I need to be around people. Find a tavern, restaurant, someplace to just sit for the night."

"Odd," she said. "You don't seem like a particularly social person."

"I'm not," he said. "I can't stand talking to people, but I like to watch them, listen to them, to figure out what makes them think the way they do—but from a distance." He tapped his temple. "I like to get into their heads. It's strange, but hey, you asked."

"No, I understand," she said. "I sometimes find myself doing the same thing. It sharpens one's investigative skills."

"That's part of it, sure," he said, nodding rapidly and popping the pipe back into his mouth. "You can't do that on a little ship like *Karia Naille*. Everyone knows each other. Everyone's too easy to read. Except Dalan, and he's too much trouble."

"True," Eraina said with a small laugh.

"And you," Zed said. "I don't quite have a handle on you, yet."

She looked at him. "Why do you require a handle on me?"

"I reckon I don't," he said. "I just like knowing which way people are likely to swing when trouble hits, and with you I really can't tell. One day you're threatening to muster allies and bring the law down on us, the next day you're cleaning out the cargo bay and healing our wounds."

"What is your point?" she asked.

"I've known more than my share of paladins, Marshal," Zed said. "You're a fair shade more complex than most of them, to put it gently. Most of them are a lot more blunt. They see evil, they smite it. They see a foe, they pursue. You're a lot more subtle. Flexible."

"Faith is not a symptom of ignorance, Arthen," she said. "A mortal can champion the gods without setting her brain aside."

"Fair enough," he said, "but to be fair, faith and ignorance are usually bunkmates, even if they're unrelated. You may be the exception, Marshal. Like I said—I don't envy you."

She laughed. "Because I am a paladin, but I am no fool?"

"Maybe," he said. "You remind me too much of myself."

They walked deeper into the sleeping city. Though Vulyar was a center of commerce between Karrnath and the Talenta Plains, few of the locals were abroad in the streets. It was too early and too hot to be working. Those who were about took the time to pause and stare at the two strangers who had entered the city. They cast nervous looks at Zed but seemed reassured by Eraina's presence. One man even whispered a brief prayer to Boldrei before hurrying away. Zed watched the man go, a sad, bitter look in his eyes. Then it all made sense.

Eraina looked at Zed intently. "You were not merely a Knight of Thrane, were you?" she asked. "You were touched by the Flame. You were a paladin."

"I never said anything like that," he said.

"But you were," she said. "Weren't you?"

"You don't know what you're talking about," he said, scowling at her.

"Yes or no," she said. "That's all you need to say."

"Why, so you can tell if I'm lying?" Zed said. "You need to drop this, Eraina. Is that clear? It's not something I like to talk about."

Eraina looked away. "Fine," she said softly. "Then let us speak of something else."

"How about something useful, then?" he asked. "We're both investigators. Why don't we try to figure out how Marth keeps following us?"

"He can't follow us now," she said. "His flagship is demolished."

"Until he repairs the *Seventh Moon,* you mean," Zed said. "Tristam is sure that's only a matter of time. So let's use the breather we have to figure out what's going on. Ever since Wroat, Marth has known where the *Karia Naille* was going to be as soon as we did. We still don't know how."

FLIGHT OF THE DYING SUN

"He is a powerful artificer," Eraina said. "Could he not use magic to find us?"

Zed sighed. "You're smart enough to know what a lazy answer that is," he said. "Magic isn't all-powerful. It isn't infallible. Most important, magic is on our side too. If there was some way that Marth could predict our course with magic, don't you think Tristam would have found some way to block it? Or at least warn us about it?"

Eraina nodded thoughtfully. "What other explanation could there be?" she asked. "A traitor?"

Zed sneered. "It has to be," he said. "There's a leak of information somewhere, that's for certain. I can only think of one significant thing that has changed for the *Karia Naille* since she left Wroat, and that's Seren."

"No," Eraina said, predicting Zed's line of thought. "Seren Morisse is not responsible. My father would not have adopted a traitor. I have seen no deceit within her."

"I don't really believe she would do it, either," Zed admitted. "I'm grasping at anything here. Maybe it's Dalan? He's worked with them before."

"Whatever Dalan's faults may be," Eraina said, "I believe he is sincere in his desire to stop Marth. It is only his methods that I find suspect."

"That's not what I mean," Zed said. "Dragonmark heirs are expected to send regular reports while on missions abroad, right? Just so their house knows that they're safe. We already know Baron Zorlan d'Cannith has some sort of unusual interest in our mission. Maybe he's been keeping tabs on Dalan and feeding information to Marth?"

"A bold leap of assumptions," Eraina said. "Too many maybes, and Dalan is no fool. His ship does not even bear his House's crest. I would be surprised if any other member of House Cannith knew where he was."

"True," Zed said. "It's a terrible theory, but it's the only one I could think of. The other members of the crew are trustworthy. You've vouched for Seren, and you . . ."

"I am an idiot paladin, incapable of betrayal," Eraina said.

"I didn't say that," Zed said.

"Of course you did not," she said with a small grin.

Zed stopped outside the door to a small tavern. "I think this is where I stop," he said, looking at the sign above the door. "The Beaten Mule," he read. "I wonder what poor mad poet dreams up the names of places like this."

"I will return when I have attended my duties here, Arthen," she said. "Perhaps we could discuss this further over whatever passes for drink here."

"Water," he said.

She looked at him curiously. "Temperance is not a virtue I expected you to retain."

"It's the only one I have left," he said with a dry chuckle.

The inquisitive pushed open the door of the Beaten Mule and disappeared inside. Eraina looked at the door briefly, weighing some internal decision, then continued on her way.

CHAPTER
FOUR

The steady crystal song of trickling water filled the cavern. Pure streams cascaded down curtains of stone to fill deep, clear pools. Small motes of magical light hovered in the air, illuminating the natural beauty of the tunnels. The walls glistened with more colors than could be named, flowing like cloth in subtle patterns. It was amazing how something as simple as untouched stone could hold such beauty. A little time, a little moisture, and the mundane became extraordinary.

Coming here always brought him peace. There were other reasons to dwell upon this place, of course, but it was the sound, the shimmer, and the calm that somehow brought him some measure of balance. As the changeling knelt beside the pool and bound his wounds, he sought that balance now.

"Betrayal," whispered a sibilant voice from the darkness. "Nothing stings quite as deeply."

Marth peered over one shoulder. The pink scars that covered his right cheek glistened, as if freshly burned. A new light shone in the darkness, a sphere of copper flame that hovered in midair. A monk in robes to match the fire stood at the edge of the shadows, cupping the radiance in his hand. The light shone upon the walls deeper in the caverns, reflecting the twisting scripts painted there. He removed his hand from the flame and stepped away. It remained hovering where he had summoned it.

The monk looked down at Marth with sympathy.

"Brother Zamiel," Marth whispered. His voice was still dry with smoke, and he bowed his head in respect. Obviously his visitor could have been none other than the prophet. The guards would not have allowed anyone else this deep within his stronghold without violence.

"So cruel a barb," the monk replied, inclining his head in recognition. "No matter how often it wounds us, it is never any less painful or unexpected. There is no defense, no prevention for betrayal save not to trust—and a soul that does not trust is truly lost. Would you not agree? I sense the weight of betrayal heaped upon your shoulders." Zamiel gestured at the thick bandage that bound Marth's upper back. "It has taken quite a literal manifestation, in this case."

"I killed Kiris Overwood," Marth said, his voice thick. "Tristam Xain and his allies turned her against us."

"A shame," the prophet said, nodding sagely. "Kiris was a fragile, foolish girl, but her insight was useful." Zamiel frowned. "How did this happen?"

"We crippled the *Mourning Dawn* on her way to the Boneyard, but the ship escaped before she was destroyed," Marth said. "You were right to put a spy among the Ghost Talons, Brother Zamiel. Not only were they monitoring Kiris's activities on behalf of House Cannith, but they also made a deal with Dalan d'Cannith to repair his airship."

"And Xain discovered Kiris," Zamiel said. He sat at the edge of the pond, staring into the depthless water.

Marth bowed his head. "Obviously he poisoned her mind against me," he said. "The only kindness I could spare her was a swift death, lest her knowledge be turned against us. I am uncertain what Xain learned from her, but apparently House Cannith was also using the Ghost Talons to monitor us. I took Dalan d'Cannith alive to use as leverage against his house, but the *Mourning Dawn* attacked and boarded us."

FLIGHT OF THE DYING SUN

Zamiel coughed in surprise. "Boarded you?" he asked, incredulous. "Ridiculous. *Mourning Dawn* is no match for *Seventh Moon*. I thought you said you had crippled her?"

"The fault is mine," Marth said. "You were right to warn me against mercy. Xain is a great deal more resourceful than I imagined. He rescued d'Cannith, shattered the *Moon's* elemental containment core, and fled. Fortunately most of the crew survived the crash, and the elemental was dispatched after it had slain no more than a dozen soldiers. Repairs have already commenced. My own mobility remains unhindered, due to my magic, but not having a crew at my disposal forces me to act more cautiously abroad."

"Understood," Zamiel said. "How soon before your flagship can be repaired?"

"Binding a new elemental is a long and difficult process," Marth said. "Only the Zil'argo gnomes have truly mastered it, and coercing a skilled craftsman into assisting us could be difficult. It may be months before the *Moon* flies again."

"But not an insurmountable problem," Zamiel said. "What of Tristam Xain?" He looked at Marth curiously.

"Still alive, for now," Marth said.

The prophet looked at Marth quietly, his question unspoken.

"I have called in a favor," the changeling said. "Shaimin d'Thuranni has agreed to aid us."

"A single assassin where your entire crew failed?" Zamiel asked, rising and pacing slowly about the cavern. "I do not like that."

"He is a Thuranni," Marth said. "They do not fail."

"I know of his family's reputation," Zamiel said. "Even without their dragonmarks, their deadly cunning is without parallel. All the same, you must have a great deal of faith in this man to entrust an outsider with your enemy."

"We have a history," Marth said. "Thuranni House upholds its obligations. He can be trusted."

"Very well," Zamiel said, though he sounded unsatisfied. "And what remains for us to do before the Legacy is complete?"

"It is already complete," Marth said, his voice distant. He reached beneath the folded jacket that lay by his side and drew out a small cylinder.

It was an unimpressive, simple thing—an unadorned tube of pure black metal that seemed to absorb light. It was no longer than a foot, no thicker than a man's wrist. Yet the prophet's eyes widened when he sensed the power lurking within it.

"That is a working replica of the Legacy?" Zamiel said in a hushed voice. "How is that possible? I thought that Ashrem's remaining notes were imperfect, that there were still pieces of the mystery that remained to discover."

"There are," Marth said. "Yet I am not completely bereft of skill with artifice. I have taken what we have learned and made deductions, filled the gaps with my own knowledge. I believe that I have reproduced the Legacy much as Ashrem intended. It is unstable, imperfect, but workable."

"Then why are you still concerned with Xain and the others?" Zamiel asked with an excited chuckle. "They can no longer bar you from your destiny. Let us proceed to Sharn and remake the world as it should be."

"No," Marth said, shaking his head vigorously. "Not yet. The time is not right. The Legacy is not yet ready to use on the scale we intended. Even more curious, its purpose remains unclear."

"You know its purpose, Marth," Zamiel said. "You know better than anyone, save Ashrem himself."

"Yes," Marth said, "but I still don't know why a man like Ashrem d'Cannith would ever create such a thing. It does not seem right. It makes no sense. I do not trust it, and an untrustworthy tool cannot be put toward such an important task. If the Legacy has a hidden purpose, something other than what I expect, then how can I rely upon it to perform as I desire?" The changeling sighed. "I suppose my babblings must not make a great deal of sense to you, prophet."

FLIGHT OF THE DYING SUN

"More than you realize." Zamiel chuckled. "Perhaps you are right to be wary. A test may be in order."

"Agreed," Marth said. "Though I must be cautious. I cannot test the Legacy in an uninhabited area, or there will be no way to determine if it truly produces its effects on the scale we intend. Yet if I reveal its power too recklessly, the threat it represents would be diminished. If others are aware of what the Legacy can do, they might prepare against it and find ways to defend against it."

"True," Zamiel said. "But Eberron is a vast place, populated with many ignorant fools. Surely there must be some area where you could test the Legacy and no one of consequence would witness it, or have any reaction other than pointless panic."

"Surely," Marth said quietly, but his voice was troubled.

"I leave it to you," Zamiel said. "The appropriate opportunity will present itself in time."

The prophet bowed and receded into the darkness without a sound.

* * * * * * *

Power.

Power was a commodity that wavered under scrutiny and invariably waned when it was revealed. True dominance could not be measured merely by the possession of power but also by one's willingness to keep that power in secrecy until it was needed. Such was a lesson Zamiel had long ago learned, and thus he was cautious, even in Marth's presence. The prophet valued Marth—as much as he was capable of valuing anyone other than himself—but that was no reason to be lax. Caution was key. The Prophecy appeared to favor Marth. The Prophecy was never wrong. However, it could be misread. Zamiel had no illusions about his own fallibility. He had been wrong too many times before to indulge such arrogance. Entrusting too much faith in fickle mortals was a waste of time, and thus he concealed the extent of his knowledge and abilities even from allies such as Marth.

And so it was that the prophet walked a good distance from the caverns before drawing upon his magic. He spoke a single word, and then was somewhere else. Zamiel stood in the shadows of a dirty stone building, leaning slightly off balance from the passage of time and shoddy construction. Cities were a curious thing. There were too many sights, sounds, smells, all colliding at once. With so much clamoring for attention, to even try to pay attention was pointless. Focus on one thing and it would quickly be supplanted by another, equally meaningless sensation. It was all so . . . temporary. Zamiel squinted his nose in annoyance and ignored it all.

A presence close behind drew the prophet's attention. He peered over his shoulder just as a heavy wooden board collided with the back of his head. The prophet fell to one knee from the force of the attack. A second blow struck him across the back before he recovered his senses enough to turn and pluck the weapon from his assailant's hand. An unshaven man in shabby clothing stared in blank surprise, his hands now grasping empty air. Zamiel rose unharmed, looming much taller than he had only seconds before.

"Why did you attack me?" Zamiel asked, his voice shining with curiosity. His eyes gleamed with a strange eagerness.

The dirty man turned and ran. Zamiel smiled faintly and watched him depart. He weighed the possibility of stopping the vagrant, perhaps even killing him for the unprovoked attack, but what purpose would that serve? It wasn't as if the man had accomplished anything, and it was not Zamiel's duty to remove garbage from these human streets. He dropped the wooden bludgeon amid the piled refuse and stepped out of the alley.

Better to be done with his business and be gone than to waste undue time. He strode through the city with a purpose, his sharp eyes flicking from one person to the next, analyzing their worth and then discarding them. The crowd unconsciously parted around him, never taking note of his presence and returning to their business after he passed.

The prophet turned a corner and entered a broad thoroughfare, sloping upward to the north. The streets were cleaner, more orderly. Marble representations of the Sovereign Host loomed over the passing citizens, looking down with expressions of love, determination, or patient indifference. Zamiel paused to study the craftsmanship, allowing himself a small smile as he approached the man who waited in the shadows of Kol Korran's sculpture.

"A fitting place for us to meet," Zamiel said, looking up into the eyes of a broadly grinning dwarf. "God of wealth, commerce. Patron of merchants, bankers, thieves, and all those who desire more than they deserve. I can only wonder why the Host would allow someone like Kol Korran in their midst. Like mortals, I can only assume they will allow any manner of devil in their midst as long as he proves sufficiently useful, and fear that he would be far more dangerous as an enemy."

"Does your brotherhood encourage such blasphemy, monk?" the man said, eyes widening in surprise.

"The members of my brotherhood, for lack of a better name, think for themselves," Zamiel replied with some amusement. "We respect the gods, as we respect all things powerful and ancient, but we do not fear them. The gods are content to remain distant from the world, seeking nothing more than the adoration of small minds. They did not create this world. They do not control this world. Their wrath cannot be predicted or assuaged. There is no more sense in fearing them than there is in fearing a thunderstorm—the storm will do as it wishes whether one fears it or not. Likewise, there is no reason to cower before divinity."

"You should not say such things," the man said, glancing at Kol Korran nervously.

Zamiel chuckled darkly. "My words make you uncomfortable, spy?" he asked. "Then let us speak of something else."

"Yes," the other man agreed, glancing about quickly, "but not here." He ducked into the alley between the statues of Kol Korran and Boldrei. The prophet followed, shrugging his arms into his thick sleeves as he walked.

"There is little point in such measures," Zamiel said as he stepped into the shadows. "If I do not wish us to be overheard, it will not happen."

"If you say so," the man said. "Forgive me if I'm a little more careful than you. I have a reputation in this city."

"Naturally," Zamiel said, with an indulgent smile. "Now share with me what you have learned."

"The *Karia Naille* makes her port in Vulyar," the man said.

"Vulyar?" Zamiel replied. "Why such a remote location?"

"The ship was badly damaged in battle," he replied. "They put in for repairs lest it collapse upon itself. I don't know for sure how it became damaged. I was not told."

Zamiel frowned thoughtfully. "Do you think they suspect your betrayal?"

"I am beyond suspicion," the man said with an arrogant laugh. "The last message was short because there was little need for an in-depth report."

The man fell silent. Zamiel sensed he was waiting for him to inquire further, keeping a valuable revelation in reserve, savoring it. The prophet resisted the urge to roll his eyes and indulged the game a bit further. Tools like this were easier to use when they felt some measure of control. "Why no need for a report?" he asked.

"Because my contact will soon be arriving personally," the man said.

The prophet smiled. This was good news. "The *Karia Naille* is coming to Korth?" he mused.

"As soon as she is relatively airworthy," he said. "Several of her crew members, including my contact, have business here. She should be in port here for at least a week."

"Very interesting," Zamiel said. He reached into the pocket

FLIGHT OF THE DYING SUN

of his left sleeve and drew out a small, dense bag. He pressed it into the spy's palm, and he accepted it eagerly. "May your house prosper," he said.

The spy nodded eagerly. "How soon?" he asked. "When will the war begin anew?"

"You will know when I do, my friend," Zamiel said, allowing himself a small smile.

Zamiel's contact nodded eagerly and stepped away, pausing only to glance around for eyes and ears that were not there. The prophet watched him go with a bored, patient smile. As soon as he was alone in the alley, he spoke another word of magic and was gone.

Chapter
Five

If there was a word to describe the city of Korth, it was "uninviting." Centuries of building and development had turned the streets of Korth into a meandering, confusing mess. Recent attempts to rebuild and restore order to damaged parts of the city had only made matters worse. Massive square buildings stood in even rows along well paved streets only blocks away from snarled webs of dead end streets. Karrnathi pride was obvious in its architecture, as all buildings, old and new, featured the grim statuary and delicately twisted wrought iron so common in this land. Compared to Wroat, Seren was amazed at how dark the city was. Her first impulse was that it seemed to be a very cold, unyielding place. The murky gray clouds and steady drizzle of rain cast the city in a mournful light. This was a place of strict, unflinching law.

The sooner they were gone from here, the better.

"It has been some time since I have visited a leader of my House," Dalan mused, joining Seren at the railing. He held the same thick ledger he had been carrying so often of late, toying idly with a stick of charcoal as he sketched on a page. "I doubt Zorlan will be eager to see me. He was good friends with my uncle, until the end."

"I'm guessing Zorlan was one of the ones who didn't approve when Ashrem acquired a taste for peace?" Zed asked.

"Certain words were exchanged between Zorlan and my uncle

FLIGHT OF THE DYING SUN

on several occasions," Dalan replied. "Suffice it to say that the Baron's disrespect encouraged me to throw my support behind his rival, Merrix. I may not have agreed with my uncle's philosophies, but neither will I endure slander heaped upon him."

"I hesitate to posit such an uncomfortable question, Master d'Cannith," Pherris said from the helm, "but what if Zorlan is in league with Marth? The changeling's ship is crippled just as ours was. If Marth is forced to seek repairs and Zorlan is his ally, Korth will probably be his destination as well."

"I haven't ruled out the possibility," Dalan said, eyeing the city below thoughtfully. He clapped the book shut and tucked the charcoal into his pocket. "Yet I think it is unlikely. Zorlan is not the sort of man to consort with mercenaries—he has plenty of his own loyal troops. Further, Zorlan lost all respect for my uncle's work when Ashrem turned his attention away from armaments of war. As I said, he was quite vocal in his denouncements. I think Zorlan would be too proud to use the Legacy to secure his own bid for power. Using one of Ashrem's inventions to secure his bid for power would be too much like admitting he was wrong. He would be more likely to destroy the Legacy altogether, if he knew about it."

"So what do we expect to find here, Master d'Cannith?" Pherris asked.

"Clarity, Captain Gerriman," Dalan answered. "Now take us down."

Karia Naille soared downward, weaving between the heavy structures of Korth toward the sky towers near the river bank. A pot-bellied dock officer waddled across the bridge to inspect their vessel. Dalan took the man aside and, after a few quiet moments of discourse, pressed a small pouch into the man's hand with a grin. The officer glanced over the ship a final time, smiling eagerly, and disappeared back into the tower.

"Docking fees, so to speak," Dalan said. "I have tipped the man to be incurious." Dalan glanced over the crew with a smug grin. "You are all free to do as you like. I have no idea how long we will remain here. At least long enough to conduct our repairs. Our next destination still waits for us to find it. Omax, if you would be so kind, I would appreciate your attendance as I go to meet with the would-be master of my House. We must hurry."

The warforged looked over sharply from his daydreaming. Seren noticed that Omax seemed distracted of late. The injuries he had sustained on the *Moon* still scarred his metal chest.

The warforged inclined his head. "Do you expect danger, Dalan?" he asked coolly.

"Not from the Baron himself," he said. "If Zorlan had hostile intents, there is little we could do, save flee. His resources and manpower dwarf nations. However, I do not believe he is our true rival."

Omax's eyes flickered. "Then who?" he asked evenly.

"I do not know," Dalan said. "Thus we must hurry, so he will make a mistake and reveal himself."

"I'm going too," Tristam said, stepping onto the deck. His reading spectacles were still perched on the bridge of his nose. He snatched them away absently and tucked them into his coat. "I want to hear this."

"You are required here, Tristam," Dalan said, his voice edged with impatience. "Only you can direct the ship's repairs."

"And we can't repair the ship without proper materials," Tristam said. "I gave Gerith the list. He'll gather them while we meet with the Baron. By the time he returns, we'll be done."

The halfling had been chewing absently on an apple. He looked up happily at the sound of his name, flashing the hastily written list he clutched in one hand.

Dalan's gaze rested heavily on Gerith, then returned to Tristam again. "I do not have the energy to argue, Tristam," he said with a sigh. "Accompany me if you must."

"And Seren, too," Tristam said.

"Khyber, why don't we all go?" Dalan snapped, throwing his

hands in the air. "I'll bring the dog too. Aeven can come. We'll make a holiday of it."

Tristam's face darkened.

"It's fine," Dalan amended, interrupting before Tristam could utter his angry reply. "Bring her. Follow me."

Dalan crossed the bridge and entered the tower, shrugging into his hood to ward off the misty rain. Omax, Tristam, and Seren followed, descending the stairs and stepping out onto the road. Dalan was waiting, looking back with a curious glint in his eye.

"If you would accompany me," he said, hurrying down the road once he saw they were following, "I must ask that you abide by my conditions."

"What conditions?" Seren asked suspiciously.

"First, do not speak unless someone asks you a question," Dalan said. "Answer with yes or no, if possible. If more information is needed, answer with as few words as you can muster."

"What?" Tristam said. "You want us to shut up?"

"A focused front is required for all negotiations," Seren said. "Jamus always taught me that."

"Ha." Dalan said smirked. "And who do you think taught him that? Me."

"So we pretend to agree," Tristam said. "Even if we don't, just so that we are not divided further."

"Precisely," Dalan said. He glanced up and down the street, searching for an available coach. "I trust your expertise in matters of magic. You must trust me in matters of politics. The most basic tenet of politics is not to speak needlessly around men who hear more than you mean to say. Any arguments can be reserved for a later time, in private."

"That makes a great deal of sense," Tristam grudgingly admitted.

"My second condition," Dalan said, "is that you listen carefully to me. If I use the name 'Old Ash' in reference to my uncle, that is a signal. I will not say it by accident, for I never called my uncle by that ridiculous nickname."

"Signal for what?" Seren asked.

"To argue against me on whatever topic we happen to be discussing," he said. "I'm certain none of you will find that too onerous a task."

"Why?" Tristam asked. "What's the point of that?"

"A focused front is a significant strength," Dalan said, "but sometimes it is useful to appear weak. It can lead the opponent into overconfidence."

"I think I'm thankful my mind isn't as tangled as yours, Dalan," Tristam said.

Dalan ignored the comment. "Just remember. Such trickery is generally unnecessary, but I prefer to lay contingencies in place."

They hurried through the labyrinthine streets of Korth. The path was busy and more than one stranger studied them as they walked past. Seren felt strangely ill at ease. She peered about as she walked, her instincts screaming that something was amiss. She searched as cautiously as possible, hood shading her eyes so that her search would not be obvious. One hand rested unconsciously on her dagger's hilt. She was uncertain what she was seeking—only that it was there.

Tristam noticed her unease and looked around urgently. "Something wrong, Seren?" he asked.

Then the warning faded as quickly as it had come. Seren furrowed her brow in confusion and shook her head. "No," she said. "It was nothing."

Dalan finished his negotiations with a coachman and climbed aboard the vehicle, curtly gesturing for the others to follow. The coachman gave Omax a wary sneer as the warforged lumbered aboard, but said nothing.

"To the d'Cannith estates, at all possible speed," Dalan said as he sat back.

The driver nodded and drove the horses to a gallop with a crack of his whip. The vehicle rode smoothly through the grim capital, moving toward the busy streets of the Commerce Ward. The busy mumble of shouting merchants swallowed the silence. The air was filled with the rich scent of cooked bread and sweet spiced meats. The coach rumbled to a halt before a large estate near the center of the ward. Above the heavy steel gates was emblazoned the gorgon seal of House Cannith. Dalan pushed his cloak back over one shoulder, and now wore the same Cannith crest openly on his blue robe. The guild master steadied the small, square cap on his head and advanced toward the gates.

"I am Master Dalan Cannith, on urgent business from the City of Wroat," Dalan announced. "I wish to see Baron Zorlan at once."

The guards looked at each other uncertainly.

"Do you have identification, friend?" one asked.

"Would you prefer to see my papers or would this suffice?" Dalan asked. He drew up his loose right sleeve, displaying the twisted dragonmark pattern that covered his right shoulder.

"We will announce your arrival at once, Master d'Cannith," one of the guards said, quickly opening the gates.

An elderly servant in slate black livery was already approaching. He greeted them with a bow.

"Master d'Cannith, you are expected," the man said.

"Indeed," Dalan replied.

"The Baron is currently occupied," the servant said. "However his representative, Gavus Frauk, will attend you until he becomes available."

The guards quickly returned to their posts, gratefully resuming their uninteresting duties.

"My business is only with Zorlan," Dalan said sharply.

"Understood," the servant said in a mild, disinterested voice. "If you are too impatient to conduct an appointment through proper channels, you are free to depart and await the Baron's convenience in a local inn. We shall gladly dispatch a messenger to notify you when he is available. It may be days, I fear. This is a busy time."

Dalan gave a tight, joyless smile. "I apologize," he said. "I am too impatient to renew the bonds of family. I have been away from my kinsmen for a long time. I only assumed Zorlan would be eager to pay hospitality to his cousin, who served him during the War. Is this not so?"

"I am certain he will be pleased to meet with you," the servant replied with an equally thin smile. "But you visit us unannounced. The Baron is in the midst of an important meeting with several international clients. Should I interrupt and request that your arrival take precedence over the business of House Cannith?"

Dalan chuckled. "Of course not," he said. "Sometimes I overestimate my importance. A few small successes can leave even the most undeserving man to feel he is a master of the house." Dalan looked around the small courtyard idly. "Incidentally, Baron Merrix sends Zorlan his regards."

The servant studied Dalan blandly, ignoring the veiled barb. "Master Gavus awaits," he said. "If you are ready."

"That will be fine," Dalan said.

The servant bowed perfunctorily. "Follow me."

He led them into the estate, turning down a side hallway and leading them down the stairs. The interior of the building was as austere and dark as the outside, sparing little effort for decoration. The faint rhythm of a ringing anvil resounded elsewhere in the building, mixing discordantly with the voices of unseen chanters. The air smelled electric, alive. Magic lived here and was given form by the hands of artificers and magewrights. Tall statues lined the walls at intervals. Seren paused to study the plaques mounted beside a few. They were representations of former patriarchs of the guild or master artificers who had invented one legendary creation or another.

As they continued deeper, the busy sounds of the House of Making grew more subdued. The servant finally led them to a heavy door framed by shining magical stones in wire sconces. He spoke a word and gestured at the door, causing it to swing open. A small library waited within. A semicircle of bookcases surrounded a small group of stuffed velvet chairs. A single statue stood at the rear of the chamber, depicting an elderly artificer wielding a sword in one hand and a lantern in the other. A thin little man in pale white robes reclined in the chair beside the statue, peering up at them through his spectacles as they entered. His wispy hair was streaked with gray, and his face was lined with age. The room was strangely silent.

"Master Dalan d'Cannith of Wroat," the man said in a bored voice. "Finally you arrive. I am Gavus Frauk, one of the senior magewrights of the household. I would be pleased to keep you company until the Baron can make time to speak with you."

Dalan gave a short bow. Gavus offered a vague nod in reply. The servant slipped out and closed the door behind them.

"These are my associates," Dalan said, gesturing behind him as he sat in a chair across from Gavus. "Tristam Xain, Seren Morisse, and Omax."

"Tristam Xain," Gavus said, looking at Tristam intently. "I know that name. You were one of Ashrem d'Cannith's students."

Tristam paused halfway into another chair. "You've heard of me?" he asked, surprised.

"I am a great admirer of your late mentor's work," he said, gesturing at the statue behind him. "Isn't it obvious?"

Dalan looked up at the statue blandly. "Is that meant to be my uncle?" he asked. "It's a poor likeness of Ashrem. Too much chin. Eyes are too narrow. He would never wear a robe with sleeves that loose. They would drag in the ink and chemicals while he worked. Had this sculptor ever seen my uncle?"

Gavus' smile froze. "*I* was the sculptor," he said. "In point of fact, I knew Ashrem, and I think it is a good likeness."

"Ah," Dalan said. "Well, art is art, and there is no truth in art, is there? There is only what one likes and what one does not. Eye of the beholder and whatnot."

"A rather coarse and uncultured belief," Gavus said tersely. "That which has value is obvious to all those with a mind keen enough to perceive it."

"How did you know my uncle?" Dalan asked, changing the subject.

"Ashrem was a student of diverse schools of artifice and magic," Gavus said. "When he wished to know more about the nature of constructs, he came to me. I maintained correspondence with him, albeit irregularly, until his death. I considered him a friend."

"Constructs?" Seren said. "Did you build warforged?" Omax looked up curiously.

"No," Gavus said, looking at Omax with obvious unease. "I have fashioned parts that were used to construct warforged, but never participated directly in their animation. My expertise lies in the field of golemcraft."

"Mindless constructs," Dalan said.

"Quite," Gavus said. "The results are inflexible but more reliable, in my humble opinion. Warforged have a penchant for stubborn individuality. Golems do as they are told." He smiled briefly.

"And warforged think for themselves," Seren said.

"Not an altogether positive trait, for a weapon," Gavus said.

"A charming outlook," Dalan said.

"Do not misjudge me," Gavus said. "I am sure your Omax is a courageous fellow, but my goal has ever been to create tools—not life. The creation of the warforged was a grave, arrogant error. They are distinctly inferior to true golems, sacrificing power and durability for the same intelligence that only makes them so difficult to control. Their freedom to act without direction is more a burden than anything else. They are no better than the men they were built to replace. Their existence complicates an already complex world, but what is done is done. They are here now, inferior creations they may be, and we must make room for them, yes?" He looked at Omax brightly.

The warforged stared back without a sound.

FLIGHT OF THE DYING SUN

"But I babble too much," Gavus said with a light chuckle. "Tell me more of yourself, Master Dalan. I heard you were dead, and by all accounts, Tristam Xain is your killer."

"Dead?" Dalan said, sounding impressed. "I have never been dead before. How exciting! I never saw it coming. Well executed, Master Xain. You are a man of unexpectedly cold blood."

"You find this humorous?" Gavus asked archly. "You are a guild master of House Cannith, a dragonmarked heir, no less. I do not think you should take such news so lightly."

"Why should such obvious fabrications concern me?" Dalan asked. "Such clumsy lies cannot harm me. They only fool those beneath concern. After all, my own house was clearly so certain I had survived that the Baron dispatched a tribe of halfling barbarians to collect me and return me safely home. Incidentally, Chief Rossa recently died at the hands of Cyran mercenaries. The Baron will need to find a new representative to monitor the house's interests on the plains. I recommend Koranth. He seems an able fellow."

A nervous flicker passed behind Gavus's eyes. Tristam glanced past the magewright, studying the statue behind him. "I would not know anything about such things," Gavus said.

"Of course not," Dalan replied. "And though circumstances separated me from my earnest halfling guardians, I hurried here forthwith to thank the Baron for his kindness. Do you have any estimate when he will be free to attend me?"

"I cannot say," Gavus said mildly.

"Just as well," Dalan said. "I saw many interesting sights upon my journey and am eager to share them with a kinsman. The halflings are such a fascinating people. Their customs are an intriguing mixture of superstition, family loyalty, and pragmatic cunning. One, in particular, may interest you. Are you familiar with the *hmael*?"

"I am not," Gavus said.

Dalan smiled mirthlessly. "I would not think you were," he

said. He chuckled, knuckling his forehead with one hand. "The translation of the term escapes me. Seren, do you remember?"

"The golden lie," she said, eyes fixed thoughtfully on the magewright.

"Ah, yes," Dalan said. "Thank you, Seren. A *hmael* is an obvious and blatant lie, crafted to draw attention away from an uncomfortable truth. Both parties know the truth, but they use the *hmael* as a convenient shield, allowing them to discuss the truth without embarrassment. For example, I could tell you that the Ghost Talons said that they were working for Baron Zorlan d'Cannith. The halflings believed this to be true. Yet you and I both know it to be a lie. Don't we?"

Gavus's eyes narrowed. "You are a rude man, Dalan."

"You still have clay on your robes," Seren said.

"What?" Gavus asked. He looked down at the hem of his robe, quickly hiding the gray stains among the folds.

"You have a keen eye, Seren," Dalan said. "This is not your workshop, Gavus. By the spotless condition of the furniture in this room, I can assume you do not regularly come here to read without cleaning yourself first. Why would you rush here from your golems simply to entertain me until the Baron arrives? Any number of servants could have done that."

"You are paranoid," Gavus hissed.

"You have no idea," Dalan said. "Regardless, you are no random emissary. Allow me to theorize. I think after our escape from the plains, the Ghost Talons rushed a messenger to Vulyar. Via speaker, he informed you that we would soon arrive. You posted a runner at the sky towers to watch for our vessel, but when we arrived, we gave you little time to organize a reception. You drew us here to delay us while you determined your next course of action, because you do not wish Baron Zorlan to know you have been wielding his authority unauthorized."

"Why would I do any of that?" Gavus asked.

"I have absolutely no idea," Dalan said. "I'm more interested

FLIGHT OF THE DYING SUN

in knowing how you learned about the Legacy, and why you interfered with our search for it."

"Dalan," Tristam said, a warning tone in his voice. His eyes were still on Ashrem's statue.

"Not now, Tristam," Dalan said. "What do you know about the Legacy?"

"Enough," Gavus said. "You're right, Dalan. I have monitored the Boneyard for many months now, through my Ghost Talon agents. They were seeking Kiris Overwood so that they might remand her to my custody. It was only random fortune that they discovered you instead."

"How did you learn about the Legacy?" Seren asked.

"Ashrem told me himself," Gavus said. "On the day he drew my promise to ensure it was never again completed."

"On that end, at least, we agree," Dalan said. "But there are others far closer to that goal than ourselves, and we cannot stop them unless we follow the same path."

"You expect me to believe you would seek out the secrets of Ashrem's work, but not use the Legacy for your own profit, Dalan?" Gavus asked. "Your greed and ambition are well known."

Dalan rose from his seat. "Insult me if you wish," he said. "You are insignificant, so I am hardly offended. However, if you interfere with my business again, I shall inform Baron Zorlan of your insolence and he—not I—will deal with you. Understood? That is all I wished to say. We are finished here."

"Sit back down, Dalan," Gavus said.

"Dalan," Tristam said again.

"We have nothing more to discuss," Dalan replied. He turned toward the door and jiggled the handle, finding it locked.

"Sit down," Gavus repeated. "I do not wish to resort to violence."

Dalan laughed. "Omax," he said. "Open this door."

The warforged rose and turned with a fluid creak of wood and metal. He moved toward the door and lifted a heavy clenched fist, knocking the door crooked on its hinges with a single blow.

"Omax, be careful," Tristam said more urgently. The artificer rose, still watching Ashrem d'Cannith's statue.

A sound of grinding stone hissed from the depths of the statue. Omax looked back. The sculpture had begun to move, lumbering toward them slowly with its blade and lantern held high.

"A golem," the warforged said.

"Ashen, do not allow these people to leave," Gavus said, standing and quickly moving behind the golem.

The stone servant staggered forward with an obedient groan, a sound like fire crackling in the heart of a great cave. Its eyes shone a baleful yellow as it moved toward Dalan. Omax darted into Ashen's path, but the golem bashed the warforged with its lantern, knocking him back against the wall and flattening a bookcase. Dalan looked up in blank fear, quickly moving away from the door. The golem immediately ignored him, turning back to face the others. Seren rose and drew her dagger but was uncertain what to do with it against the stone creature. Tristam readied his wand and pointed it at the golem uncertainly.

"Don't waste your magic, boy," Gavus said. "Your master must have taught you that golems are immune to such things."

Omax surged to his feet with a metallic roar. Ashen turned slowly to face the warforged, lifting its sword high. Tristam spoke a word of magic, unleashing his wand's lightning, toppling a bookcase onto the golem. Ashen stumbled, giving Omax the opportunity he sought. The warforged collided with Ashen's chest, ramming it against the wall and shattering another bookcase in a cloud of torn paper. Seren pulled Dalan out of the way as debris exploded across the library.

Omax clutched the golem's face with one hand, his thick fingers boring into Ashen's wide eyes and open mouth, crushing and twisting, spreading cracks across its face. Omax rammed his other fist into the golem's body, punching him repeatedly. The golem reeled under the attack, dust and splintered stone exploding from each hit. The creature wrapped its arms around Omax's chest and squeezed. The sound of bending metal and cracking wood came in reply.

Tristam closed his eyes in concentration and clutched Omax's shoulder, directing his magic to mend what damage he could. Omax's wood and metal body twisted back into its proper shape, only to be immediately crushed once again. Sparks erupted from the warforged's chest, but Omax only grunted in pain and continued his assault. The golem pushed itself away from the wall, keeling over and collapsing heavily on Omax as Tristam narrowly dodged out of the way. The warforged heaved and twisted his wrist, wrenching Ashen's head free with a crack of tortured stone and hurling it at the door, shattering the wood. The golem continued squeezing the warforged mercilessly, ignoring the injury. Glimmering yellow smoke boiled from the hole left behind by its decapitation.

"I can't stop it," Tristam said helplessly. "I can't repair Omax fast enough. It's killing him!"

"The warforged should not have begun a fight it could not win," Gavus said, wiping one hand on his robe with a bored frown. "So much for their vaunted intellect."

Seren appeared behind Gavus, grabbing the old man by the robes and pushing him against the wall. "Call the golem off," she hissed. Her dagger drew a white line across the wrinkled folds of Gavus' throat. The old magewright's eyes filled with terror. He cried for help, and Ashen immediately rose, leaving Omax where he lay. The headless thing turned to face Seren, lifting its stone sword as it advanced. Seren turned, moving Gavus's skinny body between herself and the broken golem. It stopped, unable to harm its master and uncertain what to course of action to take.

"Stupid girl," Gavus hissed. "Kill me and Ashen will kill you in return. It can wait, quite literally, forever. We are locked in this impasse."

"*We* are locked in an impasse?" Dalan asked.

The guild master sighed and turned to leave the room in no

particular hurry, gingerly stepping through the shattered timbers. The golem spun, stepping over Omax's fallen body in its haste to stop Dalan from escaping. It hesitated, looking back at its master, uncertain which order to pursue. Dalan looked at Ashen and gave a quick, satisfied smile. Omax rolled into a crouch, seizing one of the golem's legs in both arms and twisting hard as he pushed the statue off balance. Another crackling moan issued from deep inside Ashen's body as Omax tore one leg free of its housing. The warforged spun the leg in both hands and jammed its jagged edge down with all his strength, shattering the larger construct's chest.

The golem gave what sounded like a final, tortured sigh, the sound of wounded magic escaping, the mournful call of imitated life extinguished. The golden smoke that boiled from its neck drifted away. The mutilated statue of Ashrem d'Cannith lay still. Tristam looked down at the broken sculpture in numb shock, his wand clenched in one hand. He whispered another quick infusion and placed his hand against Omax's chest, directing the magic that animated the warforged to repair some of the damage to its body.

"Impasse resolved," Dalan said, kicking aside a pile of scattered books. Above them, the chants and rhythmic hammering continued. The rest of the household was oblivious to the battle. "I will issue you a bill for the damage you have inflicted upon my warforged."

Seren released Gavus, roughly pushing him away. The old man leaned against a bookcase, gasping for breath.

"Dalan, there was no call to become violent," Gavus said, rubbing his throat and coughing hoarsely. "I panicked when you attempted to depart, but with the Host as my witness—I only wished to speak. I would not have harmed any of you."

"I do not respond well to intimidation, Frauk," Dalan said, stopping at the door but not looking back.

"Ashen was commanded only to bar your exit," Gavus said,

staring at his shattered bodyguard. "There was no need to destroy it."

"It tried to kill me," Omax said, clutching his injured chest.

"You are not alive," Gavus said.

A deep rumble echoed within Omax, but Tristam held a calming hand toward his friend. "And what if our designs on the Legacy were as dark as you fear?" Tristam asked, his own anger obviously only barely held in check. "What would you have done then?"

"Ashen would have contained you here indefinitely," Gavus said. "This library is abandoned and has been enchanted to contain sound. The door has magical wards. This room could serve quite well as a prison."

"Or a tomb," Dalan said meaningfully. "Keep talking, Frauk."

"I was foolish and desperate, but I had little choice," Gavus said. "The Legacy is too powerful, too deadly for mortals to possess. If you rebuilt it, it would do to the Five Nations what it did to Cyre."

"What did the Legacy do to Cyre?" Tristam asked.

Gavus scoffed. "Are you a fool? Look at the Mournland. That is Ashrem d'Cannith's true legacy. Ashrem told me himself. It begins with cold and lightning. The smell of wretched smoke suffuses everything as the energy of life is sucked from the world. Magic dies. The works of wonder crumble. The creatures of arcana and divinity die. Ash and mist expand to fill the void . . . Is that not what became of the Mournland?"

"Impossible," Tristam said. "The Legacy nullifies magic. The Mournland seethes with magic. The Legacy could not have been responsible for that."

"So you hope," Gavus said.

"Know this, Gavus," Dalan said. "I do not intend to rebuild the Legacy. As you say, it is far too dangerous. However, the secrets of its creation must be recovered. If left in the shadows, it *will* be found. I fear the ones who slew the Ghost Talons are already close to its completion."

Gavus grew pale and trembled visibly. "The Cyrans?"

"No," Dalan hissed. "They are no true Cyrans, though they bastardize the crest of that proud nation."

"You said you promised Ashrem that you would bar others from completing his work," Tristam interrupted, drawing an annoyed look from Dalan. "When did you last see him?"

"Only a week before the Day of Mourning," Gavus said. "As he prepared to depart for Metrol. He drew our oaths that we would do everything within my power to prevent the Legacy's construction."

"We?" Dalan asked. "Who else made this oath?"

"Norra Cais, Bishop Llaine Grove," Gavus said. "There were a handful of others . . ." Gavus trailed off, eyes wide.

"What happened to the others?" Tristam asked.

"They are gone now," Gavus said. "Vanished or killed, one by one. Norra and I were the only ones left, and I have not seen her in weeks."

"Norra Cais?" Dalan asked. "She has been missing for months, not weeks."

"She was wise enough to go underground when the others began disappearing," Gavus said. "I was one of Ashrem's more obscure associates, so I took the risk of remaining public while she conducted secret research. But then she disappeared, and even I have lost contact with her."

"Where did she go?" Tristam asked.

Gavus shook his head. "I will not tell you that," he said. "I will say only that I believe she still lives, but I will not betray her to you. If you seek her insight into Ashrem's Legacy, you will seek her without my aid."

"Fine," Dalan said. "We do not need you, but if you interfere with our search any further, my earlier promise holds. Baron Zorlan will learn how you impersonated him. I suspect the Ghost

Talons are not the only informants who believed they worked on his behalf."

The old magewright looked helplessly at Dalan.

"And clean this mess," Dalan said, gesturing at the spilled bookcases and shattered golem. "This is a d'Cannith library you have ruined. If you continue to treat it as whatever pigsty birthed you, I will see that you are returned there. Good day, Master Frauk."

Dalan exited the chamber with Tristam, Omax, and Seren following close behind. Once they were a good distance from Gavus, Tristam hurried to catch up with the guild master.

"I think he knows more, Dalan," Tristam said, glancing back. "He could tell us where Norra Cais is. If anyone can tell us more about Ashrem's work, it would be her. She was his most brilliant student."

"I agree that locating Cais should be our primary objective," Dalan said, "but I think questioning Frauk would be a waste of time. He knows nothing we cannot easily discover on our own. He is a fool, and we are better off without him. I do not enjoy relying on the help of ignorant bigots."

"Agreed," Omax said quietly.

"So we're just letting him go?" Tristam asked. "He's a valuable lead."

"He's already told us Norra is alive, and that she was here weeks ago," Seren said. "Zed and Eraina can track her down with that much to go on."

Dalan nodded. "Precisely my thought. Keeping an inquisitive and a Sentinel Marshal among us has its uses. It is obvious that Ashrem chose Frauk to safeguard his secrets only because the magewright has no imagination. Frauk follows orders with the same mindless stupidity as his golems. Tristam, return to the ship and tell the others what we have learned so that Arthen and the Marshal can begin their search. Omax, attend me and we shall see to your repairs while we are here in a House of Making."

"I can repair him," Tristam said, slightly offended.

"Ah, but I promised I would bill Gavus for his unprovoked attacks," Dalan said with a wicked smile, "and Cannith craftsmanship is *expensive*. Meanwhile, I sorely need you to focus your talents on repairing the ship and studying Overwood's journals."

"What about me?" Seren asked.

Dalan looked at the young thief blandly. "What do I care?" he asked. "So long as you cause no trouble, you are free to do as you like." The guild master took a deep breath and plucked his cap from his head, smoothing one hand over his balding scalp. "Enjoy Korth, Seren. I think we may be here for some time. The rest will do us good. This has been a most exhausting journey."

Dalan nodded at Omax and turned a corner, heading deeper into the House of Making with the warforged in tow. Tristam looked at Seren sheepishly.

"What?" she asked him, grinning a little and stepping closer to him as they walked.

"I feel like such an idiot," he said quietly. She slipped her hand into his, and he felt much better. He offered her a crooked smile.

"Why do you feel like an idiot?" she asked.

He shrugged. "I was so angry at Dalan back on the Plains," he said. "At how he'd used us, manipulated us. Now here I am, taking orders from him again. Nothing ever changes, Seren."

"That's not true," she said. "You've changed."

"For the better?" he asked, arching an eyebrow.

"I think so," she said.

They stepped out through the doors of House Cannith and into the street. The guards cast bored expressions at them and did not move from their station, huddled under awnings against the misty rain.

"How have I changed?" he asked, unconsciously huddling closer to her for warmth against the rain.

She laughed softly. "When I met you were loud and cocky, but had no confidence," she said. "Now you're the opposite. Not as loud . . . but now you do what's right without even thinking about it."

"Don't be fooled, Seren," Tristam said with a chuckle. "I have no idea what I'm doing."

"Let me illustrate," hissed a voice from behind them. "You are dying."

The assassin leapt from behind, sliding twin daggers into Tristam's back.

Chapter
Six

It was a curious trait that most halflings adopted easily in human cities. This was not to say that halflings were truly invisible, as if through magic, but that humans usually pretended that they were not there. To the average human, a halfling was not unlike a child, and the comparison extended beyond mere physical resemblance. The typical halfling's energetic attitude and constant need for attention drove humans to treat halflings with the same selective blindness they reserved for other people's noisy children. They were there. You saw them. You just pretended you didn't notice them and hoped that they would get bored and go away.

For many halflings, this phenomenon was extremely irritating. Halfling merchants found it a constant stumbling block, and halfling diplomats often became infuriated at the polite condescension they were offered in human arenas. For a halfling like Gerith, on the other hand, it was a blessing far more often than it was a curse. He had only had to share stories about his day for a mere ten minutes before the meat vendor bitterly shoved a free mince pie in his face to shut him up. Now he sat cross-legged at the side of the road, munching happily. He was oblivious to the drizzle, appearing to enjoy the rain rather than let it bother him. Though the streets were busy this time of night, the crowds parted around the little halfling who had decided to sit down on the street corner. Invisible.

FLIGHT OF THE DYING SUN

One man walked directly toward Gerith. He was clad in a shabby coat with a short pipe clenched in his mouth. Gerith grinned and gave a little wave, but did not stop eating.

"Busy, Snowshale?" Zed asked, looking down at Gerith curiously.

"I love Karrnath," Gerith said, mouth full of crust and meat. "It's such an ugly place, but the food is wonderful. They fry everything! Anything tastes better fried."

"Fantastic," Zed said. "Aren't you supposed to be doing something?"

"I'm keeping an eye on her," Gerith said. He nodded at a rooftop across the street.

Zed looked up. Blizzard sat hunched in the shadows at the edge of a rooftop, watching the far street with beady black eyes.

"That bird is trained to tail people?" Zed asked, impressed.

"He's not a bird," Gerith replied, a little insulted. "And yes, glidewings are very clever beasts. Kind of like flying dogs. My people originally domesticated them as guardians. It wasn't till centuries later that we bred them big enough to ride. Blizzard is even smarter than most."

"Remarkable," Zed said.

The little scout beamed proudly.

Zed shrugged, plucking his pipe out of his mouth and sighing a plume of smoke into the night air. "No signs of Marth or any of his Cyrans in the shipyards," he said. "If they are repairing the *Seventh Moon*, they're not getting supplies to do it here."

"How would you know he's here?" Gerith asked. "He's a changeling."

"Because it doesn't matter how well you hide your face, people notice when you buy a few small fortunes worth of soarwood to repair an airship," Zed said. "The only people in Korth who've been placing orders on that scale are Lyrandar merchant vessels." Zed paused. "And us, of course. All the same, if we can go a few days without seeing that damn warship drop out of the clouds on us, I think we'll be a little happier."

"They say it's the little things that really make you happy," Gerith agreed. "Pie. Sunsets. Girls in short skirts. No Cyran warships blasting you out of the sky."

Arthen laughed. "How's the story coming, Snowshale?"

"Oh, I have high hopes for this one," he said, swallowing the last bit of pie and wiping his hands on his vest. "We're in a slow bit right now, but that happens with every story. If there's nothing but action, then it's not interesting anymore. You need boring bits to make the rest taste better, like stew needs peas."

"So I'm peas?" Zed asked.

"A little bit," Gerith asked. "You need to pick a fight or something, Arthen, or this scene is getting cut out when I tell it to my grandfather."

"You can't write me out," Zed said. "I'm the hero."

"Pfft," Gerith said, rolling his eyes. "Seren's the heroine. You're the comic relief."

"Seren?" Zed asked. "I thought she was your winsome damsel."

Gerith sighed melodramatically. "Would that it were so," he said, bowing his head. "As comely as she is, I fear I'm too much for such a fragile lass. She would not endure. Seren will have to settle for Tristam."

Zed laughed. "I need to visit your tribe some day, Snowshale," he said. "I need to see what sort of family coughs out something like you."

"I'm the quiet one," Gerith said.

Zed looked at Gerith blankly.

"I have seventeen sisters."

"You're kidding."

"I'm not," Gerith said. "I'm the youngest, too. Bunch of troublemakers, every one of them. Why do you think I left home?" Gerith looked around with a bored expression, then suddenly changed the subject. "Does Eraina know that we're following her?"

FLIGHT OF THE DYING SUN

"No," Zed said, watching the glidewing.

"Oh," Gerith said, pondering that for a few minutes. He looked up at Zed curiously. "Why are we following her, then? Don't we trust Eraina?"

"You trust everyone, Snowshale," Zed said. "I don't trust anyone."

"But she's a paladin," Gerith said. "They have to be good."

"Exactly," Zed replied.

Gerith looked confused. "Paladins are picked by the gods," he said. "They can't be untrustworthy, can they? I mean if they were, the gods would just pick someone else, right?"

"Gods can be stupid too, Snowshale," Zed said. "Divine favor doesn't make you immune to mistakes. Paladins have a way of not watching where they're going because they think the gods are watching over them."

"Aren't they?" Gerith asked.

"Doesn't really matter," Zed said with a shrug. "If Boldrei isn't keeping an eye on Eraina, I am."

Above them, Blizzard suddenly sat up, alert. The glidewing flapped across the street onto another rooftop, watching something in the street below.

"She's moving," Gerith said.

"Follow her," Zed said. "I'll meet up with you later."

"Aye," the halfling said, scrambling to his feet and rushing off as fast as he could, trying to keep his pet in sight.

Zed tapped out his pipe and tucked it into his coat. He walked down the street, searching for the building the glidewing had been watching. A crest hung above the door, emblazoned with a chimera's head below a mailed fist clutching a double-bladed sword. This was a House Deneith holding, a bastion of the Sentinel Marshals. Zed peered about casually but no one appeared to care much about his presence. He strode toward the bastion, stepping aside just as the door opened. A thin man wearing a Marshal's seal on his chest stepped out, lifting a hood over his face to shield against the rain.

"Evening, Marshal," Zed said, nodding at the man as he walked toward the door.

The Marshal nodded, paying no attention to Zed. "If you are a client or wish to assist with an investigation, please see my subordinates within," he said, pushing past Zed and making his way down the road.

"Thanks very much," Zed said.

The inquisitive stopped at the door, peering over his shoulder and watching the Marshal hurry away down the crowded street. He followed casually, keeping his eye on the man without seeming to. The Marshal wasn't paying much attention, so it wasn't difficult. Either he didn't care that he was followed or the idea that he could be followed had never entered his mind. He cut a direct path through the randomly twisting streets and alleys of Korth. Not only did the man know exactly where he was going, he had obviously gone this way many times before.

The man turned a sharp corner and stepped into a small building. It was a speaker post, a place where dragonmarked Sivis couriers could transmit messages to distant lands via magic. Zed took up an unobtrusive position across the street and watched the building patiently. After several minutes the Marshal emerged and headed back the way he came, again not even glancing to see if he was followed. Zed felt almost insulted that he had made such a professional effort not to be seen by someone who obviously was making so little effort to watch his trail. He sighed and snatched up a heavy wooden beam from the garbage strewn alley and circled around a side street. Hefting the beam over one shoulder, he waited for the Marshal to round the corner. When the Marshal appeared, Zed lunged forward. The man only had time to gasp in surprise before the beam took him across the temple.

Zed dropped the beam and lifted the unconscious Marshal, hooking his arms under the man's shoulders and dragging him deeper into the alley. Instinctively, he glanced behind him, sensing

FLIGHT OF THE DYING SUN

someone approaching. An embarrassed smile creased his weathered features when he saw the woman facing him.

"Eraina," he said, leaning the unconscious Marshal against the wall and standing with an embarrassed expression.

"What are you doing, Arthen?" she demanded.

"Sightseeing," he said lamely. "Your homeland is very lovely. Very . . . gray. Your comrade here has injured himself."

She folded her arms across her breasts and scowled. "You know I sense your lies," she said. "Are you *trying* to infuriate me further?"

"I was trying to be funny, really," he said. "He's just unconscious."

She stepped toward him. A startled caw sounded above them. Zed looked up to see Blizzard perching at the edge of the roof with Gerith mounted on his back.

"Erm . . . everything all right?" the halfling asked in a small voice.

"Go back to the ship, Gerith," Eraina said.

"Aye," the halfling said in a relieved voice. Waiting for no further explanation, he flapped off into the night.

"This isn't what it seems to be, Eraina," Zed said, gesturing at the unconscious Marshal. "No one on the *Mourning Dawn* is a traitor, I'm sure of that. So I guessed that someone must be intercepting our communications. The thing is—we don't really have any communications. None of the rest of the crew keep in touch with anyone outside the ship except for Gerith, Dalan, and you. Gerith doesn't send anything but love letters to a dozen girls in random cities. He never mentions anything about what we're doing. Dalan's speaker posts are always financial, and always travel through such convoluted, circuitous routes that anyone tracking us would never find the source."

"That leaves only my regular reports to House Deneith," Eraina said.

Zed nodded.

Eraina sighed, leaning on her short spear and closing her eyes in frustration. "Do you think that I am stupid, or did you forget that I am a Sentinel Marshal?"

Zed blinked. "I don't follow you."

"You aren't the only one with the power of deductive reasoning, Arthen," she said. "Since our conversation in Vulyar I have been thinking about the information leak." She looked at him, her eyes blue, clear, and sad. "I was Bishop Grove's bodyguard, and his friend. I failed to protect him from Marth and have hunted him ever since. Yet every time I find a promising clue or lead, it crumbles. It wasn't until Wroat that I truly believed there was a chance. Then Marth found us, again and again." She bowed her head, her face growing dark. "And always, he found us shortly after I had dispatched one of my reports to Korth. Those reports were always delivered to this man, Marshal Killian."

Zed sighed. "So you knew Killian is a traitor, but you reported to him anyway? That was foolish."

"You are quick to judge, Arthen," she said, glaring at him. "It is no wonder that you fell."

Arthen opened his mouth to spit an angry retort, but hesitated. His expression softened. "Tell me what happened, then."

"I did not know Killian was a traitor, but I suspected," she said. "So I gave Killian my report. I said that the *Mourning Dawn* had sustained such damage that only a miracle would allow her to fly again. I told him that the Ghost Talon halflings were apparently working for Baron Zorlan d'Cannith, who would likely turn his efforts toward blocking Dalan's progress. I told him that Marth was last seen trapped in a flaming airship, battling a rogue elemental, and that his survival was highly unlikely. I told him that the last person who could have translated Ashrem's journals for us had been murdered. I told him that the surviving members of the crew would be returning to Korth."

"So you told the truth," Zed said. "Just not the whole truth."

Eraina looked pained. "Do not mock me, Arthen," she said.

FLIGHT OF THE DYING SUN

"My vows do not tolerate lies. Falsehood, prevarication, and omission are all facets of the same sin. It sickened me to deliver that report, just as it sickens me to allow Killian to draw another breath wearing the tabard of a Sentinel Marshal." She looked down at the unconscious Marshal. "I gave him that report to gauge his reaction, hoping that I would be wrong. Then he immediately leaves his post to visit a speaker station in the middle of the night."

"I thought that a bit odd, too," Zed said. "I was about to ask him why."

"I will wake him," Eraina said, kneeling over Killian.

"Wait," Zed said, resting a hand on her shoulder. "Why not just leave him? Keep sending your reports. Keep Marth misinformed, off his guard. Killian doesn't know he's been found out yet. He could do more good than harm."

"You warned me about splitting hairs," Eraina said. "After one false report, Marth will suspect the truth and cease relying upon Killian. My lies will serve no further good and a corrupted Marshal will continue to preside over Korth. There is only one recourse now." She extended one hand and pressed her fingers to Killian's temple. "And that is the truth."

Eraina whispered a brief prayer to Boldrei and her fingertips glowed white. A shivering gasp issued through the unconscious Marshal. Killian sat bolt upright, instantly awake, his eyes wide.

"What happened?" he said, looking around in confusion. "Eraina?"

"Killian," Eraina said. She rose, glaring down at him coldly. "Why?"

He looked at her blankly, glancing past her for a moment to peer at Zed curiously. "What do you mean?" he asked. "Why what?"

"Why?" she repeated, more tersely. Her hand tightened on her spear. "Why did you betray us to Llaine Grove's killer?"

"I didn't . . ." Killian began, but the dangerous gleam in the paladin's eyes made the lie die in his mouth. "You don't understand, Eraina. Your view is too narrow, too naive. Eberron is not ready for peace. Zamiel will ignite the war anew, and the world will be as we all remember it again."

"Remove that seal," she said, pointing at his Marshal's badge with her spear.

"Am I under arrest?" he asked. "I have done nothing that you can prove. You have no grounds to accuse me, Marshal."

Eraina removed her own Marshal's seal, casting it onto the cobblestones. "It is not a Marshal who accuses you. It is not House Deneith's judgment you face, traitor. The Host judges you now. Boldrei's eyes are upon you."

"Damn paladins." Killian hissed, staggering to his feet.

"Indeed," Zed said. "Need help, Eraina?"

She shook her head, eyes still fixed on Killian.

Marshal Killian drew his sword and lunged at Eraina with a fierce cry. She parried his blade with the haft of her spear and drew her shortsword across his stomach. Killian fell to his knees with a wet cough, blood streaming over his legs. He looked up at her in helpless pain, hand shaking as the sword dropped from his grasp. Eraina flipped the blade in her hand and drew it back in another swift stroke, slashing the fallen Marshal's throat. He fell dead in the filth and refuse of the alley. Eraina knelt beside him, wiping his blood from her blade with a scrap of white cloth as she uttered a short prayer to the Hearthmother.

"You're quiet, Arthen," she said. "More advice?"

Zed rested a hand on her shoulder. Eraina looked up, her eyes widening when she saw he held her Marshal's seal in his hand. She hesitated a long moment before accepting it, pinning the badge back in its accustomed place on her cloak. He helped her to the feet and together they made their way back through the rain toward the Sentinel bastion.

CHAPTER
SEVEN

Seren saw a flicker of movement, but too late. She seized Tristam's arm and pulled him to the side, but the shadows opened and a small, thin man lunged out and drew twin daggers, stabbing at Tristam's back. Tristam hissed in pain and fell to one knee as the blades drove into him. The assassin daggers fell again, the left hand blade slashing out at Seren. Seren saw the weapon coming, but her eyes were on the right blade, lifted high, prepared to finish Tristam. Rather than dodge aside, she dropped, kicking up with one leg as she fell. Her foot collided solidly, and the mysterious attacker recoiled with a groan.

She lunged forward into a crouch and sprang, her own knife appearing in her hand. Her target recovered, standing straight and spinning in a pirouette to one side. A knife lashed out, tracing a path of red pain across her hip.

Seren turned to find the assassin pacing away, watching her carefully. He was a small man with short, curly blonde hair. His ears tapered into long, slender points and his almond eyes gleamed with excitement.

"Unexpected grace and complexity. Like the first snowflake," the elf said in a deep, oddly musical voice. "If I touch you, will you melt?"

Seren glanced down at Tristam, huddled in pain on the ground. The assassin seized upon her distraction, leaping in with both daggers again. Seren returned her attention to him instantly. His eyes widened as he realized he had fallen for her feint. Seren rolled aside and her dagger slashed down, slashing a gouge across his back. He hissed and somersaulted away, throwing one of his daggers as he rolled. The blade slashed her thigh and tumbled into the darkness.

"No longer intriguing, snowflake," he said, drawing up to his full height and sneering at her.

The assassin ran at Seren, blade low and to one side. Seren held her dagger ready to meet his charge, but he cartwheeled to one side at the last moment, leaping toward Tristam. The artificer fell backward, drawing out his wand and unleashing a bolt of lightning at the elf. The assassin dodged the blast with an annoyed curse. The energy struck the side of a temple, scattering stone in a noisy explosion. Muffled shouts and startled hoof beats resounded in reply, as well as the ring of a guard's alarm bell.

The assassin stood straight, looked at Seren and Tristam, and sighed.

"Annoying," he said.

The shadows billowed outward, wrapped around him, and swallowed him. Seren and Tristam were alone in the darkened street. Tristam collapsed on the cobbles, wand tumbling from his hand. Seren ran to his side, calling out for help.

"Who was that?" Tristam groaned. "What was that?"

"He's gone now, Tristam," Seren whispered, her eyes scanning the streets to make sure that was true. "Just hold on."

Tristam fumbled in his coat, but his hand refused to obey, too wracked with pain to move normally. A pouch tumbled out of his pocket onto the street. "That bag," he said. "I have potions. They'll numb the pain till we can find a healer."

"You actually brought useful potions this time?" Seren asked in a gently mocking tone, though her voice quavered with worry. She opened up the pouch and found a small pouch of crystal vials. They contained a thick, bubbly purple liquid. She uncorked one and offered it to Tristam. The artificer drank desperately, some of the potion dribbling down his chin and mixing with the blood. He tensed as the effects took hold, then ceased trembling. His dark eyes became slightly glazed. He smiled faintly and leaned back against her. She cradled his head as his rapid breathing became more even.

"What was in that?" Seren asked suspiciously.

"Just a . . . healing draught," Tristam said with a chuckle. "But . . . you have to mix it with whiskey . . . or it clots in the bottle."

Seren sniffed the empty vial. To her nose, it seemed as if there was more whiskey than potion, but she wasn't one to tell an artificer how to do his craft.

She heard heavy boots approaching and looked up. A group of armed guards approached them. Some were White Lions, the Korth City Watch. Seren recognized the guards from the nearby House of Making as well. Other curious bystanders appeared as well, watching from windows and doorways. Seren deftly tucked her dagger into its hiding place in the back of her belt before the guards noticed it, along with Tristam's wand.

"What's going on here?" demanded one of the watchmen, glancing sharply from the injured artificer to the roof of the building across the street, now smoking in the rain.

"He's been stabbed," Seren said. "We need a healer."

"Out of the way!" shouted an imperious voice. "This man is under the protection of House Cannith."

The watchman turned, his expression annoyed as a group of Cannith guardsman approached. Dalan himself led the group.

"I represent the House of Making," Dalan said, flashing his signet ring at the guard. "Please stand aside. This boy has pending membership in the Fabricator's Guild. His welfare is my responsibility."

"Wait," the guard said, stunned. "What happened here? What was that explosion? Why is that roof on fire?"

Dalan held out one hand, cupping the rain as it fell. "In Wroat we often have thunderstorms," he said. "They are frightening events, to be sure, but our City Watch has long since ceased trying to arrest them."

The watchman gaped. Dalan pressed his advantage, sending two of the guards to help Tristam to his feet and carry him back to the House of Making. The dumfounded watchman opened his mouth to speak again, but Dalan interrupted.

"If you need to question the boy further, simply report to the Cannith house and inquire my name," Dalan said.

"Whatever is happening here, Baron Zorlan will answer for this, d'Cannith," the guardsman promised.

"I'm sure he will," Dalan said. He patted the guard on the shoulder and hurried off.

Seren followed. "You never gave him your name."

"I know," Dalan said. "The White Lions are altogether too curious and vigilant to give them that sort of useful information. So what happened? More Cyrans or just Tristam being Tristam?"

"It was an elf," Seren said. "He appeared from nowhere, then vanished into a cloud of darkness when Tristam's lightning alerted the guards."

"An elf?" Dalan said, eyes widening. "You say he ran into the darkness?"

"No," Seren said. "He summoned shadows and stepped into them. It was magic."

Dalan looked around nervously and quickened his pace. "Let's waste no time, gentlemen," he shouted to the guards. "The night is unfriendly."

"What's going on, Dalan?" she asked.

"You've described a Thuranni," he said. "A dragonmarked assassin."

"I thought the Thuranni were dancers and artists," Seren said.

"Of course they are," Dalan said with a humorless laugh. "And I'm just a humble merchant. Now let's hurry inside before he returns to dance for us again."

The guards deposited Tristam in a small guest bedroom near

FLIGHT OF THE DYING SUN

the entrance. Dalan posted two men at the door and sent another to find a healer. Tristam lay on the bed, sweat beading on his face. Seren sat beside him, clutching his hand with a worried face.

"What if he's poisoned?" she asked.

"If a Thuranni poisoned him, he'd already be dead," Dalan said. "Fortunately, many of their agents don't use poison—it's too easily traceable. Better to just strike accurately and leave the target dead than pump him full of chemicals that an inquisitive could use to track you down." Dalan frowned. "The entire existence of the House is something of an oddity. I consider them to be the worst kept secret in Khorvaire. I imagine it must be difficult to pretend your house is a band of entertainers and sculptors when you kill people for money—how's anyone supposed to hire you if they don't know what you really do? Anyone of questionable morality who possesses the financial means to dispose of his enemies will inevitably 'discover' the truth of the Thuranni's existence. It's amazing how many wealthy nobles believe they are the only ones who know the truth." Dalan laughed dryly.

"Why would he attack us?" Tristam asked. "Are they enemies of the Canniths?"

"No," Dalan said. "They are neutral. Professional killers who will take any contract. Presumably Marth has discarded subtlety and now simply seeks to remove the threat Tristam poses. Quite a clever move, in my opinion. Tristam, do you realize that you are the only member of the *Karia Naille*'s crew, including myself, who is indispensable? Without you to maintain the ship and decipher Ashrem's clues, we would be lost. We are all fortunate that you survived."

Tristam didn't speak for a time. "You told the guards I had pending guild membership. Was that just a lie so they would get out of their way?"

"Yes," Dalan said, "though only because I've not yet had a chance to speak with the Baron and officially sponsor you. If you are still interested, I think the House of Making could benefit a great deal from your presence. You bear a mix of talent and wisdom that has been sorely lacking since my uncle's death."

"Thank you, Dalan," Tristam said, shocked.

"No need to thank me," Dalan said. "Bringing such a brilliant talent into the house will boost my own standing as well. Now just try to stay alive so that you can accept the sponsorship when this is all done."

"Will Tristam be all right?" Seren asked.

"Oh, I'm not worried for his wounds," Dalan said, "He's safe enough here. Once the healers arrive he will be fine. Especially if we can find Eraina. She has a talent for patching us back together. I only worry for future attacks." Dalan looked at her intently. "As should you, Miss Morisse."

"Me?" she asked.

Dalan pointed at the cuts on Seren's hip and leg. She had forgotten her own injuries completely. "You fought a Thuranni assassin and survived," Dalan said. "Not only did you survive, but you denied him his target. I smell bruised elf pride, Miss Morisse." Dalan smirked. "I commend you for your feat, but you must be more cautious now."

"This is serious, Dalan," Seren said. "There's an assassin hunting us."

"And only days ago an army of assassins hunted us," Dalan said, shrugging. He rose and moved to the door. "We're alive, Seren. Exult in it. Mock your enemies while you retain the breath to do so."

The door opened and two halfling women in the livery of House Jorasco healers entered. One carried a small basin of fresh water. The other carried a leather satchel. They smelled distinctly of the fragrant herbs they used in their medicines.

"Your patients, Doctors," Dalan said, gesturing at Seren and Tristam. "Please forward the bill to Baron Zorlan d'Cannith."

The halflings pushed past Dalan with a mumbled acknowledgment, more concerned with their work than payment for the time being.

FLIGHT OF THE DYING SUN

"Just remain vigilant, Miss Morisse," Dalan said as he closed the door. "You have made a powerful enemy."

Seren stared at the closed door for some time. The halflings quietly asked her about their injuries and what sort of medicine Tristam had already used, all while conscientiously avoiding any questions about her attacker. Seren wondered how frequently the Jorasco healers had to deal with such suspicious injuries. She supposed in their place she would learn to be incurious as well. After cleaning and bandaging Seren's relatively minor wounds, the elder healer politely shooed Seren from the room. She stopped only long enough to set Tristam's wand atop his discarded coat, then slipped out into the hall.

Seren walked aimlessly through the halls of the House of Making. Her mind wandered over past events, and how much her life had changed of late. She opened a door and stepped out into a large, well-appointed courtyard. The drizzly rain had finally begun to die away, leaving the garden coated in a fine mist. Seren breathed deeply and sat on a stone bench near a bubbling fountain across from a weathered statue. She laughed at her own distraction when she saw the statue move, looking at her with shining blue eyes.

"Omax," she said, smiling at the warforged. "Do you feel any better?"

"I have not burdened the House artificers yet," he said. His head tilted and his eyes pulsed, radiating concern. "You are injured. What has happened?"

"Tristam and I were attacked in the streets," she said.

Omax rose, fists clenching with a metal clang. "Where is he?" the warforged demanded.

"He's fine now," Seren said in a soothing voice. "He was badly injured, but the healers have him now."

Omax's hands opened. He looked at his reflection in the water. "Our lives are much more dangerous than they once were, Seren," he said. "I fear it will only grow worse."

Seren frowned. "Omax, if you're going to try to talk me into leaving, it's too late for that."

"Leave?" Omax looked up at her intently. He looked at *everything* intently. "That was the furthest idea from my mind, Seren. I was going to thank you for staying."

"Oh," she said, uncertain what to say.

"We have been given a great gift, Seren," the warforged said.

Seren's brow furrowed. "What do you mean?"

"Do you remember the War, Seren?" he said. "Truly remember it?"

"I never saw any battles," she said. "I was too young. But I remember the look in my father's eyes when he would come home to visit. He was a little sadder, and a little more tired each time." Her voice became choked. "And I remember the day the messenger came with the black envelope for my mother, and my father stopped coming home."

Omax nodded. "Then you understand. The Last War was the greatest evil this world has ever known. It devoured nations, ruined lives great and small, and scarred the land more deeply than any other tragedy manufactured by mortals. The War is not over, Seren." The warforged sat, folding his arms across his lap.

"What do you mean?" she asked. "The War has been over for years. The Treaty of Thronehold—"

"Is nothing," Omax said. "The warforged do not sleep, Seren, and we do not dream. Yet, when all is still and the world is quiet . . . my mind wanders. I feel the pulse of magic in the earth. I feel the song of battle in my soul. I feel the soul of war, deep within the earth. War may slumber, Seren, but it never dies. The Last War has not passed from this world. It only waits."

The warforged removed the woolen cap from his head, twisting it between his rough-hewn hands. He slumped, shoulders sagging from an invisible burden. Seren watched him silently.

"I believe the *Mourning Dawn* exists for a purpose, Seren," he said. "Think upon it. Every soul in its crew has been touched by war, darkened by it."

"Even Gerith?" Seren asked. "He seems so happy."

"Gerith has wandered for longer than you think," Omax said. "For each joyful tale he tells, he carries ten tragedies. It is to his credit that he does not allow his memories to burden him. He is part of Ashrem's legacy."

"What do you mean?" Seren asked.

"Not Ashrem's terrible invention," Omax said. "His true legacy. His desire to preserve peace." Omax placed the hat back on his domed skull. "I believe we are that legacy, Seren. A band of scattered souls who have been injured by war, driven to solitude. We are now family." He looked up at her again. "The war stirs, Seren. It will send its servants to divide and destroy us. Now, more than ever, we must remain strong. Remain together."

Seren looked away, staring back into the fountain.

"Is something wrong, Seren?" he asked.

"I was thinking about Dalan," she said.

Omax chuckled. "Dalan needs the rest of us more than anyone," he said. "It was a noble thing that Tristam did, to rescue him from Marth."

"Maybe too noble," Seren said. "He's as deceitful as he ever was."

Omax cocked his head in surprise. "Would you have abandoned him?"

"I still don't trust him," Seren said. "Since we learned he was in league with Marth, he's been going out of his way to flatter and compliment us. It's like he's trying to distract us from something."

"Or he has realized his former arrogance serves no purpose," Omax said. "We should rejoice in the change. To ingratiate himself with others is his nature."

"I'm not sure that's entirely it," she said. She reached into her cloak and drew out an envelope, affixed with a broken Cannith seal.

"What is that?" Omax asked.

"The letter he asked me to give Kiris Overwood if she refused to help," Seren said. "It forced her to come with us. If not for this letter, she never would have come to the Ghost Talon village. Marth wouldn't have killed her."

"What does it say?" Omax said.

"I don't know," Seren said, standing and looking around the courtyard. "Kiris burned it, but I gathered the ashes before we escaped. If there's any place to fix it, it's here."

"Do you require my aid, Seren?" Omax asked.

"Not for this, Omax," she said, smiling at him. "I should be fine."

The warforged bowed his head, returning to his meditation.

Seren walked back into the main estate, stopping the first servant she passed. The servant directed her to an office deeper in the house. There, a tired old Cannith clerk looked up at her blearily. From the collar of his robe she could see his dragonmark, the mirror image of Dalan's own, crawling up the side of his neck. He took the envelope from her, glancing at its contents briefly before returning it with a frown.

"I am sorry," he said. "My meager talents can do nothing to repair this. The damage is too great for magic to repair."

Seren felt her heart sink. She nodded at the old man and mumbled soft thanks for his aid, then discarded the envelope in his fireplace. She walked back out into the hall.

A servant met her, offering to escort her to the chambers that had been prepared for her stay. She nodded her thanks and followed. She was shown to a small bed chamber, identical to the one where Tristam was still recovering. Seren removed her cloak and let it drop heavily on the floor.

One hand moved to her dagger when she felt eyes on her from the doorway. She turned to see Dalan standing there, his broad face expressionless.

"If you wished to know what my letter said," he said, "you could have asked me."

"Are you spying on me?" she asked.

Dalan laughed. "You are allowed to be suspicious of me, but the reverse is some dreadful sin? Hypocrisy. I wish to be honest, and all you do is insult me." Dalan smirked. "I cannot say I do not deserve such treatment. You and the others have risked much to aid me, and I have been ungrateful."

"Then tell me what you told Kiris to change her mind," Seren said, a hint of anger in her voice.

Dalan reached into his pocket and produced a white envelope, affixed with a fresh seal identical to the broken one that marked the old envelope. "I have a keen memory, and remember my words precisely," Dalan said. "Read it, if you must."

"How do I know you aren't lying again?" she said.

"You do not," he replied, setting the letter on the small table beside the door. "However, I believe the contents will leave little room for doubt."

Seren took the envelope cautiously, as if it were some dangerous thing. She broke the seal and drew out the letter.

Miss Overwood

> *You remember me from the days of the Last War, when you served my uncle in his doomed quest for peace. You may recall that I am not a man given to empty threats, so look well to my words.*
>
> *You followed Ashrem d'Cannith into ruin. What motivated you to offer your life for him, I cannot say. Now my uncle is dead, and you labor in the service of a madman.*
>
> *I know Marth. I know the depths of his insanity. What's more, many of the channels I used to contact him when we were allies remain open. As you serve his quest and interfere with mine, reflect upon this—it would be all too easy for me to convince him that you have turned against him.*
>
> *If you have spent any length of time in his presence, you must know how that will end.*

It is your choice. I cannot promise you safety among the crew of the Mourning Dawn, *but I can promise you death if you deny me your aid.*
The choice is yours.
Destroy this letter.

Dalan d'Cannith

Seren looked up at Dalan coldly.

"At the time, it still served my purposes to conceal my history with Marth," Dalan said. "Thus I wished for her to destroy the letter. Now that we all know that uncomfortable truth, hiding the truth serves no further purpose. Do you believe what you have read is a lie?"

"No," Seren said in a low voice. "How could you do this, Dalan? Kiris was manipulated. She was an innocent. You would have set that murderer on her."

"She set that murderer on herself," he said. "She was a foolish girl, who bound herself to a horrible man because she believed she could repair him. I have no patience for such idiocy. Marth would have killed her eventually, as he later proved. Remember that I offered you that letter as a last resort. No matter what you may think of me, I do not enjoy threatening people. What I said to her was necessary." He smiled faintly. "Just as your warning to me on the *Karia Naille* was necessary."

Dalan walked back in the hallway, looking back over his shoulder for only a moment. "We are not so different, Miss Morisse," he said. "In times of crisis, you are all as manipulative and pragmatic as I am. You simply refuse to see it. Reflect upon that."

CHAPTER
EIGHT

Raylen paced between the dusty crates with a fretful expression. The air in the old warehouse was dead, choked with stale dust from years of neglect. A single lantern hung from a beam, casting unsettling shadows across the room. This place had not seen any life since the end of the Last War, save the rats who made their homes in the crates of surplus military uniforms and other mundane supplies. It was a place no one remembered, which made it a good choice for the business at hand.

Raylen was not a young man, nor was he an old man. He was a lean, greasy, entirely unmemorable sort of person. The military surplus warehouse reminded him distantly of his youth, when he had served in the Karrnathi army just long enough to get himself wounded in battle and discharged. After that, he had floated about Korth for most of his adult life, taking whatever odd jobs were offered. Most of the time he simply acted as a city guide. Though few people remembered Raylen, he remembered everyone. He was good at putting people in touch with whomever or whatever they wanted to find in the city. Though that sort of work didn't pay well, at least it was consistent. Someone was always lost in Korth. More frequently, Raylen's employment was not quite so legitimate, helping thieves find a safe place to sell their stolen goods, or helping visiting nobles with questionable morals find what they required to sate their appetites. As a man of rather limited conscience, that sort of thing rarely bothered him. What good did ethics do a man who was starving to death?

At least that's what he always told himself.

These people, however, made even Raylen queasy. He hadn't quite realized what he was getting into when they had offered him the job. It seemed a little strange, sure, but a man like Raylen couldn't afford to be too picky. Some wealthy clients had odd tastes. It was just something you had to accept. When a man hands you gold and asks you to dig up some corpses, you don't argue. It wasn't as if the Karrnathi graveyards were particularly short of corpses. When Master Jiazen offered Raylen two gold crowns for a fresh human corpse, it seemed as if a small fortune was a short walk and a quick dig away.

But the disturbing stranger kept coming back, fixing Raylen with his steady gaze and listing his demands in a cool, delicate voice. The more corpses Raylen brought, the more Jiazen asked for. The pay increased each time, but each time the demands became more specific. A cadaver of a certain height, a certain gender, a certain nationality, or even of a specific pigmentation. Once the strange fellow even asked for a satchel of finger bones and a half dozen undamaged blue eyes. It was growing to be too much for Raylen. He began visiting different bars, taking different routes through the city, hoping to avoid Jiazen. The strange man always found him, always smiling that too-intense smile. He would eagerly list off the materials he required, paying Raylen in advance, always assuring Raylen that he trusted him to uphold his bargains.

As tempted as Raylen was to flee the city with the money, he was afraid of what would happen if he did. Jiazen had no trouble locating him. Could he track him as well? What if Master Jiazen was some sort of demon, or worse, a wizard? What sort of terrible purpose did he have in mind for the corpses Raylen delivered? If he tried to escape, would Jiazen kill him and add him to the heap?

Raylen shuddered. If he vanished, he would never be missed.

FLIGHT OF THE DYING SUN

He had no family, few acquaintances, and no close friends. Most of the other vagrants he spent time with in the taverns didn't even know his name. Jiazen had probably chosen him just for that reason. Whether he fled or not, the dark stranger would probably kill Raylen once he no longer required him. Considering the rather specific nature of what Jiazen had ordered this time, Raylen feared that this would, in fact, be his last job.

Raylen's teeth chattered loudly as a quaver of fear washed over him.

"This is damnation," he babbled to the empty air. "I know it is. The Host has cursed me as a thief and coward. I've wasted my life, and now they're taking it away from me while I'm still alive."

"The Host has better things to do than worry about scum like you," came a gruff voice from among the crates. "Get it together, Raylen. We can't let Jiazen know anything is wrong."

"I can't d-d-do this," Raylen stuttered. "I don't want to do this. The deal is off."

"You'd rather live in fear forever?" the voice said.

"I've been afraid all my life," Raylen said.

"Then if you die here, you haven't lost anything worthwhile," came the reply. "Consider this a turning point. A chance for redemption. You don't get those every day."

Raylen opened his mouth to reply, but the sound of a creaking floorboard beyond the warehouse door froze the words in his throat. He looked around quickly. The rear door was still open. He could run. He could still get away. Maybe Jiazen wouldn't find him. He could start again somewhere else, maybe Karrlakton or Rekkenmark. A man who knew how to fit in could vanish forever in either of those places. Maybe even a wizard couldn't find him there. Maybe. He took a single step toward the door.

And he stopped.

The fear remained, but Raylen ignored it. He didn't think about why, or how. He just didn't let himself back down. He cleared his throat, turned, and faced the door.

"You know what to do?" the voice said.

Raylen nodded.

The doors slid open, and four men-at-arms stepped inside, each carrying a long halberd in one hand. A small lantern hung from the haft of each spear, dangling just under the blade. They were dressed in silver armor with black, featureless tabards. Plain, black-enameled visors covered their faces. Raylen wondered how the men could see. They fanned out, watching Raylen cautiously while the others searched the warehouse. Raylen tensed as they passed the stack of crates behind him, but they apparently saw nothing. One faced the door and clapped a mailed fist against his breastplate.

Master Jiazen entered in no particular hurry. He wore a finely pressed suit of cobalt blue with a matching cloak draped over one shoulder. His eyes were lined with dark paint, intensifying the paleness of his skin. He smelled faintly of wet earth and vanilla. His lips quirked in an unsettling smile as he gave Raylen a short bow. Two more of the silent warriors followed him, watching Raylen patiently.

"Master Raylen," Jiazen said, his voice low and sibilant. "I am pleased that you contacted me so soon. I feared that I might not hear from you again. What I asked was difficult."

Raylen laughed nervously. "You know me, Master Jiazen," he said. "I don't back out of a contract. I have a reputation in this city."

"Of course you do," Jiazen said with a condescending smile. "If you are not offended by my curiosity, how did you procure such uncommon materials so quickly?"

"Only uncommon if you sit and wait for them to die," Raylen said. "With the money you paid me, I thought I might take a bit of . . . erm . . . what's the word?"

"Initiative?" Jiazen asked, flashing white teeth.

"That's it," he said. "Initiative."

"Astounding," Jiazen said. "You may have a great deal more

potential than I imagined. Where is she?"

"Right over here," Raylen said, beckoning to the dark stranger as he walked toward a long crate in the back of the warehouse. He kicked off the lid, revealing the contents.

Jiazen's smile broadened as he studied the crate in the light of a silent warrior's lantern. Within the box, a young woman lay on a bed of straw. Long brown hair fell loose about her shoulders. Her eyes were closed, and her skin was pale. She wore a simple white dress, her hands clasped across her chest in a posture of repose. She might have looked very peaceful, if not for the bloodstains that covered one side of her dress.

"Immaculate," Jiazen said in a breathless voice. "I hope she is as . . . undamaged as she appears."

"It was a clean wound," Raylen said. "Knife just under the ribs, here, to the side." Raylen pointed at his own back. "She made a lot of noise while she was bleeding out, but no one heard. She's in good shape."

Jiazen nodded clinically. "Yes," he said. "That would certainly suffice." He reached leaned over the crate, drawing a long leather glove from his cloak and stretching it over his right hand. "Allow me a moment to inspect her, and our business shall be concluded."

Jiazen extended his hand toward the corpse, but he stopped short with a gasp when she fixed him with dark eyes. The woman opened her hands, revealing the complex golden octogram of the Sovereign Host. "By the light of the Hearthmother," the girl whispered, "burn."

The holy symbol shone. The warrior beside Jiazen released a mournful wail and staggered backward, smoke boiling from his armor. He fell to his knees, ashes spilling from the joints beneath the plate, crumbling in a heap of empty metal.

"What is the meaning of this?" Jiazen shouted, backing quickly away.

"In the name of House Deneith," the girl said, rising from the crate and plucking her spear from the straw beneath her. "By the authority of the Sentinel Marshals, you are under arrest."

"Vol, kill them both!" Jiazen shouted. He reached into his pocket and began chanting words in an arcane language.

"Careful, he's a wizard," warned a voice from above. A small crystal sphere dropped from the rafters. It shattered at Jiazen's feet and ignited the powder strewn on the floor. The warehouse filled with blinding light and an explosive crack shattered Jiazen's concentration.

When the light faded, they were there.

Omax burst from the crates beside the warehouse door, seizing one dark warrior's halberd and clutching another by the helmet in one wide hand. Seren dropped beside another of the armored men, slashing at his knees with her dagger. Gerith's crossbow took another in the skull, but the undead soldier remained standing upright.

Jiazen blinked rapidly, trying to restore his vision. He looked up in time to see Zed Arthen striding toward him with a grim scowl. A dark warrior stepped into his path but was cut down with a single blow from his massive sword.

"Wizards and zombies," the inquisitive growled. "I hate zombies."

"Could be worse," Tristam said, hopping down from the rafters beside Zed. "Could have been a vampire, like Eraina suspected."

"True," Zed admitted. He rolled his eyes at the wizard. "Don't do it, Jiazen."

Master Jiazen began casting a spell.

Zed Arthen punched Jiazen in the throat.

The wizard fell, choking and clutching his neck.

"I warned you, damn it," Zed said, turning and cutting down another of the zombie soldiers.

In moments, it was done. The undead warriors were no more, reduced to ashes by Eraina's holy magic or torn apart by the furious warforged. Eraina removed her bloody dress, revealing her customary armor. She knelt and bound the wizard's wrists behind his back.

"Impressed you took him alive, Arthen," Eraina said as she dragged him toward the door. "The White Lions may even have a chance question him, once he can speak again."

"I do my best," the inquisitive said. He glanced around the warehouse, searching for the shabby grave robber. Raylen stood just under the sputtering lantern. He held an undead warrior's halberd in his hand. A scrap of a black tabard hung from the tip of its blade. He stared at the floor in numb shock.

"Didn't notice you actually joining the fight," Zed said, impressed. He clapped the man on the shoulder. "You're free now, Raylen."

Raylen's jaw worked for several seconds before he could speak. "By the Host," he finally said. "Thank you."

"I doubt the Host have a lot of good feelings toward me, but you're welcome," Zed said, lighting his pipe and popping it into his mouth.

"What do I do now?" Raylen asked.

"You uphold your part of the deal and tell us what you know," Zed said. "After that, I really don't care. Like I said, I'm a big admirer of redemption, but that's really up to you."

"Right, right," Raylen said, nodding quickly. "The deal. It was four weeks ago. That woman you asked about wanted to charter an airship to Stormhome. Very urgent."

"Stormhome?" Zed asked. "Are you sure?"

"Very sure," Raylen said, scowling bitterly at the memory. "She was really pushy about it, too. Didn't tip very much, either."

"Did she say why?" Zed asked.

"I didn't ask," Raylen said. "People like me learn not to ask."

"Thanks," Zed said. "Now get out of here."

The greasy little man nodded, mumbling a final, effusive thanks before running off into the night and, possibly, a new life.

"Khyber," Zed said. "Why Stormhome, Tristam? Does that make any sense to you?"

"Unfortunately, yes," Tristam said. "According to Kiris's journals, the Boneyard wasn't the only place where Ashrem studied the Draconic Prophecy. There were others, as well. Places of power hidden around the world, where the Prophecy is very old and very strong."

"And Stormhome is one of those?" Zed asked.

"No," Tristam said, "The Prophecy wouldn't be very strong in a place like that. It tends to resonate in places far away from mortal life, often in places we fear to go."

"People are scared of the future," Zed said with a dark chuckle.

"Maybe," Tristam said. "Or maybe the future doesn't like to be disturbed until it's good and ready to arrive."

"So then what does the Prophecy have to do with Stormhome?"

"It's the northernmost port city on the continent," Tristam said.

Zed looked at Tristam seriously. "Host, Tristam, I hope you're not implying what I think you are."

Tristam gave a quirky smile. "One of those places of power was Zul'nadn, an abandoned ruin deep in the Frostfell."

Zed groaned and exhaled a cloud of smoke. "Khyber," he swore. "I hate the cold."

Chapter Nine

The city of Stormhome teemed with people. Travelers from a dozen different races and a dozen different lands crowded the wide streets. Twin flags bearing the Aundairian dragonhawk and the House Lyrandar Kraken flapped proudly from nearly every building, boasting the twin masters of this city. Unlike most port cities, which often stank of fish and pitch, the inner streets of Stormhome smelled distinctly of cinnamon. The Lyrandar boasted an impressive mastery of the winds and were not above flaunting that mastery to make their city more palatable to visitors.

A single majestic tower rose against the sedate Stormhome skyline. This single massive docking tower was equipped to deal with all of the city's airborne visitors. During the city's time as an Aundairian military outpost, most of Stormhome's structures had been built with an eye for simplicity—squat and close to the ground so that they might weather the frequent sea storms. When House Lyrandar took command of the settlement and transformed it into the hub of their vast merchant network, they added the tower for docking their fleet of elegant airships. Dozens of colorful burning rings pierced the dense morning fog around the tower, the idle energy of the elementals that held the Lyrandar fleet aloft. Captain Pherris Gerriman's eyes fixed nervously on a familiar ring of pale blue.

"Don't worry, Captain," Dalan said, clapping the old gnome on the shoulder. "The *Dawn* isn't going anywhere without us."

Pherris's bushy eyebrows rose. "Am I so obvious?" he said wistfully. He looked back at the path ahead, following the others as they walked through the busy street. "We only just put her back together. I would hate to lose her in a place like this."

"I wouldn't worry," Dalan said, winking. "The Lyrandar will keep a close eye on the ship while we're here, if only to make sure we don't cut in on their business. There's no watchdog quite as keen as a sailor who thinks you might be after his share. Aeven is still there as well. I pity any thief that tries to sneak on board."

Pherris shrugged. "I know," he said with a sigh. "I'm a silly old man sometimes. I just can't bear to be away from her."

Dalan looked down at Pherris for a long moment, wondering if the old gnome was talking about his ship or the dryad. He changed the subject. "We need you here, Captain," he said. "The Frostfell is a perilous frontier. We need your expertise if this journey is to be successful."

"I meant to ask you about that, Dalan," Zed said. "I know almost nothing about the Frostfell, and I hate not knowing what we're getting into. I know it's cold, it's on the far side of the ocean, and no one ever comes back. That's about it."

"I think you know a great deal more than most," Dalan said. "The Frostfell is a low priority for most explorers. Most deem it far more trouble than it's worth, considering the profit to be had in less dangerous and more accessible areas."

"I don't like the sound of that," Pherris said, grumbling under his breath. "I don't recall ever hearing of a successful voyage to the Frostfell."

"There was only one large expedition that ever journeyed into its depths and returned," Dalan said.

"One *known* expedition," Tristam corrected, looking back over his shoulder at Dalan.

"Quite," Dalan said, nodding. "I am not surprised to learn that my uncle apparently made his own secret forays into that land, but if we wish to follow, we must seek the wisdom of those who made their exploits popularly known." Dalan paused, surveying the streets around him. A small grin split his broad features as he found the building he sought—a small, two-story home surrounded by a low fence. "Masters Ijaac and Lemgran Bruenhail are friends of the family. They both accompanied Lord ir'Dayne's expedition into the Frostfell. If we wish to journey there safely, we should seek their advice."

"Do you need me for this?" Gerith asked. The halfling shifted from foot to foot, looking at Dalan and Pherris with an anxious expression.

"What's got into you, Master Snowshale?" Pherris asked, offering Gerith an irritated look.

"Me?" Gerith asked, feigning surprise. "I'm not up to anything." He looked around sharply, eyes moving from one thing to the next with an eager intensity. "It's just that I've never been here before. I've heard a lot of stories about this place. I want to see it."

"Stormhome has a reputation as a den of spies, pirates, and debauchery," Dalan said with some amusement. "Your curiosity fails to surprise me."

Gerith shrugged lamely. "I guess maybe I was a little curious," he admitted, "but I thought I might start looking into gathering supplies. Frostfell is a long way away."

"Good idea, Master Snowshale," Pherris said. "I doubt in your current agitated state you would add much to this meeting."

Gerith grinned.

Pherris smiled. "Take Omax with you, just to be safe," he said.

Gerith frowned.

The warforged looked down at Gerith and released a metallic sigh.

"You don't really expect to carry all those supplies by yourself, do you?" the captain asked.

Gerith pursed his lips in an annoyed pout. "I guess not," he said. "Come, Omax." The halfling walked off toward the docks, shoulders slumping slightly. The warforged loped along behind him, blue eyes scanning the streets for danger.

"Remind me to apologize to Omax for any trouble Master Snowshale topples down upon them," Pherris said, watching them go.

Dalan laughed as he opened the gate and entered the small garden beyond. There were few plants; the garden was mostly fine stones of black and white, placed carefully upon the earth and combed in intricate patterns. A stocky little man knelt on the path near the house, smoothing the stones with a long-handled rake. He peered up as they approached. His wizened face was framed by thick gray brows and an explosion of salt-and-pepper beard.

"D'Cannith," the old dwarf said, rising and carefully leaning his rake against the house. He erupted in wet, hacking coughs for several moments before composing himself and eyeing Dalan shrewdly. "How did I know you'd come?"

"I need information, Lemgran," he said. "I will pay."

"Oh, you will," the dwarf agreed. He looked at the rest of them with a cautious eye, then turned and opened the door, gesturing for them to follow.

The inside of the house was dark and smelled richly of incense. The walls were adorned with faded maps and dusty hunting trophies. Half-eaten plates of food sat stacked about the bookcases and furniture, discarded and forgotten. The old dwarf led them to a low table surrounded by overstuffed chairs and a long couch. He sat down heavily and watched them enter in keen silence, muffling a cough behind his handkerchief.

"I won't take much of your time," Dalan said, settling on the couch across from the dwarf. "Allow me to introduce my associates . . ."

"No," the dwarf said, eyeing Zed Arthen warily. "No names. Your friends have the look of people I'm better off not knowing. Just ask your questions, d'Cannith. You're here about the Frostfell?"

Dalan nodded. He looked around the room thoughtfully. "Your brother Ijaac has gone there, hasn't he?" he asked.

"Why do you say that?" Lemgran asked, his voice rough as he stifled a new fit of coughing.

"Your brother was always the tidy one," Dalan replied. "By the looks of your home he has not been here in weeks."

Lemgran scowled. "Ijaac's a fool, and he always has been," the dwarf said. "Always running off on any stupid adventure, Bruenhail honor be damned. I told him the Frostfell was no place for an old dwarf, but he was too stubborn."

"Has Norra Cais been here?" Dalan asked.

Lemgran nodded. "She was the one who wrapped him up in promises of adventure," he said. "Ijaac left with her weeks ago on a ship bound for the north."

"But you stayed here?" Dalan said.

"I don't regret our adventures, but I put them behind me," the dwarf said sadly. "Ijaac was always hungry for one more trip, but the Wayfinder Foundation never really needed us. They have plenty of young fools to die on their trips to Xen'drik, Argonnessen, and Q'barra. Sure, we have experience, but nobody ever wants to go to the Frostfell."

"Except for Norra," Dalan said. "And my uncle, Ashrem."

"Aye," Lemgran said with a bitter smile. "Our experiences in the Frostfell were what brought Ash to us all those years ago. He found something in the Draconic Prophecy that pointed him toward the Zul'nadn ruins. We helped him take the *Dying Sun* to that forsaken temple." Lemgran fell silent for a long moment. His dark eyes were haunted. "When Ijaac and I went north with Lord ir'Dayne and his crew, we saw some strange things, but that was nothing compared to what Ashrem d'Cannith showed us in Zul'nadn."

"You've been to Zul'nadn?" Tristam asked eagerly.

Lemgran sneered at Tristam. "Aye."

"We need to go there," Dalan said. "We need a guide."

The dwarf looked back at Dalan. "Give up now, d'Cannith," he said. "There's nothing out on the ice but death. Even were my health not in the sad shape that it is, I would not go there with you. You have the wrong Bruenhail."

"What did you see in Zul'nadn that filled you with such fear?" Dalan asked. "I thought you were an explorer."

"Fear?" Lemgran said with a laugh, though the laugh dissolved into a short fit of wet hacking. "Fear is what fills you when you don't know what to do. I know exactly what to do about Zul'nadn—leave it lost in the snow where it belongs."

"Ijaac clearly wasn't so ready to give up," Dalan said.

"My brother is dead by now," Lemgran said. "Whatever you're seeking out there isn't worth it. Give up."

"We can't," Tristam said. "We need to know what Ashrem saw."

Lemgran sighed. "Listen to me, boy," he said. "I see that fire in your eyes, and because you're young, I'll excuse it. You sense secrets and you want answers, but some things are forgotten for a reason. Zul'nadn isn't one of those mysteries that needs to be solved. It's a cursed place. The dwarves that built that temple were not normal folk. They weren't sane. Thousands of years ago, they went out there seeking the Prophecy, but the powers of Xoriat crawled into their heads and changed them. Raw madness forced them to build a living nightmare, a place of power, a temple designed to unravel the world."

"What happened to them?" Zed asked.

"They died, thankfully," Lemgran said, clearing his throat with a pained expression. "The Fellmaw was born out of their twisted magic. It crawled into their temple and froze them dead. You can still find them there, hunched over their altars, kneeling in their dormitories, trapped in ice, praying to demons who repay their faith with nothing but oblivion. Some of them still walk out on the ice . . ."

"Alive after all this time?" Eraina asked, incredulous.

"Hardly," Lemgran said. "The darkness they served seeped into their corpses. They don't live . . . they just hunger." The old dwarf shuddered at the memory.

"What is the Fellmaw?" Dalan asked.

"A living storm," Lemgran said. "We found a few writings about it in the temple. Apparently the cultists created it on purpose, believing they could control it. It prowls the plains and canyons of the Frostfell, devouring any life it sees. It's like a blizzard that never dies. It hounded the *Dying Sun*, hunting us, howling in the night and spraying green lightning across the sky whenever it couldn't find us." The old dwarf shivered.

"A living storm?" Zed asked dubiously.

"I've been to the Frostfell twice, human," Lemgran said with a sneer. "I saw terrible weather on my first expedition with Lord ir'Dayne, but it was nothing like the Fellmaw."

"Maybe you were just lucky on the first trip?" Zed asked.

"Zed," Pherris said softly, "I've been a sailor all my life. In my experience there's no surer path to death than laughing at someone else's nightmares. If Lemgran says that he saw a living storm, then that is what he saw."

"Nature itself doesn't want anyone finding whatever is inside Zul'nadn," Lemgran said, eyeing the gnome shrewdly. "I'm still not sure how Ashrem got a few of us out of there alive."

"It's not inconceivable," Tristam said, pondering the dwarf's words. "If the Zul'nadn priests truly worshipped the demons of Xoriat, the boundaries between the planes would be thin there. A powerful rogue elemental could easily have slipped through one of their summoning rituals and become enraged at its entrapment in our world. An elemental has no concept of time or reason. It would perceive any living being as an ally of those who brought it here and lash out in vengeance. A large enough air elemental could manifest itself as a storm."

"Pointless," Lemgran said. "Does explaining things make you feel better, artificer?"

Tristam blinked. "I'm only trying to help," he said. "If we know what we're up against, we'll be better prepared to face it."

"The Fellmaw doesn't care or know where it came from," the dwarf said. "It doesn't care if you understand it. Go there and it will kill you. You can't reason with a storm."

"In that regard we may be in luck, as storms have always been kind to us," Pherris said. "All the same, we will be cautious."

"Any help you could offer would be most appreciated," Dalan said. "Maps, suggested courses, advice on what sorts of supplies we should bring and what sort of hazards we might expect to face outside of the obvious occasional ravenous storm." Dalan reached into his vest and drew out a small velvet bag. He leaned forward and set it on the table in front of Lemgran. The dwarf picked up the bag, weighing it in his hand.

"Money is a good start," Lemgran said, his voice so low it was nearly a growl. "But you . . ." He looked at the gnome captain. "The boy called you Pherris. Would your last name be Gerriman, by any chance?"

"It would," the gnome said.

"*Dying Sun*'s first mate was a boy named Haimel Gerriman," Lemgran said, coughing softly. "He spoke very highly of his father. He said that Pherris Gerriman was the finest airship pilot to ever sail the skies of Eberron."

Pherris smiled sadly. "Haimel had a tendency to exaggerate," he said, "but he was my son. He flew with Ashrem to Zul'nadn?"

"He did," Lemgran said, studying the gnome carefully. There was a strange, hopeful light in his eyes. "Tell me, Captain Gerriman, how quickly could your ship reach the Frostfell?"

"If the winds favor us, five days," the gnome said. "And the winds always favor us."

"No Lyrandar airship would agree to take Cais on her doomed expedition," Lemgran said. "The winds in the Frostfell are too wild for all but the bravest pilots. She and my brother were forced to journey by sea. You may yet have time to intercept them. Though

FLIGHT OF THE DYING SUN

I will not go with you to the Frostfell, I will give you everything you need, Captain Gerriman. I only ask one thing." He pushed the pouch of coins back across the table toward Dalan with a serious expression.

"And what is that?" Pherris asked.

"That you find my foolish brother, Ijaac," Lemgran said in a thick voice. "And, if he lives, bring him back home."

Chapter Ten

Gerith Snowshale sat at the edge of the docks, his small face creased with a frown. Omax settled beside him, his enormous metal body making little sound. The warforged deposited a heavy sack of supplies with a solid thud. The docks were busy at this time of day, with dozens of sailors, merchants, criminals, and other assorted citizens going about their daily business. The weather was fair. A warm yellow sun blazed in a cloudless sapphire sky. The wind mildly caressed the docks, carrying the raucous cry of soaring gulls. Rumor claimed that the priests and wizards who served House Lyrandar used their magic carefully to cultivate an area of fair weather around their port, just as the mages within the city warded away the smell of the docks. Ships moved in and out of the busy bay. Though most bore the seal of House Lyrandar, vessels from every seafaring nation could be found.

The Lyrandar stormships and wind galleons were easily distinguishable from the rest. A sleek tower rose from the back of each ship, linked to a swirling ring of shimmering silver mist. Much like *Karia Naille* and other airships drew upon bound fire elementals to soar through the sky, these sailing vessels drew upon air elementals for a steady source of wind. The ships were a gorgeous combination of magical innovation and shipbuilding artistry. Many travelers spent hours on the Stormhome docks, just watching the elemental ships come and go. Gerith cared nothing for the show. The halfling sat hugging his legs against his thin chest, looking unusually forlorn. Omax looked at the halfling, his blank adamantine face somehow radiating concern.

"Is there a problem, Gerith?" the warforged asked.

"Of course there's a problem," the halfling said with an irritated frown. "You're making my job way more difficult than it needs to be."

"Difficult?" Omax asked, peering about himself in confusion. "What do you mean? What am I making difficult?"

Blizzard landed on top of a nearby post with a leather snap of wings. The glidewing shifted from foot to foot, making himself comfortable, and settled in to patiently watch his master.

"I'm here looking for stories, Omax," Gerith said, mildly exasperated. "I'm always looking for stories, so I can finally find the best one. That one unique story that my grandfather's never heard. Look at all these people, all going interesting places, coming from interesting places, doing interesting things. They must have stories, but none of them are going to talk to me or let me overhear anything interesting with you looming around like that."

"Looming," the warforged said, tilting his head. "I was unaware that I loom. Shall I endeavor to cease looming?"

Gerith blinked. "Now you're making fun of me."

"Certainly not," the warforged said.

"You know what I mean," Gerith said. "You can't help it. The Host knows you're a decent and honorable soul, Omax, but you were built to scare people. You are an intimidating person. Just look around us." Gerith gestured vaguely.

Omax looked over one shoulder compliantly. He was not surprised to find the crowded, busy dock had left avoid for a safe distance around him. "Not unusual," he said, tracing a finger along the jagged scars on his chest. "The presence of a warforged fails to inspire trust in all but the most forgiving and sympathetic souls. It is a simple fact of my existence, and not a stereotype that is entirely unjust."

Blizzard suddenly dove from his perch with a triumphant caw, disappearing over the side of the dock with a splash. The glidewing soared back up seconds later, clutching a struggling fish in its beak. The creature settled back on its perch and shook the water from broad wings, eliciting some muffled curses from startled passersby. Blizzard pinned his catch beneath one talon and began pecking at it contentedly.

"Doesn't that ever bother you?" Gerith asked, ignoring the familiar display.

The warforged looked at the halfling, his shimmering eyes questioning.

"That people assume you're a killer," Gerith said.

"I am accustomed to it," Omax said. "It was, in fact, what I was built to be. I am not without blood on my hands."

"I don't think it's right," Gerith said. "The same thing happens to me. Outsiders look at me and assume I'm a thief and a troublemaker because I'm from the Plains." He looked at the water, thinking for a long moment.

"You *are* a troublemaker," Omax observed. "You exult in it."

"But I'm not a thief!" Gerith protested. "Not for weeks. It's unfair."

"In your case, perhaps arguably," Omax said. "But why should people not fear me? Though I avoid violence, it comes easily to my kind. Why should they not assume I am a danger to them? It is safer for them to assume I mean harm, considering the ease with which I could inflict violence upon them."

"That isn't the sort of person you are," Gerith said.

"Not of late," Omax answered, returning his attention to his injuries. "I have earned some measure of trust from you and from the rest of my friends on *Karia Naille*, and I treasure that. Yet it would be all too easy for me to revert to the monster I once was."

"Are you saying that warforged are inherently evil?" Gerith asked.

FLIGHT OF THE DYING SUN

"I am not sure what 'evil' is," Omax said. "I do not believe there is any value in such an arbitrary designation. What seems evil in one instance may be quite heroic in another. Marth does not consider himself evil. He clearly sees himself as a patriot, and those who follow him believe they still serve my dead homeland. Yet to us, their actions are obviously flawed and destructive. We, on the other hand, have committed crimes and taken lives to stop him. Does that make us heroes?"

"You're talking about laws now," Gerith said. "Laws don't count when they get in the way of what's right."

"A thin distinction," Omax said.

"Laws are what other people tell us to do," Gerith said. "Other people don't always know what's right."

"And how do we know what's right?" Omax said.

"It comes naturally," Gerith answered.

"And here is what comes naturally to me," Omax said. He opened a broad, three-fingered hand and held it before Gerith's face. "These hands can crush bone and tear metal, Gerith. I do not rest, do not tire, and can struggle on when my enemies have long succumbed to exhaustion. I have been given the tools to function as an efficient war machine, a living weapon to kill mortals. I was trained and encouraged to surrender to my violent urges. It is not what I aspire to be, but it is what comes naturally to me. It would be easy for me to be a monster, Gerith. Very easy. Does that make me 'evil?' Or does it grant my struggle to do what is 'right' greater value?"

Gerith shivered. "I think I want to talk about something else now."

"Very well," the warforged said, unperturbed.

The glidewing squawked happily and threw a stringy chunk of fish guts over his shoulder. The glidewing seemed to be aiming the entrails into the crowd.

"You look injured," Gerith said, nodding at the dents and cuts that marked Omax's chest.

"I am somewhat damaged," the warforged said quietly. "It is nothing."

"I thought Dalan had commissioned the Cannith thinkers to repair you," Gerith said.

"I do not trust them," the warforged said. "I would prefer to wait until Tristam has the time to do so himself."

"And he hasn't?" Gerith asked.

"He has done his best," Omax said. "I have taken a considerable amount of damage in a short period. Given time, I do not doubt Tristam could fully repair my wounds. Warforged were designed to work in tandem with artificers such as Tristam. Their magic naturally boosts, heals, and sustains us—and Tristam is far more skilled than most artificers I have known. Yet I do not wish to tax his abilities when we need him focused on our quest."

"That's ridiculous, Omax," Gerith said. "We need you in good shape."

"Why am I needed so badly?" Omax asked.

The halfling looked surprised. "You're the strongest."

The warforged chuckled.

"What are you laughing at?" the halfling asked, brow furrowing in irritation.

"Nothing," Omax said. "I was recalling a conversation I had with Seren. Do not worry about me, Gerith. I shall ask Tristam for aid when the time is right. We have a long trip ahead. There will be ample opportunity."

"Good," Gerith said. "We don't need you falling apart on us, or breaking down, or dying, or whatever." The halfling looked puzzled. "Do warforged die? I mean, if you fall apart, can you be fixed? Or do you die just like living people do?"

"Like living people?" Omax said.

"You know what I mean," Gerith said. "I'm not trying to say you aren't alive."

"I did not take it that way at all," Omax said. "I just found it somewhat amusing that you judge the finality of death as a gauge of legitimate life. Eberron's history is peppered with individuals who prospered long after they should have been dead, and that is without even considering magic, which blurs all lines."

"True," Gerith said. "Hey, do you think Eraina can bring people back from the dead? I hear the gods give their champions that kind of power sometimes."

"I think such blessings lie beyond the sphere of a paladin," Omax said, "but if you are curious, you could always die. Then I could ask her on your behalf."

"I'm not that curious," the halfling said.

Omax laughed, drawing a mischievous grin from the halfling.

"I do think it's weird, though," Gerith said.

"How do you mean?" the warforged asked.

"I mean it's odd that we run into half the problems that we do, considering how much magic we have at our disposal."

"What seems magical to one may be quite mundane and limited to another," Omax said. "Take Blizzard, for example."

The glidewing squawked and peered down darkly at the sound of his name, then returned to nibbling his meal.

"What about him?" Gerith said.

"Your rapport with him is extraordinary," Omax said. "To the observer, almost mystical. You sense one another's moods, move perfectly in time with one another. When you fall, he never fails to catch you. It seems magical."

"Blizzard isn't magic; he's just a good boy," Gerith said, smiling proudly at his steed. The glidewing ignored him. "That's just training and good timing. It's nothing like what Tristam or Aeven or Eraina can do. Some of that stuff is nothing short of miraculous. You'd think that with magic like that, we could get an edge. We could just make our problems go away."

"We have a flying ship," Omax observed. "We have a paladin who heals our wounds and a dryad who commands the weather. Do you not consider these an 'edge?'"

Gerith opened his mouth to reply but said nothing at first. He removed his soft leather cap and shrugged. "That's a good point," he said. "I guess there are a few things I take for granted, but still—shouldn't magic make this a great deal easier than it is?"

"I am no expert in the arts of divine and arcane powers, but I have come to grasp a few of their limitations by watching Tristam," Omax said. "Many people use the word 'magic' to define and contain anything they do not understand. Thus any problem beyond their grasp can be solved by 'magic.' Yet true magic is a power with boundaries and limitations like any other."

"I know, but those boundaries are pretty loose," Gerith said. "Magic can make an airship fly, heal the dying, and let me speak languages I've never even heard before. Host—it can even create life. Look at yourself, Omax. You're a creature of magic."

"And my existence is adequate warning that one should not use an ill-understood power to resolve a crisis," he said. "The result will only give birth to more unforeseen problems. The men who created me and my brethren, for example, wanted slaves—not a sovereign people who wish to seek their own destiny. There is a reason no one builds any more warforged."

Gerith stood, dusting his small hands on his leather trousers. He leaned one elbow absently against Omax and rested his head against his fist as he studied the ships at the docks. Omax did not appear to mind, tending his injuries and occasionally flicking a scrap of burnt, twisted metal into the water. Above them, Blizzard finished his meal and flung the now clean fish skeleton into the bay.

"Now that the war is over, what does a warforged do?" Gerith asked.

"The same as any soldier does, I imagine," Omax said. "Enjoy the welcome respite, or wait for the next battle."

"Eh, I'd rather not wait," Gerith said. "Even during the War I avoided fighting. Most halflings know better than to get wrapped up in that sort of thing."

"Yours is a wise people," Omax said.

"Eh, it doesn't make as much of a difference as you would think," Gerith said, a forlorn note in his high-pitched voice. "People I knew still died, or even worse, just disappeared." He was quiet for a time. "Still, I found some of the best stories during that time. I just hate the endings. Stories should have happy endings, and the War left far too few of those."

"Agreed."

The halfling drummed his fingers against his scalp. "I don't think it's over, Omax," he said. "They say it's over, but it's not. Just look around. People don't trust each other. The Five Nations, the dragonmarked houses, the other assorted kingdoms, they're all still always trying to find ways to pick fights with each other. Is this the way things are supposed to be?"

"Hard to say," Omax said. "After a century, too few remain who remember life without war. I think it will take some time for the world to accustom itself to peace."

"Maybe," the halfling admitted. "I just worry about all the other Legacies that might be out there."

"Other Legacies?" Omax asked.

"How many other leftover memories of the Last War," Gerith said. "Dangerous weapons, like Ashrem's Legacy. Charismatic madmen like Marth. How many sparks are still bouncing around out there, looking rekindle the war?" He looked at Omax seriously. "And are there enough people like us to put out all the sparks? What if we can't do it, Omax?"

The warforged's heavy shoulders shifted. "I do not know, Gerith," he said. "I wish I could reassure you."

The halfling sighed. "I guess we should return to the ship," he said morosely. "Maybe we should stop on the way to pick up some more furs and blankets. We'll need as many as we can get."

"Aye," Omax said, rising with a hollow clank.

"I keep feeling like we've forgotten something important," Gerith said. "I always forget something important."

"I cannot say," Omax said. "Other than that your recent

introspective turn has left you no time for mischief. Captain Gerriman will be most disappointed if you leave him no reason to scold you."

"Oh, I haven't forgotten," Gerith said with a sudden mischievous grin. "We still have to cross half of Stormhome to get back to *Karia Naille*. I have plenty of time to get into trouble."

"Excellent," Omax said. "I shall strive to keep my looming to a minimum as we continue."

"Good," Gerith answered. "You do that."

Chapter
Eleven

Stormhome was an unusual sort of city. Due to the thriving trade and tourism that flowed through the city, over half the people at any given time were strangers. Even many of the citizens who kept houses here spent much of their time abroad as sailors, merchants, or spies. Thus Stormhome was, with the obvious exception of the nobles who ruled the core of the city, a city of strangers. Known acquaintances were rare, and friends were even rarer. Passersby, while always cordial, kept to their own affairs. Such a place was quite comfortable to Shaimin d'Thuranni. He was the sort of man who preferred to be politely ignored. It just made his life a great deal easier. The less people who remembered his face, the better. The less people cared about each other, the less likely that a cry for help would summon anyone who cared. He liked being a stranger.

Dressed simply in an oiled black coat and short gray cloak, the assassin lounged under the awning of a small tea house. He leaned against the door frame as he sipped from a steaming ceramic cup, painted with the ugliest depiction of the Lyrandar house seal that Shaimin had ever seen, resembling a tangled mess of blue yarn and jagged noodles more than the traditional kraken, lightning bolts, and pearl. The tea was terrible, truly awful. It was far too bitter for his taste and reeked of kelp. He would never endure being served such a thing in his home. At a casual gathering he likely would have spat it in the host's face and demanded satisfaction in blood. He was not the sort of man to indulge moderately—anything less than perfection was not worth his time.

Of course such quibbles didn't apply when he was on a mission. Given the current circumstances, Shaimin was actually enjoying himself quite a bit. There was a certain decadent charm in allowing himself to pretend to be so flawed, to endure such wretched treatment to maintain his anonymity. It was the truest test of his skills, that he could restrain exercising his murderous talents even against someone who would insult him by serving such refuse. He knew he was arrogant and self indulgent, but he had earned the right to be such things. Humility was for morons.

Most of *Karia Naille*'s crew had been inside the dwarf's house for a little over an hour. It had been a long time since Shaimin had seen Lemgran Bruenhail. The assassin doubted the dwarf would notice or recognize him after so many years, but Shaimin kept a careful distance from the house regardless. He wondered if Lemgran was still absorbed with self-pity and cowardice. The elder Bruenhail had always been a feeble man, a shadow haunting the steps of his more intelligent and capable brother. If Ijaac Bruenhail was dead, Lemgran was now truly and fully worthless. Shaimin could only imagine what sort of desperate state would lead Tristam Xain and his crew to seek the aid of such a pathetic soul.

As he waited for them to emerge from the house, Shaimin analyzed and categorized the situation thus far. The warforged and the halfling had already separated from the others to attend to their own business. That, at least, was a good thing. Even so, he had already been surprised once on this job, compelling him to take a more methodical approach. Impatience bred mistakes as surely as filth bred vermin. A Thuranni did not suffer filth.

Shaimin watched the dwarf's house and considered the other potential threats and strategies one by one. One thing was certain. If he was to kill Tristam Xain, it would have to be done outside the airship. In his long and glorious career, Shaimin had frequently been required to deal with that most annoying of obstacles—magic. After being unduly surprised by more than one wizard, he had commissioned a bracelet that would allow him to sense the presence of magic, as well as those who could wield it. When he looked up at *Karia Naille*, the trinket warned him of the presence of something powerful and primal. Shaimin was uncertain what it was. Given the intensity of the energies, he was unsure he even wished to know. Perhaps he could deal with whatever was on board, given time and planning, but why bother when he could merely wait for Xain to emerge?

Catching the artificer away from the ship seemed safer, but Xain surrounded himself with allies at all times. The *Karia Naille*'s crew was not large, but each member was a considerable threat in his or her own way. Shaimin considered his potential opponents one by one.

Neither the gnome captain or Ashrem's fat nephew would pose any serious threat. The gnome had perhaps been a formidable warrior in his youth, but those days were long past. His limbs were stiff, and he carried no obvious weapons. Dalan d'Cannith was only slightly more threatening. The guild master had never been—and never would be—a warrior, though he was definitely the sort of man who would turn a knife against an unwary enemy's back.

The halfling scout appeared to be a capable, alert fighter, but Shaimin doubted Snowshale would pose a serious danger. Snowshale's glidewing, on the other hand, made the assassin nervous. The creature was all sinew, claws, and teeth. Its dull black eyes radiated the mindless fury of a predator. If Shaimin were forced to confront the pair, it would be better to slay the beast first—and quickly. To kill either would likely send the other into a suicidal frenzy, and Shaimin preferred his chances against a raging halfling rather than a frenzied dinosaur.

The presence of a Deneith Sentinel Marshal, much less one who wore the trappings of a Spear of Boldrei, was intensely puzzling. To serve a goddess and a dragonmarked house would already require a questionable balance of loyalties. Shaimin wondered what would inspire such a champion to ally herself with such a questionable group. Whatever the reasoning, her presence irritated him. Divine magic was extremely frustrating to a person in his line of work. After going to all the preparation required to deal a perfect killing blow, nothing was quite as galling as to see a paladin wave her hand and wipe the injury away. It was the sort of thing to ruin a man's faith. Did the gods have nothing better to do than interfere with his livelihood? The very idea of paladins and clerics made Shaimin bitter. If the paladin interfered, he'd have no choice but to attack her first, optimally striking her at the throat so that she could not call upon her goddess. She would be a formidable opponent. Once engaged there would be no option but to fight until she was confirmed dead. Paladins were stubborn sorts, and could recover from extraordinary wounds if an assassin was neglectful.

Zed Arthen was another curiosity. Most inquisitives that Shaimin had encountered were bookish, awkward creatures. Arthen had the eyes and bearing of a veteran soldier. His name was vaguely familiar, and Shaimin cursed himself for being unable to recall the reference, but the man was definitely more than he appeared. Shaimin considered hiring random thugs to pick a fight with the inquisitive, simply to gauge the man's abilities. He was probably just as well off waiting for Xain to separate from him. Xain's relationship with Arthen was cold at best. The two rarely spent more time with one another off the *Karia Naille* than they had to.

The warforged, Omax, was definitely an opponent to avoid at all costs. Shaimin had slain his share of constructs in the past. They generally took far more effort than they were worth. Warforged fought to kill, asked no quarter, and survived brutal damage. Even victory was a dubious accomplishment, as they frequently left their opponents in no shape to fight again. Even more important, they knew how to wait. As an elf, Shaimin was virtually immortal. His long lifespan had granted him inexhaustible patience, a wealth of experience, and a unique perspective of time. He was willing to wait for days on end to draw an enemy into a relaxed and vulnerable state. The tactic worked well against humans, who were frequently impulsive and foolhardy. Such an advantage was of no use against a warforged. Though none of the constructs were more than a few decades old, they were literally immortal and neither slept nor rested. They were more patient than elves, and the idea that they would one day outlive elves as well was mildly insulting to Shaimin. Judging by the scarred, weathered condition of this warforged, Omax had survived many battles. He would be a deadly enemy, but he radiated overconfidence. Shaimin noted the unsteady, pained twitch in the warforged's gait. Omax was injured, and more badly than he admitted. All that remained was to find those wounds and exploit them.

Then there was the girl.

Shaimin's face darkened at the memory. He was not the sort of man who enjoyed losing, and he definitely did not enjoy surprises. Surprises were for men without imagination. He liked to believe when he embarked upon a mission that there was no contingency he had not considered. That girl—that foolish, random, stupid human girl—had shattered his preconceptions. Though she had not stopped him, she beat him in every way that counted. She noticed him tailing Xain through the streets of Korth when he did not intend to be seen. She acted before he could strike a killing blow. She had distracted him long enough for Xain to bring his powerful magic to bear.

She had made Shaimin bleed.

She was untrained and inexperienced. He had seen that in her movements. Yet she had nearly undone him. Such instinct. Such talent. In a human!

It was intolerable. His failure was inexcusable.

She was so very intriguing. He needed to know more.

A sudden burst of movement within the house drew Shaimin's attention. He sipped his disgusting beverage while he nonchalantly pretended not to be watching the door. From the corner of his eye he saw seven figures emerge. One waved and returned to the house. That would be Lemgran. The others split, three heading up the street in one direction while the rest headed the other direction, back toward the docking towers. Shaimin looked up more intently, searching for details now that it was less likely he would be noticed spying. Tristam, Seren, and Pherris composed the group that moved back to the airship.

Shaimin briefly considered entering Lemgran's house and questioning the dwarf, finding out why Xain had come to Stormhome and what he was seeking in the Frostfell. The assassin carefully stamped out his curiosity as a traveler stamps out a campfire before it becomes dangerous. He didn't know the full story of why Orren Thardis, or Marth as he wished to be called now, wished Ashrem's former apprentice to die. He didn't know what the changeling sought or why the boy wanted to stop him. He had enough problems of his own. He merely wished to repay this debt and be done with it. He smiled at the serving girl, let the teacup fall on the stone floor with a chink of shattered porcelain, and carefully followed Tristam and his companions into the streets of the city.

The assassin was more cautious than usual, following at a safe distance and melding with the flow of the crowd. That had been Shaimin's biggest mistake back in Korth. He had been careless. For the last few years, his jobs had been rather boring and simple: eliminating old widows, merchant competitors, curious reporters, and other inoffensive quarry. Since the war had ended, his career had been stagnant. Gone were the days of sneaking into a fortified camp and slitting the general's throat in his sleep. Stealing into a besieged castle to deposit poisoned meat in the water supply was simply a fond memory. Life as an assassin during peacetime was dull—you never got to kill anyone interesting. He should have realized from the start that Thardis—Marth—wouldn't have called upon him for a mundane task. This would require effort. It was a welcome change, to be sure. It was merely an adjustment in his recent lazy habits.

The trio paused at the door to a small papermaker's shop. Shaimin smoothly stepped into an alley and pretended to busy himself wiping nonexistent stains from his coat with a handkerchief. The gnome stopped to speak with the merchant while Tristam and the girl waited nearby. Shaimin concentrated upon the dragonmark upon his back and felt part of his soul step away from his body, extending his senses across the street.

"Three hundred sheets of fine vellum," the gnome said. "The waterproof kind, if you can manage it. I'll need it by the morning."

"That's a tall order," the merchant replied.

The gnome held up a bronze seal.

"Cannith?" the merchant replied, impressed.

Buying paper. How boring.

Shaimin moved his senses to his target and the girl.

"I can't help it, Seren," Tristam said, answering some question that Shaimin had not overheard. "I just want to get moving. We're so close now."

So her name was Seren.

"Relax, Tristam," Seren said. "This trip won't be easy. We need to prepare."

Shaimin chuckled. Seren advised Tristam to relax, but Shaimin could see the tension hidden just beneath the surface, the taut muscles in her back and calves. Her eyes watched the windows relentlessly. She was looking for him. The assassin smiled.

"I know, Seren," Tristam said. "I'd just rather not be wasting time buying paper."

"There are better ways to spend your time, I guess," Seren said demurely.

"I could be doing all sorts of things," he said, flustered, missing her cue entirely. "I could be doing the final launch maintenance on the ship. I could be studying Overwood's journals trying to get an idea what we'll see in Zul'nadn. I could be trying to get

Omax to hold still so I can finish repairing him. I could . . . erm . . ." He blushed darkly at her. "You weren't talking about ship maintenance, were you?"

Seren smiled and whispered something in Tristam's ear. They both glanced at Pherris to see if he overheard, then moved a bit closer to each other with the mischievous grins of young lovers.

Shaimin chuckled darkly as some things fell into place. Marth had told him that Xain and his crew shared a mutual quest, but he had not told him—or perhaps had not even realized—the bonds these people shared with one another. Love made enemies dangerous, but it also made them predictable. Seren and Tristam would be watching each other, protecting each other—and Shaimin could use that against them.

The merchant finally came to some agreement and shook hands with the gnome. He led the three of them inside. Shaimin continued watching, his invisible eyes and ears following the merchant as he moved into the back room to fill the gnome's order. Shaimin let the power of his dragonmark fade. Without another moment's hesitation, he strode across the street, opened the door, and stepped inside. The low building was filled with dark iron printing presses and heavy wooden shelves piled with stacks of paper.

Seren recognized Shaimin instantly, drawing her knife and stepping to block his path to Tristam. Shaimin moved erratically, darting the other way and snatching Pherris Gerriman by the back of his coat. The elf held his long dagger against the gnome's neck. Tristam drew his wand a few seconds later, his reflexes much slower than Seren's. Pherris' eyes widened, peering down at the blade pressed against his wrinkled skin.

"Khyber," Xain swore. "You again."

"Good evening, Master Xain," Shaimin said, executing as much of a bow as he was capable of while holding the struggling gnome. "I am not from Khyber. The devils of that forsaken place only wish they had my immaculate sense of style."

"Put him down," Seren said.

"Why?" Shaimin whispered. "If you yell for help, I will kill him and vanish. If you attack me, Seren, I will kill him and vanish. Tristam, you cannot safely use your magic on me without harming your friend as well. If you fail to kill me with your wand, I will certainly kill him and vanish. Now put your weapons down."

"So you can kill us?" Tristam asked.

"And vanish," Shaimin added, waving his dagger with the rhythm of the phrase.

"If you hurt Pherris," Xain said in a cold, steady voice, "even your dragonmark will not hide you from me." He set his wand carefully on the floor.

Seren looked at Tristam uncertainly, then did the same, putting down her knife.

"A reasonable opponent is such a rare thing," Shaimin said with a pleased sigh. "Master Xain, please take off your coat as well. I am well aware of the sorts of accoutrements you artificers like to tote about in your pockets."

Tristam scowled and drew the garment off his shoulders, letting it fall to the floor with a heavy clink.

"Tristam, I'm sorry," Pherris said helplessly.

"It's all right, Captain," Tristam said, rising, eyes fixed on the assassin's. "Nothing you could do."

"Now kick everything well out of your reach, if you please," Shaimin asked.

Tristam did so, booting his rumpled coat and the weapons toward the assassin. "Let Pherris go," he said, voice quavering.

"Not yet," Shaimin said. "Seren, please step away from Master Xain. Into the corner."

"I won't let you kill him, Thuranni," she said.

He looked at her, impressed by the murder he saw in her eyes. Properly tempered, she would make an excellent assassin, for a human. Sadly, she probably would not forgive him for this. "Seren, I realize death is the sort of thing that is quite difficult not to take personally," Shaimin said. "I am afraid there can be no other arrangement. Facing both of you together is too irritating. If it pleases you, I might permit you a desperate leap for your knife after Tristam is dead—at which time I will kill you as well."

Seren's scowl deepened.

"Seren, listen to him," Tristam said. "I'm not worth it."

She looked at him in surprise for a brief instant, then their eyes met. Something passed between them, and she relented, stepping back into the corner.

"Now put him down," Tristam said, holding his hands open to his sides. "You have what you want, Thuranni."

"Not yet," the assassin said, smiling as he set Pherris on the ground. He glanced down at the floor. He smiled as his bracelet pulsed, quietly warning him of the explosive ward Tristam had activated in his coat. "Captain Gerriman, please move Tristam's discarded clothing out of my path. I would not wish to trip."

Tristam paled as he saw his last hope fade. Pherris looked up at Tristam fearfully. Tristam shook his head, trying to warn Pherris away.

The door at the rear of the room opened and the papermaker stepped in, carrying a thick ream and a small knife. Seren lunged at him, ripping the parcel from his hand and twisting, scattering a cloud of fluttering paper across the room. The merchant shrieked and ran back out of the room. Seren dove toward Shaimin with the papermaker's knife. The assassin sighed, ducked under her attack, and sank his own weapon deep into her side, twisting. She cried out and collapsed to her knees. He knocked her aside with a lazy kick. Tristam cried out in rage and snatched his wand from the floor, filling the room with white lightning. Shaimin sighed as he flipped to one side, dodging the worst of the blast.

"I can afford to be patient, Xain," the assassin said with a sigh. "Hide behind your friends, and watch me carve them away one by one."

A cloud of shadow enveloped the small room. Tristam shouted

FLIGHT OF THE DYING SUN

words of magic and burned the darkness away with a sweep of his wand. Shaimin was already gone.

Tristam hurried to Seren's side, falling to his knees and cradling her head in his lap. A thin stream of blood trickled from her mouth. He reached desperately for his cloak, the explosive ward canceling at its master's touch.

"Where in Khyber did he go?" Pherris said, looking around the room fearfully.

Tristam dug through his pockets and drew out a healing draught, tipping it between Seren's lips.

"Why are the Thuranni after us, Tristam?" Pherris asked shrilly.

"Captain, find the Marshal," Tristam said coldly. "She can still save Seren."

"What if he comes back?" Pherris asked.

"Then there's not much we can do, is there?" he said. "Find Eraina."

The captain looked back at Tristam. For a moment, he looked very old and very helpless. "I'm sorry, Tristam," he whispered roughly. "I should have done more. Maybe I should have stayed on the ship."

"Just find Eraina, Captain," Tristam said softly. "I'll be fine till then."

The little gnome nodded sadly and hurried off into the streets of Stormhome.

And from the darkness of a nearby rooftop, Shaimin d'Thuranni watched with a patient, calculating grin.

CHAPTER TWELVE

Orren Thardis drew his sword and stepped into the threshold, barring the chamber door. The captain's face was grave, his pale eyes searching the empty halls for any sign of approaching movement. The twisted amethyst wand pulsed softly in his left hand, casting the frozen ruins in an eerie purple light.

"We must hold our ground here," he said, his voice reverberating in the vast emptiness. "Old Ash needs as much time as we can purchase."

The other crewmen murmured their assent with the exception of the elder dwarf. "What is that old fool doing?" Lemgran demanded in a low voice. His beady eyes flicked toward the shadowy fissure in the rear of the chamber. A pale, shifting light rose from far below, the only sign that Ashrem d'Cannith was still alive. "Whatever's down there can't possibly be worth our lives."

A tortured, gurgling roar rolled through the halls beyond. It was followed by the sound of jagged claws scraping on ice and stone. The sound was familiar to all of them by now. It had taken only two of the creatures to kill four crewmen earlier. Now it sounded as if many more approached. Behind him, Orren heard Kormas mumble a desperate prayer to the Silver Flame. Kormas had never struck Orren as a particularly religious man, but then he had never really cared to ask. He envied Kormas, in a way. At

FLIGHT OF THE DYING SUN

times like this, Orren wished he still had any faith in anything other than himself and the man who had disappeared into the ruins beneath them.

The hideous sounds drew nearer. Now pinpoints of light could be seen in the darkened hallway—the baleful radiance of eyes that had never known true sunlight. There were over a dozen of the ravenous undead creatures.

"How many are there, Captain?" Haimel asked.

"At least six," Orren said. It was a harmless lie. They were likely all doomed anyway.

"We can never beat so many," Lemgran wailed plaintively. "Ashrem d'Cannith has led us to our doom! I know you have magic, Thardis. Teleport us out of here!"

"By the Host, toss that dwarf into the hall if he complains again!" spat one of the other crewmen. "I, for one, will be a great deal happier without his wretched moaning."

"Quiet, both of you," Orren said, glaring back at the assembled crew sharply. "We hold hope in our hands."

The crew all looked at Orren in stunned silence. Outside, the shrieking ghouls drew steadily nearer.

"Do you even realize what Ashrem seeks here?" Orren said. His hands tightened on his sword and wand until the knuckles shone white with his anger. "I know each of you must have a friend, a son, a father, a lover who marches into battle somewhere in Eberron. The knowledge lost in these ruins could end the Last War forever. We do not fight for our own lives here, but for the future of our world. Even if we die, even if Ashrem fails and none ever know our fates, can any of you say that our deaths were not worthy? Would you rather live a long life in a world of orphans and widows when you had the means to fight? Even your cowardice cannot be so great, Lemgran Bruenhail."

"I . . ." Lemgran could say nothing more. The dwarf was stunned, his blue eyes blinking rapidly in shame and surprise.

Just then Lemgran's sibling climbed out of the fissure, his

wizened face beaming. "D'Cannith is almost there," Ijaac reported. "He's found the Eye. He only needs a few more minutes."

"Then stand with me, sons and daughters of *Dying Sun*," Orren said, casting a commanding gaze over them all. "And one day, when Eberron knows peace, all of us will remember that this was the final battle of the Last War, and that we did not falter."

Orren turned and stepped into the hallway to face the maddened ghouls. He felt the crew move as one behind him, even cowardly Lemgran.

Time rippled around him. Memory faded away. The crew was gone, but the ruins were the same. The intervening years had changed very little, though the charred and shattered corpses of the ghouls still lay where the wards had slain them. Orren Thardis's weapons were the same—the Cyran longsword and amethyst wand. The man himself however, was different. He now wore the black uniform of a Cyran soldier. The guise of Orren Thardis melted away with his memory, replaced with Marth's pale, scarred face.

Marth stared into the forsaken corridors of Zul'nadn, only the faint light of his wand reflecting off the ice and stone. He tried to remember the man he once was.

"You never needed them," whispered the timeless voice. "You are the conqueror."

But he could not remember the man who hated the War with such passion. That man was dead.

The Prophecy released him and the visions faded, returning him to the caverns beneath his stronghold.

There was too much pain, too much loss, too much burning need for revenge. The man named Orren Thardis may have forgiven the world, but that man was a mask—and that mask was no more. There was only Marth—the conqueror. The changeling sheathed his sword and touched his face, tracing the scars he had earned on the Day of Mourning. They still burned. The raw magical fire had left wounds that would never fully heal. They matched the shadow cast upon his soul.

FLIGHT OF THE DYING SUN

"Introspection can be a dangerous thing, Marth," Zamiel said, appearing at the end of the corridor. "Worthy deeds are always difficult, and doubt makes that which is difficult impossible. Doubt lays legends low."

"I do not doubt," Marth said, pulling his hand away from his face. "I merely . . . wonder if there might have been another way."

"Ask Ashrem," Zamiel asked. "Your old master wavered at the moment of his destiny and was destroyed for his arrogance. What must be must be. The future will come no matter what we do. We can only prepare and herald its coming. You know that, Marth. Do not resist your fate. Embrace it, as a sail embraces the wind."

"Yes," Marth said. He sighed deeply. "Yes, you are right, of course."

"But I have not come all this way to reassure you," Zamiel said. "Our eyes and ears among Xain's crew are no more. Our spy has been discovered and slain."

"Slain?" Marth said. "I did not expect such brutality from Tristam. He could hardly bring himself to attack me when I faced him, even after all that I have done."

"I doubt it was Xain," Zamiel said. "More likely it was one of his allies—probably the paladin."

"Which paladin?" Marth asked.

Zamiel looked at Marth curiously. "Eraina d'Deneith," the prophet said. "What other paladin would I mean?"

"Never mind," Marth said.

"Things will be far more difficult," Zamiel said. "We have no way of predicting where they will go next. Your assassin has failed."

"They will come here, in time," Marth said. "Dalan knows far too much. But they will not come here yet."

"Where?" Zamiel asked.

"The only destination of importance Kiris could have revealed to them," Marth said. "Zul'nadn."

"They must not reach the Eye," Zamiel said.

"They will not."

"How will you stop him without an airship?" Zamiel asked.

"There are only so many ports from which *Karia Naille* could embark upon a journey to the Frostfell," Marth said. "They are bound for Stormhome, no doubt."

"What will you do?" Zamiel asked.

"Do as you suggested," Marth said. He reached into his long cloak and drew out a short black cylinder, turning it over in his hands. "Conduct a test."

CHAPTER THIRTEEN

Eraina closed the hatch softly and looked up at Tristam with a reassuring smile. "I will not lie to you, Xain," she said. "The wound caused a great deal of bleeding, and Seren is in a fragile state. She has fallen to a fever, but I believe you brought her to me in time to save her life. A few days of rest and, with Boldrei's aid, she will be as fit as she ever was. I will watch over her."

"Thank you, Marshal," Tristam said softly. He bowed his head in relief. "Thank the Hearthmother, as well."

Eraina's eyes widened with mild surprise. "I am unaccustomed to seeing such piety among this crew," she said with a light laugh.

Tristam shrugged. "I guess you're the first real servant of the Host I've ever known," he said. "All you've ever done is help us. Why shouldn't I respect your goddess?"

Eraina said nothing, though her face flushed slightly. She clasped Tristam's arm with one hand and moved off down the corridor toward her cabin. Two shimmering blue lights appeared in the darkened hold behind Tristam, and he looked back with a grim expression as Omax appeared. The artificer nodded silently at his friend and moved above deck, the warforged in tow. He had almost reached the docking bridge before Zed Arthen stepped into his path, gray eyes squinting in irritation.

"Where are you going, Xain?" he asked.

"After the elf that tried to kill Seren," Tristam said. "Come along if you want." Tristam tried to push past Zed onto the bridge, but the inquisitive stopped him with a hand on his shoulder.

"Pherris said the assassin wasn't after Seren," Zed said. "He was trying to kill you."

Tristam glared at Zed. "Seren nearly died."

"Think it through, Tristam," Zed said. "Seren is safe now, and that assassin could be anywhere. We can't waste time looking for him. We need to be gaining ground on Marth while we can."

Tristam's scowl deepened. "Do you suggest we just let him get away?"

"Not at all," Zed said. "I wouldn't worry, Tristam. If he's really a Thuranni, he'll find you again."

"That doesn't make me feel any better," Tristam said. "Stay here if you want, Zed. Let's go, Omax."

"I think Arthen is correct, Tristam," Omax said.

Tristam looked up at the warforged in surprise. "What?"

"This assassin is toying with you," Omax said. "Where he cannot kill you, he tries to weaken you—taking Pherris hostage so you will not use magic to defend yourself, wounding Seren to infuriate you. Do not succumb to impatience, Tristam."

"Impatience?" Tristam snapped. "I can't believe you would say that, Omax. After everything Seren has done to help us, you would do nothing to defend her?"

"An impulsive mistake is no way to repay her friendship and bravery," Omax said. "She was injured protecting you from that assassin. Delivering yourself to him would be pointless."

Tristam glared at Omax angrily, unable to find any words. The warforged looked down at his friend impassively. Zed folded his arms across his chest and stepped back, letting Tristam make his own choice.

"Well, I can't go alone," Tristam said bitterly.

"Good," Dalan said, appearing at the hatch of his cabin. He held a thick ledger under one arm. Gunther paced in small circles around his master, tugging at the short leash Dalan held in one hand. The dog was eager to leave, though it wasn't sure where it was going, as all dogs are. "If that's settled, let begin making preparations for takeoff. Gerith, make sure everything is secure."

The halfling rose instantly from his apparent nap, scrambling below deck.

"We're leaving now?" Tristam asked, shocked.

"Why wait?" Dalan asked. "We have all the maps, supplies, and rations we require. Norra Cais is already weeks ahead of us. Thus we have no time to dally. And what better place to shed your Thuranni admirer than the heart of the Frostfell? Better than giving him time to plan a second attack. If he can follow us to the frozen north, then perhaps he deserves to kill you."

"I agree it's time we were gone from here," Pherris said, emerging from the galley and climbing up to study the ship's controls. "If Marth's assassin knows we are here, then Marth cannot be far behind. We don't have much time before he realizes our intent and moves to stop us."

"It just seems a bit hasty, is all," Tristam said.

"Understandable," Dalan said. "I do not know what awaits you in Zul'nadn, but I would wager it is a large part of why Marth knows more about the Legacy than we do. Remember, he was the *Dying Sun*'s captain."

Tristam cursed himself for not making the same conclusion. "Marth went there with Ashrem," he said. "Marth has known about Zul'nadn since before any of this even started."

Dalan nodded. "I'm quite confident that whatever you find there will illuminate our path," he said. "I wish you all luck."

"Wish us luck?" Zed asked, looking at the leash in his hand. "It almost sounds like you aren't coming with us, Dalan."

"I am most certainly not," Dalan said. "Why would I? I have no illusions about my talents in such a physical arena as arctic exploration. Even if I were to remain on board the ship the entire time, I would, at best, be a drain on your rations. I can serve us better here."

"How?" Zed said. "By not getting in the way?"

"In part," Dalan said, "but primarily by completing the project I've been working on since my rescue from *Seventh Moon*." He took the thick ledger from under his arm, opening it and displaying the pages to Tristam and the others. Dozens of small sketches covered the interior, mostly variations of the Cyran coat of arms.

"What are those?" Tristam asked.

"Personal crests," Zed said, looking at Dalan intently. "Marth's soldiers?"

"Heraldry has always been one of my favorite hobbies," Dalan said. "During my captivity I took careful note of the badges Marth's subordinates wore, committing them to memory. I have spent the time since methodically transcribing them in this volume."

"You remembered all of them?" Pherris asked dubiously.

"I remember everything," Dalan said, slightly offended that any other possibility might be suggested. "A soldier's greatest fear is that his sacrifice will not be remembered, thus heraldry is of utmost importance. All variations, even the most minor, are carefully recorded. A personal crest boasts a soldier's identity and history even should a grisly demise render him otherwise unrecognizable. It is a living memory. The House Lyrandar archives here in Stormhome have extensive heraldic archives. Such resources are useful if a wealthy passenger dies in transit and they need to know where to ship his effects . . . or to collect on an unpaid tavern bill."

"So you hope to find out who Marth's soldiers are?" Zed asked.

"Indeed," Dalan said. "Even Marth cannot weave an army from nothing. The soldiers who follow the changeling seem to, for the most part, hail from the 87th Legion. That unit was was abroad when the Day of Mourning occurred, but he seems to

FLIGHT OF THE DYING SUN

have acquired some new recruits as well. If I can learn who these former Cyrans are and how they came to serve him, then perhaps we might find his headquarters."

"Smart," Zed said, though the admission was somewhat grudging. "Need a hand, Dalan?"

"I can manage well enough alone. Your talents will be more useful in the Frostfell, Arthen." Dalan grinned wickedly. "I know how much you enjoy the cold. Have a marvelous time."

"Thanks," Zed said dryly.

Dalan nodded as he stepped onto the tower bridge with his dog in tow. "Good luck to all of you," he said. "Give Miss Morisse my best wishes. I am relieved that she was not permanently harmed."

"Thank you, Dalan," Tristam said sincerely. "Do you think we should leave her here to recover?"

"I most certainly do not," Dalan said. "I can think of no safer place for her than aboard the *Mourning Dawn,* close to you. Move her to my cabin if you like. It has an actual bed rather than the canvas-bound boards I supplied the rest of you." Dalan looked at Tristam evenly. "Take care of her, Tristam."

The young artificer nodded quietly.

A sudden rush of soft wind whispered over the deck. Suddenly the dryad was there, seated on the rail beside the figurehead. She was hunched against her likeness, arms wrapped around her thin chest as she shivered uncontrollably.

"Aeven?" Pherris called out, alarmed.

"Something has begun," she said hoarsely.

"What's happening?" the gnome asked sharply. "What's wrong?"

The smell of burnt ozone and bitter smoke drifted on the wind. Pale blue lightning crackled in the cloudless sky. Even the bright yellow sun looked darker, as if hidden behind a gray haze.

"The wind trembles," Aeven whispered. "The chains the Lyrandar have placed upon the storms are weakening. Magic is dying."

"By the Host, no," Tristam said. "This is just as Frauk described it."

"The Legacy," Dalan whispered.

"I'm taking us out of here," Pherris shouted, hurrying to the controls. "All hands prepare for takeoff. Master d'Cannith, get back on board, if you please."

"No," Dalan said, though his voice echoed with fear. "I have too much to do here. I have no magic to speak of. I will be fine."

"As long as an airship doesn't fall out of the sky on you," Zed said.

Dalan glanced up nervously. Gunther whined and huddled behind his master's legs.

"Pherris, hurry," Aeven whispered. "Leave this place."

The gnome nodded, leaning into the controls. A high-pitched whine surged through the ship's elemental ring. For a brief moment, the blue flame flickered and the ship dipped dangerously, as if she would fall. Then the fire flashed with a sudden defiant roar and *Karia Naille* lunged into the sky. Tristam ran to the rail, looking down at the city as the ship soared upward. A swirling finger of blue mist had erupted from the center of the city, swirling rapidly outward toward the sky tower. As it expanded, the elemental rings surrounding the airships sputtered and died. The sound of thunder erupted repeatedly below them as the proud Lyrandar airships crashed into the earth. Fires erupted as the mighty fleet crumbled, followed by the confused screams of the citizens as chaos spread through the port. The sky overhead cracked in reply.

"What's going on?" Eraina asked, rushing onto the deck.

Karia Naille shuddered. Veins of sickly green flame shot through her pure blue ring. Omax fell to his knees with an anguished groan, greasy smoke spilling from his joints. Aeven shook violently and slipped from the rail with a moan. Zed leapt to her side, seizing the tiny dryad in his arms and pulling her onto the deck. Eraina knelt beside Aeven, whispering a healing prayer that died in her mouth.

FLIGHT OF THE DYING SUN

"I cannot hear Boldrei," she said, terrified. "The Hearthmother is silent."

"My magic is dead too," Tristam said, kneeling beside the anguished warforged. "I can't heal Omax or remember my infusions."

"Omax and Aeven are dying, Pherris!" Zed shouted, looking fearfully at the ship's shuddering elemental ring. "Get us out of here."

The gnome nodded grimly.

A web of blue lightning covered the sky, now rippling with the same sickly green electricity that tainted *Karia Naille*'s fire. A rush of wind surged past them as an airship toppled from the sky, plummeting past them into the city below. She was followed by another dying vessel, then a third. The last ship passed so close that Pherris was forced to bank to starboard to avoid collision. Tristam could see the terrified faces of the doomed sailors, clinging desperately to the hull. He could hear their helpless screams. *Karia Naille*'s elemental ring passed through the void where the other ship's ring had once been—and for an instant, a faint circle of fire crackled around the falling ship. The falling airships plunged like stones into the city, disappearing in clouds of smoke and flame. The winds roared as storms long kept in check rolled over the city.

"How in Khyber are we still in the air?" Gerith said. "Why is everyone falling but us?" The halfling eyed his glidewing nervously, clearly ready to hop overboard and fly for his life.

"A mystery to consider at a later time, Master Snowshale," Pherris said. Sweat beaded on his forehead as he urged the airship to greater speed. "Master Xain, any suggestions for how to escape this crisis would be welcome."

Tristam nodded. Rain scoured the deck. It was as if the elements were making up for lost time in Stormhome. He returned to the rail, staring down at the city skyline in horror. Fires now burned throughout the city, marking the crash sites of the

Lyrandar airship fleet. The bay was scattered with elemental galleons, now drifting helplessly with no source of power. At the western edge he could see silver trails as three stormships sped away from the city under the power of their bound elementals.

"That way, toward the sea," Tristam said. "The Legacy's power doesn't seem to extend very far over the water. We can escape."

Pherris nodded and turned hard into the controls, forcing *Karia Naille* to bank and speed out to the north. Lightning sizzled the air around them. For a tense minute, the elemental ring crackled and blurred. Then, as quickly as it had begun, a rhythmic hum resounded from deep inside the vessel. The fire burned steady again. The air grew calm. The storm receded behind them. Omax sat up with a sigh, his eyes shining with a faint but steady glow. Aeven coughed sickly and struggled to her feet, leaning heavily against Zed.

"No wonder Ashrem wanted to bury that damn thing," Zed said, rubbing his unshaven face with one hand as he stared back at the burning city. "I hope Dalan will be all right in the middle of that."

"Master d'Cannith is a survivor," Pherris said, though the words lacked confidence.

"Why would Marth do that?" Gerith asked. The halfling's eyes were moist as he looked back at the burning city. "Why would anyone unleash something like that?"

"To cripple our ship as we crippled his," Tristam said. "To stop us from finding Zul'nadn."

"All this just to stop us?" Gerith asked, horrified. "People are dying down there."

"If the Legacy can do that, I fear that Stormhome is only the start," Pherris said. "There are others who rely on magic far more heavily than the Lyrandar."

"I can't even comprehend what we just saw," Zed said gravely. "How would you stop a weapon like that? If you can't even use magic against it, what do you do?"

FLIGHT OF THE DYING SUN

Tristam didn't answer. He looked away from the retreating city of Stormhome and went back below deck, shoulders slumping from the weight of what he had seen.

Chapter
Fourteen

Ringbriar was certainly not a large town. It was hardly even a village, more a muddle of huts where the local farmers and woodsmen lived in close proximity to one another. Ringbriar wouldn't have had a name if a Brelish cartographer hadn't passed through a few decades past, felt that section of the map was somewhat bare, and assigned a name as thanks for the warm meal he had been offered that evening. The name didn't even mean anything. There was no ring to speak of, nor did the village have any profusion of briars. It was just a pair of random words strung together. Ringbriar wasn't an important place unless you lived there. The only folks who ever moved away joined the Brelish army—but those who took that route were seldom heard from again. In recent years, the war had been particularly fierce on the Brelish borders. Life for a young recruit was dangerous and usually short.

So when Seren looked up from tending her mother's garden, she did not expect to see a lone, tired man walking down the main road. He wore the tattered uniform of a Brelish soldier and slung a heavy satchel of supplies over one shoulder. He limped slightly and was hunched from exhaustion, but pushed onward with the stride of a man who knew a well-deserved rest lay ahead. Seren gasped. The shears slipped in her hands, neatly beheading an innocent rose. She hardly noticed, dropping the tool on the soft earth before running toward the traveler as quickly as he could.

FLIGHT OF THE DYING SUN

He only had time to say, "Seren," before she collided with him, arms wrapping tight around his waist. She buried his head against his chest and sobbed quietly.

"Don't leave, Dad," she whispered. "Don't go away again."

"I'm not going anywhere," he said in a thick voice. He wrapped his free arm around her shoulders. The embrace quickly turned to support when Seren realized how exhausted he was. She let him lean against her, helping her father hobble back toward the house.

"Are you on leave?" she asked.

"Something like that," he said.

"Has the fighting stopped?" she asked.

"For a little while," he said.

"Can you help me practice dueling?" she asked.

"Maybe later," he said, laughing. "I'm a little tired of fighting at the moment."

She laughed and looked up at him, grinning as a tear rolled down her cheek. "I missed you, Dad."

He was briefly silent. "I missed you too, Seren," he said, not meeting her eyes.

Seren looked past him, studying the surrounding houses. It was strange that no one else was around. Usually there were at least a few children in the streets, or the usual gaggle of old men gossiping about days gone by. A returned soldier usually caused quite a stir, with everyone hoping to be the first to greet their hero. Today everything was quiet. It was only the two of them.

Seren's face became pale. "Dad, where is Mom?" she asked.

"She's fine," her father said. He stopped walking, turning Seren to face him. "She's exactly where she should be, but that isn't important, Seren. It's you I'm worried about."

"Me?" Seren asked, confused. She felt an itch in her side. She moved to scratch it, but her father gently pulled her hand away, clasping it in his own. She felt confused, as if she was forgetting something.

Her father's hand tightened. "Seren, I'm proud of you," he said. "You're a young woman now. You're a hero, much like I wanted to be."

"A hero?" she asked, confused.

Memories blurred through Seren's mind, visions only half-remembered. She saw a ship surrounded by a ring of blue fire. She saw a pale figure with a shifting face, hunting her. She saw a kind young man with sandy hair. His shoulders were slumped and his eyes were troubled, but when he noticed her, he smiled.

"You don't belong here, Seren," her father said. "You aren't needed here."

She closed her eyes. "I'm tired, Dad," she said. "So tired. It's harder than I thought it would be."

"It always is," he said.

"I don't know if I can keep fighting," she said. "I'm not strong enough."

"You're stronger than you think" he said. He smiled. "And you're not alone anymore."

"I miss you, Dad," she said.

"Don't," he said. "I'm never far away."

The village melted from view, and Seren's head swam. Her vision blurred as the memories fell back into place and sorted back into reality around her. She opened her eyes blearily, finding herself lying on an overstuffed bed. It was Dalan's cabin, slouched with thick bookcases and a disorganized desk covered with paperwork. Tristam slumped on a stool next to the bed, arms folded tightly, chin propped against his chest as he dozed. Tristam's homunculus perched on the edge of the desk. The lumpy clay man looked up with shimmering golden eyes as Seren stirred. It quickly turned and poked Tristam with the sharp end of a pencil, causing him to jerk from his nap and nearly fall backward off his seat.

"Wha?" he said, blinking in confusion. "By the Host, Seren!" This time he did fall in a confused tangle of limbs. He quickly regained his composure, staggering into a kneeling position beside the bed. He impulsively reached for her but stopped several inches away.

She looked at him, surprised. "Tristam," she whispered.

"How are you?" he asked, nervously glancing at the bandages bound around her waist. "I mean, you were out for days with fever. Are you still hurt?"

She laughed and wrapped her arms around Tristam, pulling him close and kissing him soundly on the mouth. She felt a faint twinge from her side but didn't particularly care. She pulled away to look at him. He stared back with a broad, stunned grin.

"I was so worried," Tristam said. His voice was thick. "We were all worried," he added quickly. "Even Dalan volunteered his cabin before he stayed behind in Stormhome."

"Sorry to be a burden," Seren said weakly. She felt drained. Her side still ached where the assassin's blade had twisted inside her. But she felt whole. She was healing. Eraina was probably to thank for that.

Tristam laughed. "Never a burden, Seren," he said. "You saved my life. There's something I want you to see." He stood, offering his hand to her.

Seren looked at him curiously, then accepted, letting him lift her from the bed. Despite his lean frame, he was much stronger than he looked. When her legs wobbled and failed to support her, she leaned into him.

"Don't forget this," she said, taking his wand from the homunculus and handing it to him. She looked at the weapon curiously. "It looks different. I don't remember these quartz crystal settings."

"You noticed?" he asked, blushing slightly. "It's new. I incorporated some of the things I learned from the Cannith libraries in Korth with my own theories. I think the overall calibration of the arcane matrix . . ." he stopped, noticing Seren's polite but confused expression. "I'll tell you about it later. Like I said, I have something to show you."

He pulled a thick felt cloak over her shoulders and opened the hatch. A sudden burst of freezing air and brilliant white light filled the room, making Seren gasp. She squinted at Tristam suspiciously, but he only smiled and led her out onto the deck. All around them, the world shone a brilliant blue. The sea stretched beneath them, a field of sapphire studded with chunks of ice like white diamonds. Above them, the sky was pure and clear. The sun hovered above them, a pale white flame. It was as if the whole world was made of crystal—pale, cold, and serene. A thin dusting of wet frost covered the deck of the *Karia Naille,* but it melted as soon as it set due to the ship's flaming elemental ring.

"I always see you sitting at the rail whenever we go somewhere new," Tristam said. "I didn't think you'd want to miss this. Even Gerith has never seen this place before."

Seren had no words. She was awed by the beauty of the Frostfell. She moved to the bow of the ship. Tristam stayed near, offering his support.

"It does my heart good to see you up and about, Miss Morisse," Pherris said from the ship's helm. "We were somewhat overdue for good luck, I think."

"Good morning, Captain," Seren said, smiling at the old gnome. Pherris's goggles were partially frosted. The little man was thickly bundled in wool and furs.

"It's almost midnight, actually," Zed said from where he stood at the opposite rail. His usual bulky coat was supplemented by a fur cloak and a thick scarf. "The sun doesn't ever seem to set around here. Maybe it doesn't bother, since there's no one here to see."

"It has to do more with the angle of the sun relative to the world's axis," Tristam said. "The angle of incoming radiant energy also has a major impact on the climate, creating perpetual winter . . ."

"Save it, Tristam," Zed said, holding out a hand. "I know how it works. I just like my explanation better. If you want to put your knowledge to good use, do something about this cold."

FLIGHT OF THE DYING SUN

"I already have," Tristam said. "The elemental is already warming the ship considerably. It should be much colder than this."

Zed looked slightly sick. He returned his attention to his pipe.

Pherris chuckled to himself. "Considering the number of things you take in stride," he said, "I find it amusing that something as simple as cold weather bothers you so much, Master Arthen."

"Nothing simple about it," he said. "I spent the first six years of my service to Thrane stationed at Flame's Refuge in Thaliost. The north winds would come right down the Scions Sound and freeze everything in their path. In the middle of winter you could spit off the top of the dam and hear it shatter when it struck bottom." He took the pipe from his mouth and exhaled a long plume of smoke. "I did everything I could to get transferred out of that place, but the bastards kept promoting me. I ended up the master drill sergeant before I got called away." He smirked. "Took a miracle to get me posted somewhere else."

"You were a drill sergeant?" Tristam asked, laughing.

"You find that funny, Xain?" Zed asked sternly.

"Yes, actually," Tristam said. "It explains much."

The inquisitive gave Zed a long, humorless glare.

"The winds are strong and untamed," said Aeven's cool voice. The dryad was perched in her customary place by her figurehead. Her green eyes were clear and alert, showing none of the weakness that had overcome her in Stormhome. "I have importuned them to be merciful, and they have complied. Even so, the journey will be rough. A lesser vessel would not survive this journey. I only hope I can maintain the wind's favor."

"Do all that you can, Aeven. I have faith in you," Pherris said.

"Did the winds say anything about Lemgran's Fellmaw?" Zed asked with a dark chuckle.

"Zed, please," Pherris said. "We can worry about such things when . . ."

"They did," Aeven interrupted. "They whisper of a storm born long ago, a storm that will not die. It is a thing of fury and hunger. It hunts the mortals who drew it to this world, unaware that they are long dead. Its rage is reserved solely for the monks of Zul'nadn, but it will ravage any other life it finds so long as it cannot hunt them. The Fellmaw moves swiftly, but the winds will warn me of its approach. It is there." She pointed at the eastern horizon. The faintest flicker of green light reflected in the sky there. "I believe we can avoid it."

"Then that's more good luck," Pherris said, relieved.

"How do we expect to find one person in all of this?" Seren asked, looking out at the frozen waters. "All of this ice and water looks the same."

"Norra Cais is using Ijaac Bruenhail's charts," Tristam said. "His brother Lemgran's maps are an exact copy. So we're following the same course she did, just higher up. If we keep on this heading, we'll find her eventually."

"Seren?" came Eraina's sleepy voice. The Marshal stepped out of the lower hold, blinking as her eyes found the light. Her eyes were hollow with exhaustion. She shivered in the unaccustomed cold. "You're awake?" the paladin said. "I'm glad to see you have finally recovered."

"Thank you, Eraina," Seren said quietly. "For everything."

The paladin smiled faintly. Behind her, Omax emerged onto the deck. He gave Seren a careful look, bowed his head respectfully, and looked past her, eyes studying something in the sky above.

"Halfling incoming," he said, pointing.

A shrill caw sounded above them and Blizzard landed on the rail with a heavy thud. The glidewing's chest heaved desperately. The creature gratefully climbed down onto the deck as Gerith rolled out of the harness, covered head to toe in thick furs and leathers. He rubbed the back of his steed's neck and whispered something in his native tongue. The glidewing cawed gratefully and scrambled off into the galley, seeking warmth.

"How did the ointment work, Gerith?" Tristam asked.

"Great," the halfling said, gasping for breath as his mount did. "Kept most of the cold off him, though he's still not happy about the thin air. He can't fly very long out there."

"Welcome back, Master Snowshale," Pherris said. "Did you find anything interesting?"

The halfling pulled off his thick goggles and blew on his hands, trying desperately to warm himself. He held up one reddened finger as he collected himself, letting his breathing grow regular. After a few moments, he pointed off to the west. "That way," he said between labored breaths. "I found Norra Cais's ship on the shore, but it's in bad shape."

"Bad shape how?" Seren asked. She didn't like such a tone of trepidation from the usually fearless halfling.

"The ship is beached," Gerith said. "Lots of bodies on the ground. I didn't see much more . . . I was inclined to keep my distance until I got help." Gerith looked at Tristam nervously. "I don't think you're going to like what we see."

Pherris grumbled something under his breath and worked the ship's controls, causing the ship to bank and veer to the west. Beneath them, the ice flows began to grow larger and more frequent. The occasional spire of a glacier broke the waves. Ahead of them, the Frostfell gradually shifted from frozen water to frozen earth. The crew fell silent as they saw what awaited them. Where the sea met the land, a ship lay scuttled upon the frozen beach. Its mast was shattered and half its hull was torn away. Bodies lay scattered about the ice on pools of bright red frost.

"Captain, put us down a safe distance away," Tristam said, his voice unusually steady.

"I'm not even going to attempt to land in this forsaken place," Pherris said, "but I'll get you close enough to take the ladder down."

"That will do," Tristam said.

"Have a care, Master Xain," Pherris warned. "Whatever destroyed that ship may still be down there."

Tristam frowned. "Then we'll deal with it," he said.

The gnome nodded silently. The airship turned in a slow arc, circling down toward the frozen earth. The elemental ring burned clear white, leaving a plume of sparkling steam as the ship descended. Seren adjusted the knife at her hip and reached for one of the thick coats lying folded in a crate near the galley. She caught sight of Tristam watching her with a pensive expression.

"You aren't going down there, Seren," he said softly. "You're still hurt."

"Trying to protect me?" she snapped at him, though the weakness in her voice was obvious.

"Yes," he said. His eyes were intent. "For once, would you let me?"

Her sharp retort died in her mouth. She nodded wordlessly. Tristam blinked, seeming surprised by her agreement.

"Probably best that I remain here as well," Eraina said. "My energy is at a low ebb, and I would like a chance to make certain Seren is fully recovered."

"Fair enough," Tristam said. "Zed, Omax, Gerith, come with me." He climbed down the ladder back into the cargo hold, pausing only to glance up at Seren one last time.

"Be careful, Master Xain," Pherris said. He nodded at the tiny woman huddled in the front of the ship. "Aeven does not like this place. I have learned to be wary when she is wary."

"I will," Tristam said. "I'll be back." He offered Seren a reassuring smile and disappeared into the hold.

CHAPTER
FIFTEEN

Omax had already opened the bay doors and lowered the ladder. Tristam pulled a thick furry coat over his shoulders and wound a woolen scarf around his face before climbing down. The cold wrapped around him, seeping through the thick layers of clothing, numbing his flesh. He gasped sharply, but his thoughts on the matter were quite aptly summed up when Arthen landed next to him, loosing a trail of expletives unlike any Tristam had heard in his young life.

Omax hopped down from the ladder, regarding Arthen with interest. In addition to his usual soft woolen cap and loose trousers, Omax had donned a thick felt cloak to keep the harsh wind out of his joints. A faint, warm haze emanated from his metal skin.

"What?" Arthen demanded from within his small mountain of furs.

"I am uncertain how to react, other than to be impressed," the warforged said. "I was not even aware that a few of those conjugations existed, or that you spoke the hobgoblin tongue."

"Cold weather makes me creative," Arthen growled. "I don't know how I'm going to fight in this, if we have to. I guess I'll just snap off pieces of myself and throw them."

Gerith alighted next to them. Blizzard's wings shivered visibly. The glidewing's pure black eyes held an even more dangerous gleam than usual.

"How can your mount even survive in this, Gerith?" Zed asked. "Aren't reptiles cold-blooded?"

The glidewing snapped angrily in Zed's direction, coming away with a piece of his sleeve. Arthen quickly backed away, grasping his hands as if making certain his fingers were intact.

"Not a lizard," Gerith said. "This way." He pointed with two fingers before whistling and taking to the air again.

They trudged forward across the frozen earth. The snow was hard and crusty beneath their feet, more like gravel than the soft powder more common in Khorvaire. There was no sound save their footsteps and a baleful wail as the wind raced over the earth and sea. The dead ship was easy to find, a mass of black wreckage on the white plain. The bodies of the crewmen were scattered in a wide area around the vessel. Zed knelt by the first one they encountered, two hundred yards from the ship. He pulled up his goggles to investigate more thoroughly.

"Impossible to tell how long he's been dead, frozen like that," Zed said in a low voice. "Claw marks deep in his chest, like some sort of huge animal. Whatever it was, he died terrified. Didn't even bother to draw a weapon." The inquisitive looked at the ground between the ship and the corpse. It was mostly flat and even. The corpse lay at the end of a shallow groove in the snow. "No trail, and no fresh snow. The body was thrown here, all the way from the ship."

"If there are survivors, we must find them," Omax said.

"Aye," Tristam agreed.

"I found some tracks," Gerith said, landing nearby. "Some kind of creature, something big." The halfling scratched his nose nervously.

"Tell us the rest, Gerith," Zed said carefully.

"The tracks lead into the ship," Gerith said, "but they don't come back out."

"Damn it," Zed hissed. He pulled the heavy sword off of his back, struggling to pull it out of its scabbard with his thick gloves.

FLIGHT OF THE DYING SUN

"Careful Zed," Tristam said, leading the way slowly. "We don't even know if a sword will help."

"It makes me feel better," Zed retorted.

Tristam nodded, admitting the point. He reached into his coat and drew out his wand before proceeding. They moved closer to the ship, finding many more bodies like the rest. They were scattered like forgotten toys, savaged by claws and left lying in the snow. A large cavity gaped in the side of the ship, where she had been cracked open and torn apart. Large sections of the ship were now encased in pure ice. The ground was gouged and torn around her hull. Deep claw marks pierced the wood in several places. The mast was cracked and the sails hung in limp shreds. It looked as if the entire ship had been hauled onto land and crippled as her crew was methodically killed.

Tristam realized then that he was trembling. Something about this dead ship, this carnage frozen in time, terrified him. There had been no defense. There was nothing these people could have done to save themselves. Yet somehow he found his voice.

"Is anyone there?" he called out, his voice echoing over the icy plain.

Zed winced at the echo and held his sword ready.

"Is anyone alive?" Tristam added.

A long, reptilian snarl resounded from the depths of the ship, making Tristam take a step back. Omax moved in front of his friend, his heavy metal fingers clenching into fists. A red light pulsed within the cavity on the ship's side, illuminating a pair of faceted black eyes. A long, slender head emerged from the darkness, like an impossibly enormous centipede. Segmented antennae swayed from its brow and upper mouth, curling in the air as they tasted the scent of intruders. A pair of gossamer fins spread from the back of its head and down its long neck, pulsating with a faint crimson light. Its body moved with sinuous grace as it emerged from the darkness, contrasted by the dozens of short, scrabbling legs that jutted from its underbelly. The creature was half the size of the ship, large enough to take any one of them in a single bite. It slid out onto the snow, casting aside a half eaten corpse with the flick of a leg. It turned, coiling on itself as it regarded the intruders warily.

"Remorhaz," Gerith said, hunching low in his glidewing's harness. "Just back away, Tristam. This is his territory now."

"What if there are survivors?" Tristam asked, watching the beast warily.

"There won't be," Gerith whispered. "They're very territorial. He has plenty of food, so he won't want to fight unless we threaten him. Let's just get out of here."

"For once I agree with the halfling," Zed said. "Let's not start this fight."

Tristam nodded, backing away. His foot met something slick and the ground slid under him. He fell onto one of the half-eaten corpses, landing heavily on his side with a sickly smack. The remorhaz's eyes narrowed into slits. The fins on its back extended, pulsing a bright, angry red. Its hideous mouth folded open and released a terrifying screech. It lumbered forward to defend its food.

"Khyber," Tristam swore.

The artificer pointed his wand, desperately releasing a bolt of white lightning at the creature. The blast seared its flesh and shattered two of its forelegs, but it kept advancing, heedless of the pain. Omax leapt into its path, clasping his metal fists together and delivering a powerful blow to the creature's chest. The creature shrieked in pain and snatched Omax in its forelegs, clutching the warforged against its body with the sizzling smell of burning wood and melting metal. Omax grunted in pain and seized one of the creature's lower antennae, pulling its head down. Zed charged at the opening Omax had offered, swinging his sword in a broad cleave and slashing the monster across the face.

It shrieked and recoiled as Zed's blade shattered its carapace, skittering backward and dropping Omax in the snow. Gerith

FLIGHT OF THE DYING SUN

loosed a crossbow bolt, lodging the missile in the creature's left eye. Blood-red steam boiled from the creature's wounds as it danced away. It began scrabbling at the ground with its legs, tearing through ice and stone. In moments, it had rent a hole in the icy crust and slid into the tunnel, the wispy tendrils of its tail waving in the air for a moment before it vanished. The creature's mad, pained shrieking could be heard descending into the earth.

Tristam ran toward the tunnel, drawing a clay flask from his coat. He twisted the cork, forcing a plume of gray steam and yellow sparks to erupt from the bottle before he hurled it into the hole. There were several moments of silence, followed by a reverberating thud and a tremble in the earth. Oily smoke belched out of the remorhaz's tunnel, and the creature was heard no more.

"Omax," Zed said, pointing at the collapsed warforged.

Tristam quickly ran to his friend's side. The intense heat of the remorhaz's body had seared Omax's armored skin. The adamantine covering his left arm was now a twisted, melted mess. One side of his face was now misshapen, like a melting wax statue. But what concerned Tristam more were the jagged injuries in his friend's chest.

"I thought the Canniths had repaired you, Omax," he whispered. Tristam spoke a quick infusion and his hands glowed briefly. Omax's face straightened. Much of the metal and wood in his chest bent back toward its intended arrangement.

"I am . . . fine," Omax said, his voice a pained growl.

Tristam sighed. "Gerith, go back to the ship and tell Pherris to come to us," he said. "Omax can't walk like this." He looked down at the warforged angrily. "Why did you ignore your injuries?" he asked. "That was foolish."

The warforged said nothing, and could not meet Tristam's gaze.

"You'd best hurry, Gerith," Zed said. "As scary as that was, that creature didn't do any of this."

"What?" Tristam said, looking at Zed in surprise.

"That remorhaz couldn't have thrown the bodies so far, or dragged that ship out of the water," he said. "Even if it had, the corpses would have been burned from touching its skin. They're not. A few of them are frozen solid, in fact. That monster didn't kill the crew . . . it just came along to feed after whatever did this left the corpses behind."

"So what did this?" Tristam asked.

"I don't know," Zed said, his eyes scanning the crash site intently, looking for any clues. "Something big. Something that didn't care to feed on the dead, or that was too concerned with something else."

"Like what?" Tristam asked.

Zed pulled his scarf down over his chin. A slow grin spread across his unshaven face. He pointed with his sword, past the wrecked ship. A rowboat lay overturned in the snow and, beyond it, a pair of footprints tracked off into the icy wastes. "Why don't we find whoever left that trail," he said, "and ask them?"

"Good luck, gentlemen," Gerith said, climbing onto his glidewing. "I'll try to catch up to you as soon as I can."

"Yeah," Zed said. "We'll need your expertise, Snowshale."

Gerith paused for a moment. "Really?" he said. "Are you serious?"

Zed looked at the halfling blankly. "This place may be new to us, but you're still the best scout on *Karia Naille*," he said. "We're a little more suited to cities and laboratories."

The halfling's tiny chest puffed out with pride. "I'll be back as soon as I can," he announced.

Zed nodded, giving a tiny salute as the glidewing leapt into the air.

"Should have known better than to tell Snowshale he was useful," Zed said ruefully. "We won't hear the end of his bragging for a week."

"You think he'll finish that soon?" Tristam said, still studying Omax's injuries.

FLIGHT OF THE DYING SUN

"I'm an optimist," Zed said.

Tristam laughed, drawing another annoyed look from the inquisitive. "Omax, will you be all right here until the ship arrives?" Tristam asked.

The warforged groaned. "I am fine to come with you, Tristam," he said. "These injuries are as nothing."

"You can barely stand, Omax," Tristam said, irritated. "You have to stay here so that you can be taken back on board."

"I do not wish to stand by idly when we are so close to something this important," Omax said.

"Then maybe you shouldn't hide your injuries like a fool," Tristam said, angry now.

Omax's mouth closed with a metal click. Tristam looked away, his face darkening with frustration. Zed pointedly studied the tracks, ignoring the outburst.

"Tristam, I am sorry," the warforged said.

"Don't," Tristam whispered. "Don't be sorry. Just . . . just do as I say. Please. You're in no shape to help me."

Omax nodded silently. Tristam rose and moved to follow Zed. The two of them marched off through the snow. Zed glanced back at the solitary warforged. He still sat on the snowy earth, clutching his injured arm. The light in his eyes shone as he watched Tristam go. The artificer did not look back.

"You did the right thing," Zed said, sheathing his sword over his back. "Seen his type before. Old soldiers get weighed down by what they've seen, stop caring about themselves, fight on for everyone else while they fall apart. Omax is a little older than most, and falling apart is somewhat literal in his case, but it still holds."

"It's my fault," Tristam said. "A warforged doesn't heal. He must be repaired. I know how stubborn he is. I know how badly hurt he is, but I've spent so much time trying to figure out what to do next . . . It's my fault he's so badly hurt."

"It's not your fault he didn't let the Canniths fix him when Dalan told him to," Zed said.

"Why were you called away from Thaliost?" Tristam asked, changing the subject.

"This again?" Zed said. "Don't get into this. I'll talk about my past when I choose to, but I don't appreciate being grilled about it."

"I just never knew you used to be an instructor," Tristam said.

"Add that to the heap of things you don't know about me," Zed said. "I guarantee it's pretty substantial. Suffice it to say there are only a handful of things that will throw you to the top of the list for reassignment in Thrane. The Silver Flame is one of them."

"The Flame?" Tristam said. "You were called by the gods?"

"I was called by *a* god, not *the* gods," Zed said. "A meddling, unforgiving, and judgmental god." He glared at Tristam bleakly. "Like I said, let's not get into it."

"Right," Tristam said, pulling his cloak more tightly around his body as the wind kicked up.

"So what do you know about Norra Cais?" Zed asked. "Did you ever meet her while you were studying with Ashrem?"

"We met a few times," Tristam said, scowling uncomfortably.

"Doesn't sound like you remember her very fondly," Zed said.

Tristam looked up in surprise. "I didn't think I was that obvious."

"Give me a little credit. I'm an inquisitive, and you're a terrible liar."

Tristam sighed.

"I'll get to the point," Zed said. "Is she crazy like Overwood is? I don't know if I have the patience to pry another piece of this puzzle out of the brain of a lunatic."

"No, she's very sane," Tristam said. "Brilliant, in fact. I guess I was always jealous of her. She was about my age, but Ashrem always treated her as an equal. She was a prodigy, trained as a sage and artificer by the Zil'argo masters. Back during the war, she worked as a traveling correspondent for the *Korranberg Chronicle*.

I suppose that's how she came into contact with Ashrem. Both of them moved around a lot and traveled in the same circles."

"What kind of person was she?" Zed asked. "I know she's supposedly not on Marth's side, but would she try to use the Legacy for herself? Or stop us from getting it?"

"I'm not sure," Tristam answered. "She was always a little arrogant and dismissive. Never had much time to talk to me. I remember that much. She seemed pretty dedicated to Ashrem's quest for peace, though. I never really got much of a chance to know her. She served mostly on *Dying Sun*."

"While you were on *Seventh Moon*," Zed said.

"Mostly," Tristam answered. "Ashrem and I stayed on the *Moon* a lot, but he moved us around from time to time, using the other ships for certain missions. Sometimes he took me along."

"Makes sense," Zed said.

"What does?" Tristam asked.

"Splitting his time among the three ships," Zed answered. "Keeping all three crews in the dark about the Legacy so that none of them knew everything. That's probably why he didn't tell you anything, Tristam. You were the only one he took with him from ship to ship."

"No," Tristam said with a laugh. "That's Dalan's way. Ashrem wouldn't do something so duplicitous."

"Or maybe Dalan just gets caught more often than Ashrem did," Zed said with a wry grin.

Tristam gave the inquisitive a dark look, and he let the matter drop. They kept following the trail as it crested into a wide valley. The sight below caused both men to stop dead in their tracks. Neither spoke for a full minute as they struggled to take in what they saw. Beneath them spread a vast valley of sheer ice. In the heart of the valley rose a pair of jagged glaciers. Between them, rising from the icy surface of the earth, yawned an impossibly enormous skull. It was unclear whether the structure was carved from ice or stone or was truly the remnants of some ancient and colossal humanoid. The eyes and mouth shone with some supernatural fire. Deep within the skull, something stirred, a shadowy flicker of movement.

"By the Host," Gerith said from between them, making both men jump.

Zed sheathed his sword, which had been half-drawn before he stopped himself. "Damn you, Snowshale," he said, catching his breath. "I'm still not convinced I shouldn't have killed you for scaring me."

"Sorry," Gerith said, climbing down off his glidewing as he stared down into the valley.

"Good timing, though," Zed admitted. "I was starting to have trouble following the trail."

"I can track it, no problem," Gerith said casually. He nodded at the enormous skull. "Is that Zul'nadn?"

"It had better be," Zed growled. "Xain, please tell me we're looking at Zul'nadn, because if something that weird has nothing to do with us being here, I'm going back to the ship."

"No," Tristam said, his eyes wide. "That's Zul'nadn, though I'm as surprised to see it as you are. Overwood's journals described it as 'the resting place of giants.' I didn't expect that definition to be so literal." He blinked several times, taking in the view. "Or so . . . giant."

"I've seen a few giants," Gerith said. "They aren't really that big."

"Well it looks like whoever survived that wreck was headed that way," Zed said. "Let's keep following."

They descended into the valley. The smooth terrain gave way to jagged rocks and spires of broken glacier, like a forest of ice and stone that cast the valley into deep and unmoving shadows. Gerith remained on foot as he studied the trail, his glidewing hopping along behind him. The winds grew more intense toward the base of the valley. They cut through the yawning skull on the horizon, producing a bizarre, blaring noise like a bagpipe being mashed at random. The cold grew more intense as well, drawing more muttered complaints and unique epithets from Zed. Halfway to the yawning skull, Gerith stopped. His tiny face creased in an expression of puzzlement.

"What's wrong, Gerith?" Tristam asked. The chill of the valley was intense here, and the winds had taken on a strange, wailing edge. He hugged himself for warmth, but found none.

"There are more trails here," Gerith said, kneeling on the ground and studying the earth. "Fresh ones. About a dozen of them. They look like humanoids, but they're not wearing any shoes." He squinted. "It looks like they have claws."

"Shifters?" Zed asked. "Maybe kobolds?"

"Too big for kobolds," Gerith said, "and I think even shifters would wear shoes on this ice." The halfling stiffened, looking quickly at the glidewing beside him. The creature's body was tense, its wings half open, as if it were prepared to take to the air. It peered slowly from side to side, its black eyes alert and fierce.

"Now?" Zed asked quietly.

Gerith nodded very slowly as he reached for his crossbow. He quickly lifted the weapon and fired at the peak of a nearby spire. A surprised screech erupted from above. A gangly figure fell from the shadows above, collapsing on the ground with a crossbow bolt in its neck. It lay still for several moments before rising again. It looked like it had been a dwarf at one time. Its flesh was pale, hairless blue and striated with purple veins. Its eyes were hollow and rotten, leaving nothing but burning yellow pinpoints. Its lips had been torn away, revealing a mouth filled with sharp, uneven yellow teeth. It hunched onto its hands and feet like an ape, staring at them with a fearless, hungry glare. One arm had been shattered by the fall, but it did not appear to care.

One clawed hand roamed to the bolt in its throat and tore it away. A chunk of skin and muscle came free with the missile. The creature looked at the tip for several seconds before deliberately plucking its flesh from the tip and tucking it between its teeth, chewing rapidly, eagerly, like a rodent. Its teeth made a sickly, rattling sound that was immediately echoed from the stones all around them. A second pair of glowing eyes appeared in the shadows, followed by a third, then a fourth. A gurgling, growling sound rose around them.

"Ghouls," Gerith said.

Zed drew his sword. "Don't let them touch you," he warned.

"Poison?" Tristam asked, his voice worried.

"Worse," Zed said. "They paralyze a target with their touch. Then the whole pack springs to eat you."

Tristam frowned and tucked his wand back into his coat, drawing out the new one. The first ghoul scuttled toward them and rose up on its hind legs, leering at them with a twisted, lipless grin and beating its chest with a screech. The other ghouls circled in a frenzied dance, echoing their pack leader's cry with an arrhythmic chatter. Zed held his sword ready but kept a safe distance away from the creature's reach. Tristam pointed his wand at the ghoul and spoke a word of magic. A roaring burst of golden lightning seared from its tip and consumed the creature, leaving its silhouette painted in ash upon the ice. The other three ghouls immediately ceased their chattering, peering at one another in bewilderment. Tristam looked stunned as well.

"Upgrade?" Zed asked, impressed.

Tristam nodded, unable to speak, surprised at the results.

"Tristam," Zed said in an extremely calm voice, watching the ghouls as they circled. "Can you please do that three more times?"

The other three undead overcame their shock and rushed forward, charging at Tristam. Tristam unleashed another blast, searing through a second ghoul's torso and sending it flying back across the ice. Zed slashed another of the creatures from shoulder to hip, cleaving it in two pieces. The third lunged onto Tristam, claws grasping at his throat and bearing him to the ground. Gerith shouted, and his glidewing leaped into the air, diving over the ghoul, raking his claws across its back and pulling it off Tristam. It rolled several times and fell into a low hunch just as Zed swung his blade again, taking off the creature's head. The inquisitive turned quickly, gray eyes scanning the area for any more enemies.

"Tristam!" Gerith shouted, leaping off his steed and running to the fallen artificer's side.

Tristam was doubled over in pain, hands clenched into shivering fists. His wand lay discarded on the snow. Gerith quickly picked it up and tucked it back into Tristam's pocket.

"Try not to bite your tongue and you'll be fine," Zed said, kneeling by Tristam's side and sheathing his sword. "Shouldn't do any real harm, but it'll take a few minutes to pass. We'd better keep moving before more come along."

"You think there are more?" Gerith asked.

"There are always more," Zed said, still looking around warily. Zed grabbed Tristam's wrist, pulling the artificer's arm tight around his shoulders and hugging his waist. Zed lifted Tristam easily and hurried on. Gerith ran along behind, reloading his crossbow and glancing about furtively as his glidewing hopped beside him.

"I think . . . I can manage," Tristam said after a few minutes, though his voice was shaky and his breath came in gasps.

Zed nodded, releasing Tristam to stand on his own. The artificer wobbled as he sought his balance. He limped forward with hesitant, ginger steps. Zed watched him to make certain he was not seriously hurt.

"They way you spoke, it sounded like you've both fought these sorts of things before," Tristam said.

"Ghouls are a pretty common form of undead, as those things go," Gerith said. "Though to tell the truth I haven't really fought them before. One of the advantages of having Blizzard around is that I can usually just fly away."

Zed murmured his agreement. "Those sorts of things were

more common during the War," he said. "Packs of them used to haunt battlefields, looking for an easy meal. I'd usually get sent out with a few of the other knights to purge them." He grimaced. "I wish we'd brought Eraina along. She could handle these things better than me."

Tristam gave Zed a questioning look but was interrupted by a burst of chattering teeth from the north. The trio drew their weapons and huddled together, prepared for a second attack, but the noise appeared to be getting farther away.

"Are they running?" Tristam asked.

"Ghouls don't run away," Zed said. "Ghouls don't get scared. They're chasing easier prey."

The inquisitive broke into a run, following the sound. Gerith climbed into his saddle and kicked Blizzard into the air, soaring above the maze of stone for a better view. Tristam hobbled along, feeling more flexible by the second as the ghoul's touch faded. They turned a sharp corner and found the bodies of three ghouls on the path, charred and sizzling. Another lay nearby, a throwing axe lodged deeply in its skull. The body of a human lay near the ghoul, steam rising from the savage wounds in his throat. He wore the same uniform as the dead sailors from the scuttled ship. Zed ignored the bodies and kept running. The corpses of two more ghouls and three more sailors lay strewn about the path. Now the chattering of ghouls was joined by the startled, desperate cries of the living.

They rounded a corner and came upon a narrow cave. Gerith waited for them at the mouth, glancing back fearfully. Four ghouls lay dead at the mouth, burnt like the others had been. Within the cave, a dozen more were advancing deeper into the tunnel, their backs to Tristam, Zed, and Gerith. They scuttled over loose stones and ice formations, seeking something deeper within. At the far end of the cave lay several more dead ghouls and as many dead sailors. An old dwarf in battered armor hefted a gleaming morningstar, casting the cave in a pallid blue light. He stood defensively over an paralyzed woman, steel eyes fixed on the ghouls without fear.

"By the Host, there are so many of them," Tristam whispered. "What do we do?"

Zed looked at Tristam grimly and sheathed his sword. He snapped off the tip of an icy stalagmite and turned it over in his hands, studying the shape of it. He stepped into the cave mouth, holding the twisted plume of ice high in one hand and extending a mailed fist forward.

"By the just glory of the Flame," he shouted, voice echoing through the cavern, "I command thee, foul abominations, to begone from this world."

The chattering immediately ceased. As one, the ghouls all turned and looked back at Zed with hateful eyes. Nothing had happened.

Tristam looked at Zed curiously.

"Old habits," Zed said, a bit breathless. He drew his sword. "It was worth a try."

The ghouls shrieked and charged in a pack, rushing toward the inquisitive. Tristam stepped in front of him, holding his wand in both hands as the tip flared brilliant white. The next few moments passed with agonizing slowness as he waited for them to reach the mouth of the tunnel, barely a few feet away, climbing over one another in their haste to be the first to escape the narrow passage. Then a cone of golden fire exploded from Tristam's wand, filling the cave mouth, washing over the tangled mob of ghouls. An instant later, the light faded, and the undead were nothing but ash on the chill wind. An eerie silence descended with the death of the ghouls, broken a few seconds later by Gerith's excited clapping.

"What was that all about, Zed?" Tristam asked, looking at the inquisitive.

"Just a distraction," Zed mumbled. He let the twisted chunk of ice fall in the snow.

"Balinor's hand itself, ye are," said the dwarf, hurrying to the cave mouth with a wide grin. He tore off his helmet and let it fall in the snow, revealing a wild mane of pure white hair. "I thought that'd be my last moment for certain." He drove his morningstar into the ground, tore off his leather glove, and extended a thick, sweaty hand toward Tristam. "Ijaac Bruenhail, Journeyman Wayfinder. At your service and in your debt."

"Tristam Xain, of the *Karia Naille*," Tristam said, removing his own glove and letting his hand be crushed in the dwarf's merciless grip. "These are my friends, Zed Arthen and Gerith Snowshale." The dwarf eagerly shook their hands as well, looking into each of their eyes with a manic, grateful intensity. Zed shook the man's hand and walked off to the mouth of the cave to sit alone.

"Xain," the woman said, sitting up weakly. "I remember you."

"Norra," Tristam said. He entered the cave and knelt beside her. She had a thick splint tied to one leg but didn't seem otherwise badly injured, though it was difficult to tell through the thick furs she wore. She was Tristam's age, but her severe expression and haughty demeanor made her appear years older. Her blond hair was tied back in a tight braid, though loose hairs now hung frayed over her face from her ordeal. "Don't worry, you'll be fine. The paralysis is temporary."

"I know what a ghoul does," she snapped. "I'm no novice."

Tristam blinked.

"What are you doing here, Tristam?" she demanded. "If you think I will help you steal Ashrem's Legacy, you're a fool."

"Prying us from a ghoul pack's lunch pail from the looks of it, Norra," Ijaac said with a hearty laugh. "We can afford to be a little civil, eh?"

Norra frowned deeply at Ijaac, then looked back at Tristam. "Thank you," she said with forced cheer.

"There we are. Civil," Ijaac said, clapping his hands together briskly. "That's much better. I wish you'd showed up a few minutes earlier, but I can't complain. That was a fair impressive display of magic there, lad. Now let's get to work with the explosives."

Tristam coughed in surprise. "Explosives?" he asked.

"Got any?" Ijaac asked. "You tinkers always have a few, don't you? Norra was about to use the last of hers to bring the cave down on us before they paralyzed her. Better buried in the ice than letting those ghouls eat us, aye?"

"I do have some explosive reagents," Tristam admitted. "Why do you need them now?"

"I want to drag the lads that died back into this cave and collapse it," Ijaac said. "Doesn't feel right leavin' them out there for the ghouls to eat, or worse yet, shuffle back up as more undead. Closest we can come to a proper burial, given the situation." The dwarf looked at the bodies silently, his eyes sad as he looked at his fallen friends. He quickly cleared his throat and collected himself. "I felt bad enough leaving the others behind at the wreck, but nothing to be done for it now. It was too dangerous to stay out in the open."

"Why do you say that?" Gerith asked.

"On account of the dragon," Ijaac said.

"Dragon?" Zed said, looking back in surprise. "There's a dragon here?"

"Don't tell me it didn't give you any trouble coming in here," Ijaac said in wonder. His eyes brightened. "Don't tell me you got this far and still have a *ship?*"

"*Karia Naille* was one of Ashrem's airships," Norra said. "The dragon was watching the seas. She probably never even saw them, or just couldn't catch up."

Ijaac cackled. "You really have an airship, lad?"

Tristam nodded.

"And you'll take us out of here?"

"Once we finish our business here," Tristam said.

"I'd kiss you if you were shorter," Ijaac said. "Now lend a hand. We've got a lot of bodies to move."

Chapter
Sixteen

Though he was not the sort to brag, Pherris Gerriman had seen a great deal of the world during his distinguished career. The old gnome had flown through every conceivable sort of weather. He had fought through airship battles and survived his fair share of crashes. He had explored the skies of every nation in Khorvaire as well as a fair bit of Xen'drik. He was proud of *Karia Naille* and her crew, and was quite confident that they could handle most any crisis that confronted them. Yet as he stared down at the skeletal face of Zul'nadn, he could not help the sense of dread growing within him. What was this place? If it was so old, so remote, and so mysterious, how did Ashrem ever learn about it? Ijaac Bruenhail's latest news only made him even more wary.

"A dragon?" the captain asked, looking at the dwarf dubiously. Pherris turned the ship's wheel expertly, driving *Karia Naille* higher into the sky.

"Aye, that's what I said," Ijaac answered. The dwarf leaned against a large crate, cupping a bowl of steaming broth between his hands. "I wouldn't believe it myself if I'd not seen it. Tore the ship apart. Would have died with the rest of the crew if we hadn't already been exploring on the shore. I didn't think dragons wandered this far from Argonnessen."

The rest of the crew members were assembled on the deck as well, both to see the ruins and meet the survivors. Even Seren had risen from Dalan's cabin, looking entirely rested and recovered from her injuries.

"Why is it so surprising?" Norra Cais asked tersely. She limped about the deck on an improvised crutch Gerith had fashioned out of spare lumber. "Dragons go where they please."

"Encountering dragons is normal for you, Norra?" Tristam asked.

She sighed. "Of course, not, Xain," she said, "but Zul'nadn's entire significance stems from the Draconic Prophecy inscribed in the caverns spread throughout its foundations. You know that—or at least I hope you do, otherwise I wonder why you would have traveled here. Dragons have traditionally expressed an interest in the Prophecy. Thus its name. I would have thought that much was obvious."

Seren looked at Norra calmly. "If a dragon's presence here was so obvious," she said, "then why did it kill your entire crew?"

Norra glowered at Seren. "Admittedly I did not expect a dragon," she said, "but the crew knew the risks of my mission."

"You didn't say a word about dragons," Ijaac said. "Truth be told, this trip took a wee bit deadlier of a turn than I expected, and my expectations for the Frostfell are fairly terrible. Finding this lot was the first spot of good luck since we saw the coast." He glanced over the rail nervously. "All things considered, our situation has much improved!"

"I'm not entirely convinced of that, Ijaac," Norra said. She looked at Tristam coldly. "What are you doing here, Xain?"

"Looking for the Legacy," Tristam said. "Just like you are."

"Then you are a fool," Norra said. "I'm not here looking for the Legacy."

"Odd place to not look for it," Pherris said, still peering down at the enormous skull.

"No sense in being secretive, Norra," Ijaac said, finishing off his bowl with a slurp. "We're in their debt. If their intentions were dishonorable, do you think they'd have taken us onto their ship?"

"Perhaps," Norra said, looking archly at Tristam. "Xain was always Ashrem's worst student. He probably needs me to figure out what's going on."

"That may be, but I'm just a useless old dwarf, and they just gave me the best bowl of soup I've had in years." Ijaac waggled the empty bowl hopefully. Gerith scampered over and grabbed it, running back into the galley to fetch seconds, buoyed by the dwarf's praise. "They might want to use you, but they got no need to be nice to me. So I'm of a mind to trust them."

"You should let me tend your injured leg, Miss Cais," Eraina said, nodding at her splint. "I can heal that."

"Keep your blessings, paladin," Norra said. "I don't intend to be indebted to your goddess."

"Boldrei asks nothing in return," Eraina said.

"The gods only ask for nothing because, to them, we are nothing," Norra said. "I can tend to myself."

"Let her limp, Eraina," Zed said, shrugging.

"Norra, I'm not your enemy," Tristam said, quickly losing his patience. "Please lose the arrogance. You're just wasting your time and mine."

Norra's eyes narrowed.

"I know you were collaborating with Kiris Overwood," Tristam said. "You know that Marth is reassembling the Legacy. Kiris trusted him, but you didn't. She hoped that she could help him become the hero he used to be, but you've always been cynical. You kept tabs on her, but you disappeared as soon as he killed Llaine. You've been working on a way to stop Marth, haven't you?"

"I don't work on problems, Xain," she said. "I resolve them."

"How?" Tristam said. "What did you hope to do here?"

"It doesn't matter, Xain," she said. "I've failed. I can't finish this mission with a broken leg."

"Then let us help you, damn it," Tristam said. "We want to stop Marth, too."

She glared at him suspiciously.

FLIGHT OF THE DYING SUN

"What other hope do you really have?" Tristam asked. "We're here. You can't go into Zul'nadn alone. You may as well trust me."

"Norra," Ijaac said. "If what you came here for was so important, give the boy a chance to help. He did save our lives."

She continued to glare at Tristam steadily for several moments, then sighed and reached into the satchel at her hip. She drew out a metallic silver sphere, studded with small black gems.

"I came to the Frostfell to use this," she said.

"What is it?" Tristam asked, looking at it curiously.

"Zul'nadn houses more than just the Draconic Prophecy," Norra said. "High Priest Zoltan and his cultists came here all those millennia ago seeking something else. The ruin exists in a unique manifest zone, where the boundaries between the planes are unusually thin. The cultists came here seeking to commune with Xoriat, the Realm of Madness, but the ruins touch upon several other elemental planes as well. The connection between this world and those is embodied by an ever-burning flame in the caverns beneath the temple. It was the same source that the cultists used to summon the Fellmaw."

"Aye," Ijaac said. "I seen that flame when I came here with Old Ash. He called it the Dragon's Eye."

"The unique energies within that fire are critical to controlling the Legacy," Norra said. "Without them, the resultant effect is unstable. It may last only a few seconds. It may become permanent. More commonly, its effect will be buffered or negated by strong elemental energies."

"Like what we saw in Stormhome," Pherris said. "The Legacy's effect faded over the water."

"Marth has used the Legacy already?" Norra said, shocked.

"He tried to crash our ship with it," Tristam said. "That's why we're here, Norra. Now what does that sphere do?"

"It is a less powerful, but more specialized, version of the Legacy," she said. "It is intended to feed upon the energies of the Dragon's Eye, to draw them into a continuous feedback loop, turning the manifest zone upon itself and collapsing the boundaries between the planes."

"That sounds dangerous," Tristam said.

"It is," Norra whispered. "When cast into the Eye, the effects will be both explosive and catastrophic. Zul'nadn and much of the surrounding area will be sundered and scattered throughout the planes."

"How long before it takes effect?" Tristam asked.

"A few minutes, at most," she replied.

"How did you intend to escape Zul'nadn after you used it?" Zed asked.

"I did not," Norra said.

Ijaac looked up at Norra in surprise, soup spilling down the front of his armor. "You never told me that bit, Norra," he said.

"Noble sacrifices aren't so noble when you take unwilling people with you," Zed added, chewing on his pipe.

"It was necessary, Ijaac," Norra said, looking at the dwarf sadly. "You have no idea the damage that the Legacy would do to the world. If Marth can neither be reasoned with nor delayed, then the means by which he can perfect his creation must be destroyed. It is worth any sacrifice."

"Well if you think it's worth killing me for, maybe you should tell me what sort of damage it would do," Ijaac said, eyes wide with alarm.

Norra sighed. "So much in our world relies on magic. With the Legacy, Marth could drive airships from the sky, crash lightning rails full of innocents, slay creatures of magic—such as the warforged—outright, or destroy entire cities whose buildings rely on magical architecture to remain intact—such as Sharn itself. Was that worth risking your life to stop? I say yes."

"And you call Master Xain Ashrem's worst student, Miss Cais?" Pherris said, disgusted. "You intended to sacrifice every one of those men who came with you, and already killed all of them but one."

FLIGHT OF THE DYING SUN

Norra ignored the gnome. "I had no alternative, Xain," she said. "Believe me, I searched for one."

"I should have listened to my brother," Ijaac grumbled. "He said you were trouble, Norra."

"Give the sphere to me," Tristam said, extending his hand. "I'll enter Zul'nadn and destroy the Eye."

"Tristam, no," Seren said, worried.

"Don't worry, Seren," he said. "A few minutes should be long enough to run back to *Karia Naille* and escape."

"You think I would trust you with this?" she asked.

"By the Host, give it to him, Norra," Ijaac snapped. "You want an alternative? This is it. You don't even know where the Eye is, anyway. You needed me for that, and at this point I'm not sure I'd help you." He looked at Tristam. "Are you sure you can get us back out of there in time, boy?"

Tristam nodded.

Norra frowned. She gave Tristam a long, wary look and held out the sphere. He took it in one hand, turning it over and examining the surface.

"How does it work?" he asked.

"Just throw it into the Eye," Norra said. "It will activate automatically. I suppose you could get back to the airship if you were quick and lucky."

"We excel at quick and lucky, Miss Cais," Pherris said.

"Put us back down, Pherris," Tristam said. "As close to Zul'nadn if you dare, but get back out fast if you see any sign of the dragon."

"Aye," Pherris said. *Karia Naille* veered and banked downward, her elemental ring blazing a brilliant turquoise.

"Zed, Gerith, I'll need you both again," Tristam said. "Ijaac, you said you would help us?"

"What are we doing again?" he asked.

"Collapsing a doorway between worlds and trying to stop a madman from reigniting the War," the artificer said.

The dwarf let that sink in. "Seriously?"

Tristam nodded.

"And you're sure we'll survive?" Ijaac asked.

"Fairly sure," Tristam said.

"Eh, why not?" the dwarf chuckled. "I was ready to die down there in that cave. For what you did for me, I can take one more stupid risk."

"Eraina should come too," Zed said. "If we run into more ghouls, we may need her."

"I would like to help," Eraina said. "Seren is fit enough to travel and fight again, as well."

"Good," Tristam said, smiling confidently at both of them. "We'll need all the help we can get. I'd be grateful to have you both beside me."

"And me?" Omax said. The warforged sat near the bow of the ship, head bowed.

Tristam hesitated. "Stay here and guard the ship, Omax," he said, not looking at the warforged. "You're too badly hurt to help us."

Omax looked back at the deck. "Aye," he said.

"Come, then," Tristam said, climbing down the ladder to the cargo bay. "We need to hurry before the dragon notices us."

"Or before the Fellmaw arrives," Aeven said. The dryad had appeared at the ship's bow again. She perched on the railing, looking toward the east with a pensive expression. The sky flickered a faint green.

"Is the storm coming?" Pherris asked.

"Yes," Aeven said. "We have a few hours, perhaps."

"Then we'll hurry," Tristam said, dropping below deck.

The others filed after him. The warforged watched them go in silence.

"Xain is as much a fool as he always was," Norra said. "Why would he go into battle and leave a warforged behind?"

"He fears that I will come to greater damage," Omax said. The warforged rose and walked back toward the cargo bay, clutching his chest. He staggered slightly as he climbed down the stairs. His blue eyes flickered in pain, but he pressed on.

Once Pherris and Norra were alone on the deck, the gnome turned to look at her. He pushed his frosted goggles back onto his forehead and gave her a polite smile. "Miss Cais, I understand that you have endured quite the traumatic ordeal," he said. "As such, I was prepared to offer you a modicum of patience and politeness. Interestingly enough, you have already exhausted that gesture."

"You intend to judge me as well, gnome?" she asked.

"That I do, human, and as long as you stand upon my ship, that is my right," he answered, returning his attention to the ship's controls. "Thus far Master Xain has saved your life and offered you a viable alternative to your crazed suicide mission. He deserves better from you than to be treated a fool."

"I . . ." Norra's voice was heated, but she trailed off quickly. "I suppose we shall see," she finished, looking slightly ashamed.

Pherris grunted noncommittally. "Be aware that while you are welcome to remain with us and enjoy our hospitality until such a time as we return to civilization," he said, "I then expect you to remove yourself from my ship immediately upon our return to Khorvaire." He looked back at her. "Is that understood?"

"Aye," she said quietly.

"Until then, I recommend that you repay the generosity that Master Xain has shown you by making yourself of use," he said. "I understand you are an artificer?"

"I am," she said.

"Then I have a request."

Chapter
Seventeen

Tristam stood before the gates of Zul'nadn, staring up at the giant skeletal maw in wonder. The empty eye sockets shone with a faint golden fire, staring upward into space with an expression of timeless anger. The inner structure of the ruins stood just within the mouth, with the lower jaw and skull serving as an outer wall.

"Why would the dwarves build something like that?" Seren asked, standing close to Tristam as he studied the massive skull. "And how did they build it out here?"

"Not entirely sure they built it, lass," Ijaac replied. He trudged past them, morningstar slung over one shoulder. "According to some of the inscriptions Old Ash found inside, Zoltan's cult just sort of found the skull and moved in without asking too many questions."

"So then who built it?" Seren asked.

"Who says anyone did?" Ijaac replied with a mad grin. "Someone definitely built the inner walls, but I think the skull is just what it appears to be. Take a good look when we get close. It's more like bone than stone or ice."

"No creature is that big," Gerith said.

"Not anymore," Ijaac replied.

Tristam looked down at the halfling scout. He was nervous, fidgety, constantly jumping at imagined sounds and clinging close to his glidewing. He remembered how Gerith clung to the

FLIGHT OF THE DYING SUN

halfling superstitions about the Boneyard. This place, an enormous monument to some forgotten supernatural entity, was not so very different.

"Gerith, maybe you should get on Blizzard and patrol out here," Tristam said, laying a hand on the halfling's shoulder. "Someone should keep an eye out for the dragon, if it comes here."

"Aye," Gerith said gratefully. He cast the ruins one last suspicious glance, made a quick sign against evil, and flew off on Blizzard's back.

"Sense anything, Eraina?" Zed asked. The inquisitive had drawn his sword, and held it ready.

The paladin nodded. "There is evil here, intense and pervasive," she said. Her face glistened with sweat. "I can sense it without even attempting to do so. I feel it senses us as well."

"Was afraid you'd say that," Zed said. "Let's hurry this up a bit."

"Your instincts are sharp, Arthen," Eraina said, looking around carefully. "I sense ancient evil makes its home here."

"Show us the way, Ijaac," Tristam said.

The dwarf nodded pertly and stomped off through the gap in the jaw that served as a gate. He paused briefly, tapping the tip of his morningstar against the bone. The weapon's spike head took on a bright blue glow, illuminating the path ahead. Tristam twisted the head of a ring on his right hand, causing it to glow brightly as well.

"Showoff," the dwarf said with a chuckle.

The courtyard between the outer wall and the inner ruins was littered with bones and debris.

"Most of these aren't animal bones," Zed said, looking at the refuse as he walked. "How is that possible? I thought only Lord ir'Dayne and Ashrem d'Cannith ever went to the Frostfell."

Ijaac laughed darkly. "People come here all the time," he said. "They just never go back home."

"Comforting," Zed said.

"You did notice that all the ghouls weren't dwarves, right?" Ijaac said. "The original Zul'nadn undead have bolstered their ranks with the odd hapless explorer over the years. S'why I was so eager to make sure my friends got as proper a burial as we could muster."

"Something is following us," Seren whispered. She did not look back. She followed Ijaac at a calm, even pace. Her dagger was in her hand and her eyes flicked to one side, indicating the direction. "Several of them, moving through the shadows."

"Ghouls?" Ijaac asked. His voice shook. His hands tightened on the haft of his weapon.

"No sense in waiting to find out," Tristam said. He reached into his coat, drawing out several small clay flasks. "Run for the entrance and don't look back."

The others complied, running for the door just as Tristam hurled the flasks toward the gap in the gate. The shrieking chatter of ghouls rose behind them as the undead saw their prey attempt to escape. Tristam's bottles exploded in a chaotic swirl of light and sound. The ghouls howled in confusion. Tristam used the precious seconds of distraction to dash after his friends. Seren had waited for him. He took her hand and ran. They ran through the narrow doors of the inner ruins, hounded by the scrabbling sound of bare claws on stone.

"Help me with this," Zed growled, throwing his shoulder into the heavy wooden doors.

The others complied, forcing the massive doors to slowly grind shut. The mad cries of the ghouls grew closer. Shining yellow eyes appeared in the shadows beyond the door, drawing near. Eraina stepped back, holding her spear and sword crossed at length before her.

"By the light of the Hearthmother—burn," she whispered.

There was a moment of silence, then a wave of warmth washed out from the paladin. A few of the ghouls cried out. Pain wracked their twisted corpses as the goddess tore the semblance of life from

FLIGHT OF THE DYING SUN

them. The rest threw themselves into the doors, shrieking in pain, ignoring the paladin's power. Twisted hands probed through the cracks in the door, seeking flesh.

"I can do no more," Eraina said, worried.

"Get away from the doors!" Zed shouted.

They fell back as the ancient wooden gates flew inward. The stench of stale, raw flesh filled the halls of Zul'nadn. The ghouls clambered through in a chaotic mass, some of them clinging to the wood like monkeys. There were even more than before. Tristam's wand was already in his hand, unleashing fire over the undead. A hollow, twisted roar erupted from the mass, dying quickly as the ghouls were reduced to ash. A half dozen survived, now loping directly toward Tristam. Eraina and Zed stepped into their path, sword and spear slashing through them. Ijaac's morningstar fell heavily on another from behind, crushing its back. The wounded creature struck the dwarf across the face. He fell, limbs stiffening, just as Seren darted in and buried her dagger in the ghoul's chest.

"Help him," Zed shouted, pointing at the dwarf. Seren snatched Ijaac's morningstar off the floor and wrapped an arm around his trembling shoulders.

The last of the ghouls had fallen. Eraina knelt beside one of them, her dark eyes searching for answers. "Will there be more?" she asked.

"With ghouls, there are always more," Zed said. "Eraina, we have to hurry." He held his sword ready and watched the courtyard, shoulders tense.

"Here," she said, tearing something from one of the undead dwarves. She held out an ancient amulet of blackened metal, depicting a complex circle of writhing tentacles. "Touched by the dark powers of Xoriat. Look." She pointed at the undead bodies scattered beyond the door. "The ones who fell when I called upon Boldrei were not dwarves—probably sailors or explorers who were reanimated by the cultists in the years since. The rest were protected from Boldrei's holy power by these amulets. I could not turn them."

"All of the ones in the cavern earlier were wearing those," Zed said, looking at the twisted metal, pondering some unspoken thought.

"If it's a magic problem, then magic can solve it," Tristam said, kneeling and plucking an amulet from one of the corpses. "I can study this later and maybe find a way to pierce the protection."

The sound of more maddened shrieking echoed from somewhere outside, drawing slowly closer. Zed pushed the wooden doors closed and let the bar fall. "Eraina and I can wait here and hold the door," he said. "Find the Eye fast, Tristam."

"Aye," Tristam said, tucking the amulet into his pocket.

"That way," Ijaac said, nodding stiffly as Seren helped him walk.

The three moved deeper into the ruins. The Frostfell's pervasive cold quickly faded, replaced by a sticky heat so warm and intense that they were forced to remove their extra layers of bundled furs and leather. The walls of Zul'nadn hummed, radiating an unnerving living energy. Tristam felt the strange sensation that there was something deep within the floor beneath him, watching them, waiting. It was a maddening sensation, invasive and alien.

"I feel it too, lad," Ijaac whispered. The dwarf's face was pale behind his wild beard. "Let's finish our business and be done with this place."

"Which way?" Tristam asked.

"Keep going," Ijaac said, nodding at the hall ahead. "There's a stair or a ramp somewhere. Been a few years since I was here last, but this was the . . ."

Without warning the floor gave way beneath them with a crack. Seren jumped back instinctively, but Tristam and Ijaac tumbled forward into the void. Everything went dark, and Tristam felt himself falling for several seconds. He hit the earth with a

FLIGHT OF THE DYING SUN

jarring thud. He crawled to his hands and knees, finding himself in a rough earthen cavern. The light of his ring reflected against the walls, spattering fitful shadows everywhere. Ijaac lay on his back beside Tristam, muttering pained curses to himself in the Dwarven tongue.

"Yep. I think this is the place," Ijaac said, finally sitting up with a grimace.

"Seren!" Tristam shouted. He scrambled back the way he had come, climbing up the rocky slop toward the hall above.

The pale light of his ring shone through the hole into the darkened hall above. Seren lay at the very edge, her arm outstretched, grasping toward Tristam. He leaned toward her but couldn't reach.

"No rope?" Ijaac asked, looking up at Tristam with a frown.

Tristam looked back at Ijaac and shrugged uncomfortably.

Ijaac sighed and trudged off to explore the cavern.

"I can't reach you," Seren said, her voice panicked. "I'm not sure I could even pull you up."

"It's all right, Seren," Tristam said, studying the way he had fallen. "It looks like the hole collapsed a bit after we fell anyway. I don't think we can go back that way. There has to be another way out." He pulled off his ring, tossing it up to her. She caught it deftly in one hand. "Go back and help Zed and Eraina. We'll find our own way back to you."

"Are you sure?" she asked quietly.

Tristam nodded and smiled reassuringly, ignoring his gnawing fear.

Seren looked uncertain but returned his smile. "Come back to us, Master Xain," she said, her tone lightly mocking.

He laughed and felt a little less afraid. "I will, Miss Morisse," he promised.

"Adorable," Ijaac grumbled, peering around the cave by the light of his morningstar. "I'm touched. Can we keep moving? I don't like not knowing the way out."

"Sorry," Tristam said. He looked back up at Seren, but she was already gone.

Tristam climbed back down. He drew his wand out of his coat, speaking a word of magic that made it glow with a warm golden radiance. He gasped as the light filled the cavern. A hundred lights shimmered in reply, filling the darkness. The shine of his wand reflected off of twisting scripts that covered the stone walls.

"The Draconic Prophecy," Tristam whispered.

"Aye, part of it," Ijaac said. "It's all over the walls down here."

Tristam barely heard the dwarf's reply. The words surrounded him, pressed down on him, forced themselves into his mind. The Prophecy really was alive . . . and it had been waiting for him. Images swum through his vision. He saw an army of demons battle an army of dragons over the skies of the Talenta Plains. He saw an ancient giant, standing alone in a vast field of emerald green, fighting to hold the world together with will alone as everything unraveled around him. The giant fell, alone and unmourned, leaving behind only his burning heart as a reminder of his vast power as the ice embraced his bones. He saw a mortal conqueror take up the weapon of the fallen dragons, temper it in the giant's fiery heart, and turn its power against the nations of man, elf, and dwarf. The conqueror wrought death and destruction against those all who stood against him. The conqueror was cursed as a villain, decried as a madman.

And in the end, there was everlasting peace.

"Xain," Ijaac said, shaking Tristam's shoulder. The dwarf's eyes were wide with worry.

"Huh?" Tristam said, blinking. He was lying on the stone floor, though he didn't remember falling. His throat felt raw and dry.

"You've been lying there screaming for ten minutes," the dwarf said.

"Sorry," Tristam said, mussing his hair as he rubbed his aching head. "Not sure what happened. I had some kind of reaction to the magic here."

FLIGHT OF THE DYING SUN

"Magic'll do odd things if left to itself," the dwarf agreed. He peered around the cavern, holding his glowing morningstar high. "I've been trying to figure out where we are. I thought this is the same cavern where Old Ash and I found the Dragon's Eye, but it's been a long time. It should be right there." He pointed at a large formation of pure white ice in the center of the chamber. "Afraid my memory isn't what it used to be, Master Xain."

"It's all right, Ijaac," Tristam said. He staggered to his feet and snatched his wand from the floor, holding it up for a better view of the cavern. "It has to be here somewhere."

"If you pardon me asking, you said some strange things while you were out," the dwarf said. "I know my way around foreign languages, at least well enough to ask where the privy is in most of the places I've been, but I've never heard that one before. What was that?"

"I'm not sure," Tristam said. "I don't remember saying anything."

"I would think the answer was obvious," rumbled a deep voice from the depths of the cavern.

What had appeared to be an icy boulder moments before now shifted. A slender neck detached itself from its heart, tapering to a blunt head crowned with a sharp crest. Its scales, so dense and white that they had appeared to be pure ice, now shimmered in the light. A thick, powerfully muscled forearm emerged, grinding the stone beneath its claws. Two broad wings unfurled, casting a gentle wind over Tristam and Ijaac. The creature stretched lazily as it emerged from its slumber. A throbbing blue flame burned on the floor at the center of where it had lain. Tristam recognized it from his vision—the Dragon's Eye—though it seemed smaller than before.

"The human spoke my language," the dragon said. "The human spoke Draconic."

Chapter
Eighteen

Dalan grunted uncomfortably as he climbed up the stairs. His feet ached terribly, and his back was sore. His vision blurred from hours of poring over heraldic manuscripts. He was no longer a young man and had never been a fit man. He detested walking and had done far too much of it in the past few days. Since the Legacy had released its power over Stormhome, the city had been a mess. Coach services were entirely disrupted. Most horses had been committed to help with hauling debris from the sections of the city where the damage had been most severe. Dalan was not quite loose enough with his money to meet the exorbitant fees the few remaining hostlers required.

Dalan paused at a window to look out at the city. It was amazing how rapidly the Lyrandar had recovered from Marth's unprovoked attack. The burning rings of airships hovered over the city again, and the streets were crowded once more. The differences were subtle but significant. Squads of armored Aundairian soldiers now patrolled at every street corner. At least one wizard or artificer accompanied every group, alert for any signs of suspicious magic. Though the Lyrandar wished to portray the image that their business would continue unhindered, they had not forgiven the injury done to them.

Memories of the night still weighed heavily on Dalan's mind. He had known that Marth was a wicked man, a murderer who

FLIGHT OF THE DYING SUN

imagined himself a patriot. Even this seemed beyond him. To cause so much destruction, to kill so many simply to hinder an enemy, it was unthinkable.

Worse, it was sloppy. Marth's gambit had failed. It was the first obvious mistake the changeling had made, and an enemy's failure always smelled of opportunity.

Stormhome flew an Aundairian flag, but Aundair did not rule here. Stormhome was a House Lyrandar city, and Dalan knew how the dragonmarked houses operated. Their pride was of utmost importance. If other houses and nations did not respect them, conduction business across the lands of Eberron would become impossible. Having restored order to their city, maintaining face would be House Lyrandar's primary concern. They would be seeking retribution against the enemy who had wounded Stormhome.

Given his standing in House Cannith, Dalan could easily arrange an audience with the Lyrandar matriarch. From there, it was only a matter of revealing just enough to drive a Lyrandar thorn into Marth's side without interfering with his own search for the Legacy. Already he had overturned a few interesting names and locations. A bit more research and he would have all the information he would require. So long as *Karia Naille* returned safely from the Frostfell, Marth's act of thoughtless violence may well result in his losing substantial ground.

Such meddling would have to wait. There was a good possibility that Marth was still within the city, waiting and watching. Without the security of the *Karia Naille*, Dalan was forced to move cautiously, using one of several well-cultivated aliases. Once Xain had returned, he could begin to pull the strings once again. Dalan allowed himself a self-congratulatory chuckle as he opened the door to his rented apartment. His pleasure faded quickly. He saw Gunther's eyes shining in the darkness underneath his bed. Usually it was all he could do to keep from being knocked prone by his pet upon returning home. Something was wrong.

"Hello, Dalan," said a mellow voice from inside. "Please, come in. You know me well enough not to run."

Dalan tucked his key into his pocket and sighed. He stepped into the tiny room, closing the door behind him. A small, blond man in an elegant black suit lounged in a chair near the window. His keen blue eyes watched Dalan carefully over the rim of a crystal goblet.

"Time has not diminished your exquisite sense of taste, Dalan," the elf said, nodding at the wine bottle on the table. "Let the fools argue the merits of Aundairian wine. Darguun hides hidden treasures of the vine that the Five Nations will never grasp. Rhukaan Taash bloodwine is divinity given form. I suspect it is the sole reason that the Sovereign Host tolerates the existence of a goblin nation." He closed his eyes and sipped, a rapturous expression overcoming his handsome features.

"Did you break into my room just to steal my liquor, Shaimin?" Dalan asked, sitting across from the assassin. Gunther crawled timidly out from under the bed, hiding behind his master. Dalan scratched the old dog's ears gently.

Shaimin sneered. "Please, Dalan," he said. "The security in this hovel is so lax that you may as well have left the door unlocked. Besides, would you not have shared your drink with me if you knew I was visiting?"

"That depends," Dalan said. "Did you come to kill me?"

"Not today," Shaimin said.

"Then, by all means, let us drink," Dalan said. He took a small cup from his nightstand and poured the wine into it, then held it up toward the elf.

"A toast?" Shaimin asked with a light laugh. "To what are we drinking?"

"To my uncle, Ashrem," Dalan said. "To his brilliant legacy."

The elf's eyes narrowed, and then he smiled. "To Old Ash, then," he said, lifting his glass and letting it clink faintly against Dalan's cup. The two men drank silently for a moment.

FLIGHT OF THE DYING SUN

"How did you find me?" Dalan asked.

"I was watching when *Karia Naille* took off," he said. "I saw you remain behind. I have been following you ever since, save for the occasional intermission to enjoy the local theatre. Even in the wake of recent events, the play schedules remain unaltered. Don't you find that extraordinary?"

"If you intend to use me as a hostage," Dalan said, ignoring Shaimin's tangent, "then you overestimate my value. Tristam Xain would not risk his life for me."

Dalan watched the elf carefully, weighing his reaction. If Shaimin knew Dalan's words were a lie, then the assassin had been working with Marth all along and knew about the *Seventh Moon*'s crash on the plains. If not, then he had only recently entered to the game. The difference was subtle, but significant.

Shaimin shrugged. "I never presumed Tristam would save you," he said. "No offense, my friend, but you aren't the sort of man for whom others would risk themselves."

Dalan smiled bitterly. "No," he said. "I suppose that I am not. What do you want, Shaimin?"

"To renew the relationship that benefited us both so greatly all those years ago," Shaimin said with a bemused grin. "An equal exchange of information."

"Equal?" Dalan asked. "You don't have anything information I want—at least nothing you would volunteer. The only questions I have regard Captain Marth, and I know you won't betray an employer."

"Betrayal is a strong word," the elf replied. "I return the faith that is placed in me. Captain Marth has offered me very little."

"What do you mean?" Dalan asked, intrigued.

"I know that our mutual associate was responsible for the chaos in Stormhome last week," Shaimin said. "He issued me a warning only a few hours previous so that I might move to safety." The elf's handsome face twisted in a scowl. "The captain was quite upset that your vessel was somehow unaffected by the Legacy, but my sympathy was limited. I do not appreciate being commissioned for a task and then not being trusted to complete it unaided. Marth should have left it to me. Had his rash act not expedited your ship's departure from Stormhome, Xain would be dead now."

Dalan scoffed.

"You doubt me?" Shaimin asked. "Your paladin, the Marshal, was quite the creature of habit. She left *Karia Naille* every day at dusk to pray at Boldrei's shrine near the northern docks. She would have been alone and unprepared. Most of her divine power would have expended tending to the wounded girl, because you have no other healers on your ship. When Eraina did not return, Tristam would have become nervous, desperate, and set out to find her. That would have been all the opportunity I required. The inquisitive, the halfling, the warforged, none of them could act quickly enough to stop me from striking a single killing blow."

"Oh?" Dalan asked. "Seren did. Twice."

The elf's face darkened. "Which brings me to the purpose of this conversation," Dalan said. "Seren. Who is she?"

"Do I detect wounded elf pride?" Dalan asked, tossing back the rest of his wine and pouring himself another cup. He held the bottle toward Shaimin and lifted an eyebrow curiously.

Shaimin smiled gratefully and tipped his empty goblet under the bottle to be refilled. "Perhaps you do," the assassin admitted. "I am not a man who is well accustomed to failure, and this assignment has been curiously difficult from the beginning. I like to fancy that I am a flexible sort of fellow, quite able to rapidly adapt to a variety of situations. To be deflected by such a . . . such a *nothing* . . . is quite galling."

"Believe me, I sympathize," Dalan said, setting the bottle down. "Seren Morisse is a great deal more complex than she appears. She is Roland's student."

Shaimin's eyes widened. "She was trained by Jamus Roland?"

"She was something of an apprentice to him," Dalan said,

frowning into his cup. "Until Marth murdered Roland several weeks ago. Marth hired Roland to perform a task on his behalf. Roland did not perform to Marth's expectations, so Marth killed him."

Shaimin said nothing. His blue eyes were lost in memory. The corner of his mouth twitched in an uncomfortable frown. "You know the danger Xain is in," Shaimin said. "You would say anything to leverage my emotions, to try to save him."

"Indeed," Dalan agreed, "but that does not change the fact that Marth *did* kill Roland."

"If you mean to imply that I will suffer the same fate as Roland, you underestimate me," Shaimin said.

"Nothing of the sort," Dalan replied. "I remember when you were Roland's comrade, as I was. I should think you would not appreciate his murder."

"That depends if what you say is true," Shaimin said, "and it does not alter my obligations. Once my debt is repaid, I shall have words with the former Captain Thardis. Until then, Tristam Xain's death is merely a matter of time."

"Isn't everyone's?" Dalan asked.

Shaimin chuckled. "I have missed your cold pragmatism, Dalan," he said. "No other man in Eberron could sit and drink with me while I calmly discussed murdering his friend, well aware and unperturbed that there was nothing you could do to stop me."

"Or perhaps I am confident that there is no need to stop you," Dalan said. "What ties you to Marth, Shaimin? Did he save your life?"

Shaimin laughed. "My life?" the elf asked. "I would not grant my services in return for my life. My life is not worth so much."

"Then what?" Dalan asked. "You offered an exchange of information, but you have given me nothing."

"I would have thought that simply asking you for help would be treasure enough, d'Cannith," Shaimin said. "You were always a man who learned a great deal more than was said to him."

"Not always," Dalan replied. "You have always been difficult to read, thus I have learned little. So tell me this."

"If you wish," Shaimin said, setting his glass down carefully on the table. "Years ago, I was working in the embassy of the Cyran ambassador to Breland, acting as a private political adjutant for certain anonymous Thrane interests."

"A spy," Dalan said.

"How crude," Shaimin said, frowning. "Please, don't interrupt."

"My apologies," Dalan said.

"At any rate, my primary contact was exposed without my knowledge," Shaimin continued. "To save his own life, he sold my identity to a particularly brutal Brelish constable. I was captured, tortured, and interrogated at length." Shaimin drummed his fingers gently on the table as he dwelled upon the dark memory. "Marth—Orren Thardis at the time—delivered me from my imprisonment. After I had wrought vengeance upon the good constable, Captain Thardis offered me safe haven among the crew of *Albena Tors* until such a time as the Brelish authorities abandoned their search for me."

"I thought you said Marth didn't save your life," Dalan said.

"An irrelevant side effect," Shaimin said. "Marth salvaged my reputation—that which endures long after we are gone, the name which I borrow from my ancestors and must return upon my death. Revenge is very important to my House, d'Cannith. No slight can go unpunished. I told Marth that I owed him a life, and after all this time he has come to call in his debt."

"I see," Dalan said.

"So surely you can see why Seren's interference is so perplexing," Shaimin said. "I feel now as I did back in Breland—as if forces outside my control have rendered my skills inadequate for the task to which I have directed myself."

"Then you were wise to seek my aid, Shaimin," Dalan said.

Shaimin looked surprised. "What is this, d'Cannith?" he asked. "I sense trickery."

FLIGHT OF THE DYING SUN

"Not at all," Dalan replied. "To my own surprise, I agree with you. We are both rational men. We like things simple. Complexity has polluted our lives. I believe we can help one another."

"My help is expensive," Shaimin said.

"Fortunately I have money," Dalan said.

"Interesting," Shaimin said. "Tell me what you have in mind."

Chapter
Nineteen

Tristam had never seen a true dragon before. The creature radiated power and majesty. He towered over them as he advanced from the darkness, gazing down with detached curiosity. He moved with sinuous grace, pacing in a wide circle around them, eyes fixed upon the two intruders. The creature's body rippled with muscle, sheathed in scales of pure white. A crown of short horns curled from the brow of his large, blunt head. Piercing eyes of sparkling silver bored down at them as his lip curled to reveal rows of small, sharp teeth. His short, thick tail stood straight behind him, serving as a balance for the dragon's long neck. A pair of leathery wings gently fanned the air as he stretched lazily.

Tristam tried to will himself to move, to run, to use his wand against the dragon, anything, but could not. Fear suffused him, pinning him in place. Ijaac's morningstar shook in his hands. Fear had paralyzed the old dwarf paralyzed.

"What is your name, human?" the dragon demanded.

Tristam's mind raced. There was no hope of fighting such a creature physically. Fortunately, the dragon appeared curious and hesitant to kill him. For the moment, it seemed he had a chance. He remembered the vision he had experienced upon his arrival, and a mad idea came to him.

"I am Tristam Xain," he said. "I am the conqueror as foretold in the Prophecy."

FLIGHT OF THE DYING SUN

The dragon considered his words for a long, agonizing moment.

"Welcome, Master Xain," he said, taking a step towards him. His claws tore gouges in the hard ice floor. "Zamiel told me you would come one day."

Tristam wasn't sure whether the dragon's reaction was relieving or even more terrifying. Marth had mentioned the name Zamiel when they faced each other on *Seventh Moon*.

"Where is the prophet?" the dragon asked. His voice was smooth and sibilant, reverberating through the caverns in and endless stir of echoes. "I find it odd that he would leave you to wander the ruins alone."

"Though no man can rise without guidance, the conqueror must ultimately find his path alone," Tristam said, lifting his chin and meeting the dragon's gaze. It sounded like something Omax would say.

The creature tilted his head and drummed one claw on the stone. "Quite so," he said. "Or so Zamiel tells me." His eyes moved to the dwarf. "But why did you bring *this* thing with you?"

"An insignificant servant," Tristam said, shrugging. "His destiny is too small to hinder mine."

Ijaac looked at Tristam blankly, then at the dragon. "Aye, servant, that I am!" the dwarf said, nodding eagerly as he dove into the lie. "Been with Master Xain for years now. Ask me? Couldn't have picked a finer conqueror. With Xain, consider it conquered, and that's that."

The dragon's mouth twitched in irritation, revealing the tip of one long fang. "Do I know you, dwarf?"

"That will do, Ijaac," Tristam said, looking down at the dwarf.

"Aye," Ijaac said contritely. "Forgive me, Master," he added for good measure.

"Xain," the dragon said, the word resounding through the caverns. "I am Mercheldethast, guardian and steward of Zul'nadn.

You are welcome here, as your predecessors were, so long as you remember your place. Know that the Draconic Prophecy has destroyed conquerors who have failed to meet their destiny. I have seen many like you fall without ever meeting their potential."

"Many?" Tristam asked. "How long have you been here?"

The dragon regarded him suspiciously. "It has been our eternal duty to safeguard this place," he said. "I have admitted no mortal into the presence of the Prophecy or the Eye without the prophet Zamiel's sanction. Only he determines who will rise."

"No mortal?" Tristam asked.

"None," Mercheldethast answered. "Though many were not aware of their destiny, or of my presence. How little has Zamiel told you? I thought he already learned the lesson of ill-guided conquerors."

"He has told me very little, but I know better than to question," Tristam said. He pointed at the pulsing flame in the center of the chamber. "May I study the Dragon's Eye?"

The dragon reclined upon the stone, studying Tristam patiently. "In time," he said. "Who are those other mortals upstairs? I heard you fighting the undead vermin."

"My crew," Tristam said.

"The conqueror willingly allies with paladins?" Mercheldethast asked.

"The conqueror uses whatever tools he finds," Tristam answered.

"I see," Mercheldethast said. "I would be wary of allying yourself with such beings. Their dedication to abstract purposes often restricts their actions."

"Understood," Tristam said. "May I see the Eye?"

"No," the dragon said, exposing his sharp teeth in a grin. "I think it would be best if we waited for Zamiel's return. I think I would be interested in hearing the details that led to your predecessor's death."

Tristam fought to keep the fear and tension from his face. It was obvious that the dragon was beginning to see the holes in his poorly woven lie. Now it was only a matter of time before this Zamiel returned and exposed him. Time, unfortunately, was not something he possessed in abundance. He looked around the cavern, studying the smooth rock formations and the arcane scrawl of the Prophecy.

With a final sigh, he sat down on the stone floor, trying to appear relaxed. Ijaac looked at him, confused. Tristam gave him a calm smile and gestured at the stone beside him. The dwarf looked uneasy, but sat, hands still tight on his morningstar. The dragon nestled his chin upon his massive talons and watched them patiently. Tristam turned his wand over in his hands and stared into its crystal depths.

"Please don't contemplate anything stupid," Mercheldethast said. "I doubt you could do much more than irritate me with that mortal toy. If you wish to die, please, wield your magic against me. I am highly resistant to such clumsy forms of magic."

"Odd that you claim to have such low regard for mortals," Tristam said, looking at the dragon.

The dragon said nothing.

"You serve Zamiel, don't you?" Tristam said. "He is mortal."

"Flaunting your ignorance is a poor idea," Mercheldethast said. "Perhaps you should remain silent."

Tristam looked into the dragon's eyes. He watched him with a bored, predatory gaze. Somewhere, far above, he could hear the sounds of fighting again. He looked at Ijaac. The dwarf's lip curled in a weak smile. He nodded imperceptibly at Tristam. Whatever the artificer was planning, the dwarf was ready to go along with it. Anything was better than waiting here to die.

Tristam flipped the wand end over end in his hand. The dragon watched him, one eye twitching in anticipation. Tristam caught the wand by one end, balancing it between his fingers. The dragon watched intently, waiting for Tristam to attempt using his magic. Tristam grinned and spoke a word of command, unleashing a bolt of golden lightning into the ceiling above the dragon's head. At the same moment he passed Norra's silver sphere to Ijaac.

"Hurry," Tristam whispered.

The dwarf nodded.

Mercheldethast roared as debris exploded down upon his head. He flapped his wings frantically, clawing at the ice and stone. He roared, more in outrage than in pain. White steam roiled from his nostrils. Though Mercheldethatst had been confident in his ability to resist Tristam's magic, the ceiling was not quite so invulnerable. Tristam ran to the left, away from the Dragon's Eye, firing another blast at the ceiling and raining more debris upon the dragon. Ijaac dove to the right, holding his mace to light the way through the swirling dust.

The dragon shook himself violently, shrugging off much of his burden. He turned with a snarl. Tristam ducked as a massive claw sliced the air, shearing off a chunk of his cloak. Tristam hurled a vial to the ground, erupting in a cloud of smoke and light as he retreated quickly away. The dragon surged forward. Tristam edged toward the hole in the ceiling where he had fallen and let himself slip as the dragon's claw shot out again. He looked over his shoulder and saw that Mercheldethast had torn the opening wide enough to climb out. If only he had a chance to scramble through, just a moment's distraction, the beast would be unable to follow him through the narrow tunnel.

A deathly rumble echoed through the cavern. On the walls, the Prophecy's glowing script became shot through with sick green energy. Mercheldethast stopped, his eyes narrowing into angry slits. The dragon's head whipped around. Ijaac Bruenhail stood beside the Dragon's Eye. The Eye's energy flickered and pulsated erratically. The dwarf looked up at the dragon in sheer terror.

"What have you done, dwarf?" Mercheldethast roared, his voice exploding through the halls of Zul'nadn.

"Run, Tristam!" Ijaac shouted. "Run now!"

FLIGHT OF THE DYING SUN

Tristam looked back. The way was clear. He had his chance.

Mercheldethast's tail swept through the tunnel, striking the dwarf and throwing him back against the wall. Ijaac cried out in pain and collapsed, morningstar toppling from his hands. Then Tristam was there, white fire lancing from his wand into the dragon's side. Mercheldethast hissed as the force of the blow singed his perfect flesh, made his knees buckle. He rounded and glared at Tristam, surprised at his strength. He reared his head as he took a deep breath. Tristam scattered a handful of dust in the dragon's eyes and rolled between his legs as he coughed a cloud of searing frost through the cavern. The breath became a scream as the acidic powder burned the dragon's eyes.

"Stupid boy," Ijaac growled as Tristam ran to his side. "Thank you."

Tristam grinned and pulled the dwarf to his feet, holding his arm to help steady him as they ran. Ijaac grabbed his morningstar, and they ran as the dragon turned again. Tristam blasted Mercheldethast with his wand again, causing him to rear back reflexively. They dashed madly toward the hole in the ceiling, their escape into the ruins in sight. The dragon flapped his wings, scattering rock and debris with a violent wind. Tristam felt his legs betray him as the rough slope collapsed under his feet. A cloud of smoke rolled through the gap in the ceiling, robbing them of even their last glimpse of freedom.

Tristam reached out toward nothing as he fell. He would die here, and no one would ever know how or why. He only hoped that he had done enough, and that the others would escape.

Then two blue lights shone through the smoke. A three-fingered metal hand clasped Tristam's arm. Tristam tightened his grip on Ijaac as he was hauled upward into the temple. A tall figure sculpted of adamantine and darkwood stood before him, wearing a shapeless woolen hat. It was Omax, his body whole and strong once again.

"Omax," Tristam whispered. "How?"

"Seren told me where to find you," he said. "We must hurry from here. The Fellmaw is coming."

"That's the least of our problems," Ijaac said, running past the warforged and down the hall.

"Run," Tristam explained, pulling on his friend's arm.

Omax nodded, following Tristam. Behind them, a frenzied roar echoed from the caverns, followed by an explosion of ice and stone. Tristam looked back and saw Mercheldethast's blunt head ram through the floor, followed by two talons, tearing at the walls as the dragon tore the gap wider, pulling himself into the hall. The creature was sleeker than he looked, sliding into the wide halls, if only just. He ran toward them, teeth bared in fury.

"Khyber," Ijaac swore. "It just gets worse."

Omax turned, fists clasped to his sides. "Go," he said.

"Right," Ijaac said, running.

Tristam stood by the warforged, wand in hand. The dwarf ran on for several steps before stopping, looking back with a shamed grimace, and returning to join them. The dragon bore down on them, bracing his claws against the walls and collapsing a pillar as he drew back his head for a breath. Omax leapt at the creature, clubbing him across the face with a powerful two-fisted punch. Mercheldethast's head snapped back, frozen breath spraying erratically into the ceiling. Omax darted in under his head, wrapping one arm around its neck and repeatedly driving his other fist into the bottom of its throat.

The dragon hissed and grasped at the warforged's back with one claw. Tristam fired another bolt of white flame, blackening the dragon's face. Ijaac ran forward and brought his morningstar down on the dragon's other claw. It deflected with a harmless metal clang. The dwarf shrugged at Tristam and quickly backed away.

Mercheldethast shrieked in pain and humiliation, finally tearing Omax away from his bleeding throat and hurling him away. The warforged rolled into a crouch next to Tristam. The dragon retreated several steps as he drew its breath again. Tristam fired his wand, this time blasting the weakened ceiling between himself and the dragon. A mass of stony debris fell just as the beast breathed, instantly frozen in place by Mercheldethast's icy breath. A biting wind washed over them, followed by a frustrated roar as the dragon vainly sought to claw through the mess and pursue them.

They broke into a run again, heading frantically for the exit. Tristam nearly fell as he burst into the courtyard, a savage wind almost driving him off his feet. A cacophonous clash of thunder filled the courtyard. He could see the sky had darkened beyond Zul'nadn's gaping maw. Dark clouds seethed and burned with green lightning. In the midst of the growing storm, just beyond the wide skull mouth, a familiar ring of blue fire burned.

The gurgling shriek of ghouls erupted around them as they ran across the courtyard. Shambling figures erupted from the shadows, seeking to intercept them. Tristam's wand blasted several off their feet. Omax seized one as he ran, lifting it bodily and hurling it into another pack. More fell into pursuit behind them, but a flurry of crossbow bolts from *Karia Naille*'s deck dropped several more. Tristam seized the rope ladder beneath the airship's swaying hull, climbing as quickly as he could. Ijaac was right behind him, eyes wide and terrified as he tried very hard not to look down. Omax brought up the rear, knocking the last of the ghouls away with a powerful kick as the airship pulled higher into the sky.

"Welcome home, Xain," Zed said, grabbing the artificer's hand and pulling him into the cargo hold with a grin. Norra Cais stood just behind him, watching with a pensive expression. "Good work," the inquisitive said.

"I don't think we're done yet," Tristam said, turning to help Ijaac climb inside.

"What do you mean?" Norra asked. "Did you fail to destroy the Eye?"

"Nay, it's destroyed," Ijaac said, helping the warforged climb aboard and hauling the ladder inside as the bay doors closed. "Its guardian was none too pleased."

"The dragon," Tristam said. "We slowed him down, but he's angry."

"Khyber," Zed swore, closing the bay doors as Omax climbed inside. "Pherris, they're aboard!" he shouted. "Get us out of here!"

A powerful whine surged through the airship as she accelerated. Tristam hurried to the upper deck, stumbling with the movement. The others all waited there. Pherris was at the controls, gray hair streaked with sweat, eyes intent on the boiling storm. Seren ran to his side, her eyes bright. He embraced her with a relieved smile.

"Thank you for sending Omax," he said.

"Thank Norra," Seren said. "She fixed him."

"She did?" Tristam asked, surprised.

"The storm is getting worse!" Gerith shouted, rolling out of his saddle as Blizzard landed clumsily on the deck. "Blizzard can't fly in this!"

"We won't be able to, either, in a moment," Pherris said.

Beneath them, the eyes of Zul'nadn shimmered brilliant green. Deep cracks shot through the skull and the earth trembled with a fury that matched the thunder. Large chunks of the ruin began collapsing inward, leaving only inky darkness behind. A white dot separated itself from the ruins, soaring up out of the eye on broad, bat-like wings.

Mercheldethast.

"Being trapped between a living storm and an angry dragon is only the latest in a series of uncomfortable experiences you have introduced to my life, Master Xain," Pherris said with his typical exaggerated calm. "All the same, it is good to have you back. Do you have any recommendations?"

"The Fellmaw sees us," Aeven said. She stood at the railing, green eyes staring out into the swirling storm. "It comes for us."

FLIGHT OF THE DYING SUN

Beneath them the dragon grew larger, flying directly toward them at incredible speed.

Tristam looked at the dryad urgently. "You can talk to the storm?" he asked.

"I can," she said. "It is consumed with pain and madness. It thirsts only for revenge. There is no reasoning with it."

Tristam reached into his pocket, an idea forming in his head. "Does it still hunger for the servants of Xoriat?" he asked. "The mortals that summoned it here?"

"Above all else," she said.

"Gerith, do you have your crossbow?" Tristam asked.

"Of course," the halfling said, surprised by the question.

"Lash this to a bolt and be ready to loose," he said, handing Gerith something. "Pherris, turn us into the storm."

"*Into* the storm?" Pherris asked, incredulous.

"Do it!" Tristam barked.

The gnome looked at Tristam in amazement, then nodded. "Oh, why not?" he said. "Not as if we can be *more* doomed."

"That's the spirit," Ijaac said, huddling behind a crate and trying not to look over the rail.

"Aeven, talk to the Fellmaw," he said. "Tell it that we wish safe passage. In return, we will guide a powerful servant of Xoriat into its clutches."

Aeven looked at Tristam suspiciously but nodded. She closed her eyes for a long moment, then nodded. "It is done," she said. "The storm says it will show us mercy, but if you lie, your torment will be exquisite, your flesh shorn by rain, your bones crushed by sleet, your organs burned by the fires of . . ."

"I get the point," Tristam said. "Now, Pherris, let the dragon catch up with us—just as we get near the storm."

The gnome's shaggy brow lifted at that, but he nodded.

"Gerith, be ready," Tristam said.

The halfling nodded, already taking position at the rear of the ship.

The yawning vortex of the Fellmaw screamed before them, all churning snow and searing lightning. Behind them, Mercheldethast sped toward them. Soon the dragon's wide silver eyes and grasping talons were visible, but when he realized that they were flying directly into the Fellmaw he paused, his laughter resounding through the storm.

"You would murder yourselves to escape me, mortals?" Mercheldethast roared. "So be it!"

"Now, Gerith," Tristam said.

The halfling took aim and loosed. His bolt flew true through the savage winds, sticking neatly into the wound in the dragon's throat. Mercheldethast twisted his head to look, barely catching a glimpse of the Xoriat amulet that now dangled around his throat.

The airship disappeared into the heart of the Fellmaw. Mercheldethast turned in midair, trying to escape. Claws of lightning, ice, and wind descended upon the dragon. In the final instant, Mercheldethast turned to pursue them, though even the dragon's considerable might was nothing compared to the storm itself.

Karia Naille shuddered as the Fellmaw embraced her. Mercheldethast vomited a cloud of searing frost that coated the back of the ship, causing her to buck dangerously. A claw of green lightning raked across the dragon's flesh, blackening its side.

"No!" the dragon roared, the anguished shriek of destiny forever denied.

Another burst of lightning vaporized the dragon's left wing. The winds carried the dragon's flailing body away. Again and again electricity sizzled into the dragon as he tumbled helplessly through the storm. The mindless hatred of a thousand-year storm bore Mercheldethast away to be consumed in a mindless vengeful tempest. Tristam watched with wide eyes, stunned at the power he had unleashed upon Zul'nadn's eternal guardian.

Mourning Dawn flew on.

CHAPTER TWENTY

The churning green clouds retreated into the distance as the ship lifted higher into the sky. It looked as if the raging storm had calmed, if only slightly.

"The Fellmaw is satisfied with our offering," Aeven said. The dryad's pretty face was twisted in a scowl. "Such lies taste sour in my mouth, Tristam."

"I'm sorry, Aeven," Tristam said. "The dragon wouldn't have let us escape. It was necessary."

The dryad stared at him for several moments, cool green eyes unflinching.

"It is not like you to say such things, Tristam," she said.

"There wasn't any other way, Aeven," he said.

She looked away, returning her attention to the sky.

Tristam gripped the rail for support as the excitement of his escape faded. A sudden wave of fatigue overtook him. Omax's hand gripped Tristam's arm, supporting him. Seren moved to his side, looking at him with concern.

"I'm fine," he said, pulling away from them both. "I just need to talk to Norra."

"She's in the spare cabin," Zed said.

Tristam nodded. He noticed Eraina standing just behind the inquisitive, watching him with a solemn, unreadable expression.

"What did you find down there, Tristam?" the paladin asked.

"I really don't know," he said as he climbed down the cargo bay ladder. "I'm hoping Norra can give me some answers."

Tristam hopped down and moved toward the long corridor beyond the cargo bay. The first hatch on his left was open. Norra sat on the small cot within, massaging her splinted leg with a pained expression. Tristam knocked softly on the hatch frame, drawing an irritated look from her.

"Save your breath and tell your paladin to mind her own business," Norra said. "My injuries are not so grave that they won't wait until a real healer can attend me in Stormhome."

"Wasn't going to bother," Tristam said, stepping inside and sitting on the stool beside her cot. "Though I do find it odd."

"Find what odd?" she asked, looking at him sharply.

"That you're so distrustful of divine magic," Tristam said. "Eraina's healed us all countless times."

"It is no matter of trust," Norra said. "I simply don't have much use for gods. Any power that cannot be relied upon to function in a logical and predictable manner is ultimately useless."

"But wasn't Llaine Grove one of your friends?" Tristam asked. "He was a cleric of Boldrei."

"He was a colleague," she said. "My opinions on religion were well known to him. It was the subject of more than one protracted debate." She smiled bitterly at the memory. "What do you want from me, Xain?"

"I want to know how you built a working replica of the Legacy," Tristam asked. "In all my research I never even came close."

"My skill is greater than yours, Xain," she said, shrugging.

"No," Xain said, with such intensity that Norra's eyes widened. "This is more than just artifice. The Legacy can unmake magic. You don't figure that sort of thing out on your own, Norra. How did you learn how to build it?"

"I think you already know the answer to that question, Xain," she said. "You just don't want to accept it."

"Tell me," Tristam said.

"Fools like Gavus Frauk believe that Ashrem's Legacy was flawed," she said. "That it was uncontrollable, untested, and that its wild magic created the Mournland. It's not true."

"Then what is the truth?" Tristam asked.

"Ashrem had a working version of the Legacy for years," she said. "I helped him build it. The original Legacy was fused with the elemental heart of *Seventh Moon*. He used it, secretly, at least six times that I remember—crippling armies, breaching magical defenses, silently granting the advantage to one side or another as he steered the course of the War."

"That's impossible," Tristam said. "All that Ashrem ever wanted was peace."

"Yes," Norra said. "The Legacy was the instrument of that peace. Brother Llaine Grove was his moral compass, advising him on how to use the Legacy with minimal loss of life. I advised him on arcane matters, determining where the loss of magic would hamper the war's progress the most."

Memories of the Draconic Prophecy flashed through Tristam's mind. He envisioned the mortal conqueror wreaking destruction upon the world, but this time that conqueror had Ashrem d'Cannith's face. He could find no words. He only stared blankly at the floor, absorbing Norra's words. He didn't want to believe her.

"Ashrem was no fool, Tristam," she said. Her voice was softer now, no longer as harsh and arrogant as before. "He was a good man in the midst of a desperate, impossible war. I do not know how he learned the secrets of the Legacy, but he seized the opportunity to fight for a better world."

"Who is Zamiel?" Tristam asked quietly.

"I do not know that name," Norra said.

Tristam's face flushed with sudden anger. He rose from his seat, scowling down at Norra. "You are lying," he said, his voice a low growl. "I am done being misled and manipulated. Tell me everything you know. Tell me who the prophet Zamiel is. What part does he play in this?"

Norra's eyes widened. "Xain, this has taken a turn from discussion to mad rambling," she said. "Please back away from me or leave this cabin. I will not endure your threats."

"Threats?" he snapped. "I haven't threatened you."

She arched an eyebrow and glanced down at the shimmering crystal wand he held in one hand. He did not remember drawing the weapon. He mumbled a hushed apology and tucked it back into his belt. He sat down on the stool, burying his face in his hands.

"Do you see now?" she said quietly. "The real danger is not the Legacy—it is within us. Power exaggerates our normal human frailties. Even the noblest soul can be consumed by rash anger. With power like the Legacy at our disposal, a rash act can end entire nations. Ashrem did not hide the Legacy from you because he did not trust you, Tristam. He hid it from you because he did not wish to burden you with such a terrible responsibility."

"Don't try to reassure me, Norra," Tristam said, looking up at her weakly. "I'm not even sure what sort of person Ashrem d'Cannith was anymore."

"He was the same as anyone," she said. "A good man who made mistakes. Are you familiar with Vathirond?"

"No," Tristam said.

"Vathirond is a city at the northeastern tip of Breland," she said. "Throughout the war it served as a military outpost, situated as it was directly between Thrane and Cyre. Near the end of the war, the Brelish army had amassed a particularly devastating force of airships, prepared to drop heavy infantry units deep within Cyre's borders. Breland was a powerful force in the war at the time, and though they avoided conflict with Cyre, Ashrem received reports that a large force was moving south through Thrane, prepared to ally with the Brelish forces and strike a destructive new offensive into Cyre. Ashrem used the Legacy to cripple the Brelish airships, hoping that the Thrane soldiers would no longer see any value in the alliance and withdraw."

"What happened?" Tristam asked.

FLIGHT OF THE DYING SUN

"The Thrane general was a particularly vicious servant of the Silver Flame," she said. "He saw Vathirond's weakness as opportunity. He quickly forged an alliance with the Cyrans, offering them a chance to strike back at Breland's arrogant might. Together, they invaded Vathirond from both sides. The Brelish soldiers were defenseless. Without their magic, they were unable to even issue a speaker post to call for reinforcements. By the time help arrived, the city was in flames. Over three quarters of Vathirond's populace died at the hands of the Thrane invaders and their Cyran allies. Through it all, Ashrem could only watch and realize that the blood of the fallen was on his hands. It was on that day that he dismantled the Legacy and determined to never use it again. The potential for grave errors like Vathirond was simply too high. Its secrets would die with him."

"And with you," Tristam said.

"I know only fragments," she said. "Ashrem only taught me enough to assist him, never enough to build the Legacy on my own. He did not trust me that far. Truth be told, I was relieved that the replica I built actually functioned properly."

Tristam blanched. "You weren't sure it would work?"

"Not entirely," she said, "but I was sure enough to take the risk."

"What if it had failed?" Tristam asked.

"What if the Fellmaw hadn't fallen for your ruse?" she asked. "We both gamble much, Xain."

"Except that my crew knew the risk they were taking, Norra," he said. "Yours did not—and now everyone but you and Ijaac are dead."

"You have no idea how heavily that weighs upon me, Tristam," she said. "Pray to your selfish, petty little gods that you never have to make such a sacrifice."

Tristam sighed and said nothing, clasping his hands and slouching on his stool.

"So what do we do now?" Norra asked.

"We return to Dalan and find out what he has learned,"

Tristam said. "Hopefully he will have found something by now."

"That's not what I mean," Norra said. "I mean what happens to me? I do not wish to remain on this ship."

"You were ready to die to destroy Zul'nadn, but now you won't help us?" he asked.

"Your captain does not want me here," she said. "None of you particularly like me. I am not needed here."

"But you know more about the Legacy than anyone save Marth," Tristam said.

"And that is what worries me most," she said. "Will you let me leave this ship, knowing what I know? I am a danger to you, Xain."

Tristam frowned. He could force her to stay. He could threaten her. Better yet, he could just delay her until Dalan returned. If anyone could find a way to obligate Norra to remain and share her expertise, it was he. The Host knew Dalan had already done the same with half the crew.

"You would have given up your life to keep the Legacy from being reborn," he said at last. "I do not believe you would rebuild it. Do as you will, Norra. Live your life as you wish. I will not interfere."

Norra gave him a long, thoughtful look. She laughed softly, drawing a confused look from Tristam.

"Did I say something funny?" he asked.

"You reminded me of Ashrem," she said. "The same odd mix of doubt and confidence. Do not worry, Xain. I do not intend to leave you to fight Marth alone—but you do not need two artificers on this ship, especially when your skills are quite adequate."

"Adequate," he said wryly. "Thank you, Norra. So what do you intend to do?"

"I will return to Morgrave University," she said. "Ashrem began his studies of the Draconic Prophecy there. Perhaps I can find the path that originally led him to the Legacy. In the meantime, you can continue pursuing Marth in a more direct manner. I will contact you if I learn anything."

FLIGHT OF THE DYING SUN

"We may be difficult to reach," Tristam said. "Even I do not know where we will go next."

"Send me a post whenever you will be in a port for an extended length of time," she said. "I will reply as quickly as I am able."

Tristam nodded as he rose. "Very well, then," he said. "I will leave you to your rest, Norra."

She closed her eyes and sat back against the wall.

"Thank you for repairing Omax," he said, still standing at the hatch. She seemed to already be asleep.

Tristam closed the hatch, running one hand through his tangled hair as he walked down the corridor. As usual, answers had only brought more questions. Discoveries only bred doubt. What was the Legacy? Who was Zamiel? What was Ashrem's part in the Draconic Prophecy? Was he right to just let Norra Cais leave?

The last question he quickly pushed away. He would not force her help. He would not become like Dalan, playing games with other people's lives.

A heavy thump from deeper in the cargo hold drew Tristam's attention, along with an oddly dank smell. He looked up to see Ijaac sitting between two large crates, wearing a loose tunic and loose cloth trousers. His morningstar and armor sat in a heap beside him. He removed his other heavy boot and massaged his bare feet with a blissful moan.

"Ijaac?" Tristam said curiously.

"Sorry about the smell, Master Xain," Ijaac said. "Feels like I've been running for days. Good to get a real chance to rest."

"You can have a cabin if you want," Tristam said. "We still have one to spare."

"No thanks, Master Xain," Ijaac said, looking down the corridor pensively. "The cabins all have portholes."

"Portholes?" Tristam asked, "and call me Tristam, please."

"Aye," Ijaac said nervously. "If I don't have to look at the sky, it bothers me less to be so high up in it."

"You're afraid of heights?" Tristam asked.

The dwarf's face flushed. "Afraid is a strong word, Tristam," he said. "Call it cautious."

"Cautious," Tristam agreed with a laugh. "Well, I can ask Gerith to find something to cover the porthole if you like. Better than sleeping in the hold."

"That'd be wonderful," the old dwarf said. "I'd be much obliged."

"So I take it we'll be dropping you off in Stormhome as well?" Tristam asked.

Ijaac looked up at Tristam, blue eyes wide. He quickly returned his attention to his feet, sighing deeply. "I suppose the *Dawn* has steel enough to defend her," he said. "If you don't need this old dwarf, I'll be happy to go on my way. Have to admit I'll be sad to leave."

"You want to stay?" Tristam asked, surprised.

Ijaac looked up again, smiling through his thick beard. "Tristam, I saw what happened back in Zul'nadn. You were free and clear. I'd given you the time you needed to escape. There aren't many men who'd run *back* past a raging dragon to save a man they'd just met."

"What else could I do?" Tristam said. "I couldn't leave you there."

"And that's what I mean," Ijaac said, snapping his fingers. "I'm your dwarf, Tristam Xain, till you need me no more."

Tristam was stunned by the unexpected show of confidence. With all of the doubt and confusion that their journey to the Frostfell had heaped on him, the dwarf's earnest trust was an odd relief.

"Thank you, Master Bruenhail," he said finally. "You're welcome to stay as long as you like."

Ijaac grinned and continued rubbing his feet.

CHAPTER
TWENTY-ONE

The prophet absorbed the scene below with extraordinary calm. Truth be told, calm was the only emotion he felt he could appropriately muster. Anger would have been a waste of energy. Sadness was beneath him—regret was a burden for weak minds. Instead, his mind focused with a fierce intensity as cool as the frozen plains that surrounded him.

He stood on an icy precipice, looking down into the valley where Zul'nadn had been. It was a yawning chasm now. Churning, oily smoke boiled from its depths. One side of the giant's skull still rose from the earth, like a shattered eggshell. The rest was gone. When he heard Mercheldethast's call, he expected trouble. The dragon never summoned him lightly. He had not expected this. He could sense magic—raw, random, fluctuating magic as it echoed through the pit. He had not expected this, and he did not enjoy being surprised.

He continued staring earnestly into the jagged pit, as if expecting the temple to rise back out of the depths and rebuild itself.

Zamiel climbed down and slowly walked toward the smoking crater. He could have moved much more swiftly if he chose, but there was no need. This was a situation best observed with care. He had no idea who could have done this or how. It galled him to underestimate an enemy. He searched his surroundings cautiously as he advanced. In the distant southern sky he saw the crackling green mass of clouds that was the Fellmaw. The storm was a powerful entity, but it could not have done this. Zamiel squinted as he studied the play of lightning through the storm's heart. His sharp eyes picked out a hint of blue light within the storm, a ring of fire moving swiftly away.

"*Karia Naille*," he whispered.

A low gurgling rolled through the jagged rocks in reply. Zamiel paid it no mind. He could feel dead eyes watching him from the shadows. As stupid as the ghouls were, they had long since learned not to rouse his wrath. Zamiel was, in turn, content to leave the undead beasts alone as long as they avoided him. They were useful in dissuading the occasional curious explorer from Zul'nadn, and had proven ridiculously difficult to exterminate. No matter how many of them he killed, they always returned to infest the temple again. Apparently at least a few of them had even survived whatever catastrophe had consumed the valley. Zamiel idly wondered if the undead would just wander the Frostfell aimlessly forever, but he had greater concerns.

Tristam Xain. They boy had grown from a minor irritant to a serious threat in a short time. Until now, Zamiel had always assumed it was some failure of conscience or indecision on Marth's part that had always allowed Xain to escape. Now he was not so sure. If Tristam Xain had destroyed Zul'nadn, what else was he capable of? Had he listened to the Prophecy and seen its visions? Did he know about the destiny of the conqueror?

The Prophecy was never wrong, but it could be misread . . .

The other mortals who entered Zul'nadn had all reacted predictably. The Prophecy was very strong in the depths of Zul'nadn. It wanted to be heard. It wanted to be fulfilled. It would speak to any candidate who was even remotely acceptable, painting images of a terrible future. Those who endured the visions invariably replied in one of two ways—either seduced or repelled. Ironically it was the latter sort who Zamiel had always found the most pliable. Those who were repelled by the destiny of the conqueror were willing to make the greatest sacrifices to avoid it—and with each sacrifice lost a bit more of their souls, making them easier to control.

None of them had done anything like this, with outright defiance, destroying the Prophecy itself rather than become a pawn of destiny. This changed everything.

Zamiel stood at the edge of a broken cliff, extending one thin arm from his robes. The black smoke curled around his fingers. His dark eyes narrowed as he studied the patterns of magic. They were broken and confused, but still quite obvious to his eyes. The means by which Zul'nadn had fallen were all too familiar. It was impossible. Xain had no access to any such power, but Zamiel knew better than to distrust his senses.

The prophet glanced to one side, his eyes catching sight of a glimmer amid the debris. He knelt, sifting the snow away and picking up a flat shard of ice. Not ice, in fact, but a sleek white scale. It shone in the cold light of the Frostfell sun, gleaming brilliantly in Zamiel's hand. One edge was ragged and dark, as if broken in a fire.

The prophet's lips parted, and he released a mournful cry. The words were strange and alien, fragments of a language never invented by man. He closed his eyes as he listened to the call echo on the wind. He bowed his head when there was no reply. Mercheldethast knew better than to ignore his call. Such a creature would not endure capture. The white dragon must be dead. Bitter anger threatened to shatter Zamiel's intense calm and he threw back his head, bellowing with such fury that large chunks of crumbling ice fell from the cliffs into the void. As the prophet's roar faded, he heard the claws of ghouls scampering to get away.

With a sigh, Zamiel collected his rage, swallowing it down, burying it with the rest. Mercheldethast had been a loyal if occasionally dull ally. Endless vigil over a frozen wasteland had been a duty well-suited to such a creature. The white dragon's loss would not be forgiven. Zamiel tucked Mercheldethast's scale into his robe and stepped out over the cliff's edge. He fell, long sleeves of his robe spreading outward and fluttering in the air like broad wings. The smoke swallowed him, enveloping him as he fell. For several seconds there was nothing but darkness as the wind whistled past the falling prophet.

Zamiel landed on the blasted earth at the base of the pit with a thunderous crash. He knelt with hand braced against the earth, but was unharmed. He stood, copper fire curling around one hand to light the depths. He was surrounded by broken ice, stone, and bone. Sparks of orange flame sputtered in the black as the vestigial remains of the Draconic Prophecy attempted to reflect Zamiel's light. The writings were unreadable now, destroyed along with Zul'nadn and Mercheldethast.

That was perhaps the most disturbing loss of all. It was rare that the Prophecy manifested as powerfully as it did in the caverns beneath Zul'nadn. The prophet had found only one place where it spoke to him more powerfully than it did here. Strongholds could be rebuilt. Minions, even those as powerful as Mercheldethast, could be replaced. Zul'nadn's voice, however, would remain forever silent.

Zamiel released a deep, exhausted sigh. He spoke a word of magic and the world folded around him, shifting and blurring as it resolved itself into a broad, grassy plain. *Seventh Moon* sat propped on a skeletal network of scaffolding as Cyran soldiers scrambled about repairing the crippled airship.

A raucous cry erupted from over the nearby hills. A pack of six Ghost Talon halflings broke over the crest, riding on bipedal clawfoot mounts. They shouted defiantly in their bizarre tongue, loosing arrows at the Cyran soldiers as they rode past. Their shafts flew true, injuring several of the workers. The Cyrans reacted immediately, falling behind wooden barricades and returning a volley of arrows. One of the clawfoot mounts staggered and fell, spilling its rider on the earth near the prophet's feet. The halfling grunted in pain and rolled nimbly to his feet just as another arrow took him in the chest,

FLIGHT OF THE DYING SUN

driving him to the ground again. The other riders hesitated, but the wounded halfling shouted, waving them off. They continued galloping, cursing at the Cyrans as they retreated.

Zamiel relaxed the magical aura that surrounded him, allowing himself to be seen. The advancing Cyrans hesitated, staring in surprise. The halfling looked up, his face twisted with pain, rage, and hatred. He lunged at the prophet wildly with a short, hooked knife. Zamiel caught the little man's wrist and looked down at him with a compassionate smile.

"Your thirst for vengeance is understandable, my friend," he said, speaking to the halfling in the little man's own tongue. "Yet you have failed your tribe, because you were impatient. Do you understand this? In your haste to avenge your kin, you have only fallen to the same power that destroyed them."

The halfling glared at Zamiel in silent hatred, blood streaming from his nose and lips. A shriek erupted as the Cyrans buried their swords in his wounded mount, setting off an anguished shriek from the halfling. He drew a second, hidden knife and slashed at the prophet's hand. The knife left no wound.

Zamiel looked down in mild surprise and seized the halfling's other wrist. He sighed, carefully placed his foot against the halfling's throat, and gently pulled on both arms. There was a brief, muffled cry followed by a wet snap. With a disappointed sigh, Zamiel let the dead halfling's body collapse on the earth.

He looked up at the Cyran soldiers, all now watching him with undisguised awe. While Zamiel was not one to broadcast his power recklessly, it was important that examples sometimes be made. He clasped his hands and bowed politely, mumbling a barely audible blessing before sweeping off toward the great hulk of the fallen vessel. There, in the shadow of the *Moon*, he found the camp where repairs were directed.

"Brother Zamiel," Marth said, only glancing up to nod in greeting. The changeling was well accustomed to Zamiel's sudden appearances and disappearances.

"What progress?" Zamiel asked smoothly.

"Very little," Marth said. "*Moon's* basic structure is nearly intact, despite the frequent incursions of those annoying Ghost Talon harriers. The guards have them well in hand, for the most part. It is the Valenar who concern me more."

"Valenar?" Zamiel asked. "Elves?"

"They invade the plains periodically," Marth said. "Some of the lookouts say they've seen scouting parties, but there has been no violence yet."

"If the Valenar sense opportunity, they will not attack until they have mustered force enough to overwhelm us," Zamiel said.

Marth nodded. "I fear they have returned for reinforcements. The men are worried. They know the elves' reputation."

"I would not give it much thought," Zamiel said. "If the elves seek booty, the halflings are much easier targets than we."

"Perhaps," Marth said, clearly unconvinced.

"Or perhaps they can be reasoned with," Zamiel said. "The Valenar are honorable souls. We can always use more allies." He looked at the wrecked airship. "When will she fly again?"

"A difficult question," Marth said. He straightened as he studied the ship, focusing on the change of subject. "The elemental containment is, as I feared, unsalvageable. After studying her workings in detail, I am uncertain that the *Moon* would fly even if we secured a new bound elemental from Zil'argo. Ashrem customized upon the gnomish construction extensively. I fear we would need his genius to make the *Moon* rise again."

"Disturbing," the prophet said. "Why do you continue to repair her if there is no hope she will fly again?"

"I never said there was no hope," Marth said with a grim smile. "Only that hope does not lie in Zil'argo. I need only wait for Tristam Xain to resurface. Ashrem d'Cannith built the *Karia Naille*. Her elemental core will serve to fire the *Seventh Moon*."

"When do you think he will reappear?" Zamiel asked.

"I cannot say when, but I know where," Marth replied. "Dalan

FLIGHT OF THE DYING SUN

d'Cannith was on the *Seventh Moon* far too long. A mind like his would have easily gathered clues enough to trace the soldiers who serve me. No doubt the *Mourning Dawn* will follow that trail to New Cyre. Over half the crew still has kin there."

"Find Tristam quickly, Marth," Zamiel said. "Each time he escapes you, he grows more dangerous."

Marth frowned at the mention of his failure, but made no excuses. Instead, he stepped away from the repair crew, pale eyes intent on the prophet. "Something has happened," he said.

"Xain has been to the Frostfell," Zamiel said. "He has destroyed Zul'nadn."

"Destroyed it?" Marth asked, shocked. "Are you certain?"

Zamiel looked at Marth patiently.

"A foolish question," the changeling said. "How did he do such a thing?"

"It seems he is not as far behind your research as you believed," the prophet said. "I sensed rampant magical energies similar to those of the Legacy. He turned the manifest zone upon itself, twisting the space between worlds and collapsing the temple."

"What of the Draconic Prophecy?" Marth asked.

"Gone," Zamiel said. "That which was written on the walls of Zul'nadn only remains here." He pressed his hand against his chest. "Fear not, Marth. I feel I spent lifetimes studying the mysteries. Though the Prophecy speaks no more, I guide you still."

"Thank you, Zamiel," Marth said. "If you have time, do you think you could speak to the men? Between the wreck, the halflings, and the elves their morale has suffered terribly. Your words would do much to inspire them."

"I will do what I can," Zamiel said. "But I shall require some time alone in meditation."

"Whatever you require," Marth said. He smiled gratefully at the prophet and returned to his work.

CHAPTER
TWENTY-TWO

Tristam staggered onto the deck, pulling his goggles away and coughing painfully. Pink smoke rolled off him, along with the stench of rotten eggs. He lurched to the ship's rail, leaning into the wind and letting the cool breeze wash over him. His goggles fell forgotten from his hand. The little clay homunculus snatched them in one hand before they could tumble through the railing and into the sky. It slung them over one shoulder and plopped down by Tristam's feet, regarding its creator with patient curiosity. Tristam clapped his hands rapidly over his sleeves, putting out the last few sparks that were dancing through his clothing.

"Research not going well?" Pherris asked, glancing over his shoulder at the artificer.

"I'm just a little flustered," Tristam said, voice hoarse from coughing. "I'm not sure what's wrong with me."

"Pretty obvious to me," Zed said. The inquisitive stood near the bow of the ship, long pipe dangling from his mouth. "I've seen this sort of thing plenty of times."

Tristam looked at the inquisitive curiously.

"Peace," Zed said with a laugh. "From the Frostfell to Stormhome and beyond and we haven't had any trouble at all. You don't know what to do with yourself, Tristam. You keep expecting something to happen, and when it doesn't, you worry. You're looking for trouble. Seen it in plenty of young soldiers who just survived their first battle. Few weeks of peace after something like that can drive a man crazy."

"Maybe you're right," Tristam said. "I'm worried about how easily things have gone since Zul'nadn. I'm worried that Norra was so eager to leave the ship and return to Morgrave. I'm worried that Dalan has been acting so strangely since he came back on board. I'm worried that no one in Stormhome gave us any trouble when we landed, though we were the only ship to escape Marth's attack."

"Dalan thinks none of the Lyrandar port authorities recognized us," Pherris said.

Tristam grunted, unconvinced.

"Anyway, what were you working on, Tristam?" Zed asked. "Smells like it isn't going well."

The artificer shrugged. "I was taking a break from Overwood's journals to tinker with a new formula," he said. "I'd been toying with it in my head for a while now. It didn't turn out quite as stable as I was hoping."

"Explosives?" Zed asked.

"Not initially," Tristam said. "I meant it to be a sleep powder. There was an unexpected reaction." He rubbed his eyes and blinked into the wind. "I still can't see straight. I guess the mixture was ineffective"

"Or just effective enough," Zed said. "That all depends how long you want them to stay asleep. Did you make any more?"

"Of course," Tristam said. He held out one hand, displaying a pink glass sphere. A gleam of gold metal shone within it.

"Looks like an egg," Zed observed. "What's that inside?"

"A calculated risk," Tristam said.

"I am glad you are not one to let a failed experiment discourage you, Master Xain," Dalan said, emerging from the galley. "I knew I was wise to sponsor you. Without curiosity, there can be no innovation." The guild master held a thick wooden platter heaped with bread and roast duck. He smiled broadly and nodded at his burden, quite pleased at the bounty. "Gerith has outdone himself today. You really should help yourselves while it's still warm." He whistled softly as he strode across the deck and disappeared into his cabin.

Tristam stared at Dalan's hatch blankly. Zed carefully tapped out his pipe on the rail and tucked it back into his coat.

"You're right," Pherris said quietly. "Dalan has been odd since he returned. Almost . . . I can't describe it."

"Pleasant," Zed said.

"That's the word," Pherris answered.

"Pretty disturbing, I agree," Zed said. "He hasn't been as nosy as usual. Kept mostly to himself."

"Perhaps he is busy organizing the information he acquired in Stormhome," Pherris said. "He's been amiable because he has a riddle to occupy his mind."

"Or he found a woman," Zed said. "Host knows Dalan needs one."

Pherris frowned in disapproval.

"It's true," Zed shrugged. "He needed *something* to cheer him up, anyway. What makes Dalan happy?"

"Plans coming together," Tristam said.

"Wouldn't be surprised," Zed said, taking a deep breath. "You should probably talk to him, Tristam. Try to find out what he's up to. Make sure he still remembers whose side he's on. You know Dalan."

"You want me to talk to him?" Tristam asked. "You're the inquisitive. Why don't you find out what he's up to?"

"Because Dalan hates me," Zed said. "He's extra careful not to give anything away because he knows I'm as smarmy, curious, and arrogant as he is. You've actually earned his respect, Tristam."

"Me?" Tristam asked. "You're kidding."

"As much as Master d'Cannith is capable of respecting anyone other than himself," Pherris said. "You should consult with him before we land in New Cyre."

"True," Tristam said.

He crossed to Dalan's hatch and knocked, but it swung open at his touch. Dalan looked up from his desk with an eager smile, still enjoying his lunch. He waved Tristam in and gestured at the seat across from him. Tristam carefully drew out the chair and sat down. The little construct sat at his feet, drawing a confused sniff from Gunther before the dog retreated beneath the bed.

"They sent you to check up on me, didn't they?" Dalan asked, eyes twinkling mischievously.

"You have been acting strangely, Dalan," Tristam said. "And you're dressing strangely. Plainer than usual. Not wearing any of your House seals."

"Ah. This is merely a disguise," Dalan said. "I believe our investigations today will go smoothly if I am perceived as a simple traveler, rather than Dalan d'Cannith. Much the same impetus that drives me to strip *Karia Naille* of all markings of ownership. As for my behavior. My brief vacation from *Mourning Dawn* has rejuvenated me. Since the events in the Talenta Plains, I must confess I have felt as if I were a burden to this crew."

"A burden?" Tristam asked, surprised at the confession.

"Indeed," Dalan said. "None of you trust me. None of you like me. I realize that the only reason that I was endured among you was because the airship belongs to me. While you all will gladly allow me to finance our expedition, I feared that none of you trusted me enough to let me wander far from your sight for long."

"We let you stay behind in Stormhome," Tristam said.

"You did," Dalan said, smirking. "And how fortuitous." He tore a small loaf in half and nibbled on a chunk. "I accomplished a great deal there. Events are set in motion that will put a severe dent into Marth's plans."

"Such as?" Tristam asked.

"Plans, plans, great and small," Dalan said with a chuckle. "I successfully identified several members of Marth's crew. A few of them have family members who do business with the Lyrandar. Apparently those families have been ordering unusually large amounts of food and supplies. It was assumed they were merely stockpiling, rebuilding resources—after all, many Cyrans escaped their homeland with no more than their names and the clothing on their backs. If they intend to continue ordering supplies for Marth, they will no longer do so on Lyrandar vessels."

"You've frozen Marth's mail," Tristam said.

"Basically, yes," Dalan said, laughing. "You may see it as a petty victory, but many wars are lost by economics. Don't worry, Tristam, I didn't waste my time. I have been quite busy. As you have been, I see. You took it upon yourself to add a dwarf to my crew." He sliced off a large piece of meat and stuffed it into his mouth.

"Ijaac is an experienced explorer and a brave warrior," Tristam said. "We can rely on—"

Dalan held up a silencing hand and smiled. "Tristam, please," he said, chewing. "That was no criticism, merely an observation. The Bruenhails are friends of my family. I consider Ijaac's presence a blessing. He told me how you saved his life." Dalan drank deeply from his goblet. "Is it true that you fought and slew a dragon?"

"Tricked would be a more accurate description," Tristam said.

"But it *is* dead, right?" Dalan said, looking at Tristam carefully.

"Torn apart by the Fellmaw," Tristam said.

"Good," Dalan said. "By all accounts, dragons have long memories and a richly honed sense of revenge. The last thing any of us need is a dragon appearing at an inopportune time to settle the score."

"No, it's definitely dead," Tristam said.

"Shame you couldn't find its hoard," Dalan said, a faraway look in his eye.

"We had more important things on our mind, Dalan," Tristam said.

"Of course, of course," Dalan said, snapping back to the subject at hand. "What else did you discover in Zul'nadn?"

"The power source that Ashrem used to stabilize the Legacy," Tristam said.

"You recovered it?" Dalan said.

"I destroyed it," Tristam said.

"Even better," Dalan said. "If Marth can't create a reliable prototype of the Legacy, then we just about have this won."

"Once we find him," Tristam said. "Even an unstable Legacy is dangerous."

Tristam wondered if Dalan was right. When the Prophecy entered his mind he saw the Dragon's Eye, burning large and bright. When he found the actual flame, it appeared somehow reduced. He had the uneasy feeling that someone had somehow removed part of it. How did you remove part of a doorway to another world? That wasn't the kind of thing a person could simply carry around.

"With luck that discovery will come shortly after we land in New Cyre," Dalan said. "Several of Marth's crew have family here. I believe our strongest chance to turn up clues will be his helmsman, Devyn Marcho. He and his elderly mother are the only survivors of a large family, all slain in the war."

"You're hoping Devyn will have kept in touch with his mother," Tristam said.

"And that his mother will be lonely enough to gossip with a friendly stranger," Dalan replied.

"Do you think the people of New Cyre are working with Marth?" Tristam asked.

"As a whole?" Dalan asked. "No. I doubt many surviving Cyrans would support Marth. After all, I am Cyran, and his actions disgust me. It takes a special sort of person to believe Marth's rhetoric. My research has shown that most of the soldiers who followed Marth have histories of crime and violence since the end of the war. In any case, I doubt Marth would seek official sanction from New Cyre. He likely sees Prince Oargev ir'Wynarn as weak."

"Weak?" Tristam said. "You said the prince organized the Cyran refugees and led them to a new home in Breland."

"And from a certain perspective, that was weakness," Dalan said. "Better to die Cyran than to live under Breland's skirt." He sipped deeply from his goblet.

"Do you think the prince is weak?" Tristam asked.

"Compromise is not weakness," Dalan said. "In adapting, we survive. I admire Prince Oargev greatly for doing what he must to preserve the remnants of my homeland." He looked at Tristam shrewdly. "Speaking of compromise, tell me what deal you made with Norra Cais to ensure her cooperation."

"There was no deal," Tristam said. "I convinced her that we do not intend to rebuild the Legacy. I promised that I would do all I could to stop Marth. She believed she could offer more help by returning to Morgrave University."

"A strangely trusting outlook, given her brusque treatment of you in the past," Dalan said. "I wish I would have had a chance to speak with her before she left the ship."

"So you could have convinced her to stay?" Tristam asked.

Dalan smiled. The steady whine of the ship's elemental ring changed tone, becoming a bass hum. The airship banked slightly, forcing Dalan to steady his cup with one hand.

"I think we shall be landing soon," the guild master said. "You should remain aboard the ship while I go speak with Devyn Marcho's mother."

"No," Tristam said. "I'm coming with you."

Dalan gave Tristam a long, unflinching look. "With a Thuranni assassin still stalking you?" he asked. "I do not think that is wise. You will be much safer aboard the ship."

"I'll bring Seren with me," he said. "She stopped him before."

Dalan laughed.

"Why do you find that funny?" Tristam asked. "She nearly died protecting me from him."

"Oh, I don't doubt Miss Morisse at all," Dalan said with a pleasant smile. "I was planning to take her with me anyway. I was merely reflecting on how quickly we have come to rely upon her. If you feel that her protection is sufficient, then I will take your word. She has certainly proven herself capable."

Tristam nodded. He felt there was something more to Dalan's reaction, but then that was to be expected. Even now, when he was being friendly and agreeable, Dalan was hiding things.

"Tristam," said Seren's soft voice. She opened the door, the morning sun shining through her dark hair as she stood framed in the doorway. "We're almost in New Cyre."

"Excellent," Dalan said. He quickly polished off the remainder of his meal and rose, swallowing his drink in one gulp. Gunther emerged from beneath the bed, wagging his tail expectantly. Dalan dropped his platter on the floor beside several others like it. The dog eagerly began cleaning the dish.

Gerith waited for them just outside the cabin. He handed Dalan a brown wrapped package with a conspiratorial grin. Dalan accepted it with humble gratitude.

"What is that?" Tristam asked, looking at the package now tucked under Dalan's arm.

"An edge for our negotiations," Dalan replied.

"Master d'Cannith, I know your opinion of the New Cyran leadership," Pherris said from the helm. "Regardless of your optimism, you do realize that we are flying directly toward a town known to house our enemy's kin? I think perhaps it would be wise not to land within the town limits."

"Agreed," Dalan said. "Just outside the walls should be fine. We'll have ample cover to mask our arrival."

"Everyone else, remain on the ship," Tristam said. "We shouldn't be long, and if things go sour we may have to leave quickly. I don't want to leave anyone behind."

Tristam noticed Dalan grinning at him silently.

"What?" Tristam asked.

"I was about to say much the same thing," Dalan said.

Tristam wasn't sure if the idea that he and Dalan were thinking more alike was reassuring or disturbing.

The ship descended swiftly, the elemental ring humming in its steady rhythm. The rolling hills of Breland spread out beneath them. New Cyre sat nestled at the base of a small range of rugged cliffs. The eastern sky churned a greasy, unsettling gray.

"I expected the city to be bigger," Seren said.

"It's a fair-sized town," Dalan replied.

"Maybe," Tristam said, "but for the home of Cyre's survivors, it's smaller than Vulyar."

"Not all the survivors have accepted it as their new home," Dalan said. "Not that there were many of us to start."

Karia Naille swooped down in a broad arc, circling well around the city and settling among the southern cliffs. Dalan, Seren, and Tristam climbed down the boarding ladder and hiked down to the main road. Tristam looked at Seren curiously. She wore a short dress of fine white silk under a long black coat, with black velvet boots.

"Why are you dressed like that, Seren?" Tristam asked.

"I'm pretending to be Dalan's niece," she said, looking at him earnestly. "I look foolish in this, don't I?"

"No," he said quickly, obviously a little dumfounded. "Not at all."

Seren grinned.

"I felt Seren would make the best bodyguard in New Cyre," Dalan explained. "She provides adequate protection without standing out as much as Omax or Zed would."

"I feel underdressed," Tristam said, shifting his baggy coat over his shoulders.

"You're fine," Dalan said as he headed off toward the road. "Just pretend you're my shabbily dressed bodyguard, or something."

Tristam shared an exhausted look with Seren, then followed.

They were almost immediately met by a farmer and his sons on the way to town with a bushel of fresh fruit. The man greeted them amiably, tossing each of them an apple before continuing on his way. A pair of bored soldiers sat at the gates, playing a game of dice. One greeted Seren with a low whistle and a friendly grin, but they seemed otherwise unconcerned. The streets were clean, straight and uncluttered. The roofs of the houses were painted in a rainbow of colors, giving the entire town a welcome, cheerful appearance.

"This certainly isn't what I expected," Tristam said.

Dalan had been watching Tristam with an expectant grin. "And what did you expect?"

"It's . . ." Tristam searched for the right word. "Cheerful? It's strange to me, after everything the Cyrans lost."

"They have one another," Seren said.

"Phrased with beautiful simplicity," Dalan said. "You live in a beautiful world, Miss Morisse, but I'm not sure that I agree with your assessment. Cyre was the gem of Khorvaire. As a nation, we prided ourselves on craftsmanship, brotherhood, and beauty. The prince has gone to great lengths to ensure that the vision of Cyre is maintained. So long as New Cyre stands as a reflection of the Cyre that was, the people can perhaps believe, for a time, that Cyre has not perished. The illusion of Cyre gives them a sense of hope. Some tragedies can only be addressed by pretending that they never happened. Thus the forced cheer and mask of friendly hospitality."

"I like Seren's explanation better," Tristam said.

"Then believe it," Dalan said, shrugging. "I am a pessimist. But enough sightseeing, we have work to do here. Follow me. I have the address we require."

They passed through the streets, pausing occasionally to ask directions. Tristam studied the people carefully as they went about their daily lives. They looked normal, happy, and cheerful, but there was a certain edge. A hesitation before laughter. A moment of regret after a smile. Families walked with a space between them, as if leaving room for someone absent. Solitary figures huddled alone where they hoped none would see, sobbing quietly. New Cyre was a town of hope—but it was a fragile hope. Tristam sighed. Was he really starting to see the world the same way Dalan did?

"This is the one," Dalan said. The small house stood adjacent to a schoolhouse. A pack of children ran and played in the yard outside, under the watchful eye of an elderly schoolmarm. Dalan approached the door and knocked briskly.

"Can I help you, strangers?" said a thin voice. The old schoolmarm had risen and walked over to meet them. She looked at each of them warily, casting extra suspicion at Seren's short skirt and leather surcoat.

"Taria Marcho?" Dalan asked, smiling brightly.

"I am she," the old woman said.

"Is Devyn your son?" Dalan asked.

Taria's face paled. One hand moved unconsciously to cover her mouth. "Has Devyn come to harm?" he asked.

"My apologies," Dalan said with a reassuring laugh. "I did not mean to alarm you. Devyn is quite well. I saw him only a few weeks ago. I am a friend of his." He proffered the brown package. "I was merely in town and felt it proper to bring his sweet mother a gift. Fresh-baked cookies. Devyn sends his regards."

The old woman relaxed, her suspicion replaced with a friendly smile. "Thank you," she said, accepting the package gratefully. "I worry about him so."

"The mother of a hero," Dalan said. "You must be quite proud. Well, I shall take up no more of your time . . ." He tipped his hat and turned to walk away. Tristam looked at him, confused.

"Wait, no," Taria said. "Please, wait a moment." She turned toward the schoolyard. "Rathen?"

One of the older boys playing looked up at the sound of his name.

"Keep an eye on the children, please," she told him firmly. "I'm going inside for a bit to speak with my son's friends. Children, listen to Rathen."

FLIGHT OF THE DYING SUN

Rathen nodded obediently and stood up, immediately assuming the aura of cocky authority that children do when given command of other children. He gave Taria a little salute. She smiled at him and stepped into the house, gesturing for them to follow.

"I apologize for appearing so unexpectedly," Dalan said as he followed her inside. "I travel a great deal and am never sure where the road will take me."

"Of course," she said sweetly. "My Devyn is the same way. His friends are welcome any time. Would you like tea? What did you say your name was again?"

"I am Tomas," he replied, taking a seat next to a small table when offered. "This is my niece, Arielle, and my bodyguard, Gorbus."

Tristam smiled stiffly at the sound of his new alias. He and Seren sat to eachside of Dalan. Tristam felt slightly dazed. As frustrating as Dalan's manipulations could be when caught amid them, it was amazing to watch them from the other side. The old schoolmarm busied herself readying a pot of tea for her guests, singing happily to herself, her mood greatly cheered by news of her son's well-being.

"Gorbus?" Tristam whispered when Taria's attention was elsewhere. "What kind of name is that?"

Dalan chuckled. "I must confess this is something of a homecoming for my friend Gorbus," Dalan said loudly, looking at the artificer with a wicked grin. "He is a lad eager to prove himself. My old war stories seem to have inspired him. He greatly admires Devyn."

Tristam raised an eyebrow at Dalan. Dalan nodded in encouragement.

"A hero," Tristam said. "I hope to one day prove to be as great, so that I may win the heart of winsome Arielle."

Seren giggled. Dalan frowned. Tristam could barely keep himself from laughing.

Taria returned to the table, smiling fondly at each of them as she poured tea into four cups and arranged the cookies. "You fought beside my Devyn, Tomas?" she asked.

"Indeed," Dalan lied as he sipped his tea and selected a large cookie. "Though the injuries I sustained at Vathirond required that I retire from active service." He patted his right leg and winced. "My only regret is that I do not continue to serve Cyre as Devyn does."

"Devyn only does as his prince commands," Taria said with obvious pride. She sat down across from them, clutching her teacup in her small hands.

Dalan looked at Tristam meaningfully. "The prince?" Tristam asked. "I didn't know that Cyre still maintained an army."

Taria looked suddenly uncomfortable.

"It's all right," Dalan said. "Gorbus is half Lhazaarite, hence his revolting name. His father was a mercenary who made Cyre his home, but his mother was a dear friend. He is Cyran, born and raised."

The old woman nodded and leaned forward in her chair, a conspiratorial grin twisting her features. "It's nothing official," she said, "but Devyn told me that the prince has been keeping an eye out for patriots—soldiers who haven't forgotten what it means to be Cyran. I was worried after the Day of Mourning. Devyn didn't know what to do with himself. We were . . ." She sipped her tea quietly and swallowed. "We were the only ones left, but it was like he just kept fighting." Her distant frown was replaced with a cheerful smile. "Now he's on a secret mission for the prince. I'm so proud."

"As well you should be," Dalan said. "It was mere chance that I encountered him. Of course I can't say where, for reasons of security."

"Of course," Taria said, happy to be part of the conspiracy.

"It must be very difficult for you, Taria," Seren said. "Has your son kept in touch with you at all?"

"He writes whenever he can," she said. She rose from her chair, returning to the kitchen and taking a small wooden box from atop the cupboard. "He isn't supposed to, of course, but since his brothers and father died he's tried so hard to stay close." The box was filled with dozens of speaker posts, all neatly stacked.

"He hasn't mentioned anything about his missions, has he?" Dalan asked.

"Oh, no," Taria said. "Of course not. Nothing like that. It's mostly poetry. He's such a sweet boy. Read some, if you like."

"Thank you," Seren said. She smiled sweetly and took the box, leafing through the crisp pages.

"Ah, curse my clumsy fingers," Dalan muttered as his cup tumbled from his fingers, spilling tea onto the floor. He drew a broad handkerchief from his vest with a flourish and knelt awkwardly to clean up the mess. "Terribly sorry."

"No, no, it's all right," Taria said soothingly. "You sit, I'll get that." She rose and walked back into the kitchen, searching for a wash rag.

Seren waited a moment to make sure she was gone and deftly snatched a few of the letters from the stack, folding them and tucking them into her shirt. She continued reading innocently as Taria returned.

"Let me get that," Tristam offered gallantly, taking the wet rags from her. The old woman smiled gratefully as Tristam began cleaning up the mess.

"These are quite good," Seren observed as she read. "Simple verse structure, but very visceral. Devyn has a talent."

"You like poetry?" Tristam asked, surprised.

"I do," Seren said, seeming slightly offended by the question.

"All women do," Dalan said. "Don't be an idiot, Gorbus."

Tristam blinked in dumb silence. Seren gave him an impish grin and kept reading.

"Odd that Devyn never struck me as the poetic sort," Dalan said. "Amazing, what you can learn about someone. We all have such depths."

"He really only started writing on the Day of Mourning," Taria said. "Petik, my oldest, was the writer. His plays were performed in the Grand Globe of Metrol. I think Devyn feels he should take up where Petik left off."

"The souls who faded on the Day of Mourning never truly left us," Dalan said, finishing his cookie.

Taria began to reply, but a the sound of a mailed fist beating urgently on the door interrupted. She looked up with an irritated frown, stood, and moved toward the door. It burst open before she arrived. The old woman drew back with a startled shriek. Six Cyran guardsmen stood at the door, weapons drawn. Their eyes searched the room urgently before settling on Tristam.

"Tristam Xain," the leader said. "In the name of King Boranel, you are under arrest for the murder of Dalan d'Cannith."

"Well, this is ironic," Dalan said dryly.

Chapter
Twenty-Three

The iron door closed with a reverberating clang. The cell was cramped and dark, with a low ceiling and only one small window to admit the light. Dalan seated himself with a long groan. Tristam ignored him, listening at the door until the guards' footsteps had receded. When they were gone, he rattled the cell door experimentally and leaned against the bars.

"Seren, can you hear me?" he called out. "Are you there?"

"I'm here," she answered from an unseen cell further down the hall. "I'm fine."

Tristam knelt and studied the lock. He patted himself down, searching for any tool he could use to probe at the door, but found nothing. His wand, coat, and tools had been taken from him, leaving him in just a loose tunic and breeches. All he had remaining was a pack of tindertwigs. He struck one against the wall, sparking a small flame as he searched the floor for anything he could use.

"Relax, Tristam," Dalan said, leaning back against the wall. "This really is not the time for heroics."

"I thought you would criticize me for not fighting the guards," Tristam asked.

"That was understandable," Dalan said. "We were outnumbered. Though I do not enjoy being imprisoned, I think you acted wisely."

Tristam looked at Dalan. "But if we weren't outnumbered, it would have been acceptable to blast them with lightning? With all those children playing twenty feet away?" He cursed as the tindertwig's flame bit his fingers. He shook it out and threw it aside, lighting another.

"Why must you be so belligerent, Tristam?" Dalan said, sighing. "There are any number of reasons fighting would have been foolish. Do not presume that yours are superior to mine. If you truly wish to take the moral high ground, consider that those guards are not Marth's soldiers. They were only doing their duty. Remember that you are still wanted for murder and have done nothing to clear your name."

"You're the one they think I murdered!" Tristam said, exasperated. "Why don't you tell them who you are and get us out of this?"

"Because it would serve no purpose," Dalan said. "Even if I told them the truth, we would be detained here until that truth could be verified. Consider our situation, Tristam. Wroat is over a thousand miles from here. No one knows me in New Cyre. Why would they have arrested you so quickly for a crime committed so far away? Those guards were spurred to action."

Tristam looked at Dalan, rising from his crouch and leaning back against the door. He shook out the twig, sucking his fingers and wincing. "You think Marth is behind this?" Tristam said.

"Clearly," Dalan said, surprised that Tristam had not arrived at the same conclusion. "Marth must have had a spy watching the homes of his soldiers here. Upon our arrival, that spy summoned the city guard to detain us on a technicality until his master arrives."

"We don't have much time, then," Tristam said, looking at the door again. He ran his hands over the metal, searching for any flaw, any weakness. He lit another tindertwig and glanced around, eyes widening as he noticed a discarded lantern under one of the rough cots.

FLIGHT OF THE DYING SUN

"I wouldn't bother, Tristam," Dalan said. "This is Cyran architecture. Even with your magic, you'd be hard pressed to escape. The doors are likely warded."

"I won't wait here and die, Dalan," Tristam said. "Seren, how are you doing?"

"Doing fine," Seren replied. "I feel like I'm back in Wroat. I miss Warden Thomas, though."

"That's not what I mean," Tristam whispered harshly. He tinkered with the lantern, twisting out enough wick to set it alight. "I mean can you find a way out?" He was quiet a moment, reflecting. "Wait. You were on first terms with the Wroat prison warden?"

"Don't be jealous, *Gorbus*," she teased.

"You should relax," Dalan said. "Be more like Seren. As crises go, this is relatively minor."

Tristam rolled his eyes at Dalan and returned his attention to the thick metal door. He peered closely at the lock, studying the tumblers inside.

"If anything, we should utilize this opportunity to assess the information we've gathered thus far," Dalan continued. "We need to plan our next move. That was a clever move, Seren, taking those speaker posts."

"How is poetry going to help us?" Tristam asked. He looked into the lantern's sputtering light, his expression thoughtful and distant.

"Like all dragonmarked craftsmen, the speakers of House Sivis are proud of their trade," Dalan said. "Their original posts all bear certain numerical codes, printed discreetly in the corner of the page. These codes verify their authenticity and also indicate their point of origin. For that reason, most spies learn to swiftly copy and destroy their original speaker posts so that they will not be traced to their point of origin. Taria Marcho, it seems, would make a poor spy."

Tristam looked up at Dalan. "You mean that we can use

Devyn's letters to his mother to find out where he's been?" he asked.

"Possibly," Dalan said. "As Marth's helmsman, most of those points of origin would mean little. Presumably he spent a great deal of time flying the *Seventh Moon*. But if we can discern a recurring location we can perhaps determine where Marth is stationing his soldiers. Zed can decipher the codes when we return to *Karia Naille*, and from there we can determine where to go next."

Tristam fell silent, staring into the lantern again. He turned and sat with his back against the door. "No," he said.

"No?" Dalan asked archly. "You have a better suggestion?"

"It all makes sense now," he said. "I know how Ashrem did it."

"Did what?" Dalan asked. "What are you talking about?"

Tristam looked up at Dalan, eyes intense. "I know how he carried the Dragon's Eye out of Zul'nadn. How do you carry fire, Dalan?"

"Enlighten me," Dalan said.

Tristam held up the gleaming lantern.

Dalan looked confused. "Ashrem put an elemental manifest zone in a lantern?"

"So to speak," Tristam said. "I think he used *Dying Sun*'s elemental containment housing. Airship cores are already enchanted to prevent elementals from returning to their home plane. Why couldn't one be modified to do the same thing to part of the Dragon's Eye? He used the heart of his own ship to fuel the Legacy."

"Incredible," Dalan said. "Are you certain this is even possible, Tristam?"

"I can't think of any other way he could have done it," Tristam said. He pondered silently for a long moment before speaking again. "There's only one way to be sure. We need to find the *Dying Sun*. If her elemental core has survived, we have to destroy it. Otherwise Marth might find use it to stabilize his Legacy."

FLIGHT OF THE DYING SUN

"Impossible," Dalan said. "*Dying Sun* crashed in the Mournland. She could be anywhere. We could search for a lifetime and never find her."

"But we already know where she is," Tristam said. "Ashrem was headed for Metrol, the Cyran capital. He took Kiris Overwood with him. Obviously the *Sun* caught up with him before the Day of Mourning began, because Marth rescued Kiris and flew back out in Dalan's ship. *Dying Sun* has to be in Metrol."

"Hardly a comforting distinction, Tristam," Dalan said. "Do you realize how large a city Metrol was?"

"We have to start somewhere," Tristam said.

The sound of a heavy thump from the end of the hall ended the conversation. It was the sound of a body hitting a stone floor.

"Zed?" he called out. "Ijaac? Omax, is that you?"

There was no reply. As he stared into the door's lock, he imagined he saw the tumblers slowly move. A heavy tick echoed inside the mechanism. Tristam jumped as the door creaked slowly open. A thin figure darted into the room and threw Tristam back against the wall, forcing him to gasp in surprise. Shaimin d'Thuranni's cold blue eyes stared into Tristam's. The artificer felt a chill of metal as a thin blade pressed against his throat.

"Shaimin, don't do this now," Dalan said urgently. "There is more at stake here than your reputation. We need Tristam."

"There is nothing of greater significance, d'Cannith," Shaimin said, though he stayed his hand. "If you can give me a reason to spare the boy's life, speak quickly."

A metal click from behind drew the elf's attention. He cocked one eyebrow and peered over his shoulder. Seren stood in the doorway, aiming a guardsman's crossbow at the assassin's back.

"Drop the knife," she said.

"That seems reason enough," Dalan said.

Shaimin looked back at her with a crooked smile.

"Thuranni," Dalan whispered. "Don't. Some things are more important than pride. I know you already have your doubts."

"You cannot manipulate me, Dalan," the elf said. He held his knife steady, his eyes locked on Seren's.

"Then consider this reality," Dalan said. "Kill Tristam first and Seren will bury a bolt in your heart. Kill Seren first and you will give Tristam a chance to call upon his magic, surrendering your advantage of surprise. How will your reputation fare when your family learns that you died at the hands of one of these children? Put your knife down."

"As you say," Shaimin said, still smiling at Seren. He let the knife fall to the floor and stepped away, hands spread loosely to his sides, as if beckoning the girl to shoot him. "I did not expect to find Xain here anyway. The opportunity will come again."

Seren's face darkened. Her finger tightened around the trigger. Shaimin's eyes gleamed.

"Seren, don't," Dalan warned. "Lower the crossbow."

"Dalan, you know this assassin?" Tristam asked angrily.

"I'm negotiating," Dalan said. "If Seren does not cease threatening Master d'Thuranni, this negotiation will take a negative turn."

Seren frowned and lowered the crossbow, setting it gently on the floor.

"Make a right out of this cell and you will find your possessions in a closet at the end of the hall on the left," Shaimin said. "The guards will not interfere with your escape."

"Did you kill them?" Seren asked.

"I don't work for free," Shaimin said. "Not unless the target intrigues me." He leered. "They guards are unconscious and will remain so long enough for you to depart and make haste back to your airship." He reached into the pouch at his belt, drawing out a thin envelope and tossing it into Dalan's lap. "The information you requested, d'Cannith." With a florid bow, Shaimin snatched up his dagger, tucked it into his belt, and darted out of the cell. "Another time, Xain."

Seren looked at Dalan, her face red with anger. Tristam

grabbed her arm gently. "Not now, Seren," he said. "We need to get out of here. Dalan, when we get back to the ship you have a lot of explaining to do."

"Naturally," Dalan replied, tucking the envelope into his vest.

The trio rushed out of the cell, stopping long enough to take their gear from the closet and equip themselves again. Tristam ran to the door, warily peering out at the street. A patrol of watchmen were picking their way through the noonday crowd toward the jail, in no particular hurry.

"Be casual," Seren said, pushing past him and walking out into the street. "None of those guards have seen us before. They don't know we're prisoners. Don't run. Don't give them a reason to chase."

Dalan and Tristam followed Seren, moving down the street in a close group. The guard patrol paid them no mind, continuing their slow path toward the jail. They rounded a corner onto a more sparsely populated street. A patrol of six mounted guardsmen trotted toward them from the other end of the street.

"Same as before," Seren said. "Just try to walk past."

They walked in a loosely knit group, casting only casual looks toward the soldiers. Tristam felt a sense of unease as the Cyrans drew closer.

When they were only forty feet away, he noticed the amethyst wand tucked under the leader's belt.

"Get down!" Tristam shouted, drawing his own wand and unleashing a cone of brilliant white lightning at the soldiers just as they began to aim their crossbows.

The lightning scattered the soldiers, blasting them from their horses. The townspeople screamed and scattered. The leader scowled as the magical energy washed around him, crackling off an invisible shield. Lightning burned his horse from beneath him, forcing him to leap to the street. He let his disguise fade, resuming his original form as he rose. Dalan swore and ducked behind a stack of rain barrels. Seren drew her stolen crossbow, eyes wide with fear.

"No tricks, Xain?" Marth asked calmly. "No desperate escape? No friend to save you?"

"Seren, get away," Tristam whispered. "Take Dalan and run."

"He'll kill you, Tristam," she answered.

"Do it!" he snapped. "Get out of here!"

"Yes, Miss Morisse," Marth said. "Please begone." He swept his wand in a broad arc, unleashing a volley of roaring flame toward Seren. She rolled backward as the blast exploded at her feet, hurling her against the wall of a church.

Tristam swore and blasted his wand at Marth again. The changeling's shield wavered but held. Marth's laugh died as Tristam leapt through the brilliant distraction, drawing his sword and slashing downward. Marth ducked to one side, catching Tristam's wrist from his awkward swing. He struck Tristam hard across the face, a flash of green light exploding from the butt of his wand. Tristam staggered backward, sword toppling from his hand.

Marth caught Tristam's sword easily and advanced. He slashed the air, leaving a trail of red across the boy's chest as Tristam dodged away. Tristam quickly drew a bottle from his coat and drank the contents, vanishing.

The changeling chuckled, peering around with a bemused expression. "Your skill has advanced since our last meeting," Marth said. "It doesn't matter if I cannot see you. You cannot touch me." He whispered, and the air shimmered around him. Transparent, whirling blades surrounded Marth on all sides. "I need not strike you. I know where your weaknesses lie." He aimed his wand toward the wall where Seren had fallen.

She was gone. He glanced around in irritation, only to see Dalan helping the injured girl limp away down the alley. He aimed his wand just as another cloud of smoke erupted, enveloping the alleyway and robbing Marth of his target. Images of Tristam

FLIGHT OF THE DYING SUN

Xain now stood on each side of Marth, both aiming their wands at the changeling.

"Arrogant," Marth said. "You believe you can deceive me while you still carry my ring?" Without hesitation, Marth aimed at the one to his left, firing a blast of green flame. The illusion exploded in a cloud of sulfurous pink smoke, rolling over Marth and biting into his eyes.

Tristam ran as his illusion faded. He whispered a word of command and felt the infusions in boots activate, carrying him swiftly away. As he circled the end of the block, he found Dalan and Seren waiting for him.

"Seren, are you hurt?" he asked quickly.

"Just winded," she said. "What about you?"

"Keep running," he answered, pulling them along beside him.

"What happened to Marth?" Dalan asked.

"He found a rotten egg with a golden ring inside," Tristam answered. He patted his hip. "I lost my sword."

"We'll find you an axe, lumberjack," Seren said.

They ran through the gates of New Cyre. The bored guards looked up in confusion and returned to their dice game. Tristam drew a short tube from his coat and fired it into the air, leaving a trail of red smoke across the sky. Only seconds later a ring of blue flame rose from the southern cliffs and flew swiftly toward them. They kept running, keeping a sharp eye behind for any sign of pursuit. Tristam followed Seren and Dalan up the docking ladder. He watched the city until the bay hatches closed, his wand still clutched in one hand.

"What happened down there?" Ijaac asked. He glanced at them with a worried expression as he folded the ladder.

"Marth," Tristam said.

"Captain Gerriman, get us out of here!" Dalan shouted. "Plot us a course due east."

"Aye, Master d'Cannith," the gnome replied. The airship banked and accelerated.

"That was quite the duel, Xain," Dalan said, clapping Tristam on the shoulder. "I was impressed. I suspect the next time you meet with our Captain Marth that the outcome shall not be so—"

Dalan's congratulations ended abruptly as Seren slapped Dalan across the face. She seized the guild master by the throat, pushing him against the wall and drawing her dagger.

"Well, that was unexpected," Ijaac observed.

"Not really," Tristam said in a tired voice.

"I hate crew drama," Ijaac mumbled.

"This is an odd way to thank me for carrying you out of that alley, Miss Morisse," Dalan said. He smiled through bloody lips and looked at the knife nervously.

"I warned you," she hissed. "I told you what would happen if you hurt him again." She pressed the knife against his stomach.

"Idiot girl, I have done everything to *prevent* Tristam from being harmed," Dalan snapped, his voice now sharp and serious. "Now sheathe that blade before you do something all of us will regret."

"Seren, please," Tristam said. "Host knows I've wanted to kill Dalan a time or two but this isn't the answer."

"I'll just go check if lunch is ready . . ." Ijaac said, quietly tiptoeing out of the hold.

Seren released Dalan and stepped back, sheathing her knife. "Talk," she said. "Why did that assassin know your name?"

"Another shadow from my checkered past," Dalan said. "Shaimin also knew Marth, and owes him a favor. This favor resulted in his current employment—the hunt of Tristam Xain. While you were away in the Frostfell, Shaimin came to me seeking an exchange of information."

"What kind of information?" Tristam asked.

"The details are irrelevant," Dalan said, glancing at Seren. "Suffice it to say that he is unhappy with his assignment. Shaimin may be a killer, but he is not part of Marth's plans. Since I knew that you would not be returning from the Frostfell for some time, that left Shaimin with little to do. I hired him to come here and investigate in New Cyre."

"You hired my assassin?" Tristam asked, shocked.

"Please, Tristam, don't overreact," Dalan said. "I didn't hire Shaimin to kill anyone. The Thuranni are spies as well as killers. He was instructed to investigate something on my behalf, and to free me when Marth's pawns attempted to capture me."

"You knew Tristam's killer would be here and you didn't warn us?" Seren asked.

Dalan looked very tired. "I did, in fact, warn Tristam," he said. "You replied that Seren was more than adequate protection. Need I remind you that you were correct?"

Tristam felt foolish and angry at once. "Why didn't you tell me that Shaimin spoke to you?" he asked finally.

"Why didn't you tell me everything you saw in the Frostfell?" Dalan asked. "I know that you have concealed something that weighs heavily upon you. I don't care. I trust you to use your discoveries wisely."

Tristam didn't say anything. Seren looked at him, worried.

"That's different," Tristam said finally. "There were things in Zul'nadn that none of you would understand."

"It is no different at all," Dalan said. "You know that, Tristam. Do not pretend your secrets are more justified than mine."

Tristam leaned back against the bulkhead, rubbing his face with one hand. The rush of his duel against Marth was fading, leaving him exhausted. Dalan glanced from Seren to Tristam impatiently.

"I don't know what to say," Tristam said.

"And I told you, I don't care," Dalan said. "Whatever you learned in Zul'nadn does not matter to me so long as you use the knowledge wisely. I trust you to do so, Tristam. It merely galls me that you do not return the favor."

Tristam looked up at the guild master soberly. "I'm sorry, Dalan," he said.

"Apology accepted," he said pertly. "Any more questions?"

"No," Tristam said. Seren continued glaring at Dalan darkly.

"Then I'll just excuse myself, if both of you are satisfied that I still deserve to live."

Neither Tristam nor Seren spoke. Dalan gave a very curt bow and strode off.

"Tristam," Seren whispered once he was gone. "What did you see in Zul'nadn that you didn't tell us about?"

Memories of the Draconic Prophecy stirred in Tristam's mind. He saw the conqueror rise above the shattered mortal nations once more, but this time he saw the conqueror's face. The conqueror was not Ashrem, and he was not Marth.

The conqueror was Tristam.

"I don't know," he said, he slumped to the floor and buried his face in his hands.

Seren stood her distance for several moments, watching Tristam with a stunned and wary expression. Then she sat beside him and took his hand. Tristam looked up at her, ready to order her away, to leave him in peace. He couldn't bring himself to speak the words.

Seren smiled, and the dark visions of the Draconic Prophecy faded back into memory.

CHAPTER
TWENTY-FOUR

Mourning Dawn blazed a trail across the Brelish sky, soaring in wide circles over the forests and plains. The crew assembled, standing in a rough circle on the ship's foredeck. Seren sat in the ship's bow and reflected how strangely different the mood was among today. For perhaps the first time since she had arrived here, they were in no immediate danger and had no destination. The uncertainty was making everyone uneasy. Even Gerith was reserved as he fed scraps of fish to his glidewing, murmuring softly in his native tongue. Omax knelt in silent meditation, staring out at the sky toward the Mournland. Ijaac sat near the warforged. The dwarf had given up on his attempts to make conversation and had instead turned his attention to looking pointedly at the deck and pretending to be on the ground. Eraina paced the center of the deck restlessly while Dalan watched her with an annoyed, impatient expression. Only Pherris and Aeven seemed entirely unfazed. The gnome stood in his customary position at the helm. The dryad sat beside him, her eyes closed as she listened to the alien song of the ship's elemental ring.

Eraina ceased pacing as Zed and Tristam emerged from the hold. The inquisitive held a sheaf of rumpled papers in one hand, a mix of Devyn Marcho's speaker posts and Shaimin d'Thuranni's reports. Dalan winced when he noticed the tangled heap Zed had made of the ordered documents. The inquisitive was still reading thoughtfully as he ascended. Tristam cast about the deck briefly, smiling and moving toward Seren when he saw her.

"I think we have something," Zed said. "It isn't much. Mostly a hunch."

"Better than the sorts of clues we usually have, then," Gerith said.

"Snowshale," Dalan said, his tone warning. "Just tell us what you can, Arthen."

The inquisitive nodded. "Well, I can't guarantee that Marth is still where I think he is," Zed said. "None of these speaker posts Seren stole are newer than six months."

"The newest ones would have been useless," Seren said. "They just would have told us where the *Seventh Moon* has been chasing us. We already know that."

"True," Zed said. "I'm just qualifying that this information could be out of date. Marth might have moved his base in the last year."

"It's better than nothing," Tristam said.

"Hopefully," Zed said dubiously. "There's a definite pattern here." He rifled through the stack of posts. "Over one-third of the posts originated from Nathyrr, a village in southern Thrane. Strikes me as odd, as thus far we haven't discovered anything related to the Legacy in Thrane."

"You think Marth's base of operations is in Nathyrr?" Eraina asked.

"You couldn't hide a Cyran army in Nathyrr," Zed said, "but the village is near the Harrowcrowns. Marth's base could be in the forest there. What's more, the forest is close to the southern border, where Thrane meets the Mournland. So old Cyre is right nearby."

"I've heard legends about the Harrowcrowns," Gerith said. "Those forests are haunted, aren't they?"

Zed laughed darkly. "According to the legends, all Thrane forests are haunted," he said. "It's a wild and untamed place."

FLIGHT OF THE DYING SUN

"What of the Thuranni report?" Dalan asked. "Did you learn anything of use?"

Zed shook the stack of papers, straightening them with a snap, and sorted till he found Shaimin's letter. "I learned that elves have very messy handwriting," Zed said. "I think Shaimin holds the pen between his teeth."

"Intriguing," Dalan said dryly. "What else?"

"There was definitely someone watching the gates of New Cyre over the course of the last several days," Zed said. "Marth does a lot of recruiting there, so he must have suspected we'd come there looking for clues."

"Paranoid," Eraina said.

"And organized," Zed said. "We still don't know how many people Marth has working for him, but if he can spare them to spy on his own city, that's a bad sign. I mean, granted, we've increased the size of our own crew by ten percent in the last few days," he nodded at Ijaac with a grin, "but signs indicate we're still enormously outnumbered."

"That doesn't matter," Eraina said. "Our fight is with Marth, not his army. Once he's been brought to justice, all of this will end. He's the only one with the knowledge to rebuild the Legacy. Without him, his soldiers will return to obscurity."

Seren noticed Tristam glance away nervously at that. She worried about him. He'd been so distant since he returned from Zul'nadn. What had he seen?

"Speaking of Marth," Zed said, "Shaimin wrote quite a bit about him."

Tristam looked back at Zed, suddenly attentive. "What?" Tristam asked. "How did Shaimin find information on Marth?"

"Marth claims to be a Cyran soldier," Zed said. "So, Shaimin looked into Cyran military records."

"Where would he find such things?" Omax said. "Cyre is no more."

"Prince Oargev has a strong interest in restoring and preserving his lost nation's history," Zed said. "He's spent the last few years hiring small salvage teams to sneak into the ruins of Metrol and recover anything with the royal seal of Wynarn on it. Everything they bring back is stored here, in New Cyre. There's a substantial cache of Cyran military records. Apparently Shaimin accessed it."

"Broke into it," Pherris corrected.

"Probably," Zed said. "I don't really care how he learned what he did—it's interesting."

"Tell us," Dalan prompted.

"Getting there," Zed said, growing impatient at the interruptions. "Apparently there have only been three changeling officers in the Cyran military within the last sixty years."

"Unsurprising," Eraina said. "I think most armies would find it difficult to trust an officer whose very identity was suspect."

"Or at least have the wisdom to use such duplicity to their advantage," Dalan said. "Changelings make terrible generals but excellent spies. It would behoove an army to keep such assets secret."

Zed frowned as he studied the papers. "The story of this changeling, Captain Eover Halloran, seems to be exactly what we're looking for."

"Eover Halloran doesn't sound like a changeling name," Dalan said.

"It isn't," Zed said. "Eover was a human, stationed in the city of Melthir on the southern border of Cyre. During a siege by the Darguun goblin armies, Eover was placed in command of a commando unit, sent outside the walls to harass and delay their attackers. During a particularly brutal part of the siege, Eover's wife, Kresthian, was wounded by a goblin arrow. She took fever, reverting to her natural changeling form. The townspeople panicked, believing that she was a Darguuni spy. Her two sons, also changelings, died failing to protect her from the angry mob. Three days later, Eover Halloran returned. The goblin assault had been

FLIGHT OF THE DYING SUN

turned aside, but rather than a hero's welcome, he returned to find that his commanding officer, Lieutenant Kieran, had condoned the murder of his wife and sons as necessary casualties of war."

"By the Host," Eraina whispered.

"Eover was to be detained for questioning, but he fled," Zed went on. "Over the course of the next several days, Lieutenant Kieran and six members of his command staff, all of whom had supported the changeling deaths, were methodically murdered. Eover, also secretly a changeling, assumed the identities of the men he killed as he worked his way through the chain of command. He was ultimately captured and brought before the Cyran military court by Ashrem d'Cannith. During his trial, Eover demanded to be recognized by his true changeling name."

"Marth," Tristam said.

Zed nodded.

Seren looked up at Tristam. The artificer stared at Zed with a mix of confusion, surprise, and anger.

"What happened next?" Tristam asked.

"The records are incomplete," Zed said. "By Cyran law, the changeling should have been executed, but there's no record of it. I'm not sure if that part of the record simply wasn't recovered from Cyre, if Shaimin just didn't find it, or if it never happened."

"Crimes?" Gerith asked. "What crimes? Marth's own comrades killed his wife and children while he was saving their city. Killing those soldiers wasn't a crime. That was justice. I feel sorry for him."

"I'm sure we all share varying degrees of sympathy, but it does not change the truth," Dalan said. "The fact is that Marth was a war criminal well before he began his pursuit of the Legacy. Further, my uncle clearly knew him for what he was. Why would Ashrem knowingly associate with such a person, much less give him command of one of his airships? I knew the old fool was idealistic, but embracing a murderer seems excessive."

"Excessive?" Gerith asked. The little halfling's face was hot.

"In Marth's place I'd have done the same thing. I'd have killed every one of them."

"Then you're a fool as well, Snowshale," Dalan said. "There are avenues of revenge that do not involve wanton murder."

"None of this has anything to do with what we're doing here," Tristam said sharply. Gerith and Tristam looked at Tristam in surprise. "We need to figure out what we're doing next."

"I confess it would grant me a degree of comfort if I knew where I was flying this ship," Pherris agreed.

"Well, we know Marth has an unstable replica of the Legacy," Eraina said. "It won't be long before he uses it again."

"But we still don't know what he intends to do with it," Dalan said. "While he is certainly an individual quite capable of wanton destruction, such random violence does not seem his style. He must have a greater plan."

"Marth is working to fulfill a part of the Draconic Prophecy," Tristam announced. "I saw the future in Zul'nadn."

The crew all looked at Tristam in surprise. Even Gerith peered over from his course, if only momentarily.

"What are you talking about, Tristam?" Dalan asked.

"Ijaac, you remember the vision I had in the ruins?" Tristam asked.

Ijaac nodded silently.

"I saw a mortal conqueror," Tristam said. "He tempered the Legacy in the Dragon's Eye and used it to strike down the mortal nations in the name of peace."

"Seems an odd way to find peace," Ijaac said, scratching his beard thoughtfully.

"Graves are peaceful," Aeven noted.

"I still don't see it," Dalan said. "Marth is a logical, methodical person. Why would he follow some vague shadow of what might be?"

"It's the Draconic Prophecy, Dalan," Eraina said. "It isn't what might be. It's what *will* be."

FLIGHT OF THE DYING SUN

"So say a thousand street corner prophets," Dalan said. "I still don't see it. You can twist any happenstance to fit a prophecy, if it is vague enough. The Draconic Prophecy is not known for clarity. Why would he embrace such nonsense?"

"Marth isn't working alone," Tristam said. "The dragon who guarded Zul'nadn mentioned Marth's master, a prophet named Zamiel. Zamiel has somehow convinced Marth that this vision of the future is reality."

"I remember the dragon saying that," Ijaac said, smiling happily for having added to the conversation.

"Marth mentioned the name 'Zamiel' before we escaped *Seventh Moon*," Seren said.

"Marshal Killian spoke of a Zamiel shortly before his death," Eraina said. "He said that the prophet would ignite the war anew, and the world would be as we remembered it."

"You are all children in the eyes of this world," Aeven said, her cool voice carrying easily over the rushing wind. "Your Last War raged for more than a century. To a warrior such as Marth, this age of peace is a strange and alien thing. The War was all he knew. He wishes to return the world to what he believes is its natural state."

"An intriguing observation, Aeven," Dalan replied. "Still, I don't know why Marth would reignite the War unless he stood to benefit."

"Not everyone thinks the way you do, Dalan," Zed said.

"They do," Dalan replied. "They just don't realize it."

"I don't really care," Seren spoke up. "Does it really matter why Marth wants to start a new war? Or why this Zamiel is helping him? Or whether the Prophecy is right or wrong? All that matters is that we stop Marth before he kills anyone else."

The crew said nothing for several moments.

"Well said, Miss Morisse," Gerith said at last. "I think we can all agree on that. So what is our next move?"

"If we want to find Marth's base of operations, the Harrowcrowns seem our best bet," Eraina said.

"No," Tristam said. "We need to go to Metrol."

"The Mournland?" Zed asked, shocked. "Why in Khyber would we go there?"

"Tristam is determined to locate the wreckage of *Albena Tors*," Dalan explained.

"I believe Ashrem used *Dying Sun*'s elemental core to stabilize and sustain the Legacy," Tristam said. "We need to find that ship, or at least keep Marth from finding it. Now that Zul'nadn is gone, *Dying Sun* is Marth's only hope to complete the Legacy."

"It is too great a coincidence that Marth was already in New Cyre when we arrived," Omax said. "Even he cannot travel so swiftly. Perhaps he is preparing to enter the Mournland as well?"

"If he does, we still have an advantage," Tristam said. "Marth still doesn't have an airship. We can get there first."

"Assuming Marth doesn't simply teleport there ahead of us," Dalan said. "He's proven capable of such feats."

"Unlikely," Tristam said. "From what I've read, magic is dangerously unstable in the Mournland. Metrol is said to be particularly wild zone. Teleportation is risky even under normal conditions. Blindly teleporting that far into the mists would be suicidal."

"Then wouldn't we be taking similar risks, flying an airship in there?" Dalan asked. "*Karia Naille* is powered by magic."

"No," Pherris answered. "*Mourning Dawn*'s elemental core is well-shielded. I'll give us a safer trip than anyone else can guarantee in that twisted place."

"Interesting," Dalan said. "Now we've gone from having no options to having too many. Do we search for Marth's base or recover *Dying Sun*?"

"This isn't a choice, Dalan," Tristam said. "It's only a matter of time before Marth recovers the *Sun* himself."

"But while he's busy there, he won't be watching his headquarters," Zed said. "There's no reason why we can't do both."

"Split the group?" Omax asked.

"I can handle the Harrowcrowns alone," Zed said. "I'll just

be looking around. There's an inn I know in Nathyrr called the Kindled Flame. You can catch up with me there when you're done in Metrol."

"I'll go as well," Eraina volunteered. "It would be unwise to go alone."

"Fine," Zed said. "Both of us will go."

Eraina looked mildly surprised that the stubborn inquisitive accepted her help, but said nothing.

"Then it's settled," Tristam said. "We can put in at Vathirond, at the edge of the Mournland. From there, Zed and Eraina can continue north into Thrane while we fly east into the Mournland and Cyre."

"Aye," Pherris said. "I'll plot a course."

"Dalan, are you sure you don't want to go to Thrane with Zed and Eraina?" Tristam asked as the others began to filter back to their posts.

Dalan looked back as he prepared to enter his cabin. "Hoping to be rid of me, Tristam?" he asked.

"No," Tristam said, "but you stayed behind when we went to the Frostfell because it was too dangerous."

"I stayed behind because I would have been a useless burden," Dalan corrected. "Remember that I am Cyran. I was born in Metrol. I may be able to guide us through what remains."

"Have you been to Cyre since the Day of Mourning?" Seren asked.

"No, Miss Morisse," Dalan said. "For much the same reason that I avoid funerals and graveyards. Such places hold nothing for the living save grisly reminders of the fate that awaits us all. I do not relish the prospect of visiting that wasteland, but I believe I can help." Dalan forced a tight smile and closed the hatch behind him.

"And what about you, Pherris?" Tristam asked quietly. "You know as well as I do that there's no guarantee the ship will be completely safe from the Mournland's wild magic."

"Perhaps," Pherris said, "but I trust Ashrem d'Cannith's work and I trust you. There is no safer ship, no finer artificer to maintain her."

"I appreciate the confidence, Pherris," Tristam said. "I only hope that I prove worthy of it."

"See that you do, Master Xain," the captain said with a chuckle.

Seren laughed at the captain's ceaseless good humor, but her laughter trailed away when she saw Aeven's emerald eyes. She followed the dryad's inscrutable gaze, fixed on the eastern sky. On the distant horizon, blue sky gave way to an endless line of dead, gray mist.

The Mournland was waiting for them.

CHAPTER
TWENTY-FIVE

For two days they had soared through the mists. Tristam spent as much time as he could at the ship's rail, staring down at the Mournland, trying to understand how magic could unleash such destruction upon the world. Seren was always close beside him, her hand covering his own when his thoughts were bleakest. It was strange. She always knew how he was feeling. Tristam was comforted by the thought, but also afraid.

The closer they drew to the end of their quest, the more Tristam knew that he was changing, and not for the better. In the last few weeks he had become colder, more pragmatic, more manipulative—more like Dalan. Tristam knew, on some level, that he had ignored Omax's injuries so that he could spend more time studying Kiris's journal. He knew that he had risked their lives flying the *Karia Naille* into the Fellmaw. He had hidden the full truth of his visions—that the Prophecy had depicted him in Marth's role as the conqueror. Now he led them on a course into the Mournland, uncertain if the risk was worth the gain he had promised. Could Seren see the changes that had come over him? Could he become the person he used to be, the simple boy that only wanted to perfect his skills and impress his teacher? Could he avoid the fate the Prophecy had promised?

There was no way to know until the Legacy was out of his life forever.

From this altitude Tristam found that the Mournland hardly even looked real. After two days of flying through the mists, he still could not comprehend that the land below actually existed. There was no sun, just a sickly shimmering mist that painted the land in eternal twilight. The earth was scorched dry and blasted white. Withered trees clawed vainly at a sun they could not see. Battlefields remained strewn with the bodies of unburied dead, untouched by decay since the Day of Mourning. Bizarre creatures scuttled across the earth, sometimes pausing to stare up at the *Mourning Dawn*'s burning elemental ring with baleful eyes.

Some towns remained entirely intact, though bereft of life. Others were ruined in strange and random ways. Houses were cracked like eggshells with their contents strewn in the streets. Skeletal ruins burned with yellow flames that would not die. In one town, nothing remained but a flat glassy plain, etched with elongated blast shadows in the shapes of houses. In the larger cities, eerie lights indicated the presence of life. Pherris steered *Mourning Dawn* in a wide berth around these places, content not to know what had taken up residence there.

For all of these strange sights, the smell was even more disturbing. The Mournland smelled strangely . . . clean. There was no cloying smell of vegetation, no smoke from human settlements, no scent of rain on the air. The only scent was the crackling aroma of raw magic. It burned Tristam's senses and tingled on his skin. The power of this place suffused Tristam, energizing him and sickening him. He felt the urge to call upon his infusions, to draw upon the Mournland's wild energy to fuel his creations. It was like a siren's song. He shook his head to clear away the urge to descend into his laboratory and noticed a flicker in the mists far below, like the wake a swift vessel left through still water.

"What are those lights?" Ijaac asked, startling Tristam and drawing his attention back to the present. The artificer hadn't realized quite how lost in reverie he was. The dwarf stood well away from the ship's rail, pointing at something on the land below. A line of faint blue lights was just barely visible through the mists, evenly spaced in a line that stretched off in the distance toward Metrol, tracing a path beside the River Melandor.

"Conductor stones," Tristam answered, clearing his throat roughly. "It's a lightning rail track."

"How can the coaches still run here?" the dwarf asked, surprised.

"They don't," Tristam replied. "They've tried to run coaches through the Mournland, and they never get far. The line is broken in too many places, though theoretically you could still run a coach over the parts that remain intact. The stones are powered by their own self-perpetuating enchantments. I've heard that some of the people that live out here use improvised coaches to travel across the wasteland."

"People?" Ijaac asked, shocked. "Who would want to live in a dead place like this?"

"Some would," Omax said. The warforged rose from the corner where he knelt in meditation and joined them. "It is said that there is a warforged nation in the mists. Warforged who cannot find their place in the mortal lands come here, seeking a godlike figure known as the Lord of Blades."

Tristam looked at Omax curiously. "You've never told me that before, Omax."

"There was no reason for you to know," Omax said. "He calls to those warforged who seek something more, who are desperate to create a world where they can become something more than slaves, monsters, or tools."

"Has the Lord of Blades called to you, Omax?" Seren asked.

The warforged nodded. "I have been called," he said, voice tinged with faint regret. "I have not answered. I will not find my place in the world by setting myself apart from it." The warforged's shining eyes searched the mists for something the others could not see.

"The sky is turning blue again," Seren said, looking to the eastern horizon.

"We're very close to the far border of the Mournland," Omax answered. He sounded grateful for the change in subject. "The mists part not far beyond Metrol, taking us back into the Talenta Plains."

There was a flap of wings from above, and Blizzard landed on the deck, depositing his exhilarated rider beside them. Gerith's hair was a wild mess and he grinned broadly as he snatched his goggles away. He spoke excitedly, the words a tangled, unintelligible mess.

"Master Snowshale, we can't understand a single word," Pherris said, looking at the gnome suspiciously. "Try that again, but breathe this time."

"This . . . place . . . is . . . wonderful!" he exclaimed, clapping his hands together excitedly. "So many strange things to see!" His excitement died off quickly when he caught sight of Dalan emerging from his cabin, looking down with disapproval.

"I'm glad the corpse of my homeland provides you with such amusement, Gerith," Dalan said dourly.

"I mean it's wonderful except for all the tragedy and everything," Gerith amended quickly. "It truly is an amazing place, like nothing else I've ever seen!"

"And we can be thankful for that," Dalan said. "Report."

"Metrol is just a few miles ahead," Gerith said. "At least I'm guessing it's Metrol, from the size of it. It's amazing. Buildings are rooted up and stacked on one another like blocks. Streets just go right up into the sky and . . ." The halfling gestured, stacking his hands one each other erratically to attempt to describe what he had seen. "And they just stop! It's like something out of a dream. And there's magic in the streets."

"How poetic," Dalan said, arching an eyebrow.

"No, I mean literally magic," Gerith said, still gesticulating violently. "Clouds of it, just wandering. Like the lightning and fire from one of Tristam's wands had just got up and walked away."

"Living spells," Tristam said. "I've heard of those. They carry just a fragment of the intellect that created them. The Mournland gives them enough power to sustain themselves indefinitely. They wander around, just following their caster's last command."

"Last command?" Ijaac asked.

"Generally, 'Destroy anything in your way,' " Tristam said.

"Ah," the dwarf said. "Let's not get in their way, then. Simple enough."

"Did you see anything else, Master Snowshale?" Pherris asked. "Airborne dangers would be of particular interest."

Gerith considered the question for several moments. "No, even the living spells seemed pretty landlocked," he said. "As long as we stay above of that cloud of ghosts, we should be safe enough."

"I beg your pardon, Master Snowshale?" Pherris asked. "What cloud of ghosts do you mean?"

Gerith looked worried. "You didn't notice them?" he pointed.

"By the Host," Ijaac swore.

Tristam looked down at the ground again. What he had mistaken as mists swirling in the ship's wake had drawn closer. It resolved itself as a swarm of shadowy faces, mouths parted in anguish. They swam through the air beneath them, pursuing them. He could hear their cry now, a shrill, piercing noise that made his hands tremble. They soared just above the ground, clawing at nothing, desperate to reach the airship far above.

"Undead," Dalan observed bleakly. "We picked a fine time to leave our paladin behind."

"Isn't it always the way?" Ijaac grumbled. He stomped off toward the cargo bay. "Let me go get my morningstar."

Tristam watched the cloud of spirits keep pace with the airship for several moments. "They're faster than us," he said, "but I don't think they can fly any higher than that. We're safe up here, but we won't be able to land with them chasing."

Gerith loaded his crossbow and loosed a bolt into the pursuing spirits. The missile passed harmlessly through the ghosts and disappeared into the mist.

"They're ghosts, Gerith," Dalan said.

"Worth a try," the halfling answered.

"Aeven!" Pherris called.

The dryad appeared at the ship's rail, one arm curled around the throat of her figurehead as she stared out into the sky. Her eyes were closed as her blonde hair swept over her face.

"Can you distract the ghosts with a storm?" Pherris asked.

"I call the winds, but they do not answer," she said. "The winds are dead. This land is dead."

Pherris's face grew pale. "You've never said that before, Aeven."

"I have never seen it before," she said. "I want to leave this place."

"Soon," Pherris promised. "Can you still speak to the ship?"

"Yes," she said. "She wants to leave as well. She says that her sister is close by, and that she is in pain."

Tristam looked at Aeven hopefully. "The elemental can sense *Dying Sun*?"

Aeven nodded.

"Can she lead us there?" he asked.

Aeven looked at Tristam, her eyes narrow. "You have no comprehension of the danger, Tristam. This place should not be."

"I just need a little time, Aeven," Tristam said. "Tell the *Karia Naille* that I'm going to release the *Albena Tors*, like I did the *Kenshi Zhann*. All I need is for you to point out where she is when we fly over the city."

The dryad nodded her assent.

The ship soared higher as the city of Metrol appeared in the distance. It was as Gerith described—a bizarre amalgam of impossible architecture. Buildings stood at odd angles or uncanny heights. Some structures seemed to move as the eye studied them.

FLIGHT OF THE DYING SUN

As in the other cities they had seen, strange lights flickered within the buildings. The swarm of tormented spirits followed them even through the city, passing unimpeded through the outlying buildings below.

"There," Aeven said, pointing to a large building beside the river. "It is there."

"Perfect," Tristam said. "Can you urge the elemental to give us a burst of speed when I call for it?"

"Yes," Aeven said. "But be swift, Tristam. This place holds death." The dryad's tone held the faintest hint of threat.

"Thank you," Tristam said, frowning apologetically. "I'm sorry we have to do this, but it is necessary."

"Nature understands necessary," she replied, "but there is nothing natural here." She stared forlornly down at the black river.

"What is your plan, Tristam?" Omax asked.

"We need weapons," he whispered, an idea forming in his head. "Gerith, circle around and pass near that building again."

"Weapons!" Ijaac said happily. "That much I understand." The dwarf hefted himself onto the deck, strapping on his armor. His shining morningstar was slung over one shoulder. He tossed Tristam a short blade. "Picked that up in Stormhome because I liked the balance of it, but then I noticed you lost your sword."

Tristam turned the sword experimentally and strapped it to his belt, nodding at Ijaac in thanks.

"Weapons don't hurt them, Tristam," Gerith said. "They're just smoke."

"I can change that," Tristam said. "Give me your bolt case, Gerith."

The halfling obediently removed the pouch from his hip and offered the ammunition to Tristam. Tristam's voice rose in a low chant, infusing the missiles with shimmering energy as he brushed one finger over their fletchings. The pouch glowed briefly, and he handed it back to the halfling.

"Try again," he said.

The halfling loaded and loosed. This time the bolt struck true, lodging in one of the spectral faces and eliciting a pained cry. A sparkle of ghostly white energy trickled from the wounded spirit as it evaporated into mist.

"Seren, your dagger," Tristam said. "Omax, hold out your hands. Ijaac . . ."

"Already magic, Tristam," the dwarf said, hefting his morningstar. "But thanks."

Tristam cast more infusions, granting a glowing sheen to Seren's dagger and Omax's adamantine hands. Dalan took his cue and quickly retreated to his cabin, sealing the door behind him so he wouldn't get in the way of combat.

"Pherris, take us as close to the river as you can," he said, climbing down into the hold. "Everyone, come with me."

"Be careful," Pherris called out.

Tristam hurried below deck, opening the cargo hold. The dark waters of the Cyre River flowed beneath them. The spirits continued their pursuit, boiling over the river as easily as they followed across the land.

"Now, Aeven!" Tristam shouted. "Gerith, take us as low as you dare and pull back up in twenty seconds!"

A jolt shot through *Karia Naille* as the ship surged forward. Aeven's rapport with the ship's elemental carried them forward at tremendous speed. The river grew closer, the waters churned an ugly black.

"We're going to jump into that?" Seren asked. "Are you sure that's even water?"

"See you on the ground," Gerith said, climbing back up the ladder. "I have a glidewing. I'm flying down."

"No more time to argue," Tristam said. "Go!"

Tristam leapt. For an instant he was weightless, the dead mists swirling around his body. Then the cold surface of the river struck him hard, blasting the air from his body. He tried to swim but was too dazed by the landing. His mouth filled with a putrid, oily flavor. His vision flickered as the waters swallowed him.

Then a metal hand clamped the collar coat and pulled hard, dragging him from the water. Tristam gasped and coughed, spitting the polluted water on the ground. Omax deposited Seren on the beach beside him, turned, and walked back into the river. Above them, *Karia Naille*'s flaming blue ring ascended back into the sky.

"Seren, are you all right?" Tristam asked desperately.

"That wasn't one of your smarter ideas," she said, wiping her mouth on the sleeve of her leather jerkin.

Omax emerged from the water again, hauling the gasping figure of Ijaac Bruenhail by one arm. Blizzard alighted nimbly next to them. Gerith rolled out of the saddle and looked at his drenched comrades for a long, worried moment. Then he burst out laughing.

"Have some sympathy, Snowshale," Ijaac said. He groaned as Omax dropped him with a wet clank. "That was the most disgusting thing I've ever tasted. And I've eaten some strange things in my time."

"Like what?" Gerith asked, instantly curious.

"You really don't want to know," the dwarf said.

"Yes, I do!" the halfling protested.

"This isn't the time," Tristam said, pointing at the advancing cloud of ghosts. Their wailing cries grew closer. "Get ready."

The ghosts swarmed around them, unleashing an unholy shriek as they surrounded their living prey. Gerith fumbled with his crossbow, bolts spilling onto the ground. Seren staggered, stabbing wildly at nothing. Omax simply froze, staring at his own trembling hands. Ijaac screamed—a raw and painful noise. The sound of the screeching ghosts seeped into Tristam's mind as well, twisting his emotions, filling his mind with dread.

He saw the prophecy's visions again. He saw the mortal nations crumble. This time it was different. This time he saw Marth's face among the fallen. The city of Wroat lay in ruins. He saw *Karia Naille*'s elemental ring flicker and die as the ship plummeted into the Howling River. Tristam stood among the ruins of the city, eyes cold and passionless as he surveyed what he had wrought.

"No!" he screamed. He clawed through the fear, ripping the wand from his belt and unleashing its lightning in a savage arc. The ghosts shrieked and recoiled. Tristam's magic tore at their ethereal forms. Several unraveled completely, tendrils of ectoplasm bleeding away into nothing. Only a few of the spirits remained, now glaring warily at Tristam.

The others snapped out of their fear, invigorated by Tristam's sudden recovery. Omax clapped his metal hands over one swirling ghostly face, clenching metal fingers in an explosion of mist. Seren and Ijaac slashed the air with their weapons as well. The ghosts shrieked and withdrew, melting into the ground, their cries fading into nothing.

"Are they gone?" Ijaac asked uncertainly.

"For now," Tristam said, breaking into a run. "Let's find *Dying Sun* and be done with this place."

They ran along the river bank, feet crunching on the gravel in eerie silence. There was no other noise save their breath and the eerie hum of the giant conductor stones that lined the riverbank. The building ahead was in remarkably good condition, a large public structure of some variety. As they approached, Tristam could see a sign hanging above the wide doors.

> House Orien Rail Substation
> Servicing Cyre and the lands beyond
> Five Nations
> One Rail

Tristam stared at the sign in momentary surprise. Metrol had once been the heart of Cyre's extensive rail system. The loss of the city's rail stations had been one of the major barriers to House

FLIGHT OF THE DYING SUN

Orien's attempts to get the lightning rail operational again. Numerous exploration parties had been dispatched to the Metrol ruins in hopes of finding the main station and its substations. All had returned without success—or not returned at all. That they had found one of the substations so easily filled him with a sense of unease.

"What is it, Tristam?" Omax asked, looking at him with concern.

"Nothing," Tristam said. "Still shaking off the effects of those spirits, I guess." He hated himself for the lie.

An explosion resounded from around the corner of the building. Tristam ducked behind the foundation of a large conductor stone, gesturing for the others to follow. A seething mass of red flame oozed around the corner of the building. It spread over the street, leaving sizzling cobblestones in its wake. Tendrils of swaying fire tasted the air like antennae. It rolled aimlessly, pausing in front of the rail station doors, waiting.

"That's one of the things I told you about, Tristam," Gerith whispered. "The living spells."

Tristam gestured for the halfling to be quiet. The fireball bumped against the doors of the rail station. The field of pure white energy flickered over the doors. The spell forced itself against the doors a second time, but the shield held. A pinpoint of brighter energy pulsed deep within the flaming mass. It unleashed violent gouts of flame in an explosive display. The shield shuddered as white energy crackled around the entire substation. Tristam flinched, ducking back behind the corner of the conductor stone. The living spell shrieked and rolled away from the door, veins of white magic tearing through its form. It tumbled aimlessly away from the building, roaring in mindless agony.

"The door is warded," Seren said.

"But who warded it?" Tristam asked, running quickly toward the station doors. He whispered softly as he traced one hand around door frame. A web of magical energy came to life, surrounding the door. He could see similar shields covering the rest of the building as far as he could see.

"It's not just this door," he said in amazement. "Every door. Every window. There's no way to get inside without triggering the shields."

"Can you dispel them?" Seren asked.

"I don't know," he said. He leaned close to the door handles, studying the protective weave of energy. "It's very powerful and complex. I've rarely seen anything like this. If I hadn't seen that living spell get repelled, I wouldn't even be able to say for sure what the ward does."

"Old Orien wards?" Omax asked.

"Doubtful," Tristam said. "The Orien wouldn't waste this kind of magic locking up a public building. This looks recent and well maintained."

"Someone is inside," Seren said.

"Marth?" Ijaac asked.

"This doesn't look like Marth's magic," Tristam said. "It's difficult to explain but it's too . . . orderly."

"If anyone's in there, they've either been in there for a while or there's another exit," Gerith said. "The only tracks I see other than our own are the burn marks that spell left."

"Then at least we got here before Marth did," Tristam said. "Everyone get back a bit. I don't want you to be close if something goes wrong opening these doors."

The others nodded and backed away, though Seren hesitated. She kissed his cheek impulsively and wished him luck before withdrawing. He gave her an encouraging smile and returned his attention to the door.

Judging from the way the ward had reacted to the living spell, Tristam knew that the magic was only dangerous if he attempted to force entry. Touching the building would do no harm. He removed his gloves and placed them on the surface of the door, hoping to get a better feel for the enchantment before attempting to remove it.

FLIGHT OF THE DYING SUN

The magical field immediately faded and the doors parted with a metal click.

"Wow, that was fast, Tristam," Gerith said. He clapped his little hands, greatly impressed.

"I didn't even do anything," Tristam said, replacing his gloves and looking back at them in bewilderment. "It just opened."

"Good enough for me," Ijaac said, stomping past him and holding out his morningstar to light the way. "Let's see what we've found."

Tristam followed the dwarf inside. A small vestibule opened into a large, grand chamber. As it happened, the dwarf's light was unnecessary. Enchanted stones shone in the torch sconces, casting a radiance that reflected in the stained glass dome that served as a roof. The floor was covered in shining marble tile, as clean and flawless as if the Day of Mourning had never been. Velvet ropes marked the course intended for prospective passengers. Tristam gasped as a group of travelers walked directly toward them and passed through like phantoms, oblivious to their presence.

The walls on each side of the station had once been exposed to the open air, but were now blocked by thick gates of sculpted iron. Three lines of conductor stones passed through the chamber, entering through the east gate and departing through the west. Three silver coaches stood ready, hovering several feet above the rail. A shimmering circle of lightning encircled the head of each coach and sparked through the stones mounted on the base of the vehicle.

"An illusion," Tristam said, putting his hand through a passing phantom.

The vision of the rail station flickered and faded, replaced by the reality of an empty, discarded ruin. The floor was littered with corpses, untouched by decay due to the bizarre magic that suffused this place. There were no living people, no light save the twilight glow that filtered through the shattered skylight. One of the lightning coaches still hovered over the tracks, the stones beneath it still crackling with faint. The second coach had fallen from the stone rail and now lay crippled on its side. The third was a demolished heap, having surrendered to years of neglect and corrosion. At the far side of the enormous chamber, the massive bulk of an airship lay among the ruins of the rail station. Its elemental ring was long doused. Tristam recognized it immediately.

"*Dying Sun*," the artificer whispered, awed that it was still intact.

The illusion of the living rail station resumed, phantom travelers passing through them in each direction. Gerith moved out of their path, his glidewing hopping nervously beside him.

"How did the *Sun* get here?" Seren asked, staring at the ship in wonder. "What is this place?"

"Doesn't look like she crashed," Tristam said, studying the ship as illusion and reality alternated before his eyes. "Her structure seems to be in good condition."

"Ashrem built his ships to last," Omax said, impressed.

"Who speaks my name?" asked a hollow voice from the shadows of a ticket booth.

Tristam drew his wand immediately, and whirled to face the voice. A tall man stepped out of the darkness, his limbs crackling with a nimbus of shimmering magic. Tristam's wand tumbled from his numb fingers and bounced noisily on the marble floor.

"Who is that?" Ijaac asked, looking at Tristam urgently. "Friend or foe?"

Tristam could not speak, so it was Omax that answered.

"That is Ashrem d'Cannith," the warforged said.

"No," Tristam said, collecting his wits and stepping toward the spectral figure. "It's not."

"A ghost?" Gerith asked, drawing his crossbow.

"I hate ghosts," Ijaac grumbled. "Always coming back from the dead and complicating things."

"It's not a ghost," Tristam said. He snatched up his wand and circled the figure of Ashrem, looking at it curiously. "Not exactly."

FLIGHT OF THE DYING SUN

Ashrem looked back at Tristam, his expression calm. Tristam put his hand through Ashrem's chest. A burst of sparking orange light surrounded his fingers. Ashrem looked down at the arm piercing his body, unconcerned. The phantom extended his own hand toward Tristam. His arm dissipated in a swirling cloud of energy as it touched the artificer's chest.

"Pure magic," Ashrem said. "Wild magic. I am a memory of what was, like the figments in this train station." Ashrem gestured at the bustling crowd around them. "I am an echo of Ashrem d'Cannith. I am a memory of who he was on the Day of Mourning."

"Like the living spells outside," Seren said. "Carrying out their last command forever."

"Precisely," Ashrem said. The phantom smiled.

Tristam drew his hand back, staring at his fingertips as motes of light danced around them. "A figment that knows it's real?" Tristam said, amazed. "Are these others aware as well?"

"No," Ashrem said. He pulled his hand away from Tristam. It instantly reformed as it had been. The phantom looked at the tips of his fingers thoughtfully. "Unlike these others, I retain enough of Ashrem's logic and arcane knowledge to recognize what I am and accept it. I am a magical construct, formed from rampant energies of illusion and abjuration, fused in this phantasmal form. Trapped here, knowing that I cannot exist beyond the magical phenomenon that has suffused this station, has been difficult. My memories are complete in many ways, but fragmented and bare in others. Ashrem d'Cannith's strength of character has given me the strength to abide, but I am not . . . real. I must say that it is good to meet you at last, Tristam."

"An abjuration," Tristam said. "So you're you the one that warded the station?"

"I am," Ashrem said. "I keep out the living spells, mournful undead, and curious grave robbers. My purpose is to fulfill Ashrem d'Cannith's will."

"So Ashrem d'Cannith is dead?" Omax asked gravely.

"Truth be told, I don't know," the phantom admitted, surprised by the question. "I don't remember dying. I remember *Albena Tors* crashing through the skylight. I remember Marth leaping down through the skylight, challenging me . . . demanding that I stop."

"Stop what?" Tristam asked.

"Stop the future," Ashrem said. "I came to stop the future." His gaze was unfocused as he remembered. His voice was distant. "I was told the Day of Mourning was approaching. The War would end. All that I needed to do was stand aside, do nothing . . . but Cyre would die."

"Told by who?" Tristam asked.

"Zamiel," Ashrem said. "Do not trust him, Tristam. Do not aid him."

"Aid him?" Tristam asked. "Why would I aid him?"

"He showed me a grand vision of the Draconic Prophecy," Ashrem said. "A mortal conqueror brought everlasting peace through use of the Legacy. In my arrogance I thought I could rise above the darker visions of the prophecy—but fate would not be denied. I tried to step away from the conqueror's destiny. I dismantled the Legacy and tried to turn my back on Zamiel. This was his vengeance. Those who will not abide by the Prophecy's demands will be ground beneath it."

"What does Marth have to do with this?" Tristam asked, looking at *Dying Sun*'s dark hulk. "Why did he follow you to Cyre?"

"For Kiris," Ashrem said. "Marth loved her. She wished to stand beside me, even at the end."

"Then why did you come here if you knew that Cyre would die?" Tristam demanded.

"I do not know," Ashrem said. "There is not enough of Ashrem left within me to remember that. Perhaps I had some plan to stop the Day of Mourning and it failed? Perhaps I had no plan and wished only to die beside my countrymen? Perhaps the true Ashrem lives and his true plan has yet to unfold."

FLIGHT OF THE DYING SUN

"What is your purpose?" Tristam pressed. "You say you exist to fulfill Ashrem's will, but you didn't say what that will was."

"To protect *Dying Sun* until the heir of Ash arrives," the figment said. "I was waiting for you, Tristam."

"Me?" Tristam said, shocked. "But Ashrem cast me out. Why would he want me to have his ship?"

"I cannot say," the vision said. "I know only that he thought of you often. As the mists swallowed Cyre, he thought of you. The last thing I remember before I became what I am is the certainty that you would put things right."

Tristam looked at the corner of the rail station. The illusions flickered again, revealing the shadowed mass of *Dying Sun*. The ship was constructed much differently from the *Mourning Dawn*. Only two struts supported the elemental ring, projecting from the sides. This granted the ship greater durability but less maneuverability. It also meant that the ship had survived all of these years sitting on its hull without snapping her struts. If the elemental was still bound to the ship's core, *Dying Sun* might well fly again. Possibilities formed in Tristam's head. He knew how durable Ashrem's airships were, how a skilled artificer could restore them from even the most grievous damage. What if he could repair the *Sun*? Tristam could have a ship of his own, a vessel that could fly free of Dalan's manipulations and machinations.

"Tristam?" Seren asked. She looked at him, worried. "Tristam, say something."

"I'm sorry, Ashrem," Tristam said, shaking his head to clear it. "I didn't come to claim *Dying Sun*. I came to destroy her so that the Legacy will never be completed."

Ashrem frowned. "Stopping Zamiel's plans is not so easy, Tristam," the figment said. "If destroying *Dying Sun* would avert the prophecy, Ashrem would have done so himself. The *Sun* was profoundly changed when Ashrem mingled her energies with the Dragon's Eye. You should not destroy her. She can help you find the truth."

"How?" Tristam demanded. "What are you talking about?"

"The elemental that sleeps within the ship," Ashrem's vision said. "It speaks to me, Tristam. There are other sources of power, like the Dragon's Eye. It can sense them. It can lead you to them. If you truly wish to end the threat the Legacy represents, then they, too, must be extinguished."

The illusory station flickered and vanished again, leaving them in darkness. Tristam scowled at the phantom in silent frustration.

"What do we do, Tristam?" Gerith asked in a quiet voice. "Are we still destroying the ship?"

"No," Tristam said. "Take Blizzard and go back to the *Karia Naille*. Tell Pherris to keep a safe altitude and wait there. And bring me my tools."

Chapter
Twenty-Six

The Vathirond dock officials were taking their time, checking each traveler's documentation one by one. Eraina and Zed had been waiting patiently in the line to board the ferry for nearly an hour. Ahead of them in line, a fat man struggled vainly to keep his two bored little boys from fighting over a bag of candy. Behind them, a happy woman clutched what appeared to be a wicker cage containing a live chicken. Zed had spent his idle time studying each of the other passengers. Without speaking a word to any of them he knew where each of them had come from and where each was headed. He was bored and mildly disappointed that nothing would surprise him on this trip.

"Something is bothering you," Eraina said, interrupting his daydreaming.

Zed looked at Eraina, trying to keep his face as blank as he could. "Why do you say that?" he said, glancing back at the front of the line.

"You haven't complained the entire time we've been here," she said. "Not even about this interminable wait. That's peculiar for you. What's more, you haven't contaminated the air with that foul pipeweed since we landed."

"Black Pit Blend isn't foul," he countered. "It's downright terrible. It's the worst tobacco in all of Khorvaire."

"Then why do you smoke it?" she asked.

Zed shrugged, shifting his shoulders in his baggy cloak. "I'm trying to quit smoking," he said. "I figured if I made the experience as unpleasant as possible, it'd be easier to stop. Hasn't worked out so far."

"Amusing," Eraina said with a faint grin. "Your attempt to change the subject has been noted, Arthen."

"I'm not trying to change the subject," Zed replied. "You asked me why I smoke." He looked around carefully, trying not to meet her eyes.

"You know I can tell when you lie," she said. "You should just try not answering the question. It works much better for you."

"Looks like we're up," Zed said as the guards waved them forward.

Eraina sighed in irritation and stepped forward.

"State your name and business," a bored guard asked.

"Sentinel Marshal Eraina d'Deneith," she said, displaying her badge and papers. "I am traveling to Nathyrr on official business on behalf of my house."

The guard glanced at her papers for a moment, then waved her through, gesturing to Zed. "State your name and business," he said.

Zed handed the man a crumpled sheaf of papers. The guard looked at the documents curiously and handed them back.

"What's the reason for this trip, Master Arthen?" the guard asked.

"Don't give me any trouble, boy," Zed growled. "I just need to go home."

The guard frowned and looked at his older partner. The other guard's expression shifted from bored to irritated.

"It's no trouble, Master Arthen," the other guard said. "If you don't want to answer our questions, you can wait until you're feeling more agreeable and get back in line. Next."

"Just a damned second," Arthen said. "I'm not getting in the back of that line again."

FLIGHT OF THE DYING SUN

The younger guard's hand moved to his sword. Zed gave the boy an appraising look and smiled dangerously.

"This man is my deputy," Eraina said, glaring at Zed as she stepped back through the guard post. "Forgive the idiot glee he takes in making others' lives difficult. He is from Thrane. They breed their asses stubborn there."

The guards nodded in understanding and waved Zed through.

Zed blinked in amazement. "Did you just say what I thought you said?" he asked as he followed her onto the ferry.

"I called you nothing less than you deserved," she said, descending the stairs to the boat's passenger cabins. "Those guards were only doing their job, and we have no reason to call attention to ourselves."

"Oh, no, I'm not arguing with that," he said. He glanced in one of the cabins and, finding it empty, stepped inside and sat down. She sat down across from him. "I'm just a little amazed that you lied."

"Lied?" Eraina asked, sounding a bit offended. "I do not lie."

"You told those men that I was your deputy," he said.

"It is within the power of a Sentinel Marshal, in time of crisis, to deputize worthy men-at-arms to aid her, both in the investigation of a crime and in the arrest of a dangerous suspect," she said. "As you are already aiding me in just such a task, you may consider yourself deputized, Arthen."

Zed scratched his chin and stared out the window at the water, his expression bemused.

"Are you formulating another lecture warning me of the dangers of splitting hairs, or other such nonsense?" she asked.

"No," he said. "I was going to compliment your flexibility. I find it refreshing. You're an intriguing woman, Eraina."

Eraina lifted one eyebrow and laughed. "Are you flirting with me, Arthen?" she asked.

"No," he said.

"Have you forgotten *again* how adept I am at sensing lies?" she asked. She removed the metal clip from her hair, letting her blonde locks fall from their tightly coiled braid.

"You are?" he asked. He blinked at her, feigning innocence. "I didn't know. And you should wear your hair down more often."

"It gets in the way when I fight," she said.

"Then cut it off," Zed said.

"I can't bring myself to," she said with a small smile. "Can I be allowed that one vanity?"

"I think Boldrei will forgive you," he said.

"You need to speak to women more often, Zed," she said primly. "If you think you're being charming, you're quite terrible at it." She propped her spear against the door and crossed her legs as she leaned back in her seat. "Remember that, as you are my deputy, I shall toss you over the side of this boat if you try to cause trouble with the guards again."

"Duly noted," he said with a grin. "I never had the chance to say I was sorry, by the way."

"For what?" she asked, laughing in surprise.

"For hitting you in the jaw back in Cragwar," he said.

"Oh yes," she said, eyes narrowing. "You clubbed me over the head, too."

"I know," he said. "Things were getting pretty heated. I just wanted to stop the situation from getting worse."

"So you tried to beat me unconscious," she said.

"Tristam's a good man, but he can be high strung, especially where his mission to recover Ashrem's work is concerned," Zed said. "Are you telling me you didn't notice him reaching for his wand when you started threatening to stop us?"

"I didn't," she said. "I thought him harmless at the time."

"He probably doesn't even remember," Zed said. "Anyway, I just wanted to apologize. I was just trying to help."

"There is no need," she said. "Don't you remember? You said sorry when you hit me the second time."

"I did?" he asked.

She nodded.

"You remember that?" he said.

She nodded again.

"Even after being knocked out?" he asked.

"You never knocked me out, Arthen," she said. "I let you think you won."

Zed looked at her in blank surprise then smiled a little. "Isn't that a bit like lying?"

"I considered it a strategic retreat," she said. "If you wish to believe you can defeat a Spear of Boldrei in two blows—that is your own stupidity."

Zed cackled. He looked out the window again, but his grin faded as he stared at the receding Vathirond cityscape.

"I know you are a private, stubborn, arrogant, introverted, antisocial, dreadful man," Eraina said, "but if you wish to talk about what's bothering you, I promise to listen."

"Flatterer," Zed said. His frown broke slightly as he looked back at her.

"You've been to Vathirond before," she said.

Zed nodded. "Long time ago," he said. "When I still served the Flame."

"So you really were a paladin, then," Eraina said.

"You already knew that," Zed said, his gray eyes boring into hers.

"And this is where you fell," she said. It was not a question.

"Therese Kalaven was my commanding officer," he said. "She was everything I thought a champion of the Silver Flame should be. Bold. Beautiful. Totally fearless. I would have followed her anywhere." Zed laughed bitterly. "I was a stupid boy back then."

"You loved her," Eraina said.

"I thought I did," Zed said. "Looking back, I think my motivations were a little more . . ." He smirked. "Basic. She reciprocated, which of course only made me all the more willing to follow her."

"Most paladins take vows of chastity for a reason, Arthen," Eraina said. "Relationships like that are doomed from the start."

"Trust me, Eraina, I've heard it all before," Zed said, drumming his fingers on the arm of his chair. "We were assigned to Thrane's front lines. Our squad had a reputation for speed, efficiency, and brutality. Therese was a brilliant commander, if totally ruthless."

Zed took a deep breath as he remembered. Eraina watched him quietly, her eyes sympathetic.

"I was blind, Eraina. I never saw what she was becoming. What we all were becoming. Therese would have rationalized any violence, any atrocity, in the name of the Silver Flame. We were dispatched to Vathirond. We were supposed to ally with the Brelish, help them wipe out some Cyran forces that had been harassing their borders. When we got to Vathirond, we found the Brelish defenses had been sabotaged. They were totally defenseless."

"The Battle of Vathirond," Eraina said. "I've heard of it. So Therese saw an easier target and chose to ally with the Cyrans instead?"

"That's not all," Zed replied. "Therese burned the temples of the Sovereign Host, convinced the priests were using their congregation to spy on Thrane over the border. She commanded us to show no mercy." Zed scowled. "I watched my brothers and sisters, Champions of the Flame, do terrible things. I saw two soldiers drag a priestess out of a burning temple into an alley. I don't know what they planned to do to her. Everything blurred. I killed them both. The girl screamed and ran for her life. I don't even know if she survived the siege. When I gathered my senses again, I couldn't hear the Flame's voice anymore."

"What did you do?" Eraina asked.

"What could I do?" Zed said. "I'd killed my fellow soldiers, but I wasn't about to turn myself in for doing the right thing. I ran. I left Vathirond behind. I figured the deeper I ran into Breland, the less chance there'd be that Therese would find me." He snickered. "Or maybe I was running from the Flame. I don't know. But any god that would strip one of its champions for saving an innocent girl is a god I'm better off without."

"Perhaps your god didn't punish you for saving that girl," Eraina asked. "Perhaps it punished you for waiting so long to do the right thing."

Zed looked out the window again. "I've wondered about that," he said in a low voice. "Would it hurt so much for the Flame to tell me what I did wrong?"

"Didn't it?" she said.

"No," Zed said, exasperated. "In fact, it didn't. It let me kill my friends, disgrace my family, and stagger off to hide in a bottle for six years. The Silver Flame gave up on me, Eraina, so I gave up on myself."

Eraina said nothing for a long time. She watched Zed sadly. He couldn't bring himself to look at her.

"What did you do next?" she asked.

"I realized I would need money to keep paying for the alcohol," Zed said. "I discovered I was good at noticing things other people missed, remembering details everyone else forgot, and my military training didn't hurt, either. I lived under an alias in Sharn, working as an inquisitive. I fell."

"But you rose again," Eraina said. "You may not be a paladin, but neither are you an anonymous drunkard. What happened?"

Zed chuckled. "Would you believe I have Dalan to thank for that?"

"Dalan d'Cannith?" Eraina was genuinely surprised.

"Dalan hired me to recover some stolen Cannith prototypes that had made their way to Sharn," he said. "While on the job, I saved his life from a hobgoblin assassin. I didn't think any more of it, but Dalan didn't forget. Say what you will about him, but he's a man who repays his debts."

"What did he do?" she asked.

"I got a letter from him four months later," Zed said. "It contained details regarding Commander Therese Kalaven's trial and execution by the church inquisitors for assorted war crimes. The warrant for my own arrest had been repealed, and I had been issued a full pardon and formal apology from the Voice of the Flame herself. Dalan had dug it all up, brought it all to light. He even arranged an invitation to return to my post in Flamekeep whenever I wished."

"But you never went," Eraina said.

"No," Zed said. "I'm still not convinced that any gods are really watching over us, but Dalan convinced me that people can watch out for each other. If even a man like *Dalan* can put a wrong thing right, then I have no excuse to hide from evil." He looked at her, his gaze clear and strong now. "So that's what I do now. I help people, however I can. Actually, trying to do the right thing gave me the focus I needed to stop drinking." He smirked. "I'm still working on quitting smoking."

"I think you are right, Arthen," Eraina said. "The Flame never watched over you."

"Angling to convert me to the Host, Eraina?" he asked. "Never had you pegged as an evangelist."

"That isn't what I mean," she said. "Aren't you the one who always touts the value of redemption? Yet you deny your own redemption, deny any possibility of returning to your role as champion."

"You don't have to be an artist to like a painting, Eraina," Zed said.

"You're a good man, Arthen," Eraina said. "The Flame never watched you because it knew you could watch yourself. You were chosen as a paladin because you did not need protection. You had the strength to protect others—and you still do."

"Then why can't I call on a paladin's holy magic anymore?" Zed asked. "Why can't I hear the Flame's voice?"

"Because you are not listening," Eraina said. "You are a man of unshakable faith, Arthen, but you have turned that faith inward. You listen only to yourself."

He looked into her eyes for a long moment, wondering, wanting to believe. Then the moment was over. His weathered face creased in a bitter sneer. He folded his arms across his chest and sat back in his chair, tucking his chin against his chest.

"I think I'm done talking about religion for one day, Eraina," he said. "Wake me up when we reach Nathyrr."

Chapter
Twenty-Seven

Dying Sun was larger than *Karia Naille,* but still much smaller than most airships. She was painted brilliant red and was far more ornately appointed than her sister ship. The entire vessel, from the railing to the ring struts, was covered in decorative pictograms. A delicate lance of pure crystal extended from the bow of the ship, a smaller version of the devastating lightning rod that *Seventh Moon* had so often used against them. As Seren stood beside the airship and ran one hand along her sleek hull, she imagined how beautiful *Dying Sun* must have been. It was no surprise that Tristam could not bring himself to destroy such a wondrous creation.

She just hoped he was making the right choice.

Deep inside the ship, Seren could hear low chanting and rhythmic hammering. Tristam worked to restore life to the *Sun*. She worried about him. The more he worked on the crippled airship, the less he spoke. Today he had only emerged to eat, smile faintly at her, and disappear back into the ship's core. For two days they had been here. Gerith appeared occasionally, delivering food and water from *Karia Naille,* but they were otherwise on their own.

Ijaac and Omax were outside again, shoveling the last heaps of dirt and stone atop the mass grave they had dug for the bodies in the rail station. It seemed almost a futile act, burying a few corpses in a city of the dead. When Seren asked why they insisted, Omax only shrugged and replied that he felt he must do something. Some of the *Sun*'s crew had been the warforged's friends, years ago. Ijaac was far more pragmatic in his motivation. In a place like this, it was just better to bury the dead before they got back up and started causing trouble. Seren had helped them dig until she was exhausted, but she could not keep up for long. She was not a frail girl, but could only match the pace of a dwarf and a warforged for so long. The door of the station opened and Ijaac staggered in with a tired sigh. The dwarf's thin white hair was streaked with sweat. His pale skin was flushed with exhaustion. Outside, Omax's digging continued with the same rhythm he had maintained for the last several hours.

"Almost done," Ijaac said with a pleased smile. He ambled over to Seren, pausing to glance at something in his hand. The dwarf looked at her soberly, his cheerful demeanor fading. "I found this on one of the bodies. You may want to give this to Pherris."

He handed her a small golden badge. She held it in her palm, studying the design. It looked like a military insignia, sculpted in the shape of an open wing. Though she didn't speak or read the language of the gnomes, she recognized the family name inscribed upon it.

"Haimel Gerriman," she read.

"I flew with him to the Frostfell," Ijaac said. "He was a good lad. He deserved better than this. His father should know what happened to him. If I were a betting dwarf, I'd wager finding out what happened to Haimel was one of the reasons Pherris got wrapped up in this." Ijaac smiled ruefully. "I think he'll take the news better from you, Seren. You're prettier than I am."

"How do I tell Pherris his son is dead?" Seren asked, tucking the pin in her pocket.

"I don't know, Seren," Ijaac said, shrugging uncomfortably. "If it helps, I think Pherris already knows. He just needs proof. He'll sleep easier, knowing what happened."

"I have no sons," Ashrem's shade said sadly. "My only legacy is a prophecy that should never have been revealed." He stared into his hand, watching as the fingers faded from view and resolved themselves once again. "My heirs believe I have forsaken them." He laughed, an almost hysterical sound. "I have no legacy. There is only ash."

Ijaac looked at the figment cautiously, then back at Seren. "That thing's beginning to get on my nerves," he said. "It's been getting more disjointed and weird since we got here, mumbling on about nothing to no one in particular."

"The phantom has almost fulfilled its purpose," Tristam said, appearing at the railing above them. The artificer tugged his goggles down to hang around his neck. "The magic that binds it is beginning to lose cohesion as I get closer to repairing the *Sun*. I wish I could find a way to stabilize it. Having Ashrem's wisdom would be a great help, even as fragmented as it is."

"Let it die, Tristam," Ijaac said. "That isn't really Ashrem. It shouldn't exist. You shouldn't listen to it. The Mournland creates things like that to drive people insane."

Tristam said nothing. He stared at the illusion of his mentor, his face unreadable.

"How's your work coming, Tristam?" Seren asked.

"Good," Tristam said, breaking into an excited smile. "I think the *Sun* could fly right now if we needed her to. She just needs more fine tuning to make sure she'll stay in the air long enough to reach a city. A ship like this can fly with a single pilot for short periods, so I hope we can . . ."

A sharp pop and the sound of snapping metal came from outside. Seren jumped as white sparks scattered over the one of the windows.

"Those damn living spells are back again," Ijaac said, sighing as he drew his morningstar from his belt. "I'd best go give Omax a hand."

"Omax?" Tristam called out. "Are you hurt?"

The doors opened and Omax staggered inside. His eyes shone only dimly. A thin plume of smoke curled from his mouth. A jagged scar bisected his chest, glowing white hot.

"Tristam, flee!" the warforged said. Omax tore the doors from their hinges, hurling them at an unseen foe. A grunt of pain accompanied a burst of green flame, exploding in the doorway. Omax flew backward, crashing into a ticket booth and lying still.

Marth stepped into the doorway, walking with a pained limp. He wore his usual uniform, though his purple cloak was now ragged and torn. The amethyst wand was still smoking in his hand. Blood trickled from one corner of his mouth. He looked at them with dead white eyes and sliced the air with one hand. The invisible wards protecting the door flashed a sickening green color and shattered.

"Omax, you never did know when you were better off not fighting," Marth said.

"Khyber," Tristam swore, leaping down from the deck and drawing his wand. "How did Marth find us?"

"Find you?" Marth asked with a laugh. "I abandoned *Dying Sun* here. I knew exactly where to look for you."

Tristam pointed his wand at the changeling.

"Hold, Tristam," Marth said quickly, extending a pale hand. "I come alone. I do not wish to fight. Give me a chance to speak my piece, or I will end your warforged friend."

Tristam looked at Omax helplessly, then glared at Marth. "What do you want?" he demanded.

"A compromise," Marth said. "I am prepared to share the Legacy with you."

"What are you talking about?" Tristam demanded.

"I first suspected the truth when I saw *Karia Naille* escape Stormhome," Marth said. "I knew I was right when I learned what you did at Zul'nadn. When you escaped me in New Cyre, I knew you would come here next. Do your friends know what you are planning? Have you even admitted it to yourself?"

"Admitted what?" said. His voice was barely a growl.

"You are no fool, Tristam," Marth said. "If you have surmised, as I have, that Ashrem bound *Dying Sun*'s elemental core to the Dragon's Eye, then surely you must have realized the rest. *Karia Naille* shares the same power. Ashrem's airships were all fueled by the same energies that infused Zul'nadn. That is why the Legacy does not affect them. Ashrem's ships *are* the Legacy, though Ashrem has since rendered them unable to perform their original function."

Tristam said nothing.

"You do not truly wish to destroy the Legacy," Marth said with a dark chuckle. "You wish to complete it. Otherwise you would have destroyed the *Sun* already. You wanted to claim this ship, Ashrem's finest creation, for yourself."

"No," Tristam said, voice quavering.

Seren looked at Tristam, uncertain what to think. Tristam would not meet her eyes.

"You don't need to lie in front of your friends, Tristam," Marth said. "There is no need to be greedy, Tristam. We are both worthy heirs. Step aside and let me claim the *Sun*. Keep *Mourning Dawn*, and unlock its power for your own ends."

"What if I don't let you have this ship?" Tristam asked.

"This is not a negotiation, Tristam," Marth said. "This is a gift, to a man I once considered a friend. I once thought you intended to destroy the Legacy. Now that I see that you wish to embrace Ashrem's most glorious and terrible creation as much as I do, I offer you one last chance to get out of my way."

"No," Tristam said, his voice pained.

Marth sighed and aimed his wand at Tristam. "I don't have time to watch you wrestle with self-doubt, Xain. You had your chance."

Seren drew her dagger, still shimmering with the light of Tristam's enchantment. The changeling smirked, aiming his wand at her instead. A deadly blast of green fire rolled toward her, but this one stopped short, reflected by a shield of white sparks.

"Marth, stay your hand," Ashrem's visage said, stepping in front of her.

"Ashrem?" Marth cried. The changeling's jaw gaped. He stretched one hand toward his mentor, only to see Ashrem's image waver in a crackle of wild magic energy. "What sorcery is this?"

Seren seized on the distraction, leaping into the shadows behind a conductor stone just as the illusion of the living rail station reappeared. Ijaac followed, crouching beside her, hands tight on the haft of his morningstar. Tristam was nowhere to be seen, lost in the phantom crowd.

"Kresthian would be ashamed to see what you have become," Ashrem's phantom said sadly. "Your sons weep for their wretched father."

Marth sneered. "I will not be judged by a memory." He stabbed the wand into the image of Ashrem. The figment screamed as ripples of green fire spread through its form. The artificer's image unraveled into spiraling trails of dust, falling to its knees as its body scattered in a cloud of shimmering motes.

Marth scowled as he prowled across the station toward *Dying Sun*, unleashing a random burst of flame in his path as he went, trying to flush them out of hiding.

"You must have seen what I have seen, Tristam," Marth called. "You know what the future holds. Why won't you let me rebuild the world as it should be?"

Seren saw movement within the airship. It could only be Tristam. She darted from the darkness, hoping that Tristam was ready for what she planned. She ran past the bow of the ship, toward Omax's prone body. Marth unleashed another burst of fire at her, narrowly missing as she rolled to one side. The changeling strode after her, his pace calm and methodical, confident that she could not escape.

It was not until he lifted the wand to blast at her again that he heard the discordant whine of an elemental flaring to life. He looked over his shoulder at *Dying Sun*, and realized that the bow of the ship was pointed directly toward him, shining bright white. Seren leapt behind the cover of a thick column just as a bolt of searing blue lightning erupted from the airship's bow, tearing through Marth with the smell of burning ozone. The changeling's seared corpse fell to the earth with a crackle.

Seren's ears rang from the blast but she kept running until she reached Omax, kneeling by the wounded warforged's side. She had never seen him so badly damaged. A smoking crack bisected his chest. One eye shone only dimly; the other was dark. His jaw worked, but he made no sound. Tristam was already running toward them, his satchel of tools slung over one shoulder. Ijaac ran beside him, staring in wonder at the enormous gouge the *Dying Sun*'s lightning ray had torn through the floor.

"Omax, stay with me," Tristam whispered, kneeling by his friend. The artificer placed his hands on the injured warforged's chest, whispering the infusions that would bind the broken wood and metal. "Omax, talk to me. I'm here."

"You made me promise . . ." Omax whispered.

"Promise?" Tristam asked, leaning close. "Promise what?"

"To tell you the next time I needed repairs . . ." Omax said with a low chuckle. "I think . . . that time is now."

"That isn't funny, Omax," Tristam said. Under his hands, the warforged's body was already beginning to bend and twist back into shape. "You've been worse than this. Remember when I found you in the monastery?"

"I remember, Tristam," said Omax. "And I thank you, Tristam. I know who I am now." The warforged lay his head back on the rubble.

"Omax!" Seren cried. "Help him, Tristam!"

"I'm doing what I can," the artificer said frantically. "He's too badly hurt, and my magic is nearly exhausted from repairing the airship . . ."

Ijaac looked around quickly, the head of his morningstar cracking on the ground as his eyes widened in shock.

FLIGHT OF THE DYING SUN

"Where did the changeling go?" he asked.

Marth's corpse was gone.

"He just vanished," Ijaac said, stuttering slightly. "I was looking right at him."

Seren looked back at the airship just as a searing ring of red fire ignited around her, extending partially into the floor.

"Host!" Tristam swore. "The same trick I used in New Cyre."

He ran toward the ship, leaping at her as she floated into the air. Tristam's fingers hooked the delicate carvings on the ship's hull and for several seconds he hung a dozen feet above the ground, hanging desperately onto *Dying Sun*'s hull. The ship banked, dropping him back onto the cracked marble. The airship continued to ascend, shattering one edge of the broken glass ceiling as it rose. Tristam held up his arms to protect himself from falling glass as he lay in the ship's shadow. He glared up at the *Sun* in rage, snatching the wand from his belt and aiming it at the airship. At the same time, the crystal rod in the ship's bow flared a brilliant blue.

"Tristam, you must live," Ashrem's fading voice whispered.

Blue lightning sizzled into the rail station, but the figment's wards flared. Explosive force reverberated through the shattering shields and rippled through the building. Ashrem's voice screamed as the conflicting energies tore the phantom's remnants apart. The rail station shuddered as chunks of the ceiling began to fall.

"Get to cover, girl!" Ijaac said. The dwarf seized Omax by the neck and hip, hauling the injured warforged over his shoulders. He turned toward the door, but Seren caught his shoulder.

"We can't run outside," she said. "Marth will kill us as soon as we go out there."

Above them, the building shook as *Dying Sun* blasted it again.

The dwarf looked at her, panicked. "We can't stay here or he'll drop the building on our heads."

The artificer still stood in the center of the station, glaring up through the smoke at the ring of red fire.

"Tristam!" Seren shouted. "Help us!"

Tristam looked at her, his anger replaced with fear and concern. He ran to her side, dodging debris as he tucked his wand back into his belt.

"We have to get out of here!" she called to him.

Tristam's eyes narrowed with a sudden idea.

"This is a rail station" he said, snatching his bag of tools. "Let's take the lightning rail."

He ran toward the surviving lightning coach and threw open the door, tossing his tools inside before returning to help Ijaac load Omax into the coach.

"Are you sure this thing even still works?" Ijaac asked.

Seren looked up fearfully. Through the dusty haze she could see the silhouette of *Dying Sun* still hovering overhead. Flashes of lightning continued to tear into the station. Obviously Marth's offer of compromise had been revoked.

"I'll make it work," Tristam said grimly.

The inside of the coach was divided into two cars, a small pilot's chamber and a passenger area large enough for a dozen customers. Much like the station, the top of the coach was constructed of frosted glass, now long since broken. Omax lay across several seats, his eye shining dimly as he slipped in and out of whatever passed for consciousness for a warforged. Seren knelt beside him, clasping one great metal hand in both of hers. Tristam whispered encouragement to his friend and climbed into the engineer's seat, grasping the controls. The artificer closed his eyes in concentration as he channeled his will into the slumbering vehicle. Seren felt a tingle at the back of her neck as the coach flared to life. A circle of electricity erupted around the front end of the car. The entire vehicle shook violently and hovered a few inches higher above the conductor stones.

"It's working!" Ijaac exclaimed over the thunderous blasts from above.

"It's starting to," Tristam growled. "These coaches are bound to elementals, like the airship, but built to react to the dragon-marked engineers of House Orien. I have to convince the elemental to help us."

A heap of rubble crashed into the floor only a few feet away. Ijaac swore and rose a hand to protect his face from spraying gravel, then slammed the coach door shut. "I don't want to be a pest," the dwarf said, "but can you hurry?"

"Trying," Tristam said. Sweat trickled down his temple as he focused his concentration on the controls. "After four years locked in a box, the elemental is a little upset. All it wants to do is run free and wreck things."

Seren looked at the wrought iron gates that blocked their path, then back at Tristam. "So let it," she said.

Tristam opened his eyes suddenly. "That's brilliant, Seren," he said.

The coach shook even more violently. The ring of electricity burned a sickly green. A savage roar rolled up out of the depths of somewhere, as if echoing from another world.

"Fly," Tristam whispered, and the word seemed to through the vehicle's metal body.

The lightning coach bucked and surged forward on the tracks in a violent release of motion. Seren flinched as the car plunged directly toward the eastern gates. The car burst through unharmed, scattering metal and stone as it exploded onto the streets of Metrol. A dancing trail of energy moved ahead of them. The conductor stones shone intensely as they approached, as if anticipating being used again.

Seren looked behind them, through the roof of the passenger car. *Dying Sun* broke through the clouds of smoke that consumed the lightning rail station, her ring burning fierce red as she soared after them. The lance burned blue, and a bolt of lightning struck the side of the car. The air elemental roared in defiance, driving the car to greater speeds. The coach turned a wide corner and dove into an underground tunnel. Behind them, *Dying Sun* soared out of view. The electric aura cast freakish patterns of color upon the stone as they screamed through the tunnel.

"Marth will catch up on the far side of the tunnel," Tristam said, stepping out of his seat. "Take the controls, Ijaac."

"What?" the dwarf asked in a surprised voice. "What do I do? I'm no artificer. I don't know how to drive this thing."

"You don't need to know how to drive it," Tristam said, standing and pushing the dwarf into the seat. "Just hold the controls so that you can hear the elemental's voice in your head. Be angry and keep the coach angry."

"Good at that," Ijaac replied. "Been married."

Omax's hand tightened on Seren's. The warforged's eye now burned with a faint red tinge. Tristam knelt beside them, looking at his friend with a worried frown. He whispered and moved his hands over the warforged's battered body, repairing the damage as well as he could.

"Omax, can you speak?" Tristam asked.

"Tristam," the warforged said. A rattle escaped his throat. Seren thought it might be a chuckle.

"Omax, I'm sorry," Tristam said.

"For what?" the warforged asked.

"For letting this happen to you," he said. "We never should have stayed here. I've ruined everything"

"Then fix it, Tristam," Omax said weakly. "As you always do."

Tristam nodded.

"Coming up on the end of the tunnel, Tristam!" Ijaac shouted.

The artificer nodded and rose, drawing his wand and staring up through the roof of the coach.

"It is strange, Seren," the warforged whispered.

"What's strange, Omax?" Seren asked, trying to keep him talking.

"I am not sure if I was ever truly alive," he said. "I am not sure what it means, to live. But now I find . . . that I do not want to die."

"You're not going to die, Omax," Seren said. "We're almost home. We're going back to *Karia Naille*."

"Home," the warforged answered, savoring the word.

"It's like you said, Omax," Seren said. "War will try to tear us apart. We have to remain together. We need you, Omax."

"I am with you, Seren," the warforged said, his head slumping against his chest. The light in his eye faded.

"Brace yourselves!" Ijaac shouted.

The lightning coach burst out of the tunnel and back onto the streets again. Heaps of rubble and awkwardly shaped buildings huddled on all sides, but the rail stretched on, unimpeded. The eerie lights of living spells burned in the shadows, gathering around the conductor stones as if seeking the warmth of their magic. The coach surged on with a defiant cry, scattering the spells as a predator scattered curious scavengers. The coach sped up the steeply sloped streets. Ahead, the tracks climbed a narrow bridge over the River Melandor.

"Where is Marth?" Tristam demanded, knuckles white on the haft of his wand.

Red fire rose from beneath the bridge as *Dying Sun* appeared before them. The ship's lance shimmered and erupted with energy, tearing into the bridge. Metal and stone exploded as the center of the bridge tumbled into the river. The water glowed green as a conductor stone vanished into its depths.

"Khyber," Ijaac swore.

"Faster!" Tristam said. "We have to jump the gap!"

"This is as angry as I get, Tristam," Ijaac said. "I'm a bit too terrified to be properly mad!"

Tristam darted back into the pilot's chamber and grasped the controls with one hand. His brow furrowed as he concentrated, glaring up at *Dying Sun* as she hovered over the bridge. The coach screamed in fury and accelerated, climbing the bridge.

The bridge cracked and snapped around them as the vehicle's weight pressed against the conductor stones. The bridge jolted and tilted suddenly to the left. Tristam tightened his grasp on the controls as they sped toward the edge of the bridge. The elemental shrieked in triumph as the coach soared through the air for one glorious moment. Half of the bridge folded into the water behind it. The coach landed heavily on the other side, the conductor stones spraying sparks in a fiery burst. They careened down the far side bridge. Seren watched the conductor stones crumble into the river one by one as the coach sped onward. The bridge collapsed entirely, as the coach barreled back into the streets, rounding a sharp corner and speeding deeper into the city.

Dying Sun accelerated, soaring after them. The crystal lance at its bow glowed blue. A bolt of lightning sizzled past them, shattering a conductor stone in their path. The coach shuddered and crossed the void, jumping the dead stone in the elemental's wild desire to keep running. Ijaac gripped the controls fiercely, muttering a stream of curses in the Dwarven tongue.

Tristam took aim at the airship and fired a blot of white lightning into the sky. *Dying Sun* banked sharply. The blast barely seared her hull.

Tristam took a step back, staring up at the airship. The blue beam seared the back of the coach, shattering the rear half of the roof. Seren threw herself over Omax to protect the wounded warforged from the debris. The *Sun* drew closer, hovering only a dozen feet from the coach, and powered up the lance again as the coach crested a hill.

Everything went dark as the coach suddenly dipped into a tunnel at the base of the hill. Sparks reflected off the walls, and the elemental's roar echoed through the earth. *Dying Sun*'s red ring followed them. Unable to veer away from the tunnel, Marth simply flew in after them.

"He can't fire," Seren realized as she saw the glow in the crystal rod fade. "If he kills us he'll crash right into our wreck."

"Calm down, Ijaac," Tristam said.

"What?" the dwarf shouted. "We need to go faster, not slower! I can barely keep this thing under control as it is!"

"Calm down, Ijaac!" Tristam shouted. "Let Marth catch up to us!"

The dwarf glanced back at Tristam in disbelief, then turned back to the controls. The elemental's shriek changed pitch, from anger to defiance. The coach shook and began to lose speed. *Dying Sun* drew closer. Tristam aimed his wand and opened fire, releasing white lightning into the airship. He unleashed his magic again and again, firing blast after futile blast. The airship flashed in the light of the wand's blasts, outlined by its own elemental fire. Tristam kept firing, screaming in fury as he poured the wand's magic into *Dying Sun*. The red hull turned slowly black but continued pursuit, growing slowly closer. The wand tumbled from Tristam's hand, now a dull black, its energy spent. The end of the tunnel drew near, and in the light of the conductor stones Seren saw the bow of the ship clearly. *Dying Sun*'s crystal rod was shattered, her weapon destroyed.

The coach sped out the other side of the tunnel, plummeting down another hill and following the rail as it made its way to the edge of the city. *Dying Sun* pulled above them and to one side, hovering patiently.

"What's he doing?" Seren asked.

"Waiting," Tristam said. "We've killed his ship's weapon. Now he's just waiting for us to stop so he can finish us himself."

"Afraid it won't be long," Ijaac said, frowning as the coach continued to lose momentum. The sparkling energy that surrounded the front of the coach slowly died down and vanished altogether. The sparks that exploded from stones began to lose intensity as the vehicle gradually slowed. Tristam drew another wand from his cloak, scowling as he girded himself for the fight ahead.

"He'll land when we stop," Tristam said. "Then he'll come after us himself."

"You sound a little eager, boy," Ijaac said, worried.

"It's time this was over," Tristam said darkly.

The coach ground slowly to a halt. Tristam stepped out onto the dry earth, holding his wand and sword in either hand. *Dying Sun* hovered over them for a long, agonizing moment, then turned about in midair and soared higher into the mists.

Tristam looked back at them in confusion. "Why did he run?"

Seren saw the answer immediately. She pointed at the sky. A ring of blue fire soared from the clouds above, racing toward them. *Karia Naille* hovered as low as she dared, boarding ladder spilling from the cargo bay. Tristam secured Omax into one of the coach seats and tied it to the ladder as they climbed, then hauled the injured warforged aboard.

"What happened to Omax?" Gerith asked in a worried voice.

"Marth came after us," Tristam said, pulling the doors shut. "He's taken *Dying Sun*."

"You should have destroyed that ship, not repaired her," Dalan said angrily. "You delivered her right into his hands."

"We're near the Talenta Plains, aren't we?" Seren said, looking at Gerith. "Are there any towns nearby?"

"Gatherhold," Gerith said. "There are healers there. Good healers. Maybe they can help?"

"Can we still catch up to Marth?" Tristam asked.

"*Dying Sun* was headed back toward New Cyre, Tristam," Dalan said. "With a single pilot, he'll be flying slower than us. We can catch him, if we hurry."

Tristam looked down at the battered warforged.

"Omax looks really bad, Tristam," Gerith said. "Will he hold on long enough for us to catch Marth and get him back to Gatherhold too?"

Tristam looked down at Omax for a long, silent moment.

"No," Tristam said. "If we follow Marth, Omax dies."

"If Marth escapes again, *many* people will die, Tristam," Dalan said. "But the choice is yours. I may own this vessel, but I have no illusions regarding who commands this quest anymore."

Tristam and Dalan locked gazes for a long, silent moment.

"Gerith, run up to the captain," Tristam said. "Tell Pherris to make all possible speed for Gatherhold."

Epilogue

The prophet folded his arms in his robes and drifted off through the camp. Many of the soldiers rose and saluted or merely nodded as he passed. Some grasped holy octagrams of the Host or emblems of the Silver Flame and whispered the names of their gods as he passed. Zamiel mumbled blessings to each of them. They knew him as a holy man, and since he never spoke against any of their gods, all of them assumed he served theirs. It was true enough, he supposed. After all, the gods all served the same power he did. Destiny. The divine guardians were like brothers to him. He considered the gods intriguing peers, and worthy of respect.

Zamiel continued on his way through the camp. The soldiers returned to their business. None noticed as he continued walking past the barricades and out onto the plains. He did not wish them to see him, so they did not. He smiled faintly as the sun set over the shifting grass. Talenta was a beautiful place. The halflings had chosen wisely when they infested these plains. The prophet tilted his chin into the wind, closed his eyes, and waited. For days he had done this, seeking any sign of the Valenar. Usually, there was nothing, but he persevered nonetheless.

Faith, after all, was everything.

Eventually it came to him. The faint but distinctive scent of horses. Halflings did not ride such creatures, so it must be the elves. It was a faint trail, one that someone had taken great effort

FLIGHT OF THE DYING SUN

to conceal. To Zamiel's keen senses, it was obvious. He followed the scent of horses unerringly across the plains.

The sun had set completely by the time he arrived at the camp. A small fire burned in the darkness. Though shielded so that it would give off little light, Zamiel saw the flame clearly. He walked directly toward the camp, holding his arms outstretched so that it was obvious he bore no weapons. He felt the elves move in the darkness as they sensed him.

"Halt," came the expected command, barked sharply in the Valenar tongue.

"I am unarmed," Zamiel said. "I am Brother Zamiel. I wish to speak to your leader on behalf of the *Seventh Moon* and the Cyran nation."

Tense silence was the reply. After nearly a minute, a single warrior stepped from the darkness. He wore a baggy coat over thick chain armor. A peaked helmet reflected the pale moonlight. He drew a slender sword and pointed it toward the prophet. "No spells," he said. "No weapons. I will slit your throat if you do anything foolish. Do you hear me, priest? Even your god will not save you if you defy us."

"I wish only peace," was Zamiel's reply, "and I am no priest."

The elf nodded and pulled a long leather strap from his waist. He bound Zamiel's hands behind his back and pushed him forward, directing him toward the camp. The prophet kept his eyes on the point of the guard's sword, always nearby. It was a fine blade. He could smell the magic woven through the steel. The elves always made such wonderful things.

Zamiel cocked his head sadly as he entered the camp. As much as he had hoped the elves were merely curious scouts, such was not the case. Dozens of warriors had mustered here, gathered around their tents and mounts. There were twice as many of them as Cyran soldiers protecting the *Moon*. This was a war party, poised to wipe out his mortal allies.

"Rouse Captain Nelethar," the elven guard commanded. "The

marooned Cyrans have sent an ambassador."

The junior soldiers hesitated, obviously surprised that their presence here was known. They rushed off to the largest tent. A light appeared within. Several minutes later a female elf emerged, dressed in fine silken robes. She studied Zamiel carefully, then shot the guard an irritated look.

"Could this not wait until morning?" she asked.

"Your servant clearly seeks only to do his duty," Zamiel said in a soothing voice. "Such dedication should be rewarded. My appearance was unexpected, and I apologize for that, but I was forced to seize the opportunity to follow your trail when I could."

"Trail?" she asked, sneering. "What trail?"

"It was faint," he said. "Your warriors have gone to some lengths to remain undetected."

Nelethar scowled. "Who are you?" she demanded.

"I am Brother Zamiel," the prophet replied. "I serve Marth, the final champion of Cyre."

"He said he wanted to negotiate," the guard offered.

"Final champion?" Nelethar asked. "Tell your friend Marth to pick a better cause. Cyre is dead."

"Marth prefers to think otherwise," Zamiel said. "He intends to restore his homeland to its former glory."

"Does he?" Nelethar asked. She was fully awake now, her tone faintly amused. She tilted her head, looking at the prophet curiously. "He sent you to negotiate with us?"

"No," Zamiel said. "I came of my own accord. I wished to discern the reason behind your presence here. I do not intend to negotiate. I do not believe you would accept such an offer, except perhaps to humor me."

Nelethar frowned. Zamiel noticed that, even in her night clothes, she wore a sword at her hip. The Valenar were an intriguing people. He regretted what would come next.

"I know the customs of your kind," Zamiel said. "Valor is your greatest virtue. The glory of battle is your greatest ecstasy.

Victory forgives all sins. The halflings on these plains offer little chance for you to truly test your mettle—but a crew of trained Cyran soldiers tending a ruined Zil'argo warship? What a discovery. Surely that would be a victory of worth, so long as you could guarantee your success through strength of numbers."

Nelethar's frown curled into a grin. "And what if you are right, Brother?" she asked. "What if we intend to kill your comrades and take their ship and her spoils for my warchief? What do you think you could possibly say that would convince me to turn our swords away?"

Zamiel looked around calmly. He could see that most of the soldiers had awakened and were watching with interest. Some exchanged quiet whispers and laughed quietly. Many of them had already drawn weapons.

"I fear there would be nothing I could say that would convince you to withdraw," Zamiel said.

"Then beg, Cyran," Nelethar said. "Grovel for Valenar mercy and I will give you water enough to run back to the human lands where you may spread tales of our glorious victory over your comrades."

"No," Zamiel said.

"No?" she said, eyes gleaming as she drew her sword. "You will not grovel?"

"No," he said. "And I am not Cyran."

"Then what land do you hail from?" she asked with a mocking laugh.

The prophet sighed and let the enchantments that bound him slip. Nelethar's green eyes bulged in terror. The whispered mutterings ceased, eclipsed by fear. The shadow of Zamiel's broad wings swallowed the moonlight. A claw as thick as an airship's strut gouged the earth.

"Argonnessen," Zamiel rumbled, taking a deep breath.

The dragon exhaled, and a cloud of roiling black acid washed over the Valenar warriors.

A world of adventure awaits

The FORGOTTEN REALMS world is the biggest, most detailed, most vibrant, and most beloved of the DUNGEONS & DRAGONS® campaign settings. Created by best-selling fantasy author Ed Greenwood the FORGOTTEN REALMS setting has grown in almost unimaginable ways since the first line was drawn on the now infamous "Ed's Original Maps."

Still the home of many a group of DUNGEONS & DRAGONS players, the FORGOTTEN REALMS world is brought to life in dozens of novels, including hugely popular best sellers by some of the fantasy genre's most exciting authors. FORGOTTEN REALMS novels are fast, furious, action-packed adventure stories in the grand tradition of sword and sorcery fantasy, but that doesn't mean they're all flash and no substance. There's always something to learn and explore in this richly textured world.

To find out more about the Realms go to www.wizards.com and follow the links from Books to FORGOTTEN REALMS. There you'll find a detailed reader's guide that will tell you where to start if you've never read a FORGOTTEN REALMS novel before, or where to go next if you're a long-time fan!

 FORGOTTEN REALMS, DUNGEONS & DRAGONS, WIZARDS OF THE COAST, and their respective logos are trademarks of Wizards of the Coast, Inc. in the U.S.A. and other countries. ©2007 Wizards.

R.A. SALVATORE

The New York Times best-selling author and one of fantasy's most powerful voices.

DRIZZT DO'URDEN

The renegade dark elf who's captured the imagination of a generation.

THE LEGEND OF DRIZZT

Updated editions of the FORGOTTEN REALMS classics finally in their proper chronological order.

BOOK I
HOMELAND
Now available in paperback!

BOOK II
EXILE
Now available in paperback!

BOOK III
SOJOURN
Now available in paperback!

BOOK IV
THE CRYSTAL SHARD
Now available in paperback!

BOOK V
STREAMS OF SILVER
Coming in paperback, May 2007

BOOK VI
THE HALFLING'S GEM
Coming in paperback, August 2007

BOOK VII
THE LEGACY
Coming in paperback, April 2008

BOOK VIII
STARLESS NIGHT
Now available in deluxe hardcover edition!

BOOK IX
SIEGE OF DARKNESS
Now available in deluxe hardcover edition!

BOOK X
PASSAGE TO DAWN
Deluxe hardcover, March 2007

BOOK XI
THE SILENT BLADE
Deluxe hardcover, June 2007

BOOK XII
THE SPINE OF THE WORLD
Deluxe hardcover, December 2007

BOOK XIII
SEA OF SWORDS
Deluxe hardcover, March 2008

FORGOTTEN REALMS, WIZARDS OF THE COAST, and their respective logos are trademarks of Wizards of the Coast, Inc. in the U.S.A. and other countries. ©2007 Wizards.

MARGARET WEIS
&
TRACY HICKMAN

The co-creators of the DRAGONLANCE® world return to the epic tale that introduced Krynn to a generation of fans!

THE LOST CHRONICLES

VOLUME ONE
DRAGONS OF THE DWARVEN DEPTHS

As Tanis and Flint bargain for refuge in Thorbardin, Raistlin and Caramon go to Neraka to search for one of the spellbooks of Fistandantilus. The refugees in Thorbardin are trapped when the draconian army marches, and Flint undertakes a quest to find the Hammer of Kharas to free them all, while Sturm becomes a key of a different sort.

VOLUME TWO
DRAGONS OF THE HIGHLORD SKIES

Dragon Highlord Ariakas assigns the recovery of the dragon orb taken to Ice Wall to Kitiara Uth-Matar, who is rising up the ranks of both the dark forces and of Ariakas's esteem. Finding the orb proves easy, but getting it from Laurana proves more difficult. Difficult enough to attract the attention of Lord Soth.

July 2007

VOLUME THREE
DRAGONS OF THE HOURGLASS MAGE

The wizard Raistlin Majere takes the black robes and travels to the capital city of the evil empire, Neraka, to serve the Queen of Darkness.

July 2008

 DRAGONLANCE, WIZARDS OF THE COAST, and their respective logos are trademarks of Wizards of the Coast, Inc. in the U.S.A. and other countries. ©2007 Wizards.